RETICENCE

THE CUSTARD PROTOCOL: BOOK FOUR

By Gail Carriger

The Parasol Protectorate
Soulless
Changeless
Blameless
Heartless
Timeless

The Custard Protocol
Prudence
Imprudence
Competence
Reticence

The Parasol Protectorate Manga
Soulless: The Manga, Vol. 1
Soulless: The Manga, Vol. 2
Soulless: The Manga, Vol. 3

The Finishing School
Etiquette & Espionage
Curtsies & Conspiracies
Waistcoats & Weaponry
Manners & Mutiny

RETICENCE

THE CUSTARD PROTOCOL: BOOK FOUR

GAIL CARRIGER

orbit

www.orbitbooks.net

Copyright © 2019 by Tofa Borregaard

Cover design by Lauren Panepinto
Type design by Chad Roberts
Cover illustration by Larry Rostant
Cover copyright © 2019 by Hachette Book Group, Inc.

Orbit
Hachette Book Group
1290 Avenue of the Americas
New York, NY 10104
orbitbooks.net

First Edition: August 2019

Orbit is an imprint of Hachette Book Group.
The Orbit name and logo are trademarks of Little, Brown Book Group Limited.

The publisher is not responsible for websites (or their content) that are not owned by the publisher.

The Hachette Speakers Bureau provides a wide range of authors for speaking events. To find out more, go to www.hachettespeakersbureau.com or call (866) 376-6591.

Library of Congress Cataloging-in-Publication Data
Names: Carriger, Gail, author.
Title: Reticence / Gail Carriger.
Description: First edition. | New York : Orbit, 2019. | Series: The custard protocol ; book 4
Identifiers: LCCN 2019007413 | ISBN 9780316433914 (hardcover) | ISBN 9780316433907 (ebook) | ISBN 9780316433921 (library ebook) | ISBN 9781549175787 (audio book cd) | ISBN 9781549175794 (downloadable audio book)
Subjects: GSAFD: Fantasy fiction.
Classification: LCC PS3603.A77448 R48 2019 | DDC 813/.6—dc23
LC record available at https://lccn.loc.gov/2019007413

ISBNs: 978-0-316-43391-4 (hardcover), 978-0-316-43390-7 (ebook)

Printed in the United States of America

LSC-C

10 9 8 7 6 5 4 3 2 1

RETICENCE

THE CUSTARD PROTOCOL: BOOK FOUR

ONE

The Doctor Floats

*W*ANTED: *Airship Doctor*

Physician welcome, surgeon preferred. Remuneration according to experience level. Education open to negotiation. Progressive philosophy and equable temperament preferred. Must tolerate explosions and cats.

Dr Arsenic Ruthven turned the advertisement over in her hand. She'd spotted it three days before, in *The Mooning Standard*, which was a very forward-thinking paper. Yet it went beyond her expectations. It was, in a word, ideal. The author of such an oddly worded advert might be convinced to overlook her greatest failing as a doctor in the eyes of society: being female.

She read it over for the hundredth time. That last line was a corker. Arsenic knew of very few doctors who would put up with both explosions *and* cats. Or explosions caused by cats. She was one of the few.

Arsenic had contacted the brokering agent and been told, curtly, to seek out *The Spotted Custard* dirigible, moored in Regent's Park at five in the afternoon on Thursday next.

Accordingly, she'd arrived by half past four. Arsenic abhorred tardiness. She was standing next to her collapsible mono-wheel with medical kit in hand in time to watch a distinguished-looking physician with prominent muttonchops and even more prominent teeth go up the gangplank. He was not particularly fit, and the colour and texture of his nose suggested a preference for, and regular indulgence in, claret of an evening – and morning and afternoon and just before bed.

He was after *her* position, if his doctor's bag and smug expression were any indication.

My position, Dr Hairy Jowls Strawberry Nose! She thought it, but she didn't let it show in her expression or posture.

Arsenic tilted her head back, pretending at a tourist's curiosity over the dirigible. It was modern, massive, and cheerfully spotted. It was also heavily armed, which was an aberration in a pleasure craft.

Her pretence seemed unnecessary as the muttonchops didn't sway in her direction. A modern young lady in outrageous dress was beneath his contempt. Medical kit or no.

Arsenic judged him for his doctor's bag more than anything else. *So old-fashioned. His techniques are likely equally so.*

Oh, she very much *judged* him.

She needn't have worried.

He came back down the gangplank a mere ten minutes later, flushed and blustering. Which made Arsenic nervous but also immeasurably pleased.

She rubbed sweaty hands over the black serge skirt of her golf costume. It was hemmed in scarlet and six whole inches off the ground. As if that weren't daring enough, she'd paired it with a scarlet blouse and black knickerbockers. It was beyond progressive, some might even say *outrageously suffrage*.

But Arsenic wasn't one to hide. She had a demanding profession and she rode a mono-wheel. It was silly to wear long skirts and fancy lace blouses, they impeded mobility and were a challenge to clean. She was a surgeon, blood and mess were part of day-to-day operations – literally and figuratively. She'd even been known to *roll up her sleeves* when the situation warranted, and scuttle the consequences!

Aye, she wanted the position, rather desperately, but she wasn't going to compromise in personality or attire in order to achieve it. The advert said progressive, Dr Arsenic Ruthven would give them progressive.

Thus buoyed, she checked her watch.

4:50 p.m.

She took a breath and, mono-wheel slung over one arm, medical kit under the other, she marched up the gangplank and aboard the aptly named *Spotted Custard*.

"How's this? Fancy, fancy. I *like* this one."

A suite of young ruffians was lounging about applying commentary to the applicants. The young lad who spoke was smudged and cheerful, lean and fit, and possibly not a lad.

"No wager on this one, gentlemen, I give even odds."

Arsenic squinted at the malcontent. *Female*, she decided after a moment's focus on skeletal structure.

"Proper stuffing, she is," agreed one of the others, chewing happily on reed or cob or something similarly tough and vegetative. He was also smudged and muscled. *Bit sunburned. I must remember to stock burn balms. I wager the boilers can scald too.*

"Definitely nibbles the biscuit," added one of the others.

Arsenic was rather chuffed by this observation. She'd never before nibbled anyone's biscuit, so she was disposed to be pleased, even when coming from the mouths of babes. Wisdom of youth and all.

"Swanky duds." The first turned bright sharp eyes onto Arsenic. *Clear sclera. Healthy.*

"Thank you verra much," replied Arsenic. "I'll do, then?"

"Not up to us. More's the pity," lamented the girl.

"Still, I'd like to know I've your approval." Arsenic was not above enlisting backers, small and scruffy though they may be.

The girl jumped down off her perch and sauntered across

the deck, hands deep in pockets, examining Arsenic with interest.

"I'm Spoo," said, apparently, Spoo.

Arsenic inclined her head. "Delighted to make your acquaintance, Miss Spoo."

"Just Spoo'll do. You got dulcet ways for a lady sporting trousers."

"They tried," Arsenic explained.

Spoo laughed. "Could be our ship's motto, that."

"No one is here to collect me just yet. Would you like to start the interview, Spoo?"

Spoo looked delighted. "Would I ever! How do you feel about candied fruit?"

"Favourably."

"What would you do if the forward ballast collapsed?"

"Stay out of your way." This girl must be a deckling, and from the way the others stayed back watching, probably head deckling.

"You good with a needle?"

"Very."

"You a leech?" Spoo had excellent upper-body musculature, probably from balloon-stimulated gymnastic endeavours. Decklings did a great deal of rigging-work.

"Never. That's well out of date."

"Allergic to cats?" One of the others asked that question. He was shorter with impressive shoulders. Those muscles were from shovelling and he was more smudged. Arsenic guessed he was a sootie.

"Nay, love them."

"Well, don't love them too much. Miss Primrose wouldn't like that." Spoo spoke with sepulchral foreboding.

"Neither would Mr Percy," said a new voice. Another young person trundled up.

This one was about Spoo's age, early teens. He, however, was meticulously clean and dressed in a dark vest and jacket with striped trousers and crisp white shirt. The attire indicated staff of some kind, a footman or valet. Although he was rather young for either position. He was also on the tubby end of the spectrum, with hair trimmed short and a grave round face. Arsenic worried about his diet.

"Are you our five o'clock?" He held himself with dignity and gravitas.

"Aye, sir." Arsenic was already confused by the nature of authority on this ship, so she erred in favour of politeness.

"I like this one." Spoo patted Arsenic in a conspiratorial way.

"Oh you do, do you?" The dapper youngster was not impressed. "Gave her good odds, did you?"

"Now don't go getting all over contrary, Virgil. You know we got to have us something out of the ordinary for this here airship."

"Do we? I should think that was the last thing *The Spotted Custard* needed – yet another eccentric." The boy squinted up at Arsenic. "Are you *an eccentric*, Doctor?"

"Only when the situation warrants."

"You aren't wearing a hat."

"Hats get in the way, except for sunshade, and I work indoors." Arsenic had strong feelings on the service application of hats. Once she stopped hiding the fact that she was female and started growing her hair, she tended towards a simple plait. This kept all her thick strands contained, but did not easily support hatpins. Besides, small hats served no useful function and large ones interfered with visual acumen. She'd given them up soon as may be.

"Oh dear," said Virgil.

"They're na practical under most circumstances." She dug in.

"Stop, before you get into real trouble," advised Spoo, grinning hugely.

"This will all end in tears," predicted Virgil, guiding her over to a ladder that led down belowdecks.

"Only for you, Virgil-love," shot Spoo at his departing back, and then added, "You playing tiddlywinks with us after dinner?"

Virgil waved a lugubrious hand at her.

Arsenic, hiding a smile and feeling far more relaxed than previously, set her mono-wheel down against the railing with a sharp look at Spoo and a small prayer that it wouldn't be tampered with, and followed Virgil into the belly of the dirigible.

"I like your ship," she said, hoping to mollify the young man.

"It's ridiculous," he replied, unmollified. "So spotty."

"I've always been a fan of ladybugs," replied Arsenic. It was true. Her father was an avid gardener who'd passed that love on to Arsenic. She'd never met a gardener who didn't love a ladybug or two. She was charmed by the fact that *The Spotted Custard*'s balloon was painted to resemble one. It was jolly, all over red and black. Besides, it matched her outfit.

Professor Percival Tunstell (sometimes erroneously referred to as *the Honourable*) was annoyed with life and bored out of his gourd.

"This is the last one, correct? Please say yes." He didn't bother to hide his annoyance. He'd no idea why he was needed for this, of all things! He'd theories to research (very important *theories*), charts to draw up (vital and interesting charts). Instead he was stuck sitting in his best suit wasting good daylight hours on an endless stream of insufferably pompous physicians.

"If he works, he's the last one. But given what's happened so far..." Primrose puffed out her cheeks. "We'll likely have to do this all over again. Run another advertisement." She was clearly vexed, but being his sister, relished threatening him with future horror.

He glared at her as if this were all her fault. Then, in case she couldn't interpret his expression after two dozen years of being his twin, he said, "This is all your fault." He suspected he sounded atrocious and too much like their mother.

"It absolutely is not! I happened to be one of the few people on this airship *not* injured over the last year."

She had a fair point.

Percy hated it when his sister had a fair point.

Rue interceded. "Stop it, both of you. It's got to be done. Perhaps I should have worded the advertisement more strongly?"

Prim sighed loudly. "You said, *must tolerate explosions and cats.* I'd think that's sufficiently strong."

"Yes, but I didn't say we'd actually be testing them with an explosion and a cat."

Primrose pursed her lips. "I'm sure Quesnel didn't mean for the sugar pot to blow up."

"He never does." Rue wore a fond smile. "You have to admit it's rather startling."

Prim rolled her eyes. "Yes, all six times. Will it be happening with the next tea tray as well?"

"Of course."

Percy added, "And Footnote didn't mean to sniff every single one of them. But to be fair, this is his airship. More importantly, this is the stateroom where there's usually food. He's always around if we're in here. I can't kick him out, that'd be rude. Right, Footy old chap?"

Footnote, who was currently leaning against Percy's left ankle with one paw on the toe of his shoe, looked up at him and gave an imperious *mew.*

Rue agreed, "It certainly would be rude."

"Perhaps it's not the advert but the profession itself that is unable to satisfy our needs?" suggested Primrose forlornly.

Percy didn't want to agree with her but she was probably correct. He had his doubts about physicians. Leeches and charlatans, the lot of them, with no foundation in good proper scientific research and . . .

A tap came at the door. Footnote trotted over to supervise whatever happened next.

"Come in," said Rue. Not rising.

Percy stood, though. He was prepared to make a slightly too shallow bow to properly greet whatever pedantic twaddle swaggered through the door. He may have strong feelings on the profession, but he was a *gentleman*.

Virgil led in the candidate.

Percy goggled.

There was no kinder way of putting it. Positively goggled like a stunned chipmunk.

Primrose let out a soft, "Oh my."

Rue rubbed her hands together. "Excellent!"

Virgil intoned, "Your five o'clock appointment, Dr Ruthven, to see you, Lady Captain."

Percy considered that he might have to wean Virgil off his current diet of gothic literature. His valet was becoming positively moribund. He didn't fret over Virgil's reading habits for long, though, because some irresistible force dragged his attention back to the new doctor.

Percy came over all queasy and flushed. *Oh dear.*

The female physician, for that was what she must be, was on the smallish side, thin compared to Rue and Prim, and a mite taller. Certainly not as beautiful as Tasherit. Yet he was riveted by her. As if she were some new unexplainable natural phenomenon, like the aetheric bubbles he'd recently written about in a widely discussed and well-received new pamphlet. Or those bright green sand fleas he'd collected in Lima. Being female, she probably wouldn't like the comparison to bubbles or fleas, but both had been absolutely fascinating.

She was serious faced and dark haired and she wore no hat. Her attire seemed odd but serviceable. Percy had no eye for fashion. He disliked that he was noticing hers.

She turned big dark blue eyes on him.

Percy froze. He was supposed to bow or something. "I'll just sit," he said, voice a little weak. And did. He'd seen a whale once the colour of those eyes. Big whale, very smooth and in the ocean and lashing its tail about and . . .

Percival Tunstell had lost his train of scientific thought.

Percival Tunstell *never* lost a train of scientific thought. This was not good.

Virgil made introductions. "This is the captain, Lady Akeldama. That is the Honourable Miss Tunstell, ship's purser, and this rude boffin is my horrible master, Professor Tunstell, ship's navigator. Ignore him. I usually do." He glared about. "Spoo approves this candidate, in case you care." He threw this last statement at Rue almost like a barb.

Rue made a note. "Of course I care."

"She isn't wearing a hat," objected Virgil.

"Not everyone takes them as seriously as you, dear. It'll be all right in the end, civilisation will remain standing."

Virgil frowned. "Civilisations have fallen for less."

Rue rolled her eyes at the valet. "Go get the tea, Virgil, do."

"Same sugar pot?"

"Yes please." Rue's voice had that forced cheerfulness it often assumed when dealing with Virgil (or with Percy himself, for that matter) in public.

Rue made a graceful gesture with her hand at the open chair across from her. She'd arranged them to sit so that she and Prim were on one side of the table with Percy at the end. The chair directly opposite Rue and nearest the door was intended for the candidate.

"Dr Ruthven, do sit down. I must say, you're a pleasant surprise."

"Aye?"

"Indeed. And I admire your attire greatly. I do so adore sportswear. Unfortunately, it's not very conducive to, well, my life..."

"Actually, I find it mighty conducive to most things. That's why I wear it."

The young doctor was very forthright. Percy found this irksome, although there was no question that it would facilitate coping with an injured Rue or any of the others aboard *The Spotted Custard*. Backbone was practically a moral imperative on this ship.

Up until that moment, if asked, Percy would have said he preferred mild-mannered soft-spoken young ladies (unlike his sister and his captain). Percy frowned. *That* is *what I prefer!* Not that he'd a great deal of experience with the fairer sex. Aside from Prim and Rue (and Tasherit and Spoo, who didn't count), Percy tended to flee females as if they represented a herd of peer reviews.

Rue squinted. "You don't know anything about me?"

The doctor looked bewildered. "Nay, should I?"

"Yes, but it's a relief that you don't. I'm rather a scientific curiosity and most of the applicants so far were more interested in dissecting me than in the position on offer."

"I assure you, I am na in the habit of conducting vivisections."

"Good to know. Shall we get on with the interview then, Dr Ruthven?"

"I'm at your disposal, Captain."

Dr Arsenic Ruthven had been in some odd situations in her life but this one took the clootie dumpling.

Aye, she was being interviewed. But not by an aged ex-floatillah officer, as she'd expected. Retired puff-men were commonly tapped to captain pleasure craft for the idle rich. Generally speaking, the idle rich did not do the captaining themselves. And yet, before her sat three individuals who were, quite frankly, the very definition of the upper crust.

The stout brunette with tan skin, yellow eyes, and decidedly cheeky disposition was actually the captain of the airship! Lady Akeldama looked robust if a touch puffy. Arsenic considered salt retention.

Next to Lady Akeldama sat Miss Tunstell, who had a stack of paperwork and a stylus, suggesting she was in charge of staffing as well as being purser. She was straight-backed and pertly serious, with dark curls and soft skin. She appeared to be in good health.

Rounding out the trio was the bonnie ginger, Professor Tunstell, who didn't seem to have much to say for himself. Usual in academics who tended to wait until they had something to say on the subject of *others*. He was watching Arsenic from under lashes that were rather long for such a fair-haired fellow. Arsenic felt rather like a specimen under his microscope. He was too pale, and could likely use regular airing and calisthenics but no doubt resisted both with every fibre of his academic soul.

They were all near to Arsenic's own age, perhaps a little younger, and looked more like they were dressed for a ball than for interviewing a physician. Even behind the table, Arsenic could make out a great deal of satin and brocade, rather too much for this time of day. Both young ladies sported elaborate hairstyles and the professor's cravat was formed into a knot of epic wonder. It was all ridiculously formal.

Arsenic had donned her finest sportswear. Never would she have guessed she'd be the one underdressed for this interview.

Another person might have found the encounter too peculiar, but Arsenic was, when it counted most, her mother's daughter. Thus her reaction to an odd situation was to perfect her posture, narrow her eyes, and remind herself that she had much to offer any crew. Then, because she was *also* her father's daughter, she smiled softly, took her chair with grace, and resolved to be charming.

"Very well. Dr Ruthven, where did you train in the fine art of medicine?" Miss Tunstell began the actual interview.

Arsenic looked to the captain, because she was, after all, *the captain*, and received a gracious nod. As if to say, *Go on.*

"My degree is through Edinburgh University via correspondence. I was trained mainly on the battlefield. South Africa." Arsenic preferred to talk as little as may be about that but she knew experience was important. The advertisement had specified.

Miss Tunstell's voice became gentle. "Did you serve?"

"As a woman? Na officially. But at least that meant, when I left, it wasna desertion." *Please dinna ask please dinna...*

"Jameson?"

Arsenic winced. News of the botched raid had reached London before she did and become sensationalized. She nodded.

"You disagree?"

Politics, already? Arsenic glanced helplessly at the wealthy aristocrats before her. She hesitated. Finally, she spoke, knowing she sounded more Scottish when attempting to master her emotions. "'Tis na ours. Nary a one is *ours*."

"The whole Empire or the African outposts?" Lady Akeldama leaned forward.

I'm na going to get this position. Arsenic's heart sank but she wasn't going to fib, either. "The Empire. It costs too much, too many lives, on both sides. I'm a surgeon, na a politician."

"So who would know better than you?" Strangely the captain seemed sympathetic.

"You dinna mind?"

"That you're a radical? Not especially. We've all gone native at this juncture."

"Native to where?" They were, after all, currently in London and Lady Akeldama had a very polished accent.

The captain only wiggled her head back and forth. "Wherever we happen to be at the time, usually. It's a supernatural affinity thing."

"Is it?" Arsenic hadn't a great deal of exposure to the supernatural set. Except, of course, the werewolf regimental attachment to the army during her time in South Africa. They'd been decent eggs. But she hadn't seen much of them as they didn't require her services. They healed themselves neatly enough. As a result, Arsenic knew very little, medically or otherwise, about supernatural creatures. Although she'd enjoyed socializing with the werewolves when given a chance. They reminded her a great deal of her da, who was entirely human but a soldier and with werewolfish inclinations towards being a big gruff softy.

Lady Akeldama shifted in her seat. "I'll explain later. Moving on. You have field training in battle wounds?"

"Almost all my experience is with such. 'Tis difficult for a young lady to set up practice in a town when there are gentleman physicians. But armies canna afford to be picky about surgeons."

"Practical training is good." The captain nodded.

Miss Tunstell was taking enthusiastic notes.

Arsenic relaxed slightly.

Miss Tunstell cleared her throat delicately. "Returning to the *proper* order of questions . . . Do you know how to extract a bullet and tend a puncture wound?"

"Of course."

"And can you stitch up a gouge?"

"Verra neatly, if I do say so myself. And bone setting is one of my fortes."

"That's good. That's very good." The captain slapped her hands together. Despite her fancy attire, a beautiful ivory dress with appliqué yellow flowers, Lady Akeldama wasn't wearing any gloves. *Interesting omission.*

"Rue," hissed Miss Tunstell. "You keep skipping ahead!"

"Sorry, Prim, do go on."

"How about smaller household ailments and illnesses?"

Arsenic strove to be honest. "I've my education to call upon and a small library, if I might be permitted to bring that aboard. But day-to-day treatment is na my strong suit. Basic medicinals and such I keep to hand, of course." She hoisted her medical kit up on the table and patted it. "But anything exotic and I'd need consult an expert." She was thinking about foreign lands, and how many soldiers she had lost to malignant fever rather than injury.

"Did you say *library?*" Professor Tunstell finally spoke up. He'd a pleasant light tenor and a distinct Eton accent. Was he married to the stiff young lady? Nay, Virgil had called her Miss Tunstell, not *Mrs*, so he must be a brother or cousin.

Arsenic strove to correct any erroneous assumptions. "Only a small collection of slim volumes, I assure you. I've travelled extensively over the past few years, and havena amassed many books. They shouldna weigh down the ship overmuch."

He gave a shy half smile, which turned him even more pretty. The smile wobbled, as if it were stiff from underuse. "Oh, we don't worry about that. You should feel free to collect further. And you may store them in my library."

"Oh might she *indeed*, Percy?" Miss Tunstell's expression was all incredulity.

Professor Tunstell blinked a moment, as if startled by his own invitation. "Yes, I do believe I actually mean it."

Miss Tunstell rolled her eyes. "Oh for goodness' sake, what is floating in your aether today? You're even more exasperating than normal. Where was I?"

"You were asking about my education and experience," prompted Arsenic. She had three sisters, thus she knew how to keep a conversation on track.

"Yes, thank you, Doctor. I believe I'm satisfied for now. Besides there is Mother to consider. She said you might do in that letter."

Everyone, including Arsenic, looked at Miss Tunstell in utter confusion.

Miss Tunstell waved an airy hand. "You don't remember the letter? Something to do with Aunt Softy? No? Why am I the only one who cares about this kind of thing?"

"Well, if it came from Aunt Softy," said Professor Tunstell, possibly sarcastically.

"Via your *mother*," added the captain, definitely sarcastically.

Arsenic was confused. "Someone knew I'd apply?"

"Someone sent you the advertisement, didn't they?" Miss Tunstell looked, if possible, even more prim.

"It was in the paper."

"And that paper arrived opened to our advert on your doorstep, did it not?"

"How'd you know?"

"Aunt Softy works in mysterious ways. So does my mother."

Arsenic wondered if her own mother had anything to do with it. She felt suddenly as if her life was being managed by others.

Not a pleasant sensation. But she still desired the position and now she had something to prove.

The captain glared at Miss Tunstell. "You could have warned me this one had Aunt Ivy's stamp."

"I didn't want to prejudice you," snapped back Miss Tunstell.

"For or against?" The captain pursed her lips and looked at Arsenic with a modicum more suspicion than before.

"Who's Aunt Ivy?" wondered Arsenic.

"The Aunt Softy connection. It's best not to worry too much about such things. You know aunts, they will interfere given the slightest opportunity."

"I have sisters, same difference."

"Too true," said Professor Tunstell, softly.

The two ladies sneered at him. *Miss Tunstell is definitely his sister, and the captain probably a childhood friend.*

Miss Tunstell returned to Arsenic. "May I please see your accreditation?"

"Of course, I've it here." Arsenic popped open her medical kit with the activation button. It decompressed and spiralled up, showing off dozens of shelves and compartments, stretching three feet tall. It was a masterwork of design and function and had cost her a small fortune. Arsenic never resented a penny. She fished out the requested paperwork from its special sleeve under the lid. She kept it easily accessible. She was accustomed to having her expertise questioned.

Miss Tunstell gave it a cursory glance. The captain waved it off, seeming more interested in the auto-telescoping function of Arsenic's kit. Professor Tunstell, however, pulled out an adorable set of spectacles and gave the paperwork a thorough read.

"*Ruthven.* Why do I know that name?" he asked, apparently of the paper, as he did not look up.

"Mother's letter?" suggested Miss Tunstell.

Professor Tunstell snorted without looking up. "As if I read anything Mother writes. No no, it's something else."

Arsenic felt her heart sink. Her mother hadn't been active for years. And never worked under the name Ruthven. She was, in fact, officially retired – although really, was that even possible? Still, Preshea Ruthven had once had a *reputation*. Arsenic's family had endeavoured to keep Mother's married name separate from her *other* married names, but it was difficult for a lady of deadly notoriety to remain entirely obscure.

Arsenic prepared to explain.

But then the professor snapped his fingers. "Oh yes, Professor Belladonna Ruthven, out of Dublin. She wrote that marvellous paper on the beneficial medicinal properties of digitalis when used in small doses. Does the medical profession run in your family then, Dr Ruthven?"

"Oh aye, I mean to say, nay. It dinna run in the family. I'm the only doctor. My sister Bella is a botanist. The micro-use application was my idea. I dinna have the patience for publication, so I let her write it up. Better if people know, aye?"

Professor Tunstell gave her his full unblinking attention. His blue-green eyes were large behind the small gold spectacles. "You let her publish *your* findings?"

"Nay. I merely mentioned to her that I'd success with small doses of digitalis to increase heart rate, rather than using it to murder people. Bella thought it a fine concept and looked into it further with me as consult." Arsenic wrinkled her nose. "'Tis what she does. We deduced some verra exciting applications." She knew she was about to start rambling, but *they had*. "To counteract constrictive breathing disorders. To allay sluggish speed malfunctions in the heart. Even atrial arrhythmias. Can you imagine?"

She trailed off because everyone was staring at her.

"My goodness" – Lady Akeldama squirmed in her chair – "she's almost as bad as Percy."

"This is ridiculous," said Miss Tunstell, although she was looking more thoughtful than annoyed. "We can't justify another one, can we? Virgil may never forgive us."

"But *listen* to her," objected the captain. "She's brilliant! And she has a lovely accent. I find Sottish tremendously reassuring, don't you?"

Arsenic flushed in pleasure and dipped her head. She was beginning to rather adore Lady Akeldama. There was no artifice to her. Which, in Arsenic's family, was unheard of. Even her beloved da, while open and loving, could be secretive.

"You didn't *want to publish?*" Professor Tunstell was staring at Arsenic as if she had spontaneously grown a third arm.

Into this mild hysteria came the welcome relief of the dour Virgil. He knocked and then entered carrying a laden tea tray.

Miss Tunstell waved him in. "Now, this is mostly for you, Dr Ruthven. Do help yourself. We've already had five portions. That's a bit much tea in one afternoon, even for us."

"Heresy." The captain looked fervent.

Miss Tunstell gave a long-suffering sigh and began to pour. Despite her comments, everyone was given a fresh cuppa. Although only Arsenic was offered the plate of scones.

Arsenic, too nervous to eat, waved it away.

The captain seemed to find this the first thing about Arsenic not to her liking. "You don't want a scone? But *everyone* wants scones."

Arsenic didn't know what to say. She didn't like scones – nasty dry things – and she hadn't a large appetite, regardless. She'd already consumed a perfectly sufficient breakfast. She wouldn't need to eat again for ages. "I'm na... That is... I'm na a verra good eater."

"What?" The captain's expression darkened and her peculiar yellow eyes narrowed.

Miss Tunstell came over all placating. "Rue darling, that'd be a nice change aboard this ship."

Professor Tunstell added, "I'm not either, to be fair." He gave Virgil an affectionate little nudge after the laddie delivered his tea. Virgil scowled approvingly back at the man.

"No one cares about you, Percy." Miss Tunstell sniffed.

Arsenic scraped her brain for something witty to say to

combat Lady Akeldama's disapproval. Then, without reason or instigation, the sugar pot exploded.

It wiggled a bit. Gave a loud wheezing *bang* and shot its lid up into the air.

The thing was made of metal, so it didn't shatter. Granules of sugar flew about. The lid clattered to the table before rolling onto the floor. Nothing serious.

Arsenic jerked in her chair and then let out a surprised laugh. The lid hadn't hit anyone but she couldn't shut down her doctor nature if she tried. "Is anyone hurt? Sugar in the eye?"

"See, there? Perfect." The captain sounded triumphant.

Some kind of test? Arsenic cocked her head, trying to decide whether to be annoyed or charmed.

"Yes, well, I see your point, Rue dear." Miss Tunstell's blue eyes were warm on Arsenic's face.

Professor Tunstell wasn't paying attention. "Not publish? *Not publish!*"

Arsenic decided to ignore him, as that seemed to be the general tactic among the ladies and she was already beginning to consider herself one of them. She *wanted* to be one of them, almost more than she wanted the position. Besides, the professor was profoundly academic. Scholars could get outlandish and unhinged.

"Weel, that was fun." Arsenic stood to find the lid, which had ended up near the door on her side of the table.

"You're a good sort, aren't you, Doctor." Miss Tunstell was decided.

Arsenic retrieved the lid and sat back down, glowing with their approval.

"It was only a *little* explosion." Professor Tunstell seemed a touch annoyed by his sister's praise.

"For show?" suggested Arsenic.

The captain laughed. "How did you know?"

"My family has interests that are occasionally subversive."

"They like tricky little devices, eh?"

"My mother's usually explode with greater purpose," Arsenic said without really thinking about it. *Oops.*

Lady Akeldama became momentarily serious. "Your mother doesn't know *my* mother, does she?"

"Who's your mother?"

"Lady Maccon."

"I dinna *think* so." The name rang some faint bells but not in connection with Preshea Ruthven. Lady Maccon was something else...political? Or scandalous? Perhaps both? Arsenic rarely paid attention to London gossip. She grew up in Scotland, never had a London season, and then promptly left in pursuit of an education.

"If her interest is in devices, she's more likely to know Quesnel's mother," said Miss Tunstell.

"Who's that?" wondered Arsenic.

"Madame Lefoux."

That was a name Arsenic knew. "Aye, of course. But that hardly makes a difference, everyone orders from Lefoux."

"True, true." The captain, for some reason, preened at this. Apparently, Arsenic had said something bang on. Really this was the oddest interview.

"Quesnel is the inventor's son, then?" Arsenic wondered what connection he had to the ship.

"Could we get through one afternoon without talking about that man?" Professor Tunstell had a pained expression on his face.

"Never!" Lady Akeldama grinned.

The professor made an exasperated noise. Then glanced at Arsenic and went red about the ears. He stared hurriedly back down at her accreditation papers, which he'd been fiddling with restlessly.

Arsenic reached over and extracted them from him.

"Righto, yes." He frowned at her gloveless hands.

Arsenic wondered what he found so continually objectionable about her. He'd barely looked at her the entire interview. And now the absence of gloves offended? She couldn't very well stitch up a wound wearing fancy-wear, now could she?

Another knock sounded, and since he was still there, no doubt collecting gossip for the decklings, Virgil opened the door.

An extremely handsome swarthy gentleman stuck his head in.

Arsenic's mother was one of the most beautiful humans on the planet, which had taught Arsenic to be wary of anyone gorgeous. Not those like Professor Tunstell, who was awkwardly unaware of his allure, but those like this man. Whoever he was, he knew what he looked like. His gaze was self-assured and direct.

Predator, thought Arsenic, noting the way he moved, how he occupied the doorway – barring it but also watching the hallway with his peripheral vision. *Trained.* He was admirably fit, too. The way he stood, so balanced. She assessed his stance. Not fencing, something rougher, closer... Knives, perhaps?

He looked away from her and at the captain. There was a passing physical resemblance between them, although the eyes were different. His were dark and fierce.

"Little cousin," he said, which answered that question, "we must make with going." He had a strong Italian accent.

Lady Akeldama introduced him to Arsenic in a matter-of-fact tone. "Dr Ruthven, this is Mr Tarabotti, my cousin. Charming man, he once tried to kill me."

The Italian made a clucking noise. "Not personal. And that time has gone."

The captain's face was inscrutable. "You shot and killed my mother's butler."

Arsenic was fascinated. What an interesting dynamic these two had.

"No no, little cousin, that was one of my men, not me. Sì, if I had known who he was and how important, I would no see him dead. But he is still here. Did you want him to see this?" He gestured at Arsenic imperiously. "I could tell him. Sì?"

"What am I going to do with you?" was the captain's almost affectionate response.

Really, was everyone aboard this ship slightly mad? Much of Arsenic's initial conversation with the decklings was beginning to make sense. All the crew seemed, in a word, *eccentric*.

Mr Tarabotti smiled. "Too late, little cousin. I stay here. You done almost? You maybe do not wish late, no? Your father, he will throw a fop."

Miss Tunstell said, "Throw a *fit*, I think you mean, Rodrigo."

"Sì?"

"Yes. He *is a fop* but he *throws a fit*."

The captain interrupted, "Yes yes. Soon. But this is more important."

"Sì?" Mr Tarabotti shrugged and left. He said something in Italian to someone waiting in the hallway as he closed the door.

Arsenic turned to look curiously at the cheerful captain. "He tried to kill you?"

"Obviously he wasn't successful."

Arsenic nodded. *Obviously.* "My mother would say that shows a lack of follow-through."

The captain grinned. "Your mother sounds logical."

Miss Tunstell added, although not critically, "And a little bloodthirsty."

It was a fair assessment. "You've no idea," replied Arsenic, because it seemed they really didn't.

The captain wrinkled her nose. "Old Cousin Roddy there is not so bad. He's been reformed through excessive reading. Percy was in charge of extensive literary recuperation efforts."

Arsenic smiled at Professor Tunstell, not quite sure what to make of this explanation, but knowing that books could be good medicine.

The man dipped his head and blushed.

The two ladies looked at him as if he'd done the most unusual thing ever.

Miss Tunstell's voice was choked in horror or amusement. "Brother dear, are you well? We do currently have a *doctor* aboard."

Professor Tunstell said, "Shove off, Tiddles," and looked at Arsenic from under his lashes.

Arsenic tried smiling at him again. This only seemed to make matters worse. He got redder, stopped looking at her, and took great interest in the tabletop.

Lady Akeldama resumed the interview. Or, more precisely, concluded it. "Well, there is only one more thing to ask, Doctor."

"Aye?" Arsenic held her breath.

"How do you feel about cats?"

"Oh! I love them."

"You do, how much?" Miss Tunstell was suspicious.

"Weel, I have yours on my lap at the moment. He's lovely."

"What?" Professor Tunstell stood in shock.

Arsenic pushed her chair back slightly so they could see the handsome black-and-white tom curled happily on her.

"Oh good, Footnote." The captain beamed. "There's no greater mark of approval. Are we in agreement?"

"Yes," said Miss Tunstell, promptly, "although there is remuneration to discuss. Leave that to me while you finish getting spiffed?"

"I'll be fine, stop fussing. Sun hasn't even set yet. Percy?"

"What?"

"Do you approve of Dr Ruthven for the position?"

Professor Tunstell went wide-eyed. "What position?"

"Of ship's doctor. Do pay attention."

"Oh yes, *that*. Certainly. She seems perfectly capable and overly qualified. That is to say, I can't think of any reason why not . . . Not *publish*? It is, of course, unconscionable, but shouldn't impact her surgical abilities, should it? Implies a certain lack of ego. Or lack of confidence in her abilities? I'm not sure . . . Not to publish . . ."

"I dinna need the world's approval, I only need to heal it."

Professor Tunstell gave her a sceptical look. "If you say so."

There was yet another knock on the door.

Arsenic might have been annoyed by the constant interruptions, but really each one was more interesting than the last. She swivelled about in her chair eager for whatever happened next, but careful not to disturb the cat, Footnote. *Such a charming name.*

A tall woman of Eastern extraction stuck her head in. Perfect skeletal structure, clear complexion, glossy hair – healthy. A little too healthy? Supernatural, perhaps? Arsenic had always thought her mother stunning. Preshea Ruthven was all English rose and porcelain doll. But this lady was desert sands and ancient sculptures, expensive silks and spices. Preshea was power in the shadows, manipulation and subversion. This woman was sunlight and command – people once knelt at her feet, unashamed.

Actress, maybe? Famous dancer or singer?

"Tash." Miss Tunstell's voice was warm and buttery. "Darling, you're awake."

The woman's liquid almond eyes swept over Arsenic, assessing, and then moved beyond her to the others. "Yes, little one, and we all know what that means?"

"Oh heavens, it's after dark! We must prepare to depart at once! We have a wedding to attend!"

That explained everyone's excessively elaborate attire.

Arsenic decided it was worth disturbing Footnote. She tipped the cat off her lap and stood. "Oh, I dinna mean to keep you. Who's getting married?"

The captain was now standing. "Me, unfortunately." Her lovely ivory gown revealed itself to be a wedding dress.

TWO

Drama Dama Damp

These people are insane and I adore them.

Arsenic hurried to shut her medical kit. "Weel, I'll make myself scarce then." It hissed as it folded and spiralled down. "When will you be notifying us all about the position?"

Lady Akeldama was making her way around the table in a cautious lumbering manner. Arsenic's physician's eye was caught by her movements. Perhaps her roundness was not dietarily dictated. *A bairn, then.*

She waddled up to Arsenic. "Don't be silly. It's filled."

"Oh aye?" Arsenic was crushed. *Then why have I been sitting here all this time?*

"By you, of course!" The captain grinned at her. "Floote approves, don't you, Floote?"

Much to Arsenic's shock, a ghost was floating next to her. He was a dour-looking gentleman in clothing from the 1840s. A ghost tethered to a dirigible, who'd have thought?

"Formerly Floote, this is our new doctor, Arsenic Ruthven. Will she do? Yours is the last vote of import."

The ghost, who seemed a little worse for wear – Arsenic would guess he was edging into poltergeist stage – gave her a regal nod of approval.

Arsenic nodded back.

The captain twirled in a cautious circle. "Do I look like a proper bride, Floote?"

The ghost nodded again. His expression was amorphous but possibly near to sentiment.

He drifted down through the floor.

"Old family retainer," explained the captain, "my grandfather's valet and then my mother's butler. He's very wise, and possibly an evil mastermind, although he'd never admit to it, even after death."

"How is he here?" Arsenic couldn't help her curiosity, it was medical in origin.

"We have a preservation tank."

Arsenic could feel her skin prickle. "You are equipped to transport supernatural creatures by air?"

"It's only for Floote, although we have used . . . That's a long story."

Arsenic was disposed to be open to new ideas, even extraordinary ones involving the ghosts of butlers.

"Now, would you like to come along to my bally wedding or not?"

Arsenic was both touched and surprised. She gestured down at herself. "I'm na dressed for it."

"My dear," said Lady Akeldama with a grin, "at my wedding we are lucky if half the company stays dressed *at all*."

Miss Tunstell added, by way of explanation, "Half the family is werewolves."

Professor Tunstell snorted. "And the other half is vampires." He gestured to his stunning cravat. "So the rest of us must be *over*dressed. I have to wear a top hat."

Arsenic shuddered at the thought. Top hats were absurd affectations. She'd had to wear one back in her *I'm na a woman, I'm a doctor* phase of training. "Ridiculous things."

The professor lost a little of his awkwardness at that. "Exactly! They wobble. Virgil has me in a stovepipe for this evening. A *stovepipe*!"

Arsenic gave him a sympathetic smile. He promptly became once more reticent. Perhaps he had taken against her, or was simply painfully shy. Pity, he was rather adorable.

Arsenic turned her attention back to the ladies, who were making their way into the hallway. The tall goddess awaited, wearing an elaborate silk robe over a long satin skirt. Her hair was down and she wore no hat and little jewellery. Arsenic didn't feel so bad about her golfing outfit if that was allowed at the wedding.

"If you and Prim can come to favourable terms, you're very welcome to stay aboard *The Spotted Custard* immediately, Dr Ruthven."

I really have the position! I'm employed at last.

Arsenic wanted to hug her new captain. "Oh, thank you! I'm sure we can come to terms." *I'm na disposed to be picky.*

Lady Akeldama smiled. "Good! Then Prim will show you to your quarters, get you settled and spruced up. Unless you don't want to come along and see the pomp and circus? For which, of course, I wouldn't blame you. I wouldn't attend myself, except that's rather the point."

"Who are you marrying?"

"Oh, it's only Quesnel."

"Quesnel?" That name again.

"Yes. He's chief engineer aboard ship, and rather a pip with devices and machines. Takes after his mother. Doesn't look like her, though. He's got this cute little button nose and blond hair and he's charming and suave. He's French, so of course he's suave. Flirts like anything. I rather adore him, you see? Well, love him, really. And since there's coal in the boiler, everyone is determined that we better had."

Arsenic arched both brows. "Seems logical."

"That's what Quesnel said."

"Are you na happy about it?"

"I think I will be, *after* the wedding. Right now it seems rather a fuss and bother."

Arsenic nodded. She'd seen many a wedding over the years devolve into crisis. Her extended mess of sisters and cousins was a mixed bag. They tended towards the dramatic when gathered together for any length of time. There was a distinct possibility she'd escaped to Africa to get away from having to attend any more family weddings. Lady Akeldama's, however, was someone *else's* family. Much easier on the nerves.

"We'll discuss your condition soon?"

"If we must. Everyone is insisting it might be complicated. It's certainly awkward." The captain patted her rounded belly, but her face showed no genuine annoyance. Then she turned away to yell, "Primrose!"

Arsenic suspected that she'd need to become accustomed to fast changes in topic and attention.

"Prim, do stop nuzzling. You're being unduly romantic. There's a wedding about to happen, romance has no place here! You must settle Dr Ruthven. Indenture isn't necessary but I want a nice tidy contract. That way no one can poach her."

Arsenic warmed to the captain further. She also tried not to stare at the way staid Miss Primrose Tunstell was wrapped in the arms of the silk-robed goddess who was licking her neck by way of greeting. *Licking!*

Miss Tunstell recollected the *staid* part of her personality and pulled away, although not far.

"Tash, stop. Later, darling. Now, Doctor, let me show you to the room we've set aside for your treatments. It's directly across the hallway from a small bedroom, we thought that might work best. You could leave both doors open when necessary. If you have an overnight patient or whatnot. You can check them both over, and if you approve, we'll discuss salary? Quickly as possible, please, the ceremony is supposed to start in an hour."

Behind her, Arsenic heard the professor say, in an injured tone, "A stovepipe, Rue, must I?"

"Virgil knows best." The captain was unmoved by his pleas.

"Virgil is a snob."

"My vampire father extraordinaire will be there, you do realize?"

"Yes but..."

"And Lord Falmouth. You know how Biffy feels about hats."

"Yes, but he doesn't care about me. He only cares about—"

"And your mother's drones, reporting back to her on every little detail."

A long sigh. "Oh very well, if you really wish it."

Arsenic turned in time to see him subtly assist the captain to walk down the hall. He might complain a treat, but he clearly had a good heart.

"Do I need a hat?" fretted Arsenic.

Miss Tunstell smiled at her. "Oh, that's easily sorted, I've plenty to spare. Have you met my Tash? Tasherit Sekhmet, this is our new doctor, Arsenic Ruthven. We're rather excited about her. She's splendid."

The stunning goddess said, without really taking her eyes off Miss Tunstell, "Splendid. Arsenic, is it? After the toxic chemical?"

"Sekhmet, is it? After the angry goddess?" Arsenic replied pertly. Not wanting to explain her mother's questionable sense of humour in naming all four of her daughters after deadly poisons.

Liquid brown eyes glanced at Arsenic and the regal head tilted.

"Tash is our resident werelioness, so you won't be treating her much," explained Miss Tunstell as if a female werecat were an ordinary run-of-the-mill kind of thing.

"Your *what?*"

But the werelioness was focused on Miss Tunstell again. "Why aren't you wearing that dress I love with the lovely ball fringe all over?"

"Because you always bat at it."

Arsenic decided to hope that everything would become clear once she learned more about her new position. She was determined to like it aboard *The Spotted Custard*. It was an awfully confusing place thus far. But, if nothing else, it looked to be an amusing situation.

Percy abhorred parties. He detested balls and shunned gatherings. He hated card games and gambling dens. He avoided everything from intimate dinner conclaves to sporting events. Anything, in fact, where one was forced into regrettably uncomfortable clothing, assembling in numbers greater than six, and making a show of being entertained by other people.

But Percy reserved his true and utter ire, his loathing above all other loathings, for *weddings*.

Quite apart from everything else, they were the one social event for which a gentleman couldn't readily form an excuse. Add that to the fact that weddings inevitably included flocks of young ladies driven to twitterpations, with marriage on the brain, and Percy within their grasp – pure torture.

It wasn't the young ladies' fault per se. Percy found the society of most people tedious. The exchange of meaningless pleasantries required by polite society was an insult to his intellect. If he had to discuss the weather *one more time* he might . . . well, there was no knowing what he might do. No doubt he would find out at this event, because weddings brought out the worst in everyone.

The only upside of a wedding was that during the first part one wasn't required to do anything but sit in an uncomfortable pew.

It occurred to Percy, while he shifted about to keep the blood flowing to his nether regions, that he was profoundly relieved his sister had a preference for her own sex. He'd have to thank her later. It meant that the chances of Percy ever having to actively participate in one of these blasted things was slim.

Percy brought along a book about jellyfish migratory patterns, which was quite fascinating. He spent the entire ceremony reading that. He wasn't a fool, though. He'd selected it in part because the outside was red and gilt, making it look biblical. *The sacred jellyfish pilgrimage.* He amused himself imagining the presiding bishop, a well-bearded elderly gentleman with unfortunate ears, wearing a mantle of jellyfish.

No doubt it was a perfectly nice ceremony. Percy chose not to notice.

As they left the church, Percy with Primrose on one arm and Tasherit on the other (for the sake of appearances), he realized his sister was crying.

"What's wrong, Tiddles? Surely it wasn't all that awful."

"It was *beautiful.*"

"Uh?" He looked hopefully at Tash for support, but even she seemed slightly overcome. Most un-catlike of her.

Prim dabbed her eyes with an embroidered handkerchief. "It went so smoothly. And *everyone* is here. Well, not Rue's blood parents or our mother but that's probably for the best. Although I'm certain Rue misses her paw most awfully. Lord Akeldama did a glorious job of escorting her, don't you feel? He looked so proud and beautiful. That outfit. Extraordinary. Like a great sparkling aspic jelly." Apparently, Lord Akeldama's apparel was sufficient to start the waterworks again.

Percy looked around, bewildered. He caught sight of their too-lovely new doctor, who seemed mostly amused at being thrust unexpectedly upon a wedding. This was good. She'd need to be relaxed about getting thrust into things, if she were to survive *The Spotted Custard.* Then he realized he was staring at her – again! – which was vexing and, evidently, a new failing of his. He looked quickly back at his leaky sister.

"Lord and Lady Maccon aren't here? I hadn't noticed."

"You hadn't noticed? You *hadn't noticed* that the bride's parents were in absentia? Oh Percy, for goodness' sake. It's not as if Lord Maccon could be mistaken for Lord Akeldama, and you know they would have *both* led her down the aisle if he were present. And it's not as if you can overlook Rue's mother, either, if she's in a room. I mean Aunt Alexia isn't exactly *quiet.* Of course they

aren't here! Rodrigo is here. Aunt Alexia wouldn't even be able to
be in the same city as him, remember? I think that's the general
breadth of preternatural effect, the weather being clear and all.
We're lucky, it being springtime."

Marvellous, thought Percy, *we're on to the weather already.*

"We're off to see them next," Prim continued in a tone suggesting Percy ought already to know this.

Percy considered. *Did I know?* Sometimes people made plans
around him while he was thinking about more important
things. Like whether time travelled in waves, lines, or cycles, or
if it was a particulate gas, like aether. *Hummm...*

"Percy? Percy!"

"What? Oh yes, where are we going next?"

"Casually floating to Egypt." That was Tasherit's amused
addendum.

Percy glared at her. "I missed the part where Rue's parents
weren't invited. That isn't odd? In a wedding? No parent?"

Prim clasped her free hand to her chest and glared at him.
But at least she'd stopped crying. They'd joined the bride's side
and were waiting to throw flowers (or shoes, or small bits of
bacon, or something equally ridiculous) at the wedded couple.
Peculiar custom.

Percy made it a point never to throw anything.

He looked around, avoiding Prim's exasperated frown, and
nodded at Madame Lefoux and Miss Imogene, who stood on
the groom's side. Miss Imogene was beaming and even Madame
Lefoux was showing dimples. They clearly approved the match.
Percy wondered if he could bend Madame Lefoux's ear about
Floote's tank at some point. His calculations suggested a few
modifications might be in order. He didn't want to discuss this
with Quesnel, because, well... Quesnel was irksome.

Prim kept talking, unfortunately. "Not invited! Of course
they're invited! But you know Rue's father can't leave Egypt
anymore."

"He can't?" Percy had lost the conversational thread.

"Oh my goodness, Percival Ormond Tunstell! Must you be so tiresome? Remember the whole trip where we floated them *to* Egypt and how we had to keep Lord Maccon in the tank because he was going mad?"

Percy nodded. "Oh yes, that's right. I see, well, good thing they didn't attend the ceremony, isn't it? Why didn't you say so at the start? Wouldn't do to have an insane werewolf at a wedding."

Prim emitted an exasperated wheezing noise.

"What was that, young Percy?" A warm voice spoke behind them.

The Alpha of the local werewolf pack and his Beta had joined their party.

Primrose turned to the two gentlemen in evident relief. "Oh, Lord Falmouth, what a pleasure. Do save me from my brother? He's so impossible. And Professor Lyall, what a delight to find you back in London at long last. Are you enjoying the move to Blackheath?"

Lord Falmouth, otherwise known as Biffy, gave Prim a small polite smile. "We are indeed. It suits the pack well. Thank you for asking. A very pleasant evening to you too, my dear, and you, Percy. And Lady Tasherit! I'd no idea you'd be staying with the *Custard*. Surely all that floating about can't be good for the supernatural constitution?"

"I manage." Tasherit looked as smug as only a feline could when confronted with a lycanthrope. *Werecats are superior to werewolves in this matter.* She didn't say it, but even Percy, who wasn't a perceptive person, heard her unspoken words. Fortunately, she wasn't looking to tease the wolves too much, as she quickly added, "The little one here gave me good reason to stay."

"Did she indeed?" Biffy's eyes ran approvingly over the two ladies. "Excellent. Lovely hat, by the way, Miss Primrose."

Prim clutched at Percy's arm and let out a small sigh. As if the Alpha's hat accolades meant something profound. Well, Percy supposed that Lord Falmouth was a noted authority on all things hat. He also possessed a great deal of social standing as London's first Alpha dandy. It was nice to know his sister had the wolves on her side, if the vampires decided to object to Prim's choices in hats, or romantic partners, for that matter.

Primrose hadn't yet told their mother about Tasherit.

Percy hoped his mother wouldn't ruin everything. He liked Tasherit and he liked Prim *with* Tasherit. It was nonsense for anyone to feel otherwise. Although, to be fair, their mother was entirely composed of nonsense.

He looked back at Miss Imogene and Madame Lefoux. They'd been together for *ages*. So it was clearly possible for two ladies to give a good showing.

The conversation had gone on, as usual, without Percy. *This is what comes of weddings*, he thought glumly. *I fritter away my considerable intellect thinking about relationships, and emotions, and my mother.*

A lull and Percy could ask something that actually interested him. "How's the research trundling along these days, Professor Lyall?"

That permitted Percy and the pack Beta a modest scientific discourse, while everyone poured out of the church and assembled to either side of the doorway.

Biffy was soon flanked by members of his pack, most of whom Percy ought to know well enough to name, but didn't. The only one he did know, the odious Gamma, Major Channing, was not in attendance. Biffy explained that Channing had something to do for the Bureau of Unnatural Registry in Hyde Park.

"Not good at weddings, anyway, our Channing," explained Professor Lyall.

Percy wondered if he himself might utilize a similar excuse going forward?

Finally Rue and Quesnel, arm in arm and safely wed, walked out. Well, *waddled* in Rue's case.

The assembled decklings, sooties, and other scamps from *The Spotted Custard* let go their dirigible candle lanterns, which floated up into the night. They also set forth a cacophony of hoots and whistles. Everyone else threw flowers, mostly snow-drops, and not bacon. Percy was slightly disappointed.

"Oh, it's as pretty as I planned." His sister pressed her free hand to her mouth in an excess of delight.

"You did good, little one." Tasherit's voice had that tone it only got around Prim. Warm enough to make Percy uncomfortable.

Biffy said, "You organized the wedding, Miss Primrose?"

"Of course she did." Percy was moved to defence by the won-der in the werewolf's tone. "Primrose organizes *everything.*" Only *he* was allowed to criticize his sister.

"That was approval, young man, not censure." Biffy was not at all riled. He was remarkably calm, for a werewolf Alpha. Not at all like Rue's father, who was, in Percy's opinion, a tempera-mental grouch.

Rue and Quesnel did look remarkably happy and pleased with life (even Percy had to grudgingly admit *that*). Following them came Lord Akeldama and a small bevy of drones. Last out of the church were Rodrigo and Anitra, who'd stood up with the couple.

They'd discussed it being Primrose and Percy in the posi-tions of honour. But Prim wanted to be in the crowd making certain everything went smoothly. Percy flat-out refused. In the end, Rue had been persuaded by the irony of it all, having the cousin who had tried to kill her stand as witness. It held a certain paradox that appealed to her sense of humour. Not to mention that Anitra, wearing her best Drifter robes, all gold fringed and *foreign*, was a jab in the eye of every British snob there.

For as long as he'd known her (and that was his entire life), Rue hated to do anything the normal way, so Percy was not sur-prised that she took her vows with an Italian preternatural best man and an aravani matron of honour – damn the consequences.

Dr Ruthven was standing with the decklings. Spoo was bend-ing her ear. Virgil was nearby, sporting an impossibly tall top hat. Percy was glad she'd company but also envious of the two young persons. She was clearly delighted by their antics, clapping as the lantern dirigibles floated up.

Professor Lyall was suddenly next to him. At some point Prim had dropped Percy's arm and taken Biffy's instead.

"The Italian who stood up with Quesnel, he looks familiar. Like someone I knew long ago."

Percy tilted his head. "Rodrigo Tarabotti. Rue's cousin."

Professor Lyall started. "Preternatural?"

"Of course. Otherwise Lady Maccon, at least, would be in attendance."

"I didn't know." Professor Lyall was usually so inscrutable. Yet his eyes were suddenly swimming with emotion. *Sad? Happy? Bewildered? Lost?*

Percy wished he were better at reading people, but he was only good at reading books so he said nothing. This was beyond him.

Professor Lyall recovered. "Floote, I suppose?"

Percy cocked his head. "He kept an eye on him, if that's what you're asking."

"And you lot found him again?"

"Not really. He found us. Tried to kill Rue, got Quesnel instead."

"What?"

"As you can see, it all worked out, in the end. Quesnel survived and we adopted Rodrigo. His character required reforming. I applied Greek philosophy and then a strong dose of *Higher Common Sense.*"

"Oh?"

Percy was quite proud of this achievement. "Rodrigo's not bad, simply soulless. We deduced that a book group might give him a strong ethical foundation. Then he fell in love, so it all worked out."

"In love?"

"With Anitra. The Drifter woman, next to him. They married at the New Year. Much nicer wedding. None of this fuss and bother."

Professor Lyall looked strangely pleased. "Yes, that would work. Love usually does, you know? With preternaturals."

Percy didn't *know*, but he'd a working theory and was glad to have it corroborated by an outside source. He'd hate to have Rodrigo go rotten again and have to come up with an entire new course of study. Giving a man a surrogate soul was challenging work. He was pleased to find the solution was to give the man a heart. And even more pleased that it had been Anitra to do so. Percy liked Anitra. She was quiet and kind and never disturbed him in his library.

"Will you introduce me to him, Professor Tunstell?" asked Professor Lyall softly.

"Now?"

"Later. At the reception."

"I'd be delighted." An odd request that a werewolf would want to meet a curse breaker. Especially one such as Rodrigo Tarabotti. The Italian had, after all, spent most of his life hunting and killing werewolves.

"And perhaps I might visit *The Spotted Custard* one night before you leave? I should like to speak with Formerly Floote."

Percy shrugged. "I'm not the ship's secretary of supernatural encounters." The Beta looked taken aback, so Percy hurried on. "You're welcome to try. He can be eccentric, like most ghosts."

"He's still cohesive?"

"Mostly. The Lefoux tank is a work of genius."

"Yes. She's brilliant."

"I think this one is mostly Quesnel's doing." Percy didn't like to give such credit to the man, but he strove for truth in all things, and Quesnel was a shipmate.

"He's also brilliant. A good match for our little Rue."

"You think?"

"You don't?"

"Mr Lefoux and I are not always of the same mind in matters of publication accreditation."

"A serious business."

"Very. But he seems to please Rue. Not that she isn't easily pleased." That might not be a nice thing to say at their wedding, so Percy pressed on. "And he is disposed to find her adorable and diverting rather than ridiculous, which is key to cohabitation, I suspect."

"Do you indeed, young Percy?" Professor Lyall looked like he might be secretly laughing at him.

Percy gave him a hard stare. "I beg you to remember who my mother is."

Professor Lyall sobered instantly. "Of course. You would know ridiculous, wouldn't you?"

Percy drew himself up. "No one is better equipped to judge tolerance for silliness than I." He nodded towards his sister as well. Who certainly wasn't as bad as their mother, but could be quite frivolous when the occasion demanded. Her dress for this evening's festivities was so replete with furbelows and frills she practically fluttered about the churchyard. Percy thought Dr Ruthven's golf outfit far more practical and flattering.

I must stop thinking about that female. It wasn't like him to notice strange women's sportswear.

He sighed at himself.

Professor Lyall was circumspect in the face of human weakness and allowed the subject to drop.

Arsenic was in awe, the wedding was massive. Hundreds of people were in attendance, yet Miss Tunstell had them herded from one location to the next with the speed and efficiency of the best brigadier – although a very ruffled version thereof.

Arsenic stuck with Spoo and the other decklings, for they had only minor responsibilities and were disposed to enjoy themselves in a less formal manner. Spoo explained that since the party numbered so many of the supernatural set, the celebration was to be held in Vauxhall Bob.

"Some of Kingair came all the way from Scotland, not to mention the London Pack. Woolsey Hive sent delegates and so did Baroness Tunstell. That means two different werewolf packs, and two different vampire hives. Add in Lord Akeldama, who's a rove. Things could get royally wigged." Spoo looked pleased at the prospect.

Arsenic was intrigued by the predatory currents. She was also relieved she'd brought along her medical kit.

Based on the hanging gardens of Babylon – or what historians thought those gardens might look like – Vauxhall Bob showcased meticulous mathematical topiary and fine symmetrical sculptures, combined with automated oscillating waterfalls and fountains. It featured exotic botanicals collected from all over the Empire harmoniously balanced against traditional herbaceous borders – ferns and palm trees in equal measure.

A marvel of modern engineering, Vauxhall Bob was also mobile (unlike its grounded compatriot, Vauxhall Gardens, which everyone thought of as terribly old-fashioned). It could crank upwards to become several stories high, providing privacy for special events, like weddings. Once deployed, steam and clockwork kept different sections rotating slowly while others raised and lowered, puffing quietly and emitting white steam out the base, which gave it the appearance of resting upon a cloud. Bob also boasted unique hydro-brolly action, should the weather attempt one of those spontaneous showers so typical of early spring in London.

It was, in the end, a work of art that could be appreciated from within or without. A visual testament to technological dominance.

Arsenic herself had never attended anything so grand as to be *inside* Bob. Those who walked arrived first, because that was the state of London traffic during the start of the season. The garden was lowered and waiting for them.

Spoo introduced Arsenic to *The Spotted Custard*'s deckhands, Bork and Willard, who were also in charge of security for the evening.

"Until Tasherit gets here, of course."

"And how does she fit with the crew?"

"Our werelioness," said Spoo proudly. "She's very fierce. She's basically first mate. Lady Captain has her in charge of military matters."

"*The Spotted Custard* isna a pleasure floater? Why *military matters?*" Arsenic had hoped to leave the army behind.

"Well, theoretically we're all play and no teeth. But we tend to get into messes." Spoo grinned. "That's why they decided to hire a doctor."

"Wouldna be cheaper to avoid the messes in the first place?"

"You'd think."

"What sort of messes?"

"Oh, you know, *all sorts.*"

Elusive child. Arsenic decided not to push, she was in it now and would likely find out soon enough.

Virgil, who'd been silently trudging behind them, muttered something about *messes being hell on wardrobes and wouldn't it be nice if they just went and visited a place for a change and didn't try to fix anything?* Spoo ignored him. Arsenic gave him a sympathetic glance.

The rest of the guests slowly trickled in. Arsenic kept feeling she ought to know who was who, because no doubt most of them were supernaturally or politically significant.

Had she not recently returned from abroad. Had she cared about London society. Had she paid better attention to her mother's lessons.

Well, she hadn't.

So Arsenic stuck close to Spoo, who did her best to explain but really didn't give a toss for the mucky-mucks. Spoo ended up playing cards with Virgil, the decklings, and several sooties. Arsenic blethered on with the sooties for a bit about the dangers of boiler work. Everyone from Arsenic's new ship seemed perfectly civil.

The only one she hadn't any luck getting to know was an

aggressive ginger female with a fierce expression. She was scrappy and grumpy and Spoo declined to introduce them on the following grounds...

"You know what a wood louse is, Doctor?"

"Aye, I do."

"The prof would come over all sniffy." Spoo nodded at Professor Tunstell, who was attempting to assist an elderly matron to climb up onto Bob, without anyone noticing he was being nice. "He'd say a wood louse is an *intransigent terrestrial isopod crustacean inclined to consume deceased flora*."

Arsenic didn't really know Professor Tunstell that well and yet, "That seems exactly like something he'd say."

"Well, it's also an accurate description of *The Spotted Custard*'s sainted head greaser, Miss Aggie Phinkerlington. Only imagine the *deceased flora* is basically all human joy."

"Really?"

"Oh yes. She's upset with me and Lady Captain, most of the time."

"Why?"

"Presumably because we continue to exist and she'd prefer we didn't."

Arsenic gave the greaser an assessing look. "She looks like she has indigestion." Arsenic wondered if the woman's mean spirit was the result of severe dyspepsia. Perhaps there was a medicinal solution to her ill-temper?

"That's the human joy she keeps swallowing. Disagrees with her."

"She dinna sound like a verra pleasant person."

Spoo's small face was morose. "Unfortunately, she's a dear friend of our Mr Quesnel, and he's aces. Even if he's got no taste. She's also awful good at being head greaser."

Arsenic nodded. "So we keep her but try to avoid her?"

"Exactly."

"Will do." Really, Spoo was a fount of useful information.

The decklings resumed their game. Arsenic decided it was a little odd to be the only adult palling about with the shipboard youngsters, so took herself off to find Miss Tunstell and ask if she required help with anything. On the way she noticed the hanging lanterns all about were shaped like cheerful ladybugs.

Miss Tunstell had everything under control. The spread of food was impressive and the flow of drink excessive. A brass band tooted enthusiastically on a special rotating platform. The newly wed Mr and Mrs Lefoux danced sedately below in a specially designed grotto, along with the more civilized attendees.

Miss Tunstell looked hopefully at Arsenic. "Are you enjoying yourself, Dr Ruthven?"

"Very much so, such a varied guest list."

"It's a bit of a crush, but between them, Rue and Quesnel know half of London."

"So it would appear."

Miss Tunstell frowned in sudden concern. "Rue is good for dancing? It's not overly energetic?"

"How far along is she?"

"Perhaps six months?"

Arsenic smiled at the fretting of a dear friend. "She'll be fine. A little light exercise is beneficial at this stage. Ensure she drinks water and sits occasionally or her feet may swell."

"Oh, I'm *so chuffed* you're coming aboard, Doctor."

"Was that one of the reasons?"

"It's one of *my* reasons. Rue's a bit wild. Hopefully she'll listen to you. We aren't sure, you see, what the baby will *be*."

"You mean boy or girl? There's no way to know."

"No. I mean preternatural, metanatural, or simply natural."

Arsenic started. "Oh." *What's a metanatural?* "I see I have some research to do on the state of our captain, before I come aboard."

Miss Tunstell looked approving. "Ask Percy. That is, Professor Tunstell. He keeps all the latest papers, even though abnormal biology isn't his particular sphere of interest."

Arsenic nodded. "Most births, in my experience, are similar, regardless of the end result." In the army she'd assisted with delivery for camp followers, hunting hounds, and even a horse. She wasn't perturbed.

Miss Tunstell's eye was caught by two newcomers – a matronly older woman in a feathered hat and a slightly less matronly, slightly less older woman in slightly fewer feathers who could only be her daughter.

"Oh lord," said Miss Tunstell, "what are *they* doing here?"

"Not invited?"

"Well, yes, of course they were invited. Only I never expected them to actually show up. And so late as to have missed the receiving line. What *can* they be thinking? That's Rue's maternal grandmother, Mrs Loontwill. She's *awful*. And that's Rue's aunt, Evylin something-or-other. She's less awful."

So far as Arsenic could tell, the two ladies seemed to represent London's bog standard lesser-aristocratic snob, displaying no greater assumed superiority or bad taste than anyone else of the breed.

Then Mrs Loontwill opened her mouth, speaking loudly to her daughter. "I see my granddaughter will let *anyone* attend her wedding, even the rabble and the poor." Mrs Loontwill was glaring at Spoo and her fellows, who let out a roar of amusement at something someone said. Cards were being tossed at the offender's head in appreciation. They looked happy.

Arsenic frowned.

Miss Tunstell's hand was to her mouth in distress.

"Mother," said Evylin, "she is Alexia's daughter, what did you expect? Quality?"

"Of course. You're right, dear, but Lord Akeldama is purported to have taste. This, *well*, this is beneath contempt!" Mrs Loontwill sneered at Vauxhall Bob and its occupants, as if they were something the fishmonger tossed.

Certainly there was a wide spectrum present, from sooties to scientists, aristocrats to actors, vampires to werewolves. The clothing ranged too, from high fashion to kilts to turbans. It was eclectic, but Arsenic couldn't see anything worth sneering at.

"Perhaps it is a fancy-dress wedding?" Mrs Loontwill contemptuously regarded Tasherit's silk robes and Anitra's embroidered scarves as the two women helped stabilize the wedding cake against the garden's movements.

"Oh no, what's Aggie doing?" Miss Tunstell panicked and moved as close as she dared to the newcomers. Arsenic followed.

The surly head greaser took up position, barring Mrs Loontwill and daughter from further entering the garden. Her arms were crossed.

"This can't be good," Miss Tunstell whispered, clutching Arsenic's arm for support.

Aggie leaned into Mrs Loontwill's bonnet-sphere and began hissing at her in low angry tones.

"Oh no." Miss Tunstell dropped Arsenic's arm and began wringing her hands. "Oh! Oh no no no. Aggie, *please* don't push the bride's grandmo... And *there* she goes!"

The head greaser shoved Mrs Loontwill hard in the shoulder, which caused the older woman to stumble backwards, and fall into a nearby fountain with a tremendous splash.

Aggie Phinkerlington stormed away and Miss Tunstell rushed to the fallen matriarch. Arsenic followed, clutching her medical kit. The fall looked to be more embarrassing than injurious, but one never could tell.

"Oh, Mrs Loontwill, I do apologize. I've no idea what came over our head greaser!" Miss Tunstell fluttered in horror.

"Are you injured, madam? I'm a doctor." Arsenic bent to perform a cursory examination while the Loontwill in question wallowed and sputtered.

"Doctor? You're female. You can't possibly be a *doctor*. Get off me, chit."

Arsenic stopped trying to help and backed away.

Mrs Loontwill extracted herself from the fountain with the aid of her daughter. "Primrose Tunstell, I expected better than *this*! Your guest list is not at all exclusive. You went so far as to allow *that* branch of the family to attend!"

"*That* branch? What? That branch of whose family?"

"Mine, of course. My maiden name is Phinkerlington. Didn't you know? The family went terribly downhill around my first marriage. Lost one of my brothers to a failed bite and the other to a ballooning accident. Haven't spoken to the Phinkerlingtons in years and here I find *a Phinkerlington at my granddaughter's wedding*. Shocking!"

"Well, that explains a lot." Miss Tunstell looked thoughtful.

"You'll have her removed immediately?" pressed Mrs Loontwill.

Miss Tunstell pursed her lips. "Aggie is an excellent greaser and a sterling member of our crew. She's a sourpuss but she's *our* sourpuss." She regarded Mrs Loontwill's damp dress. "You're quite soaked, Mrs Loontwill. It can't be comfortable for you in this chill evening air."

"You'll simply have to close over the garden and increase the temperature until I'm dry, won't you, girl?"

"Oh, will I? The entire garden? For you? And what about the werewolves? They prefer open air."

"Werewolves? Werewolves! Who cares about werewolves? And you'll be throwing that horrible violent redheaded menace of a Phinkerlington out as well, preferably when the garden is at full height."

"I will, will I?" Miss Tunstell crossed her arms and looked headmistress-ish. "Oh, Tash, good, there you are. Mrs Loontwill, do you know Tasherit Sekhmet? *The Spotted Custard*'s head of security and resident werecat?"

"Werecat? Werecat! Don't be ridiculous, child. There's no such thing as werecats."

"I assure you there are. I've intimate regular acquaintance with their existence."

Arsenic was entirely riveted by the drama, as indeed were a great many other guests. A large circle of spectators surrounded them.

The captain and her new husband, however, continued dancing in apparent obliviousness. Or more likely wilful ignorance.

Miss Tunstell turned to Miss Sekhmet, who Arsenic had to assume really was a werecat. She, too, had never heard of one, but she'd heard rumours of their discovery. Everyone in the scientific community had. As they'd heard of weremonkeys. There were supposed to be excellent *papers* on both. Probably written by a certain overly handsome redheaded professor.

Miss Sekhmet turned on Mrs Loontwill. The werecat's lip curled as if she wanted to hiss. "You're *moist*, madam."

"That female pushed me into a fountain!" Mrs Loontwill gestured widely, although Aggie Phinkerlington had long since disappeared.

"Aggie," Miss Tunstell explained.

Miss Sekhmet gave an elegant little *tut*. "Aggie is like that." She looked Mrs Loontwill up and down. "Difficult to know if you deserved it or not, with her. But in either case, the gardens will be lifting soon. You'd best climb down, go home, and get dry, madam."

"You're asking me to leave? *Me?*"

The goddess in silken robes had a toothy and not at all nice smile. "Yes, you. Go." Hers was the expression of a cat that could not lash her tail, but really wanted to.

"But..."

"Hurry along now." The werecat stepped forward. "Scat."

Apparently deciding on retreat as the better part of valour, the daughter grabbed her mother's arm. "Alexia isn't here anyway, Mother. What's the point in staying?"

"I haven't congratulated my granddaughter on her match! Not that congratulations are in order, mind you. Imagine marrying a lowly *engineer*. *Lady* Akeldama canoodling with a *steam wrangler*. It's beneath us all."

"*What* did you say, madam?" That voice belonged to a gentleman even Arsenic could identify, the superlative rove and fashion icon, Lord Akeldama.

The vampire was covered in silver brocade and ice-blue velvet. Like Mrs Loontwill, he was dripping, only with diamonds in silver filigree and Chantilly lace. Lord Akeldama glittered under the ladybug lamps.

He was looking at Mrs Loontwill as if he would like to go for her neck.

Arsenic clutched her kit and prepared to leap to the rescue.

CHAPTER

THREE

A Conspiracy of Tea

Mrs Loontwill stepped hastily back as the slim vampire approached her.

Lord Akeldama reminded Arsenic a little of her mother. Impossibly gorgeous and deadly, his beauty somehow sharp edged. He was the perfect foil for the werecat. She was all tall muscled power, full bloom and without guile. Lord Akeldama was composed entirely of guile.

He wielded both temperament and appearance with such consummate ease, Arsenic could not help but be impressed.

"Now, now, Mrs Loontwill, you must feel *so very* cold and unwell in those damp things. You'll be wanting to catch a *nice dry* conveyance home to a warm fire and the bosom of your more *dignified* family. Surely, we are too energetic and unprincipled for you."

Mrs Loontwill looked, for a moment, like she might argue with the vampire.

Her daughter tugged at her arm. "Please, Mother!"

"Mrs Loontwill." Lord Akeldama's tone became more alluring as he switched tactics. "Such a youthful dress, surely you wish to get it away and treat it for stains as soon as may be?"

"Oh, yes, well..."

"It can't be allowed to dry *on your personage*. It will be permanently damaged beyond all hope of saving."

"Oh, do you believe so?"

"I know so, Mrs Loontwill. *I know so.*"

"Well then, Evylin, why are you detaining us? We should get home immediately!" With which, the odious Mrs Loontwill and her daughter departed Vauxhall Bob forthwith.

Everyone breathed a collective sigh of relief. Including Arsenic, who felt she had just gone through a trial by in-laws. And they weren't even *her* in-laws.

Miss Tunstell said in all haste, "Bork, have them raise up the gardens immediately, please! Before anyone else related to Rue comes aboard."

"Too late for that," said a sarcastic Scottish voice from behind Arsenic.

Arsenic turned. Miss Tunstell did not.

There was a low round table with four comfortable-looking chairs to one side of the dance grotto. An elaborate tea service was set atop, with Wedgwood cups and saucers and an artfully arranged platter of food gathered from the nearby service à la française.

Three matronly females had claimed the table as their *particular* territory, and having eschewed champagne, they were consuming the tea with gusto. They had presumably watched the Loontwill drama with interest and a certain odd approval.

The oldest of the matrons was bent with age, her hair white. She looked a hundred if she was a day. The other two were closer to Arsenic's mother's age. One had short hair and wore men's clothing. Spoo had identified her as the groom's mother, the inventor Madame Lefoux. The last was the Scotswoman who'd spoken. She boasted a set of familiar yellow eyes. So familiar, Arsenic guessed she had been referring to herself as being related to the captain. She was wearing aggressively simple attire, a plaid dress, unadorned except for a large octopus-shaped chatelaine at her waist, from which dangled an assortment of undoubtedly useful objects.

Born and raised in Scotland, and clearly sharing a sense of

practicality with this lady, Arsenic was disposed to like her. She gave a polite nod.

The oldest one addressed Arsenic directly. "You have your mother's eyes, girl."

Arsenic blinked in surprise. "You are na the first to point it out."

"Do you also have her temperament?"

"I dinna think so. Would you like to test me?"

"You're at this wedding because you got the job, then?"

Arsenic blinked at her. Did they know each other? "I'm the new doctor to *The Spotted Custard.*"

The older woman cackled. "Glad that worked out."

Madame Lefoux gave the crone an amused look. "This is your doing, ma poule?"

"You think I'd meddle with Preshea's get?"

"I think you'd meddle with anyone you pleased."

The Scotswoman poured a tot of something into her tea. "Truer words."

The white-haired lady had perceptive green eyes. There weren't as many lines around them as Arsenic might expect given her age. Was the red at the lash line real or artifice? Arsenic moved closer.

There were tricks there. Her mother's tricks. Tricks to make a person look older, seem less interesting, less important. Tricks to make a lady easy to overlook. Arsenic had never used those tricks herself, but she'd sat on her mother's knee while Preshea applied face paint. Sometimes the makeup was to make her even more beautiful, sometimes to make her ugly, and sometimes to make her old.

This lady was an intelligencer.

"You went to finishing school with my mother?" Arsenic wasn't one to keep her cards close. She also knew, as a rule, that the quickest way to discombobulate a spy was to notice her and call the hand.

The old woman, who wasn't an old woman, smiled. "She taught you something, I see."

"She taught all of us."

Those sharp eyes narrowed.

Arsenic felt compelled to defend her abilities, and knew she was being manipulated into doing so. "I know eight different ways to kill a man. Becoming a doctor dinna mean I canna do it anymore. It means I now know why each way works."

"You're the youngest? Hemlock or Oleander or Castor Bean or something."

Arsenic joined them at table, sitting down in the one free chair without ceremony. "You dinna like my mother, did you?"

No answer to that.

Arsenic didn't expect one. "She's difficult to like. And aye, I'm the youngest – Arsenic."

Arsenic wracked her brain for her mother's school stories. The Scotswoman looked younger than the other two, and not by virtue of artifice but by virtue of immortality. Not to mention, those familiar yellow eyes. "You're Sidheag Maccon, Alpha of the Kingair Pack." *Britain's famous lady werewolf.*

"I am."

"I grew up verra near your territory."

"Aye. I was aware of your family's presence."

Arsenic surmised they'd never met because of her mother. It was a common occurrence. People either hated Preshea Ruthven or were terrified of her. Not much elsewise.

"Arsenic, of course." The not-old woman said it as if Arsenic's existence were in question. "You know all the players, girl?"

Arsenic shook her head, frustrated. "You misconstrue. I'm *only* a doctor."

"Oh, you're very good."

"She trained me but I never wanted it."

"Why not?" Genuine curiosity from Madame Lefoux, who was watching the conversation with a faint smile.

"Someone has to make up for what she did. What she was."

"You intend to repair the damage wrought by an assassin? How poetic." The Scotswoman looked thoughtful.

Arsenic considered leaving at that. But these women weren't her mother, so instead she looked each in the eye, one after another, direct and intractable. "I like healing people *and* I'm good at it. Someone has to be ready, with you lot still mucking about." She included all three of the matrons at the table – the spy, the werewolf, and the inventor.

"Whoa there now," said the werewolf.

Silence descended while they all analysed her words for hidden meaning. They were lost because there was none. Simplicity of truth and purpose was rare in their world. Arsenic wanted her mark of existence to be kind. She didn't think there was anything wrong or less powerful about that choice.

"You canna tell me you havena killed or injured in your time, Lady Kingair. For queen and country, for pack and metamorphosis."

Madame Lefoux dimpled at Arsenic. Her eyes were green too, but less calculating than the spy's. "And me, what wrongs have I committed?"

"Your inventions never kill anyone?"

"Touchée."

"Rectifying the sins of the prior generation. That's a big task for one small doctor." That was the intelligencer again, not breaking character, voice shaky with assumed age, for all her words were calculated to cut.

Arsenic didn't like to have her choices questioned. "'Tis better than meddling in the lives of the next one, puppet mistress."

The old-not-old lady laughed, dry and crisp. Her skills were extraordinary, Arsenic never would have seen her deception, had she not been raised by an intelligencer and educated as a physician.

"I think that moniker belongs to Lord Akeldama. When everything comes to account, I'm only a simple player and a retired one at that. His is the game only an immortal can play."

What is her name? Arsenic's mother had called her something. *Sophie, perhaps?*

Arsenic reached out and touched the woman's hair, pulled her hand back, brushing white powder between two fingers. "Oh, verra retired."

All three of the matrons chuckled.

"Run along now, girl. It's good to know my boy has a doctor aboard." Madame Lefoux dismissed her.

"That all you wanted from me?" Had they tricked her to their table just to taunt? Were they revealing themselves apurpose?

"For now," said Lady Kingair.

"You'll do, girl." Approval from the puppet mistress made her shiver.

Arsenic left the tea table of conspiracy. They probably knew the most about everyone assembled, but they wouldn't tell her anything useful. Besides, Arsenic's head was already full of Phinkerlingtons and Loontwills. She was, frankly, more interested in her new crew than old grudges. She had no desire to dabble in the machinations of intelligencers.

Another kerfuffle quickly arose. This time between some of Lord Akeldama's drones, easily identified as they were the best-dressed men in attendance. They were squared off against the Baroness Tunstell's drones, also easily identified as they were mostly Egyptian by complexion and attire.

The argument seemed to be mostly fashion related and taking place via gesticulation. Since humans were involved and cravat and turban pins were being waved at one another, Arsenic headed in their direction.

There was far too much drama at the wedding for Percy.

To be perfectly fair, that was often the situation at weddings, so he shouldn't be surprised. Emotions, those messy things, were high floating and puffed full with disastrous results. This being Rue's wedding, however, everything was swollen to bursting. Including the bride.

Heh, that was mean-spirited of me. Percy amused himself with his own wit, because he was pretty darn certain it would neither amuse, nor appear witty to, anyone else.

He glanced about, hoping that the wedding drama would distract all the resident *ladies interested in marrying Percy*. Or LIMPs, as he called them. Again, only to himself, because no one else understood his sense of humour. Least of all the LIMPs. That was a part of the problem.

Fortunately, they were, in fact, distracted. First by some feathered matron taking a dip in a fountain, and now by drones arguing over cravat pin placement. Arsenic Ruthven was in the thick of both, handling the drama with aplomb.

It started when Lord Akeldama's drones and his mother's drones engaged in a bout of pronounced (but friendly) bickering. But then a couple of the Woolsey drones got involved. And then the vampires themselves fanged their way into the fray in what could only be called a *sparkly yet threatening* manner.

Percy wasn't a fan of vampire hives. He'd been raised in one and he found the dynamic fraught with difficulty. There was always a great deal of jockeying for position. It reminded him of academia, equally bloodthirsty, only instead of pursuit of publication every drone was out to set the latest fashion, display the softest neck, or arrange the nicest bouquet. It was intolerable.

Woolsey Hive had gone so far as to send Lord Ambrose to Rue's wedding, all the way from Barking. He looked pained, as well he might with his tether stretched so far. When the drones began to argue he marched over and had words with Quesnel's other mother, Miss Imogene. She gave him a dirty look and walked away. Lord Ambrose looked around as if frustrated with life, or in his case afterlife. Percy could only sympathize.

Percy wondered idly if Lord Akeldama would get involved, but he seemed to be occupied with the fountain-diving matron at the entrance.

The band continued to play despite the fact that voices were now raised and jewellery was flashing. Rue and Quesnel continued to dance.

He overheard Quesnel say, "Oh yes, because werewolves are so full of esprit de corps."

To which Rue replied, "Oh, I see what you did there, how droll."

Then one of the Kingair werewolves was pulled into the argument, his fellows backing him up. Whatever was said to him clearly caused offence, because the Scotsman looked like he was about to drop kilt and get furry.

Percy figured it was time he brought his sister's attention to the imminent danger of sudden nudity. But Primrose was off supervising the puff up as Vauxhall Bob belted out gusts of steam and indicated lift-off.

Percy struggled with himself. He knew what he should do – try to defuse the situation, for the good of all. But he didn't know *how* to defuse any situation. Usually when he opened his mouth, he made things worse.

He cast about desperately for Rodrigo.

The preternatural was also dancing, whirling his wife about enthusiastically. Perhaps he was worth disturbing? Rodrigo could at least stop an angry werewolf from transforming.

Percy had noodled too long.

The kilt dropped and the werewolf shifted and roared. The drones produced silver cravat pins. Lord Ambrose began telling any who would listen about proper supernatural etiquette, and declaiming loudly that such things were done differently in London.

Percy decided there was nothing he could do and that he was hungry.

He mooched over to the food and regarded it with studied interest, ignoring the chaos behind him. The spread was an unimaginative array of galantines (popular when a reception venue rotated, for their demonstrative wobble), stewed oysters, mayonnaise of fowl, pyramids of sugared fruit, and various knick-knackeries of confectionery.

It bored him dreadfully.

Voices behind him were raised further. He turned in time to see Rodrigo wade in and with a spectacular dive and flip, put the Scotsman (now naked and no longer a werewolf by virtue of the Italian's preternatural touch) flat on his back in a small flower patch.

That, too, was boring.

Percy gnawed on a sugared apricot.

"Well," said a pleased voice to one side and behind him, "'tis na a wedding without a really good fur-up."

He turned to find Lady Kingair, Madame Lefoux, and one other female seated at tea, eyes avid on the drama before them.

"Lady Kingair, is that one of yours? Can't you control your pack?"

"Of course I can, Master Percy. But why on earth should I want to? This is so much more fun."

Percy sighed and moved to join the group of older ladies. He wished he were home, with a good book and a nice cup of tea.

Well, I can at least have the tea.

He plunked himself down and pushed forward an empty teacup hopefully.

Madame Lefoux graciously poured him a cup. "It's tepid."

Percy nodded morosely. "Story of my life."

"Milk?"

"Better not."

She quirked a brow at him.

"Might need it to pacify the werecat later. If she has to settle a vampire-werewolf dispute her fur will be ruffled."

Lady Kingair grinned. "You think she'll get involved? I've na seen her fight. That'd be bonnie."

Percy sipped his tea. "You're a troublemaker, Lady Kingair."

"Guilty."

"*Panem et circenses*," quoted Percy. "Or the werewolf equivalent, I suppose."

"Bread and circuses," translated the elderly woman. "He's accusing your pack of attending this wedding in pursuit of nothing more than food and entertainment."

"'Tis fair," said Lady Kingair. "Although last time we met, laddie, you threw a snit over chilies, proving that you canna behave in company either." She sat back to watch as a different member of her pack turned into a large hairy beast and charged one of the drones. He neatly avoided Rodrigo and almost got a chomp in. Then Tasherit arrived on the scene.

Percy defended himself from gastronomic accusations. "It was overly spicy."

The elderly lady cackled, "No such thing, boy!"

Percy stared at her. She seemed familiar. "Aunt Softy? Is that you? What on earth are you doing here?"

"Recognize me at last, did you?"

"You look older than I recall." Percy realized, even as he said it, that he probably shouldn't. One wasn't supposed to talk to a lady about her age.

Aunt Softy was really his Great Aunt Sophronia, but had come by the name Softy because of his childhood inability to pronounce *Sophronia* combined with Prim's inability to grasp the concept of *great*. Aunt Softy found the moniker hilarious, and insisted they keep it into adulthood. Their mother produced a series of minor fainting fits on the subject over the years, but the twins and Aunt Softy would not be altered from the path of sublime irony.

She didn't seem at all upset at his remark on her advanced age. Thank heavens for the Aunt Softys of the world. If Percy were to have a favourite relation, she'd be it. She was never ruffled by anything he said *and* she spoke Latin. A pronounced *good egg*, his great aunt. Madness that she came from his mother's side of the family.

Not that he saw her much over the years, maybe half a dozen times. That, too, made her a *good egg*, scarcity was an undervalued commodity in relations.

"I'm positively ancient, boy."

"Are you an old friend of Rue's family?"

"Not exactly, more like an old influencer."

Lady Kingair gave his great aunt an affectionate look. "She meddles."

"Does she?" Percy wasn't particularly interested in his great aunt's lifestyle choices unless *meddling* was code for *matchmaking*. "You won't be meddling with me, will you, Aunt Softy?"

"No, dear, you do well on your own. Your sister, on the other hand . . ."

Percy went fierce. "She's doing very well with Tash, you leave them be!" Who was she to judge his sister? That was for him to do.

"Not that kind of meddling."

Madame Lefoux dimpled at him. "Tasherit Sekhmet won that bout, did she?"

Aunt Softy added, "A werecat in the family? How intriguing."

Percy narrowed his eyes.

"You're a funny old thing, aren't you, Percival? One would think you didn't care for anything beyond your books. That's certainly what my son thinks." Madame Lefoux still had a touch of French to her accent, despite the fact that she'd lived in England as long as Percy could remember.

"A marked preference for one thing doesn't necessarily mean I'm unsympathetic to others."

"How perspicacious of you. Tell me, do you approve of my young auntie's match?" Lady Kingair was related to Rue in some complicated supernatural manner that made her a many times great niece of Rue's, all appearances to the contrary. Family trees got quite stunted, bushy, and ingrown when they involved immortals.

Percy tried an arch expression. "Of course, I approve."

Madame Lefoux laughed. "Even after my boy scooped your publication credit?"

Percy sniffed. "I would have done the same. In fact I did,

later. Our mutual dislike is based on professional, not personal grounds."

"You didn't want her for yourself?" Aunt Softy asked that surprising question.

"Rue? Me? What a ghastly idea." Percy shuddered. "She's basically a rounder, more excitable iteration of my sister. Plus bossier and rather exhausting. Quite apart from the incestuous nature of such a match, why on earth would I want to shackle myself to *that*?"

"And yet you serve aboard her ship, as her navigator, under her command."

"Which is better than in her bed."

Madame Lefoux looked intrigued. "Are you bent towards men, then?"

Percy had wrested with this supposition before – just because he was retiring and liked his library and not steam-biffing and whorehouses.

Fortunately, Aunt Softy interceded before he need answer. "Not now, Vieve, that's unimportant."

Madame Lefoux rolled her eyes but sat back, relinquishing the conversation to Aunt Softy.

"You see, Percy dear, you're just the person I particularly wish to talk to."

"*Et tu*, Aunt Softy?"

"What do you mean by continually spouting Latin at us?" Lady Kingair glared.

Percy sighed. "It's only that everyone seems to want to talk to me at this wedding. It's not even *my* wedding."

"Who else needs talking, grand nephew of mine?" asked his aunt.

"Professor Lyall wants words about Rodrigo. And an introduction. I mustn't forget to do that." He looked over to where the Italian was still in the thick of things, attempting to keep werewolves in human form and inside kilts. If Percy were a different kind of man, he'd find it diverting. Lord Akeldama certainly seemed to. "Once he's free of his current anti-supernatural social obligations, of course."

"Lyall won't let you forget. He's not the type. Wants to see Floote, too, I warrant." Aunt Softy spoke with confidence.

"How'd you know?"

"She gets like that." Lady Kingair put down her teacup.

"She gets like *what?*" Percy was losing the thread of the conversation. Really, if only people would be more scientific and precise with their small talk.

"All-knowing."

Aunt Softy gave a small but vicious smile. "Speaking of which, we would like to ask you a favour."

"You would? All of you?"

The three women nodded, looking grave.

"We might have approached your sister, or Prudence of course, but they're otherwise occupied. After careful consideration, I decided it would be best coming from you."

"It would, why?"

"Because it never does. So it's more likely to be taken seriously." Aunt Softy was, occasionally, unnerving. This was one of those times.

"What is?"

"A request."

"A request for what?"

"Travel."

Percy was intrigued despite himself. "Oh yes, and where am I to request we go?"

Lady Kingair, Madame Lefoux, and Aunt Softy exchanged glances.

Finally Aunt Softy said, "I think you'll find Lady Maccon will be discussing this with her daughter when you visit her in Egypt."

"Oh yes? Predict the future, can you?"

"Sometimes."

"And where will Lady Maccon want us to go?"

"Japan. Chasing rumours of yet another species of shifter."

Percy wasn't surprised by this, it seemed to have become *The Spotted Custard*'s unofficial mission, tracking down new supernatural creatures. He'd published several well-regarded papers on the subject as a result, so he was game. "And?"

"We want you to go, only we have another reason."

Percy leaned forward. "Of course you do."

"One of our friends is missing . . . in Japan."

"Oh? And why was he there?"

"*She* was there for the exact same reason, chasing rumours."

"Rumours of what?"

"Fox shifters."

Percy frowned. There'd been rumours of fox shifters in Nottingham, recently disproved. Frankly, given biological restrictions on the preservation of mass, fox shifting was improbable if not outright impossible. They'd have to be extraordinarily small people or very big foxes. "That can't possibly work given the general perimeters of physics. Not even in Japan."

Madame Lefoux chuckled. "Tell that to the fox shifters."

"I'll pass along the sightings reports." Aunt Softy came over all businesslike.

Percy found great solace in paperwork. "I think you better had. Your friend had this information and disappeared while investigating it?"

"Well over a month ago. Her airship was found in pieces." Aunt Softy slid over a photograph of an entirely unprepossessing female, matronly in the extreme, pudding faced and grave. The kind of woman doomed to unfinished crochet projects.

"Intrepid explorer, is she?"

"Don't be a brat, Percival."

"What name does she go by?"

"You'll be asking after the Wallflower. Be discreet."

"Discretion is my middle name."

"No, it isn't, it's Ormond."

Percy tucked the photo into his waistcoat. "I'll be sharing this information with Rue and Prim. I'm absentminded, ladies, but I never intentionally keep secrets. I won't play your game, whatever it may be."

Again the three women looked at one another. "We only want her home safe. She's never been out of contact for so long."

"Did you send her?"

"No. Lord Akeldama."

Percy wasn't even slightly surprised by that. Every vampire kept intelligencers on staff, espionage seemed to be granted along with one's fangs. Even Percy's ridiculous mother kept spies. Admittedly, they were mostly stationed in Paris at the couture fashion houses, but spies nevertheless.

"And does the good vampire know Lady Maccon will be asking us to float to Japan?"

"No, he'd likely put a stop to it. He wouldn't want Rue to go into that kind of danger."

"Dangerous, is it?"

"Very."

"Well, I'm out."

"Percival Ormond Tunstell!"

"Only shading you." No one ever understood Percy's sense of humour. "Danger is like catnip to Rue. She'll go for it. Also we have the advantage."

"You do?"

Percy turned and gestured at the drama occurring near the dance floor.

The situation was now under control. Between them, Rodrigo, Anitra, and Tasherit had broken up the scuffle and separated the various supernatural sets.

Anitra had Lord Ambrose's arm and was looking up at the vampire with big dark eyes, pretending deep fascination with his pontifications. He was absorbed by her attention, her exoticism, and her pointed interest. (She couldn't possibly be interested, of course, but she, too, worked for Lord Akeldama.)

Rodrigo still had his hands full, literally, although the were-wolves had calmed. Even the ones who'd shifted, or tried to, were back in kilts, if nothing else. A gaggle of LIMPs surrounded the shirtless Scotsmen. The pack did not seem averse to the attention so Percy wished them well of it.

Tasherit was off to one side, robe on (it was hard to know if she'd shifted, as she was good at getting in and out of robes), an expression of resignation on her face. She put out an arm and Primrose slid up to her and under it. His sister looked distressed, but a few words from Tash and a gentle nuzzle, and Prim relaxed.

The crew of *The Spotted Custard* had dealt with more contentious situations than this.

"They're good, aren't they? I do so admire efficiency." Aunt Softy sounded self-satisfied. "Rodrigo is an excellent addition. I always thought he would be."

Percy blinked at this but his attention was caught by a slim dark-haired figure. Their new doctor was tending to some minor injuries caused in the scuffle. Her fine white hands moved with quick competence. No doubt she was murmuring sympathetic words. No one, not even the tetchiest claviger, objected to her ministrations. One of the London werewolves seemed overly pleased.

Percy nearly stood to go over. He stopped himself and instead glared at any man fortunate enough to be the subject of Dr Ruthven's undivided attention.

The ladies at the table followed his glower.

"That's how it is, then?" Madame Lefoux sounded as if she'd had a puzzle solved.

Aunt Softy sucked in a breath. "We're sure about her?"

Percy turned back, interested despite himself.

Lady Kingair nodded. "She's solid. Preshea's man did good with the girls. No one's more surprised than Preshea, I suspect."

Madame Lefoux handed Lady Kingair a small cigar. "More of your meddling, Sophronia?"

"Goldenrod's, I think." Aunt Softy passed over a guillotine to nip the tip, and they all paused reverently while the Alpha lit her cigar and puffed. Fragrant vanilla permeated the air.

Madame Lefoux tilted her head. "I've nothing to add. I've been indentured too long with vampires, and since then keeping to myself and my inventions in the country."

Aunt Softy sniffed. "Imogene's fault."

"Yes." Madame Lefoux smiled that smile Quesnel sometimes got when he was thinking about Rue. Or Primrose when she spoke of Tasherit.

Percy looked away, swallowed down the sudden ache in his throat. He felt a twinge of unworthiness. No one ever smiled like that when they spoke of him. Quite the opposite, in fact. His name was, more often than not, coupled with a pained expression. He sipped his tea a little desperately. *Ugh, it's cold.*

Lady Kingair refocused their attention on the doctor, busy bandaging up a drone. "I shouldna make the mistake of assuming she's a pawn. But that dinna mean she's a player."

Percy was a little scared to remind them he was present, but he was curious. "Why else do you think she's solid then, Alpha?"

"Have to be, no? If she was a field surgeon *and* a woman. Any mistake at all and she'd be blamed. You fretting, laddie?" Lady Kingair sounded almost protective of Dr Ruthven. Percy supposed the werewolf woman had experience being female in a male's world.

Percy didn't doubt that Arsenic was an excellent surgeon, it was the way she affected the speech capacities of his brain that had him concerned. But he wasn't going to say *that.*

Aunt Softy's attention was caught by a flash of red hair and a sour expression skulking in the garden. "Pardon me a moment. I see someone I must consult with." She stood and vanished into the shadows with remarkable alacrity.

Lady Kingair watched her, then looked back at Madame Lefoux with a quirked brow.

Madame Lefoux nodded. "One of mine. You think I'd let my son go traipsing off around the world without keeping an eye on him?"

"Introduce me later?"

Percy sighed, this was getting ridiculous. "You're claiming Aggie Phinkerlington?" he asked the Frenchwoman.

"Someone has to." Madame Lefoux shook her head in mock irritation. "Didn't realize she knew Sophronia. Though now I think about it, Aggie did find me for an apprenticeship despite the fact that I was hidden in the countryside surrounded by vampires at the time. It'd be just like Sophronia to have pointed her in my direction."

Lady Kingair puffed on her cigar. "Honestly, I dinna know why she pretends to be retired."

"Pretends to be retired from what, exactly?" Percy pried.

"Being a tricky bit of baggage." The Alpha gave a toothy grin.

"Noble goal."

Lady Kingair laughed a little too loudly. "She claims that deceiving people keeps her young."

Percy blinked. Aunt Softy seemed the opposite of young.

At that moment, Primrose came bustling up. "Please excuse me, Madame Lefoux, Alpha Kingair, but I really must steal my brother away. There are far too many young ladies without dance partners. He must do his terpsichorean duty."

Madame Lefoux stood as well. "I can help with that."

Primrose, who'd turned over a decidedly new leaf recently, didn't flinch at the offer. "Oh good, you're likely a better lead than Percy."

Madame Lefoux gave them both an amused French look. "Of course I am."

Percy sighed. "Do pardon us, Lady Kingair."

The Alpha was clearly pleased to finish her cigar in solitary grandeur.

Percy approached the dance floor with trepidation. Despite his sister's concerns, the grotto was now swollen with dancers. Many of those who'd so recently been embattled were now spinning about the floor.

Quesnel was dancing with Miss Imogene, while his bride danced with Lord Akeldama. Lord Falmouth whirled by with Anitra.

Percy was pleased to see that. He'd been afraid the Drifter would lack partners, since her preference in clothing might result in dismissal. Tasherit could be snubbed for her robes with impunity, she laughed such things off, but Percy knew Anitra to be more sensitive. It was nice of Alpha Biffy to set a precedent of acceptance.

"What are you doing standing around gawking, Percy? Look there, go ask one of those nice-looking young ladies for her card."

Percy did not follow his sister's directive, keeping his eyes on the floor. The hairs on the back of his neck told him he'd caught the attention of the LIMPs.

He dared not move.

Professor Lyall swirled by, dancing with a wide-eyed and uncharacteristically nervous-looking Spoo. Percy hid a smile. One of the Kingair Pack, a tall overly good-looking fellow, twirled around with the *Custard*'s doctor.

Percy frowned.

The music wound down and partners were led off the floor, refreshments obtained. Primrose became fierce. "Percy, go engage Dr Ruthven for the next set. You know you wish to."

"I do not!"

"Too late anyway, Lord Falmouth has her. Oh, good evening, Professor Lyall, how are you tonight?"

"Miss Tunstell, Professor Tunstell."

Percy seized on the opportunity *not* to dance and *not* to do as his sister wished. "Ah, Professor Lyall, perhaps I might perform that introduction you requested? Now?"

"Delighted. Miss Tunstell, if you'll excuse us?"

Percy had no compunction at all about applying a werewolf as a bad guy in this situation.

Primrose made a face but would not boss Percy against a gentlemen's agreement. "Oh, very well. But, Percy, I expect to see you dance at least three dances this evening."

Percy ignored her and walked away into the gardens, Professor Lyall at his side. No doubt, behind them, the LIMPs were falling into fits of despondency.

"Aren't you going to thank me for the rescue?"

"Ah." Percy flushed. "Well, yes, thank you, Professor."

"Not fond of dancing?"

"Not even slightly. Ah, there's Rodrigo. Rodrigo, please allow me to introduce Professor Lyall, Beta of the London Pack? Professor, this is Mr Tarabotti, Rue's cousin."

Rodrigo looked without much interest at the utterly forgettable sandy-haired gentleman standing before him. "Werewolf." He gave a curt nod. He'd never learned to entirely accept the supernatural, not socially, not after his upbringing.

"Might we have a private word about your grandfather, Mr Tarabotti? He was a dear friend."

Percy was being dismissed, how disappointing. His escape tactic had failed. He gave a little bow and left the now bewildered Rodrigo with the Beta werewolf.

"What was that about?"

Rue appeared at his side, cheeks rosy and hair a little mussed.

"Are you supposed to be noticing anything beyond the glittering worshipful gaze of your new beloved husband?"

"No, but I like to keep watch on Rodrigo, even when in the throes of spousal adoration. Let him loose and he goes off and kills people all willy-nilly."

"Lot of that going around?"

"It's not unexpected."

"Professor Lyall can take care of himself."

"That your professional opinion, Percy?"

"Sarcasm is a very unattractive character trait in a bride."

"Oh, do be quiet and come dance with me then, bride's prerogative. You can tell me all about how worshipful Quesnel's eyes are." Percy could do nothing but acquiesce.

The reception, thankfully, remained calm for the rest of the evening, with only a few moments of tension. Madame Lefoux caused a stir by dancing openly with Miss Imogene. Until Lord Falmouth ostentatiously led his Beta out onto the floor. Then Lady Kingair joined them, a monumentally uncomfortable but militant-looking Aggie Phinkerlington in her arms.

When Lord Akeldama, a twinkle in his eye, offered his arm to Percy, Percy only sighed and joined them. He'd prefer a hundred times dancing with a vampire over any of the LIMPs, since he could be tolerably certain Lord Akeldama wasn't after his hand in marriage.

"Which one of us should lead?" he whispered. He was taller than the vampire, but Lord Akeldama was a great deal more bossy.

"Practical to the last breath, aren't you, *darling boy*? I've seen you dance, *plumb-bob*. I'll lead."

Percy might have stepped on Lord Akeldama's feet a time or two, which distressed the vampire via shoe smudges (as opposed to actually causing him any physical harm). Percy could dance rather well, of course, it was simply that he didn't want to and he had a reputation to maintain. Besides, one must seize upon any excuse to step on a vampire's toes, for the sake of humanity. Percy was, in the end, a man of principle.

There was sure to be scandal in the papers – ladies dancing with ladies was one thing, but *gentlemen* dancing with *gentlemen*? At a wedding? That was beyond even the supernatural set. But Rue (who was waltzing happily with Tasherit) seemed pleased with this probable outcome. Quesnel was amiable enough not to care about social standing. He swirled around with one of Lord Akeldama's more impressively dressed drones.

Percy shrugged. Ah well, they were departing London soon. He suspected Rue of intentionally scandalmongering. If she could not produce the best wedding London ever saw, she could at least produce the most outrageous.

Only one other thing of note occurred, and had Percy not been on guard because of Aunt Softy's presence he would never have noticed. Lord Akeldama, having finished their set, led Percy over to the punch bowl. As if Percy were an overtaxed young lady in need of refreshment. Percy trailed after him, obligingly.

Primrose met them, wringing her hands. "Well, that was an *excessive* display." She said it to Percy, because he was the only one she could criticize to his face.

Percy stuffed a biscuit shaped like a hedgehog into his mouth as an excuse not to answer.

Tasherit, Rue, and Quesnel joined them.

"Progress never did come easily to high society, *sweetling*." The vampire's eyes crinkled in amusement.

"I hardly see how dancing can change the course of civilisation," snapped Prim.

"Give it a chance," replied Rue, grinning.

"Come now, little one, it's fun. Dance with me next?" Tasherit nudged up against Prim coquettishly.

Primrose batted at her lover in perturbation. "What if Mother finds out about this?"

Percy rolled his eyes. "Wasn't that the point? We can't all of us be accused of deviant behaviour at once."

"Of course we can! This is *Mother* we're talking about." Prim looked at Lord Akeldama. "You'll be blamed."

"*Indubitably*, my pearl. Mr Lefoux, would you care to dance?"

"Charmed, I'm sure, but I think I want my bride back in my arms."

"As you should!" The vampire looked delighted.

"Why not ask Rodrigo, my lord?" Quesnel's voice was sly.

Lord Akeldama winced only slightly. "I think not."

"Not fond of preternaturals, Lord Akeldama?" Tasherit was grinning, catlike and pleased to be teasing another immortal.

"Not as a general rule, Miss Sekhmet."

And then the most peculiar thing occurred. It was as if the vampire and the werecat were alone, surrounded by a thousand years of stillness. The two immortals stood staring at each other.

Percy found himself holding his breath.

"It's good to see you again, Alexander." Tasherit's dark eyes were grave.

"It's been a long time."

"Too long. Still keeping the company of cats?" Tasherit's voice sounded odd.

"I've two kittens at the moment."

"Of course you do."

"Terribly high maintenance."

"Cats generally are," said Prim, fondly.

For once, Tasherit didn't pay attention to Primrose.

The werecat moved close to the vampire, a little too close. Her dark eyes searched his face a moment, looking for something. Then Tasherit lifted the long chain necklace she always wore off her neck – two charms dangled from it. They were small and not something Percy had ever had the opportunity to examine closely, but he'd always thought one was a shield and the other a sword.

Primrose gave a tiny little surprised gasp.

Tasherit handed the necklace to Lord Akeldama.

He broke the chain, sliding the two charms off. He turned them about in his hand, then shifted them in such a way that they snapped together, so that the shield became the head and the sword the body, forming a scarecrow shape.

"Ah," said Tasherit, "the ankh. Of course."

"Unopened and unbroken." The vampire tucked it into his inside waistcoat pocket. "She died well?"

"She did. A long time ago." The werecat's face was serene.

"None of us can ask for more." The vampire didn't use any pet names on the werecat. Percy wondered about that.

"That is a warrior's answer, old one. I want more. I want to die beloved."

The vampire's smile was somehow sad. "Says the warrior. That is asking for a great deal more, is it not?"

Tasherit nodded, both regal and forlorn.

"She was greatly beloved, once. She gave with such compassion. To those of us so profoundly unworthy of it. We could not have loved her more." The vampire touched the spot where the ankh now lay, under his clothing, over his heart. Lord Akeldama offered his words as if they were some kind of consolation. "Better to love with your whole soul and lose, than not to love at all."

Tasherit winced.

Ah, they're discussing the price of immortality. Percy did not envy supernatural creatures the choice they made when becoming undead. To outlast everyone dear to them, again and again.

It occurred to him to pity his sister. In taking a werecat for a lover, Primrose must confront the fact that they would never grow old together. Tasherit would eventually go forward where Primrose could not follow.

Or was it the other way around?

Percy shook off any empathic melancholy. Presumably, they'd both weighed the objections and pleasures of their match and decided the first were worth suffering for the sake of the second.

Tasherit looked away from the vampire and down at Primrose. Her dark eyes were unhappy and hungry. "Dance with me, please?"

Primrose nodded. "All right, darling heart. All right." She whirled on Percy, turning her own mixed emotions and confusion into reassuring ire against her brother. "Percy, go ask the nice doctor to dance."

And because he could see how fatigued Prim was, overtaxed with tears near to the surface, Percy turned to seek out their new doctor and ask her to dance, as ordered.

FOUR

Floating Familial Relationships

Arsenic found the wedding, in the end, a thing of dreamlike balletic chaos with Wagnerian overtones. Vampires tussled with werewolves, drones with clavigers, while other guests scurried about attempting to avoid bloodshed yet simultaneously stay close enough to learn all the gossip and eat all the food.

The fisticuffs seemed mainly in good fun, more for the sake of argument and light exercise. Arsenic's skills were called upon only to tend scrapes, bruises, and a sprained wrist. This meant she enjoyed herself, in the end. She liked to be useful.

Then after everything seemed settled, the bride turned dancing into a weapon. Except Arsenic wasn't certain what the weapon pointed at – the rest of society, perhaps?

Arsenic gave up attempting to deduce what was going on and simply enjoyed herself. The food was tasty and the conversation varied, and eventually even the recalcitrant Professor Tunstell was persuaded onto the floor.

Honestly, the man was more nervous to dance with her than he had been to stand up with Lord Akeldama. "I'm not any good," he confessed as he led her out.

He was, indeed, a sublimely bad dancer – bungling and unsure with no conversation. Arsenic did her best to make him comfortable and engage in the requisite pleasantries, searching for any topic that might relax the poor lad. Nothing helped and they parted awkwardly. Arsenic remained under the impression that he either was terrified of her, which was patently absurd, or had taken her in great disdain.

She'd seen him talking with the matrons at the tea table, perhaps they had told him horrible things about her mother. That would do it. She hoped she might have an opportunity to prove herself to her new shipmate as a worthy member of staff, then perhaps he'd not dislike her so. He seemed secretly quite kind, ceding to his sister's demands, placing glasses of water near Rue whenever she took a breather, and interceding on Virgil's behalf when the laddie caught Lord Ambrose's eye.

In the small hours of the morning, after Vauxhall Bob depuffed and the wedding guests stumbled home, Arsenic returned to her grimy lodging, exhausted. She'd gone in for a job interview and ended up at a party with bare chests and kilts and ancient immortals all on pronounced display.

I should restock my bandages, she thought, and then, *At least I'll be busy in my new position.* That had only been a wedding on home soil. Imagine what *The Spotted Custard* got up to overseas.

As she'd not been given explicit instructions, Arsenic awoke, packed what little she owned — the army had taught her to travel light — paid for her room, and made her way to *The Spotted Custard* by luncheon.

Absolutely no one was awake except the day-watch. The sentry was composed of two sooties, two decklings, and a deckhand, all of whom were drinking barley water and playing tiddlywinks.

Arsenic hollered up and one of the decklings recognized her and lowered the gangplank. *The Spotted Custard* puffed out steam and generally bobbed about in the breeze. Arsenic was ridiculously proud of herself for not falling off before she attained the eck.

"You're awake before the rest of them toff-lofties," said one of the sooties, approvingly.

Arsenic considered. "I suppose with Miss Sekhmet, they tend to keep nighttime hours?"

"Most of them bob-up just prior to sunset," agreed Bork, companionably.

Arsenic nodded. "Good to know. I'll go settle into my quarters, shall I?"

"Carry on then." They went back to their tiddlywinks.

Arsenic made her way belowdecks. She hadn't really had a chance to examine her swoon room yet, so she started there.

It was well designed, with plenty of shelves and small banks of drawers made of waxed card for lighter medicinals. There were some more sturdy facilities for liquid medicines and the like, as well as hatstands and other useful contraptions for hanging bandages and tools.

She approved, making a few notes and stowing what she'd brought with her in sensible spots. She wondered what her materials stipend was and thought she'd better consult with Miss Primrose before she spent ship's coffers on ointments.

There was a partially stocked medicine cabinet already in residence. It saw a great deal of use, if the empty compartments and half-used vials were anything to go by. She noted each carefully, both for restocking, and to understand what was generally in rotation aboard the *Custard*. Considering the captain's delicate condition, Arsenic decided to brush up on birthing procedures as well. She thought she'd best look into the captain's state of metanatural existence, too. She wasn't familiar with the term, but if it was similar to *preternatural*, it meant Lady Akeldama was mortal only with quirks. Which meant birth was a risk.

There was also the werecat to consider. Arsenic wanted to talk with both of them as well as read any papers connected to the physical ramifications of their unnatural states. This was her crew to look after now. Arsenic intended to be prepared.

She made another note to ask for a ship's manifest and to enquire if there were any other supernatural, unnatural, or undead aboard. Or actors. Actors were always injuring themselves.

Once they hit a long float inside the aetherosphere, she'd have every single one of the crew come through her swoon room for a consult and a check-up. They'd grumble, but that was what doctors did – inconvenienced people with the necessities of good health.

There was only one cot for patients. She hoped she wouldn't need more, but she thought she'd better install hooks for a hammock, in case a second bed was needed.

Arsenic was so distracted by her lists and thoughts, she barely noticed when the noises around her shifted, indicating the crew awakening. She paused only when the light became diffuse and she realized the sun had set.

The clearing of a throat at the doorway startled her.

"You must be our new doctor. I regret that we didn't meet properly yesterday."

Arsenic put down her stylus and looked up. Twinkle-eyed, charming, and blond, the groom from the night before was considerably less well dressed this evening. He sported casual attire, no jacket, only a vest that had seen better days and was blessed with an overabundance of pockets.

"Mr Lefoux, how are you this evening?" He looked to be in good health, if a mite peely-wally, probably from working indoors or from overindulgence the night before.

"Topping, Dr Ruthven. Quite topping. And you? Getting started already, I see? Are those lists? Prim will be pleased."

Arsenic relaxed. *Delightful man.* "Aye. I've three going – one requesting personal information, one for requisitioning supplies, and one on the research papers I'll need to source before we leave."

"Go to old Percy for those. He won't be kind about it, but he might have what you require already. What do you need to research so soon, if you don't mind my asking?"

"Weel, after the captain decides on our destination, I'll check local diseases and other concerns, but before that I'd like to see what's to be had on werecats, metanaturals, and childbirth."

He looked pleased by her diligence. "You're in luck on the werecats. The only paper in existence was written by our Percy, to his shame. I suspect he has several copies. Knowing him, the library won't have anything on childbirth. And no one has anything about metanaturals except the government, and they won't let you see it."

Arsenic sighed. "I was wondering why I'd na heard of the state."

"Rue is what happens when preternaturals and supernaturals breed. There's Rodrigo as well, Mr Tarabotti. He's preternatural."

"You're an eclectic bunch."

"So far as I know, basic biological functionality for both preternaturals and metanaturals is exactly like normal humans'."

"But someone said that the captain's bairn, your bairn, was an unknown x-predictive?"

"Yes, that's a little concerning." He dimpled at her. "We didn't really think it would happen at all, you see?"

"Hence the hasty wedding and grumpy bride?"

He shrugged. "She likes it. She simply doesn't want to *admit* to liking it. That'd be too much like giving in."

"Aye, of course. But you're happy?"

"Very. You're remarkably easy to talk to, Doctor, did you know that?"

"Been said before."

"I'll leave you to your lists. Breakfast in half an hour in the stateroom if you'd like to join us?"

"Breakfast?"

"First meal after sleeping, we call breakfast. Rue prefers breakfast foods over all others, except pastry, and so insists that when we wake up, even if it's sunset, we eat *breakfast*. You'll find it's easier not to argue with her."

"I find it difficult to take a stance against breakfast, as a rule."

"Good show. Bring your lists? Prim will look them over."

"At breakfast?"

"We often discuss ship's business while eating."

Arsenic gave a nod and the gentleman disappeared. He was likeable. She could see what the captain saw in him. Perhaps a touch too charming.

She winced and sighed. That reminded her she'd a confession to make. Given her encounter with the tea-table matrons, and the certain knowledge of intimacy between those ladies and members of the *Custard* crew, Arsenic had better fess up about her mother. Before someone else did it for her.

She hoped she could work it delicately into conversation, but it was a dramatic statement to make, "Please pass the toast, and did you know my mother killed people for a living?"

The dining room was full of officers when Percy arrived. The mess opposite was full of staff and crew. The doors to each were thrown wide, allowing personnel to drift between and consult with respective colleagues.

Percy breathed a sigh of relief. At least he wasn't so late he'd missed the food. He'd been reading an interesting travel journal on Japan with particular focus on pearl divers, also referred to as mermaids. Percy was, as yet, unable to determine if these were actual mermaids or if it was a euphemism. Percy hated euphemisms.

I wonder what the Latin is for mermaid?

He slipped in behind an aggravated-looking Aggie, who made a beeline for Quesnel.

Greasers, firemen, and sooties all reported to Quesnel as head engineer. He had a most companionable relationship with his people, even Aggie. He was disgustingly easygoing. Staff went to Primrose, who was in charge of the shipboard household and supply logistics. She took her duties seriously and as a result the footmen were in awe of her. Percy suspected that he'd be in awe of his sister too, except that she was his sister. Decklings and deckhands consulted with Rue. No one was in awe of Rue, but everyone adored her. She ruled with the marshmallow fist of justice – fluffy, delightful, and probably slightly too sweet and sticky, but fair.

Percy, thank heavens, had charge of no one. Theoretically Virgil was under his purview, but in reality he was under Virgil's.

He nodded to those few at the table who were not busy with crew concerns – Rodrigo, Anitra, and the new doctor. 'Course he couldn't look the new doctor full on or he'd start blushing. As if he had an allergic reaction.

Unfortunately, there was only one vacant chair, which meant Percy had no option but to sit right next to Dr Ruthven. Of course.

He inhaled, coughed slightly, tried to politely acknowledge her without actually looking at her, and sit at the same time.

It was excruciating.

"Percy? There you are! What took you so long? You've been awake for hours." Could his sister be any more annoying?

"How'd you know I was up?" He reached for a roll and served himself sausage and stewed tomato. It was nice to be back in England where breakfast made sense.

"Your cat is here lurking, has been for ages."

"Footnote gave me away? Little traitor."

Footnote, hearing his name, gave a haughty *yap* and ambled over to crouch between Percy's and Arsenic's chairs. *And now I'm thinking of her by her given name.*

"I was lost in a book."

"Should navigators get lost?" wondered Anitra.

Now even Anitra is teasing me.

Percy glowered at the Drifter and she smiled back. He watched out of the corner of his eye as Arsenic cut off a corner of her bacon and passed it down to his cat.

"He'll never leave you alone," warned Percy.

Arsenic gave him one of her allergy-inducing smiles. "Good."

Percy's breath actually stopped, until she turned her dark blue eyes back to Footnote.

"Who's the best moggie ever?" Arsenic asked, as Footnote

licked his whiskers and bestowed upon her a look of abject starvation. She immediately fed him another piece. Dr Ruthven clearly knew her way into the heart of a cat.

Who has eyes that colour? Mermaids, probably. Percy tried to figure out the name of the shade. *Darker than cornflower. Not quite indigo, more purple than that.* Then he realized what he was doing. *Eye colour, for goodness' sake!*

"What do you and Mr Tarabotti do aboard *The Spotted Custard*, Mrs Tarabotti?" Arsenic asked Anitra.

Percy realized he was also curious. Rodrigo and Anitra had been aboard for ages, and he'd never once considered asking them what they actually did on his airship.

"I signed on as a translator. I speak several languages, and Rodrigo does as well. But we both help wherever we can."

"Oh aye?" The doctor arched one perfect black brow.

"Of course it never hurts to have a preternatural aboard." Anitra looked affectionately at her husband.

"Unless you are another preternatural, sì?" Rodrigo touched Anitra's cheek with the back of two fingers. Percy liked to pretend that it was his books that gave Rodrigo a soul, but realistically it was Anitra's heart that had done the heavy lifting.

Still, results! Results were good.

"Why's that?" Arsenic pried. She'd some of Aunt Softy in her – that enforced curiosity, a need to understand in order to better control outcome.

Percy would prefer not to understand people. Humans were irrational and unpredictable. Books were better.

Anitra explained, almost proudly, "Two preternaturals cannot share the same air, without distance. There is repulsion."

Arsenic turned to look down the table to where Rue sat at the head. "'Tis na the same for metanaturals?"

Of course, she's a doctor, she's interested in how biology ties to function. Percy was staring and not eating. He glanced hastily around to see if anyone noticed. His sister, Rue, and Quesnel were all occupied with ship's business. *Thank goodness.* He began hastily shovelling food into his mouth.

"Her skills are different from mine. As are her weaknesses." Rodrigo did not elaborate further.

Arsenic pressed. "Is there anything medically significant about being preternatural, Mr Tarabotti?"

"I bleed red, Dottore, like everyone. Even the cat."

"Aye, but do you *heal* differently? That's the important part."

Rodrigo chuckled. "I am human."

"And the captain?"

"Little cousin bleeds red too."

Anitra was the one who explained. "She can heal by becoming immortal, especially now we have Tasherit aboard. But it only works at night and out of aether, since both sunlight and the grey incapacitate werecat abilities."

Arsenic nodded. "As with other supernatural creatures. Good to know. Now, Miss Anitra. You're recently married. Should you wish to discuss the precautionary arts with me at any time, you're more than welcome. Unless, of course, you intend to start a family."

Anitra, poor thing, hung her head and let her veil fall forward to hide her expression.

Percy tried not to choke on a sausage.

Arsenic said, "I do apologize. I get carried away with my medical responsibilities and forget that na everyone is scientific in their approach to procreation."

Rodrigo chuckled but didn't explain why.

Percy kept his mouth shut for a change. He'd learned the hard way not to publicly report on his crewmates, after the disastrous publication of his paper on Tasherit nearly forfeited any possible friendship between them.

The general chaos had subsided and the crew retreated to their mess to get tucked in. Which meant that everyone at the table had heard Arsenic's comment.

Prim had a hand over her mouth. Rue and Quesnel were amused.

Arsenic seemed to believe this was the result of mentioning contraception at breakfast.

Percy was sympathetic. He was often lost among company, not being of a convivial disposition. But at least with these people he'd history enough to follow the undercurrents. Their new doctor had no such advantage.

"Anyone know what the Latin is for *mermaid?*" he blurted.

Everyone stared at him.

"*Syreni*, perhaps?" suggested Arsenic.

And ... she speaks Latin, I'm doomed.

"Oh, Percy, really, no Latin at breakfast. None of us have had sufficient tea to cope." Primrose protested on principle.

Percy nodded glumly and ate more sausage.

Quesnel said to his new wife, "Goodness, chérie, you went out and got us a doctor with about as much verbal acumen as our navigator. How will we survive the sheer frank Latin-ness now endemic to our crew?"

"Or more precisely, how will Primrose survive it? I think the rest of us are accustomed to brash talk."

Prim bristled. "I say, Rue, I'm perfectly accustomed. I did grow up with Percy! It's only, I don't think I should *have* to be accommodating. A little decorum isn't too much to ask for, is it?"

"Apparently, it is on this ship." Rue grinned and helped herself to more eggs. She'd been eating lots of eggs lately. Perhaps that was why she'd gotten so egg shaped. A child couldn't possibly account for all of it, could it?

Percy opened his mouth to ask exactly that, but Prim was glaring down the table at him as if she knew he was about to put his foot in it.

What did I do?

"Percy, we're paying a call on Mother tonight."

"Oh, *I say*, that's *not on!*"

"Don't be crass. I require you to accompany me. I'm not doing this alone. And who knows when we'll be back home again."

"Oh, honestly! Must I?"

"Yes, you must."

"I hate you." Percy realized that he sounded about eight years of age. Which made him blush and stare at his tomatoes in extreme perturbation.

Arsenic gave him a sympathetic look. "Mine's awful too."

Cracking. Now I'm going to start admiring her personality along with everything else. Percy tried to think of something polite to say back. But if there was a familial trait for politeness, he hadn't inherited it. *She's kind, she speaks Latin, and she has black-currant eyes. Or should I say pansy eyes? That's the colour, yes? Pansy.* Violaceae.

"Speaking of which..." Arsenic hesitated, as if waiting for a response from him. Percy remained mute, too busy thinking about pansies.

Allergic reaction is now affecting my higher brain function.

Arsenic cleared her throat. Normally this wouldn't have worked, but with a new person, everyone around the table quieted and looked at her expectantly.

"I'm afraid there is somewhat I ought tell, before I get settled. The swoon room is lovely, by the way, Miss Tunstell. Verra well designed."

"Thank you kindly, Dr Ruthven." Prim glowed at the praise. She no doubt deserved it, but it never occurred to Percy to compliment his sister. After all, she did what she was supposed to do, only better than average.

Arsenic continued on, a wrinkle marring her forehead. "I understand if you dinna want me after. 'Tis na good and may impact your opinion of me. I willna hold you to our contract, if you give me marching orders."

The company stared at her, faces grave.

Percy picked at a scone. Hoping that whatever it was, wasn't too bad. He wanted to keep Arsenic, even if she rendered him hot and uncomfortable and non-verbal. Probably because of it.

"Doubtful," came a mutter from Professor Tunstell. Who was intently buttering a scone, the only one not staring at Arsenic.

Arsenic took a deep breath and reached for her reserves of gumption. She said in a rush, "My mother was once a skilled and infamous..." She trailed off, losing steam.

"Yes?" Miss Tunstell prompted her.

"Weel, na to put too fine a point on it..." They let her flounder. "An infamous assassin."

The captain grinned. "Goodness, is that all? Mine was, and still is, a soulless harridan with a propensity for hitting people with a parasol."

Mr Lefoux gave Arsenic the sweetest smile. Arsenic was tolerably certain chief engineers ought not to smile like that. Or be French, for that matter.

He said, "Mine destroyed half of London with an octopus."

That sounded euphemistic. Before she could enquire after the particulars, the ginger professor looked up briefly from his scone to add, with a lip curl, "And mine trod the boards before becoming a vampire queen and widely influencing the current fashion for unacceptably huge hats."

Miss Tunstell added, "And there's her book, too, but I'd rather not talk about that, if you don't mind."

"Well, assassin seems tame by comparison." Arsenic sat back, less tense, more because they didn't care about her mother's history than because of their confessions. Which seemed, quite frankly, absurd.

Mr Lefoux let out a bark of surprised laughter. "I like this one, Rue, I think she should stay."

"Yes, dear, we decided that yesterday while you were busy dressing up all pretty for me. Now, let's get something sorted quickly, shall we, Arsenic dear? May I call you Arsenic? Not to put too fine a point on it, but that's the *point*. We keep to casual naming conventions aboard ship. You may call me Rue, or if you insist, Captain Rue."

"Rue?"

"Exactly, as in you will come to *rue* the day you met me. Most do. Quesnel here prefers to be simply Quesnel. And Primrose would rather be Prim, yes? And Tash is, well, Tash or Tasherit. We aren't formal, you see? Rodrigo and Anitra have never minded that we dropped their last names early on. And Percy will take Percy and like it, since we don't much care what he thinks."

Professor Tunstell rolled his eyes at his captain and ate the scone.

"That's not too casual?" Arsenic wasn't convinced. Such blatant informality surely undermined discipline?

"We're a pleasure craft, not a military ship. You'll become accustomed to our lax ways. Altering how you address us should help with that."

"If you insist. And you'll call me Arsenic?"

"Yes, I'd like that. Good. That's settled. Although I should say Formerly Floote prefers the formality of title and we pander to his quirks."

"I've been meaning to ask about him. What happens in the aetherosphere?"

"The *Custard* boasts the best Lefoux preservation tank ever built."

"And he's trapped inside that during the grey? Interesting."

Percy muttered, "There's an excellent article, if you're interested. Mr Lefoux wrote it, sadly."

Quesnel waggled insulting fingers and gave a not nice grin. "I did build it, you ponce."

These two are intellectual rivals, Arsenic realized. That made sense. Percy was clearly a theoretician while Quesnel was an engineer, they'd be at odds due to the nature of their training. It seemed a friendly rivalry. At least she hoped it was friendly. Or tensions aboard ship could go south quickly. No one was more easily offended than a male intellectual whose expertise was challenged.

Arsenic said, hoping to stop any argument before it started, "The afterlife is na my speciality, but this new tank technology sounds impressive. I wouldna mind seeing it in action."

"You're very welcome, anytime." Quesnel was smug.

Arsenic reassessed the dining room, minimally decorated but every feature efficient, small, and lightweight. Now that she knew to look for it, she suspected this man's expert touch was everywhere on the airship.

The captain – Rue – positively glowed. "He's quite the noggin, my husband."

"Thank you, chérie!"

"Newlyweds," muttered Percy darkly.

Somehow Arsenic didn't have any issue with thinking of him as Percy. It suited him admirably.

"So, *Arsenic*, have you thoughts on supplies or other adjustments to the swoon room before we depart?" Primrose seemed always businesslike.

"Aye. I've drawn up several lists. I'd love to have a brief discussion with you before they're finalized. I understand you've been serving as medic?"

"Yes, and very ham-handed I was about it too. I'm delighted to pass the job on to you."

"Nonsense. I hear you've a way with a needle and human flesh."

Everyone around the table blanched. Quesnel touched his shoulder and winced in an unconscious gesture of remembered pain.

Arsenic corrected herself. "Apologies. Slips my mind that others are na so insensitive to bodily repairs."

"She *is* like Percy. How extraordinary." That came from Rue.

"Two of them." Quesnel pretended at awe.

Arsenic took in the bonnie professor next to her. He was destroying another scone with focus.

"We are?"

"He's unusually quiet these days. It will wear off soon. Or he's unwell. Which makes him your problem now, Doctor, how delightful." Primrose showed no concern at all for her brother's wellbeing. "So, a quick discussion after breakfast? Then some shopping for everyone, stores and restocking and hats. Then when visiting hours commence, Percy and I shall call on Mother."

Percy groaned audibly.

"And don't go hide in your gentlemen's club or I shall send Quesnel after you."

Percy snorted.

Quesnel said for Arsenic's benefit, "Much to his disgust, we belong to the same club, Avogadro's."

Arsenic nodded, the den of intellectualism. She'd belonged, until they found out she was female and booted her.

Primrose pressed on. "Look at it this way, Percy. If we get it over with now, we won't have to do it again until we're next in London. Could be *ages*."

Percy glared. "Well, I, for one, hope we are going to Japan next."

"Japan, why would we be going there?"

"Never you mind *why*. It's about as far away from England as possible, aetherospherically speaking." Grabbing up another scone, he stormed from the room.

Footnote trailed after him.

The table was left in confused muttering.

"I didn't say anything about Japan, did you?" Rue looked about, curious.

"No one mentioned it. It's only Percy being Percy. You know how he gets."

"What was that about Latin mermaids?"

"Exactly. That. That's how he gets."

Arsenic smiled into her breakfast and filched a scone, thinking she might stop by the library later to store her collection. If the laddie liked scones, she was not above a bit of bribery.

CHAPTER
FIVE

Mothers and Their Consequences

Baroness Ivy Tunstell, Queen of the Wimbledon Hive, was playing indoor croquet with books for arches and parasols for mallets while explaining to her hive, in dulcet tones, the complicated evolution of British picnic etiquette. Being Egyptian by birth, and indoor by species, the concept of *a picnic* fascinated her hive. Or it was simply that Ivy was their queen, and making the appearance of adoration and interest was always the better choice for a vampire.

The baroness looked to be about Prim's age and more her twin than Percy. Ivy's face was a little rounder and her eyes more vacant. Primrose looked, even at her best, suspicious of the world and prissy about her existence within it. Their mother, in Percy's unasked-for opinion, looked like a bewildered hedgehog. She had dark eyes and hair (both of which she had passed along to Prim), a turned-up nose (which she had passed along to Percy, curse her), and a general air of fussy distraction that drove Percy absolutely spare (and which she fortunately hadn't passed along at all).

She looked particularly hedgehog-like this evening, as indoor croquet evidently called for a bonnet made entirely of feathers. The feathers were of varying lengths and spikiness, some black, some white. This resembled hedgehog fur so precisely that Percy, who rarely noticed fashion, was struck momentarily speechless by the shocking similarity between this hat and his mother's Erinaceinae nature.

Percy himself looked like their father, who, by all reports, had been a dasher. A noted thespian, more noted for his comedic showing and physical appearance than dramatic skill, Ormond Tunstell had gifted Percy with a set of nice cheekbones and a thoughtful brow. If Percy were a vain man he would have been grateful.

But he honestly couldn't be fussed.

The most pronounced physical difference between the twins and their mother, of course, was the minor fact that Ivy Tunstell boasted large fangs, the supreme pallor of a vampire, and a lingering lisp. She currently also boasted a teacup of warm blood in one hand while she directed her drones and hive members at their game with the other.

When Prim and Percy appeared, the baroness let out a shriek of unparalleled delight.

"Oh, my babies. My precious jewels! Tiddles, Sniffles! Darlings, sweetlings, loveliest children of my heart and loins, how *delightful* to see you at last! Finally, you remembered I exist, and I am waiting. You depuffed *days* ago, *weeks*, ages, eons, and forgot all about me! Come to me now. Come to the bosom of my affection."

"Oh, good lord," said Percy.

Their mother had a wispy voice that had likely been a tad lisping even before the addition of fangs and only worsened under ever-present pointy toil. It made her sound as girlish as she looked, frozen in time. Hers was the kind of face that, even had she aged naturally, would have looked young until it suddenly gave up, descending into copious wrinkles without warning.

Primrose pasted a smile on her face and scuttled into their mother's desperate embrace. "Mother! I had a wedding to plan, as you're perfectly well aware. We came as soon as may be."

"Oh yes, I heard all about *that*. Such a scandal. All manner of shocking dance partner choices, not to mention kiltless Scotsmen!"

"Werewolves, Mother, you understand how they get."

"Don't I just. Percy dear, come give your mother a kiss."

Percy obliged said mother with a peck on the cheek but removed himself hurriedly from her clutching arms. She always squeezed a little too hard. Two decades a vampire and she was still a very young queen, unaware of her strength, or perhaps simply overly enthusiastic about the afterlife.

She barely paused to draw breath. "And I heard that Alexia's *horrible* mother showed up—"

"But we got rid of her quickly," Prim defended.

"And then there were cravat pins being wielded."

"Barely a scratch, I assure you."

"And I cannot believe little Prudence invited Lord Ambrose."

"Woolsey Hive honoured us with an actual vampire, Mother, they might have only sent drones. No one would've blamed them."

Percy lurked behind his sister, who fielded the rapidly fired insults (disguised as commentary) with consummate skill and aplomb. Really it was quite amazing to see them do battle, although also rather cringe-worthy.

"Oh, I say! I sent along three whole vampires and several drones. I was barely protected here myself last night. Although no one should be thinking of my safety on such an illuminati evening. I am nothing if not altruistic in all my endeavours."

"*Illustrious*, do you mean, Mother?"

"Oh, but Primrose, sweetheart, could you not have done something about the kilts? You're so good with Scotsmen. Weren't you engaged to one at some point? Although of course you're good with everyone, aren't you, darling?"

"No, Mother, I was engaged to an Irish—"

"Oh yes, let's not talk about that, best forgotten. Now . . ."

Percy let the two female voices fade into the background and allowed his thoughts to wander. His sister's general attitude of *hic manebimus optime* when it came to their mother was admirable. But Percy wasn't a fighter, more an avoider. He'd moved out of Wimbledon Hive as soon as possible and left the majority of the battles up to Prim evermore. He might have felt guilty, except his sister seemed to thrive on controversy and drama. One had only to consider her choices of friends and lovers.

The drones and vampires had stopped playing croquet so Percy began picking up the abused books. Poor things, it was hell on the spines and pages to be propped up like that.

"Percival Ormond Tunstell, what are you doing? We're in the middle of a game."

"Books. Mother. Really. No." Percy continued in his sacred duty to the written word.

The drones watched him with equal parts amusement and shock. The vampires had seen him grow from child to adult, they knew the familial dynamic. Most of the drones, however, were relatively new. Drones rarely lasted over a decade. No doubt they'd never seen their vampire queen so easily overruled as she was by Percy on a mission of intellectual mercy.

"Percival, really, must you!" decried his mother, but she didn't order him stopped.

"Honestly, can't you use something else for arches?"

"I could, I suppose, what would you recommend?"

"Arches."

"And how would they stay up? Can't very well sink them into the carpet now, can we?"

Percy regarded the plush, no doubt hugely expensive, Persian rug. "Get little pots, or teacups, or what have you, fill them with sand, two per arch. It'd look nicer, too. Save the books."

"But then the teacups would be in danger!" Mother pressed a hand to her chest in an excess of discomfort.

"But *the books* would be safe." Really, his mother quite lacked the proper priorities in life. Or more properly, afterlife.

"Of course, you and your books."

"In this case, Mother, they are *your* books."

She turned away from him, falling into the general pattern of those who wouldn't argue with Percy because, well, he was right.

She refocused on Prim. "Now, Tiddles darling, I understand you broke off your engagement with that nice soldier fellow, Captain Whatnot? Such pretty legs. Why would you do such an outlandish thing? And by correspondence no less. I thought I raised you better!"

Percy let his sister have it. This visit was her idea, after all. It occurred to him that hair-muffs would make excellent indoor croquet arches and his mother had quite the collection, but he didn't want to draw attention to himself again.

"If you're going to interrogate me, Mother, may I at least have tea?"

"Oh! Of course, darling, how rude of me. One forgets, you know, with no need for human sustenance — except humans themselves, of course." Mother gave a girlish titter quite unsuited to a woman of her advanced years.

She summoned the lurking butler with an imperious gesture. "Tea, please, Korpin, and cakes or crumpets or something scrummy like that. We do have such a thing in stock?"

"Yes, my queen. You have human drones, remember? They require tea and crumpets regularly."

"Of course they do." Mother whirled back around. "Anything else, darlings? Treacle tart or something significantly more sticky?"

Primrose rolled her eyes at their mother's antics and said over her head to the butler, "Whatever is easily to hand, Korpin, will suit us well enough. Frankly, the tea is the important part."

"Yes of course, miss."

Mother waved at the three vampires and assorted drones who were still skulking about in silent fascinated horror at the mother-meets-twins reunion performance. "My charming hive, you are dismissed for the time being. Practice your form, do, please? We shall resume this game tomorrow night. Let me dwell for now in the welcoming embrace of my portentous progeny. I'll be perfectly safe, I assure you."

Knowing she would be, the hive left with alacrity.

"Portentous?" mouthed Primrose at him.

Percy shrugged. No idea what word Mother really meant. Most of the time a conversation with Baroness Tunstell was an exercise in interpretation by association. Ivy Tunstell had a loose relationship with vocabulary. So far as Percy could tell, it involved groping about for a word and having about as much success as one would locating a bar of soap in the bathtub. Whatever came out of her mouth as a result was squeezed forth and landed with a splash, surprising everyone around, except her.

With no little apprehension, Percy followed his mother and sister to the sitting area. He took the chaise across from them reluctantly.

"Percy dear, where is your hat?"

Percy, who'd elected to stop wearing hats unless absolutely ordered to by his valet, gestured mildly back towards the front entrance. "Left it with the footman."

Primrose gave him a look that said, *You're a liar and I'm keeping that as ammunition in case this conversation goes pear shaped.* It was fair, as Percy had made the decision to leave his hat behind knowing it could be a point of serious contention. He shrugged at his sister in a *do your damnedest* kind of way.

"Tiddles, dearest, I know it is the custom for modish young ladies to have at least one failed engagement to look back upon wistfully – I myself have one I recall with great satisfaction. And I do realize that there is something pleasant in the certain knowledge of having left a gentleman heartsore and pining for all his days. Which is, indeed, right and proper. But *three*, dear. Three. Don't you find that's a touch excessive?" She lowered her voice. "You might even be thought" – a pause while she glanced around significantly, although perfectly well aware that they were not to be disturbed – "loose."

Primrose sighed. "*He* broke it off with *me*, Mother."

Prim's hand was instantly clasped by strong cool white fingers. "Oh, my darling, dearest child! How could he? Did he break your heart? Horrible man. Should I have him killed? I could, you know. Well, sweetheart, plenty more dishes in the sea than that nasty captain fellow. If you'll recall, I did say his knees were knobby. As a matter of interest, I did meet this charming young lordling just the other evening. Of course, he was interested in becoming undead, but surely you can overlook that small character flaw? I turned him away, as it were, I've enough drones at the moment. But he'd make an eminently serviceable husband. He seemed malleable. You'd like that, my bossy darling."

"Mother!" Primrose extracted her hand and shook it to return sensation.

"Lovely eyes he had too, and a full head of hair, and *all* his teeth!"

"Really, Mother. I don't need another—"

"Moneyed as well, I believe. Which, frankly, you can't be certain of with the aristocracy these days. They keep losing their income or selling off their estates, terribly foolhardy. Then they must marry Americans. Really the whole blue-blooded institution is going south. Or, more precisely, west. The colonies have a lot to answer for. Have you seen the new sportswear they're, well, *sporting* these days? The hats are practically bare of decoration. It really can't be conflagranced, naked hats. And then, well, he..." She trailed off, losing her thought, if she could be said to have had a thought to start with. "Oh lovely, here's Korpin with the tea."

Korpin duly put down the tray and scuttled back out of the sitting room as quick as may be. Percy envied him.

"I'll pour, Mother," insisted Prim.

"Of course you will, dear, I hardly remember how. Now, where was I?"

Primrose said hurriedly, to prevent Mother from offering up any other young men for spousal consumption, "There is someone, Mother. For me, I mean."

"Oh, dear me yes? Already? Another engagement?" If it were possible for a hedgehog to look doubtful, she did.

As if their mother had not just been trying to arrange that

precise thing herself. Percy glowered into his cup of excellent tea and relaxed back cautiously into the spindly chaise.

"Percy dear, don't slouch. Tiddles, my sweet, is he a gentleman of position? Rank? Oh dear me, you've been overseas, haven't you? Not *foreign*, is he? Please, tell me it's not someone you met while floating!"

Primrose clasped her hands together and looked up at the ceiling as if for support or divine aid.

She took a deep breath. "It's not a he at all, Mother. It's a *she*. *Her* name is Tasherit Sekhmet. She's an ancient werelioness, from the Sudan. And I'm in love with her."

Baroness Ivy Tunstell, Queen of the Wimbledon Hive, fainted.

Percy set down his tea and appreciated the silence for a long moment.

Finally he said, feeling genuinely rummy, "I didn't know vampires could faint. Isn't fainting to do with blood pressure? How would that even work in an undead body? I say! Is vampire blood pressure borrowed along with the blood? Or do you think it is regulated by some nascent unaffected post-death biological system?"

"I don't know, Percy. Why not ask the new doctor? Oh wait, you're unable to form a coherent sentence around her, aren't you?"

Mother steamed herself back up and set up wailing. "Percy's in love too? With a doctor? *With a man?* Oh good lord what have I done? How could it have all gone so profundently wrong? Both of you bent! It's because your father died while you were still young, isn't it? Primrose had no proper mortal masculine influence so she seeks the company of supernatural feline tempt-resses! And you, Percy, well, I always thought you might lean that direction. But really couldn't one of you have *pretended* and given me grandchildren?" She started fretting, her hand pressed to her forehead, eyes closed. "I've ruined you both. This is all my fault. If I had not taken the bite ... Not that it was by choice, of course. But oh, if you had not been with me ... If I'd never gone to Egypt ... If your father hadn't taken that last dramatic role ... If only ..."

Percy exchanged glances with Prim. No words needed, they sat and sipped their tea while their mother wound herself up. There was no reasoning with her when she got into this state. It was like watching a kettle boil over. It would put itself out eventually.

After several long incomprehensible monologues, she quieted, cracked an eyelid, and noted that her children were calmly drinking tea and staring at her.

"You two will drive me to an early grave." Mother glared at them.

"You're a vampire, Mother. So obviously not." Percy curled his lip at her and put down his teacup with a clatter.

"Our new doctor is a female, Mother," said Primrose.

"The one who has Percy in an un-verbal state? Oh well." Mother slid her eyes over to Percy.

"And I'm *not* in love. I'm simply slightly" – he paused, struggling – "confused."

"Then you aren't of the Lord Akeldama persuasion?" Ivy perked up, feathers quivering.

Percy sighed audibly. "Why does everyone think that?"

"Well, because you're, you know, *you*, darling."

"Thank you, Mother. I'm of a misanthropic, not homogenic disposition. I can't understand the confusion."

"Perhaps, brother dear, if you ever showed *any* interest in *any* of the young ladies paraded before you over the years ..."

"They're all so silly!" objected Percy, which was true. The last thing, the very last thing, he ever wanted in his life was to fall in love with a female akin to either his mother or his sister. In his experience that ruled out the majority of the respectable females in England. With the possible exception of the good doctor. Although to be fair, she'd been hiding in Scotland.

"Well, Mother, the new doctor drives Percy into fits of terrified silence."

As do you two, thought Percy, but he wasn't dumb enough to say it. Perhaps Arsenic shared traits with his female relations after all.

"Does she really?"

"Like that lady friend of Gahiji's who visited from Tunisia. Do you remember?"

"Oh yes, Tiddles, what was her name?"

"Malinda," said Primrose firmly.

"Nadia," Percy corrected, equally firmly. He'd been sixteen and Nadia a smart and savvy businesswoman with whom Gahiji worked to import spices from Africa into England. At first, this was to fill the desires of the Arabic staff and drones who'd accompanied them back from Egypt when Percy was still a baby. Later, because the business proved fruitful, Nadia had come to visit, spices in tow. Percy had never met a woman more beautiful, with her brilliant mind and her calm accented voice.

He'd been sixteen and unable to speak the entire week she stayed with them.

"Of course, *Nadia*." Primrose gave him one of her knowing looks.

Percy hated those looks.

Ivy Tunstell looked back and forth between her children, appearing even more the bewildered hedgehog than ever.

"Percy, really?"

Percy smiled at the memory. "Oh yes. She was awfully smart."

"So this doctor?"

Primrose smirked. "Really, Mother, don't get your hopes up. You know he'll bungle everything. He always does."

Percy privately agreed with her.

Mother whirled on Prim. "At least I stand a chance of grandchildren out of your brother! *You* are a traitor to your line! What would your father say? And with a form-shifter supernatural no less! You couldn't choose a *vampire*?"

"Oh, Mother, really. I can't very well fall in love with a vampire, that would mean a queen. And frankly there aren't enough of you. And I'd have to share. You know I've never been very good at sharing."

"But sweetness, darling . . . she's a woman."

"A large part of the appeal, I assure you," said Percy, with his own smirk.

"I *love* her, Mother!" Prim's eyes flashed and her voice took on something akin to their mother's patented dramatic tones.

Percy winced. *Here we go . . .*

"I love her with my whole heart. I'm utterly lost to her. She is the beach upon which I have cast my weary self after being adrift in a sea of masculinity that did nothing but starve me for real affection, and buffet me with unwelcome attention, and make me sticky with salt."

Percy snorted.

Primrose glared at him, as much as to say, *I'm attempting to communicate with her in her native tongue.*

Percy gestured with his hand for her to go on, and poured himself more tea in order to survive the inevitable monologue.

"She is my meal after *years* of starvation. She is flavours I have never tasted before but always craved. I resisted her precisely *because* I wanted children, wanted family."

"Well yes, Tiddles. Exactly. You want a family. So you must give over this foolishness and marry a nice understanding young man and have your werecat on the side, like a corner dish, or the occasional overindulgent pudding. No one would fault such an arrangement."

"I'd fault it! I have integrity, Mother. And I love her. I want to be with her. I am *going* to be with her. I'd marry her except, well, that doesn't work outside of Shakespeare, but she's mine and I'm hers and it's a done thing."

"But, Tiddles, sweetheart—"

"No, Mother. You'll have to get grandchildren out of Percy. Good luck with that."

Percy reeled.

Fortunately, Ivy Tunstell barely even considered it a suggestion, let alone a likely possibility.

"Oh, Tiddles, but surely every young lady wants a nice husband and her own adorable little babies. I mean to say, you two and your dear departed father were the most cherished blossoms in the garden of my mortal existence."

"Well, this particular young lady wants herself a nice werecat wife, so there! Besides, Rue is going to loan me hers as much as I like."

"Loan you her husband?" Mother blinked.

Percy snorted tea.

Prim glared at him. "Fat lot of good you are."

Percy wisely buried his nose in his cup to hide his smile.

"No, Mother, loan me her *child*. You know she'll make a terrible mother."

The baroness nodded wisely. "Too much like Alexia."

"Whatever that means. No, she's simply easily distracted by constantly saving the world and similar endeavours, and not particularly interested in children. But I would make an excellent mother. So we've generally agreed that I'll have primary care for the baby, while Rue rushes about and does captain things, and Quesnel pokes at his engines. And we'll float around as this odd sort of family. I shall have my werecat and a baby, too."

Ivy threw her head back and moaned. "Oh, where did I go so pedultuously wrong?"

Primrose sighed and reached for her own tea, waved Percy forward, passing the conversation off to him.

Percy stayed silent.

So Prim went on the attack. "Meanwhile, Mother, did you know Percy has given up wearing hats *entirely*?"

Baroness Ivy Tunstell, Queen of the Wimbledon Hive, fainted again.

"That went well." Percy finished his tea.

Primrose stood. "I believe we'd better leave now. Before she recovers her senses."

"I think any *recovering of senses* is highly unlikely with our mother."

"Percy, don't be droll. It doesn't suit."

Arsenic had a lovely night shopping for medical supplies.

General consensus was that they were off to Egypt soon, and from there to parts unknown. It appeared that the captain needed to consult with her parents, who ran a tea export business out of Cairo.

This seemed rather odd to Arsenic. Why Egypt? Why parents? And why tea? Also, why had the former head of BUR, werewolf peer of the realm, and his lady wife descended into such depths as *trade*? Given their familial relationship to her new captain, Arsenic dared not ask directly – it might be perceived as impertinent. Delicate enquiry, among those not directly related to the tea vendors in question, revealed that it had to do with Lord Maccon's *feeble condition*. Which was not a euphemism she'd heard applied to a werewolf before. Surely he couldn't be pregnant. Could he?

She wished she'd taken a course of study in werewolf physiology, but her focus had always been on the fragility of mortals. While all the *money* was in understanding immortality, Arsenic hadn't taken up medicine for the pecuniary advancements. Not like *some* doctors she could name.

She was rather pleased they were headed to Egypt, as she'd been through Alexandria several times before. She'd a good idea of their probable needs, not to mention the supplies afforded locally. She wouldn't make a fool of herself.

She did corner Rue before the captain left the *Custard* to pay a departure call on Lord Akeldama.

"May I have a quick word, Captain?"

"Of course, Doctor. What can I do for you?"

"'Tis about your condition. Six months along, aye?"

Rue shrugged. "Best guess, yes."

"Verra weel. It seems likely that we will na return to London in time for the birth." Arsenic tried to find the best avenue of approach. "I ken something about preternaturals, that they can cancel out supernatural abilities with a touch."

"That is true, but you might talk to Rodrigo if you—"

"No please, hear me out. But you are a metanatural, which means what, exactly?"

"My mother is a preternatural and my father a werewolf."

"Nay. I mean what does it mean for you *physically*?"

"Oh! If I touch a supernatural creature, at night and outside of the aetherosphere, I turn into that creature for the space of that night."

"Can preternatural contact cancel you out too?"

"Yes, Rodrigo can touch me back to human."

"If Tasherit is in human form and you touch her?"

"I turn into a lioness."

"You always take the bestial state?"

"Yes."

"Can you voluntarily change back to human yourself?"

"No, I'm only the beast."

Arsenic took a breath. "This concerns me, Captain. Since we dinna know what the bairn is, exactly. My guess is na preternatural, or the act of carrying the bairn would cause you to be unable to shift."

"Unless, of course, the water around the baby acts as a buffer?"

"Water affects metanatural abilities?"

"Yes, indeed. And preternatural."

"Hum, then 'tis possible. Still, the bairn could be damaged if you shift into a creature whose body shape is significantly dissimilar to a human. That is to say, as the bairn gets bigger inside you, it will be less and less resilient to your body re-forming around it."

Rue frowned. "You're concerned about shift-induced miscarriage?"

Arsenic nodded. "Verra. We are negotiating utterly unknown biology here. Your situation is worryingly unique. I would urge caution."

Arsenic truly wanted her captain to take this seriously. General crew attitude around Rue suggested *caution* was not her strong suit. If indeed she had even a nodding acquaintance with the practice.

Rue's expression was difficult to decipher. "I take your point. Do you cherish the same concerns if I were to change to vampire, Rakshasa, or pishtaco?"

"Vampire, or what, or what?" Arsenic was beginning to seriously doubt the adequacy of her education.

"All different kinds of blood- or flesh-consuming supernatural creatures."

"All human form, no major form-shift?"

"Essentially."

"That would depend. When you're a vampire, are you driven by a need to bite necks and suck blood?"

"Not particularly."

"But your strength and speed are enhanced?"

"Yes."

"That suggests you change physical characteristics associated with skeleton and musculature. How about your vision and other senses?"

"Improved."

"*That* is organ related. So vampire shift could impact your womb."

Rue's face blanched. "Oh, but I already have! I was a pishtaco a few months ago, and a lioness shortly before that. Have I messed up the baby?"

She looked like she might cry.

Arsenic was oddly relieved. Clearly Rue did care, she was simply facetious about it. Arsenic wondered if Rue's forced flippancy with regards to imminent motherhood was a means of deflecting a profound fear of the maternal state.

So she placed a reassuring hand to Rue's soft upper arm. "Have you felt the bairn moving about since then?"

"Oh. Yes! Yes, I have."

"Then the baby is likely fine. I would urge caution going forward. It could be that the child develops its abilities later on in the embryonic process. In which case, if your bairn is a preternatural, you'll soon find yourself unable to shift, should you try. I suggest you na try, though."

Rue nodded, biting her lip. "I shall take your advice to heart, Doctor."

Arsenic thought it likely Rue was being honest, but also that she might forget in the heat of the moment. To be able to change shape in battle or to heal on a whim, would necessarily make one rather instinctively reliant on such resources. Arsenic hoped Rue would not forget and reach for Tasherit in time of crisis.

Cautiously she added, "Would you mind if I told Tasherit and Rodrigo my concerns? Perhaps if the lioness knew to avoid contact? And your cousin could keep an eye on proximity as well, as with a simple touch he could stop any unexpected shifts."

"If you think it best. I don't want them hovering, though. Can't abide hovering."

"Are they the type to hover?"

"Not by nature."

"Weel then?"

"Honestly, you might as well simply tell Prim and Spoo, between the two of them everyone will know, easier that way. They work faster than the speaking tube. It's miraculous."

Arsenic nodded, relieved. She'd expected a battle. But if everyone might be recruited to save the captain from herself, it would be best. Arsenic had done this kind of thing before with generals and brigadiers – recruited soldiers and support staff into helping her manage them indirectly and for everyone's wellbeing.

Rue glowered. "Quesnel will hover, though. I don't suppose he could be left out of it?"

"While everyone else knows? Is that wise in a relationship?"

"I suppose you're right." Rue looked resigned to having to share vital information with her own husband and presumably went off to do so.

The Spotted Custard puffed away from London on an evening current in good time to hit the grey and float off in a southeastern direction.

Arsenic joined the rest of the crew on deck for the lift. She had no means of helping and felt out of place but it was a joy to watch her new companions work. They were smooth and confident and delightfully jocular.

Spoo and the decklings moved with lithe grace, swinging from riggings and calling out instructions, observations, and insults to one another.

"Watch your head there, Nips!"

"Oui up, Spoo, my head is none of your concern."

"I wouldn't bother but you seem incapable of keeping it on your shoulders with any surety."

"*Surety?* What are you, a banker?"

"Bank your arse in the clouds, I will, if you don't pay attention."

Arsenic did not bother to hide her smile.

Rue was in her element, waddling about the deck barking out orders, and gesticulating wildly. Arsenic didn't *think* the waddling detracted from her authority. It was amusing, though, the captain looked something on the order of a dictatorial duck. Percy seemed to have given Virgil instructions on providing captain-wobble maintenance. The valet appeared at Rue's elbow to brace her whenever she gave a particularly exuberant arm wiggle, or seemed inclined to tip.

Percy himself was the revelation. He was straight-backed

and confident, yelling out responses to the captain's queries, and barking instructions down the speaking tube to engineering with authority. Gone was the awkward conversationalist of the breakfast table. He was, Arsenic realized with a shock, an extremely good navigator. He dialled in the probe, calculated the puffs, and charted current hops with consummate aplomb.

Arsenic didn't want to admire Percy's adept handling of the helm, but she did. A capable man was really rather appealing, bright eyes focused, hands confident, cheekbones sharp. Not that cheekbones had anything to do with efficiency, but the man certainly had an attractive skeletal structure.

Primrose popped her head up to ascertain that everything was running smoothly and then retreated belowdecks about some staffing crisis or pastry shortage.

Arsenic spotted Anitra, who seemed equally adrift in the efficient chaos, and sidled up to her to ask politely after Tasherit. The werecat was still absent and Arsenic was worried about aether exposure.

Anitra said that Tash confined herself for the duration of high transit. Apparently, the werecat simply fell into a deep sleep once inside the aetherosphere, from which she could not be awoken.

They stood together at the main deck railing, next to one of the Gatling guns, and watched as London became a splotch of light below them. Arsenic was grateful for the Drifter's presence. The sweet-faced lady seemed happy to keep her company, help her stay out of the way, and answer any questions.

As they puffed up, *The Spotted Custard* let out a tremendous fart. Arsenic started. "That noise? 'Tis na a concern?"

Anitra looked embarrassed. "The ship has a digestive complaint. We've been assured by engineering that its flatulence is not an indication of anything serious."

Arsenic chuckled. "It usually isna. I would advise a change of diet but I suppose steam engines run on coal, and that's about the sum total of it. There's na blockage?"

"No need to diagnose the airship, Doctor."

"Aye. I suppose you've people for that."

"Speaking of, what does my dear husband think he's doing?" Rodrigo was trying to help the deckhands haul in and strap down for imminent current hop.

"He's a deckhand?" Arsenic was impressed, as she would have guessed the preternatural too proud for menial labour.

"No, he's an assassin. Manning an airship takes real skill. He only kills people. Well, he used to. If he's not careful, he'll do it again by accident." Anitra called out. "Darling! Come away from Bork. Poor fellow."

Rodrigo said something to her in lyrical Italian.

His wife said something sweetly back.

When that didn't work, Anitra made an obvious move towards the lower decks and cast her man the kind of coy look that suggested he had a choice to make, and better make the right one.

Rodrigo trotted after her.

Arsenic was left alone but amused.

They hit the grey. England winked out of existence and they were surrounded by nothingness.

Arsenic enjoyed the aetherosphere. Some people found it cloying and oppressive but she found it restful.

Percy moved around the navigation pit frantically as they traversed the uncharted Charybdis currents, but several farts later they'd attained their target current, the European Flow. Percy managed the smoothest series of hops Arsenic had ever experienced. She wasn't sure if that could be attributed to the technological sophistication of *The Spotted Custard*, which she was beginning to realize was top-notch despite its silly ladybug appearance, or the skill of the navigator, or both. Arsenic didn't express her admiration to the man. He was working and seemed to find her distracting, so she stayed away.

She did try to pin him down and tell him later, when the sail was safely up, and all was calm and still. But he seemed to be on a mission to avoid her as much as possible.

CHAPTER

SIX

When All Else Fails, Try the Library

They were several days travelling through the grey towards Constantinople. This was largely uneventful. Except for the decklings' particularly exciting bout of combative badminton.

Arsenic managed a medic's consultation with most of the crew and staff. Anitra had been rather a surprise. Now Arsenic knew to look, Anitra's hands were a touch large and there was a small Adam's apple under her veils. Arsenic had met a lady who was a male soldier once, but never the other way around. She understood why her worries about contraception had amused everyone and left it at that.

The only crew Arsenic failed to see were Tasherit Sekhmet, who was asleep, Aggie Phinkerlington, who was impossible, and Percival Tunstell, who was avoiding her.

After double-checking her notes against the ship's manifest, Arsenic girded her proverbial loins and decided to tackle Aggie first. Armed with her mother's training, she headed down to the boiler room.

Only an assassin, she felt, could reasonably be expected to catch Aggie Phinkerlington.

Engineering was lousy with smoke and coal dust. Arsenic made a mental note to check the breathing capacity of all those who worked the boiler room. It was hot and noisy from the heat and hiss and clang of two boilers and a great deal of associated machinery. There was also *singing*, off-key and rather bawdy, as the sooties, firemen, and greasers went about their duties.

Quesnel spotted her first and came wandering over. There wasn't much excitement at the moment, since the mainsail was up and they were coasting the aether currents with restful impunity. His people were mostly focused on keeping the gas flowing, the kitchen supplied with hot water, and suchlike activities. Real excitement occurred during a puffing. Arsenic intended to stay far away from engineering at such times. She'd never been one for soot, grease, and machinery.

Of course, she was grateful for the luxuries afforded by this new age of technology, but they tended to play hell with one's clothing upon intimate exposure. Not that Arsenic considered herself a fashion maven. At the moment she was wearing a tweed mountain-climbing outfit with a nursing pinafore pinned to the top. It was an odd combination but functional, which tended to be Arsenic's preference in life.

Quesnel grinned at her. "Doctor, to what do we owe this honour?"

"I'm looking for Miss Phinkerlington."

"Aggie? Why?"

"She has missed her appointment with me three times thus far."

"Ah yes. I see. A moment." Quesnel threw his head back and yelled, "Aggie, get yourself over here, you harridan. Someone's come for you at last."

Arsenic spotted the head greaser saunter oh-so-casually away from them and nip behind the larger of the two boilers. It looked, Arsenic realized, like a massive teakettle. *How endearing.*

She tilted her head at Quesnel to indicate where the woman had gone.

"Ah," said the Frenchman with a twinkle in his eye.

Quesnel turned and pointed three fingers in a flicking motion at two burly-looking firemen. Directing them to where Aggie was now hiding. The men understood the unspoken command and went off after their head greaser with delighted expressions. They returned moments later. Each man had one arm occupied, carrying Aggie between them, upright, while she wiggled and swore. She was shorter than Arsenic had realized. She had thought of the woman as tall, possibly a result of her grumpy attitude. Dour people always seemed like they ought to be tall.

The firemen plunked Aggie down in front of Arsenic.

"Oh yes, well, erm, Doctor?" The ginger female looked all around, desperate for an excuse to escape.

"Good afternoon, Miss Phinkerlington."

"What you want me for, boffin?" She glared at Quesnel.

"Ah, Aggie, the good doctor here says you've missed your appointments."

"Ah, well, I'm on shift right now. If I could come see you after?" Aggie's gaze darted about, everywhere but at Arsenic.

"Oh no." Quesnel was looking rather too pleased. "You're relieved of duty. Things are quiet. We can spare you for a half an hour. You get this taken care of, Aggie."

Arsenic decided that this was some previously unheard-of definition of the word *quiet*. The boiler room was nothing if not noisy. Or perhaps Quesnel was too French to really comprehend the irony of his words.

"But Q!"

"No, doudou, you go with the nice doctor."

"Oh, but—"

"Or you do not come back to work at all. I have humoured you long enough." Quesnel could clearly be quite commanding, when he liked.

Arsenic crossed her arms and attempted to look persuasively threatening.

Aggie glared at her, as if Arsenic had killed her best friend. Not that Aggie looked to be the type to have many friends. Fine, Aggie was looking as if Arsenic had lost her favourite wrench.

"It willna take even twenty minutes. I'll be verra gentle."
Arsenic tried for a soft smile. "Promise."

Aggie muttered something under her breath but when Arsenic turned to climb the ladder out of engineering, the head greaser dutifully followed.

Once they hit the corridor and were well shot of the noise, Arsenic glanced at Aggie sideways. "Bad experience or simply a general fear of physicians?"

"Leeches and sawbones, the lot of you."

"Aye? So 'tis prejudice? Bonnie. My favourite."

"Now see here, Doc. Couldn't you just mark me off as oil, and we'd go forth ignoring one another? Wouldn't that be pips?"

"You'd do that with a boiler, would you? Something vital to the safety of this ship? Simply say '*tis working fine* without checking it over properly?"

"Well, no, but—"

"This way, please." Arsenic directed Aggie into the swoon room and closed the door behind them. She thought about locking it but Aggie already looked like a trapped animal of some venomous variety.

Arsenic extracted her favourite examination lens from its new cubby.

"Come, sit." She gestured to her exam cot.

Aggie, dragging her feet, sat.

"Look up, please."

Arsenic went through the motions of checking the quality and condition of Aggie's eyes, nose, ears, throat, tongue, and breath. She palpated various nodes and checked for the usual parasites. The woman seemed in extraordinarily good health for one who so assiduously avoided care.

"You gonna have me strip down?" Aggie looked terrified.

"Something I should know? Unexpected lumps, rashes, anything along those lines?"

"Blimey, no!"

Arsenic stood back and crossed her arms. "Any disease or ailments endemic to your family?"

"No."

"Bite-survivor ancestry?"

"No." The greaser looked bitter. "We run practical. There was one death in the attempt."

Arsenic made a note in her book. "Vampire or werewolf?"

"Werewolf."

"'Tis my medical duty to inform you, as a matter of record, that recent data suggests survival rates for metamorphosis appear modestly dependent on familial history as well as presence or absence of excess soul. Thus, your chances are even less than other humans'."

"Since I'm not at all creative, Doc, I suspected that already. Nice to know I'm gonna die young, though."

Arsenic looked up at her. "Did you wish to be supernatural?"

"No."

"So you're being ornery?"

"It's my character trait of preference."

"You're verra good at it."

"Thank you, Doc. What about you? Just like cutting people open and hearing them scream?"

"'Tis all I live for." Arsenic had sisters; witty banter was practically a requirement in the Ruthven household. This ginger harridan wasn't going to get the better of her with sarcasm.

Surprisingly, Aggie laughed. "You're not so bad, are you, Doc?"

Arsenic wasn't sure how she felt about *Doc* as a moniker. "Oh, go on, call me the Grim Reaper."

Aggie snorted again.

"The calluses on your fingers here. They from work with boilers?"

"No, Doc."

"Crossbow?"

"How would you know that?"

"My mother taught me. Do you shoot regular?"

"More often than I thought I would. *Spotted Custard* isn't as quiet as one might hope."

"Want to do some targeting on deck sometime?" Arsenic was thinking she hadn't shot a crossbow in years, so she could use the practice, but also that it was likely a good way to get Aggie out into sunlight and fresh air.

"You're an odd kind of doctor if you want to join me on deck to shoot things."

"So long as 'tis *things*, na people."

"We done then?"

"We are. Was that so horrible?"

Aggie gave her a level stare. "I suspect you're warming up."

Arsenic rolled her eyes. "Refrain from being injured or ill, Miss Phinkerlington, and we'll meet but rarely."

"Optimism does neither of us a service."

"You're likely right 'bout that." Arsenic went with Aggie to the door and saw her out of the room.

"You should call me Aggie, Doc. I'll come by sometime and we can shoot something." She almost seemed hesitant. "If the offer's still good?"

"I look forward to it."

"Don't tell porkers."

Rue was standing outside in the hallway patiently waiting for one of them. She had an annoyed-looking Percy next to her.

Aggie gave the captain a nose wrinkle. Her attitude not at all subservient.

Rue snorted at her. Then looked at Arsenic. "Are you two getting chummy over murder?"

"Crossbows, Captain. What else?" snarled Aggie.

"Arsenic, do you shoot?"

"Unfortunate consequence of my upbringing." Arsenic waved a magnanimous hand at her swoon room. "You waiting on me, Captain? Come in."

Rue waddled in, dragging Percy behind her. Arsenic was impressed with the captain's strength.

"Delivery for you, Doctor."

"Just what I always wanted, my own personal librarian navigator. Sit down, Professor."

Percy gave Rue a wild and desperate look.

"Stay, Percy," said Rue, before waddling self-importantly back out and closing the door behind her.

Arsenic turned her professional eye on the man. "Sit down, Percy, please." She felt rather emboldened, using his given name. As if they really knew each other and he didn't hold her in disdain.

Percy's eyes were stark with fear and his cheekbones sharper than ever. Arsenic tried to convince herself all admiration was purely aesthetic, that her attitude was professional, and she didn't want to touch the soft skin stretched over those bones. She thought about the lump in her apron, another stolen scone. She'd taken up the habit of regularly pocketing scones for Percy. In case he ever gave her an opening. She thought it would be rather out of place to offer it during an exam, but she liked knowing she had it, just in case he needed soothing.

Percy had never before suffered such an embarrassment as discussing his own biological makeup with the most attractive lady of his acquaintance. Which was saying something with Ivy for a mother.

Not that her appearance should make any difference to her abilities, of course. But it made a difference as to how he reacted to her execution of such.

Her questions all seemed that much more intrusive, although he was in no doubt that she asked every patient exactly the same things.

The part where she looked at him through various magnification devices, his eyes and ears and such, was not so bad. The separation wrought by scientific device mitigated the sensation of her proximity. He tried desperately not to notice her breath on his face or the fact that she smelled a little like honeysuckle. Ought she not to smell like formaldehyde or some other medical pong?

Percy managed to maintain an impassive face and general indifferent air, until she went to palpate his throat and check his pulse.

Her touch was light and dry and sure. His pulse increased and he began to sweat. He thought he might faint or something equally ridiculous until he realized he was holding his breath and let it out in a *whoosh*.

"I willna bite, Professor. I assure you. I'm no vampire."

"I'm not at all scared of vampires, Doctor."

"Aye, of course na. You're related to one. Mother's side?"

"Actual mother."

"I thought that wasna permitted."

"She falls under the EEC Act. Extenuating exsanguinatious circumstances. A crisis in Egypt necessitated her metamorphosis. Prim and I were already born, obviously. So there was no undoing any of it."

Arsenic shrugged and made a note in her notebook. "These things happen. Which means you possess the possibility of conversion yourself. Have you considered immortality?"

"No. Not interested."

"You're certain? Are you at all creative?"

"Not so as anyone would remark."

"Was your mother?"

"Well, she had some innovative tendencies in the arena of hats, theatricals, and vocabulary." Percy considered his mother's horrible slim travel volume. "And some unfortunately lurid purple prose."

"A writer?"

"Of sorts."

"Do you write, Professor?"

"Only scientific papers."

"Oh aye? I'd heard this. I understand you wrote the definitive work on werecats? Considering we have one aboard, I should verra much like to read it."

He looked pleased but replied, "I doubt it will do you much good, Doctor. It's not biologically explicit."

"'Tis better than nothing. And why na? Does the physiology of shifter species na interest you?"

Percy frowned. "It felt intrusive to ask for particulars, considering Tash is practically family."

"Because of your sister?"

Percy straightened. "You object to the match?"

The lovely doctor inclined her head. "Not at all."

Percy swallowed around a sudden lump of fear. Before his sister's unexpected breach with the marital standards of polite society, he would never have thought to ask, but now he felt it polite. "You are similarly inclined?"

"Nay. Just untroubled by the relationships of others. Whom she loves dinna impact me in any particular way. Why should I mind?"

"Because society, as a general rule, minds."

"Considering society has done me no favours as a woman in a man's profession, society can go hang itself."

"Oh," said Percy, flummoxed. "You're a rebel."

Arsenic tilted her head and regarded him out of those remarkable dark blue eyes. "Is that na the verra definition of this airship?"

Percy considered that a moment. He supposed they were, each of them in their way, rebelling against something. "Fair point. Are we finished, Doctor?"

"We are indeed, Professor. May I follow you back to the library for that paper?"

Percy's tummy went tense at the thought of Arsenic in his sacred space, but he agreed in the hope that she might take what she needed away to her quarters.

Unfortunately, she found his library charming. No doubt it helped that Footnote greeted her with evident delight. Then Virgil arrived with tea, gleefully dashing off for a second cup and audibly whispering, "Sir! You have company!"

The valet returned with a second teacup and a plate of gingersnaps. It was no wonder she chose to stay.

Arsenic was polite about it. She curled into a yellow wingback chair and read his paper on werecats in complete silence. Normally the chair was Footnote's but the cat ceded it to her on the understanding that she would compensate by providing her lap. Arsenic dutifully compensated.

Percy, eventually, forgot she was there and was able to relax. He was therefore startled when, an hour later, she cleared her throat and asked if he had anything in his collection concerning metanaturals. At which juncture he was left to explain how rare metanaturals were, and there was only one other named on record, Zenobia, and that was only because of Lord Akeldama. So she asked if she might read about preternaturals, given that they had one of those aboard too.

He passed her what he had on the soulless, which also wasn't much. The two slim volumes, one of them Italian in origin, had been obtained via his club and government connections in a slightly underhanded and pleasingly illicit manner. Percy had a nefarious streak when contraband books were involved.

Arsenic sat still as she read, moving only to make a note in a small leather-bound doctor's handbook. At one point, she tentatively asked for clarification on a preternatural term. No doubt she knew of his friendship with Rodrigo. Percy was shocked to find he was more excited to answer her question and engage in intellectual conversation than he was irked by the interruption. How out of character.

Her question showed she had a sharp scientific mind and a way of thinking about the supernatural and adjacent unnatural states distinctly different from his own. Her spirit of enquiry being medically based, her insights were all bent towards the practical results of abilities on the *body* – as opposed to on the spirit or the rest of the world.

One question led to another and suddenly they were – not to put too fine a point on it – *in conversation*.

Percy found her perspective fascinating and she seemed equally enamoured of his. By dinnertime Percy was shocked to realize they'd spent the better part of *four hours* in contemplative conversation broken by long stretches of reading, supplemented with tea.

Never had he spent a more pleasing evening in his life.

Percy had even asked her opinion on a topic or two of his own interest. Much to his shock. Percy, as a general rule, never consulted anyone else about anything, unless they were long dead and had written it down.

But he found Arsenic's insight enlightening. He greatly admired her ability to simply state that she held an opinion, rather than attempt to invent information or flapdoodle over inconsequentialities.

When she stood and stretched (Percy absolutely did not note the trimness of her figure) and then excused herself to freshen up before the meal, Percy was shocked by four things.

First, she'd covertly left him a scone on his desk, which she'd obviously filched special. He remembered from her interview she didn't like scones herself.

Second, he immediately missed her company. He, who preferred to be alone!

Third, he found her charming. *Charming.* Percy never found *anyone* charming!

And finally, that the chair smelled faintly of honeysuckle, and he wished for it to remain so always.

When he sat down in her place, despite the dinner bell, the seat was warm from her slight form. He liked that she'd been there. Loved that she had chosen to spend time with him.

Footnote glared at him, since his was not the right lap. Percy was struck by a flight of fancy, imagining Arsenic in his lap, with Footnote on top of both of them. A tangle of limbs and books and cat and comfort. He was startled by the depth of his own yearning.

Percy depuffed the *Custard* into Constantinople for a refuel with even more than his customary skill. He was showing off. And he positively glowed when Rue, who was sparse with praise, told him what a good job he'd done of it – in front of Arsenic.

They headed back up into the grey and navigated due south on one of the more crowded currents. This, too, was a smooth float and Percy was pleased that the aetherosphere seemed in support of his courtship. Then he wondered if that was what he was doing. Was he floating with aplomb as some oddball form of *courtship*? To puff and depuff to the best of his abilities, as if he were a kind of puffed-up peacock putting himself on display for a suitable peahen. Was Arsenic his peahen?

Was that a romantic pet name? *Peahen?*

Despite Arsenic not being part of the deck crew, their new doctor made a point of appearing abovedecks for every major current hop. Probably for the thrill of it and the change of pace, but everyone was pleased to see her taking an interest. She was more skilled than Percy at integrating into a crew. They already liked her better than they'd ever liked him. He observed this with an odd sort of pride.

And she continued to steal scones for him.

Definitely courting behaviour.

Only Percy didn't know how to really do it. (*Peahen*, he eventually decided, was not a good name for one's beloved. He'd have to do better. What did the ancients use? Time to research.)

Percy understood the mechanics of courting, of course. One ought to write a lady sonnets, send her flowers, and purchase the odd trinket or two. But the only flowers aboard the *Custard* were the potted sunflowers to help cleanse the aether of malignant humours. They ought not to be cut and presented to doctors. Besides, Percy had never understood the notion of gifting the dead sexual organs of a plant to females. It seemed oddly threatening. Trinkets might be the way to go. Tokens of affection. If he were crafty, he might find Arsenic some expensive medicine that was rare and highly coveted. Mercury, perhaps? Or something more simple like castor oil? Or was that the daisy of the medical world? Percy resolved to investigate around Cairo for castor oil after depuff. If he had the chance.

But then there would be the awkwardness of actually giving her the gift. What would he say? How would he say it?

Here, my lovely peahen, I have brought you a bottle of castor oil. Please come sit in a chair with me in my library and don't talk too much and when you do speak, say something smart? If we're lucky the cat will sit on top of us.

He shuddered at the notion, and wanted badly to court Arsenic with nothing more than a companionable silence while reading. But presumably one had to state one's intent in matters of affection, if one ever wished to move *beyond* reading.

She'd said she was a rebel. Wasn't a silent courtship terribly rebellious?

Would she even welcome his suit? She did seem to like to look at him. And how did he feel, after spending the better part of his life avoiding LIMPs, entertaining the notion of a lady companion? He felt like he'd have to hide it all from his sister.

Such was the manner of Percy's thoughts during their travel.

Whether or not she perceived it as courting, the lovely Arsenic did, in fact, join Percy to read happily in silence, while he did the same. Whenever he was not required on deck at the helm, and she was not required in her swoon room, they could be found together in the library. They even chatted on occasion.

If the others noticed that the professor and the doctor were spending a good deal of their time together, they made no comment. This was either terribly circumspect (which Percy considered highly unlikely) or they were the subject of a great deal of gossip behind closed doors (which Percy felt was practically guaranteed). He was, of course, horribly embarrassed.

But by the time Percy realized what was happening, Arsenic took it as a given that his library, his armchair, and his cat were hers. Percy would have been far more embarrassed to come up with some excuse to boot her at that juncture than he was suffering under his sister's and Anitra's knowing looks, not to mention Rue's, Rodrigo's, and Quesnel's occasional snicker. Besides, he didn't *want* to boot her. He was beginning to hope that he himself might be added to the list of things that were hers.

Even if Virgil was absolutely horrid whenever he brought in tea.

"Tea for *two*," the valet would say, in an arch tone with an impossibly smug smile.

Percy could only hope that Arsenic didn't notice. If she did, he hoped she would realize all mockery was at his expense and not hers.

Percy contented himself with a scathing and softly muttered *corvus oculum corvi non eruit* whenever he caught one of his erstwhile friends, employees, or nominal enemies giving him a knowing look.

In the meantime, he determined to enjoy Arsenic's company and not hope for too much more while he figured out what to do about it. Any form of enjoyment was so alien to his nature that he did have to resolve firmly to appreciate it.

It was, therefore, all too soon for Percy, when they settled out of the aetherosphere above Cairo.

Arsenic had a quick consult with the customs officials in Cairo, Anitra acting as interpreter, to establish that there were no prevalent illnesses, tropical disease outbreaks, or other medical concerns at the moment.

She was informed, curtly, that all was well, so long as one did not count the God-Breaker Plague, and even that was retreating. Since the God-Breaker Plague, technically, wasn't a plague at all but more an anti-supernatural zone, Arsenic didn't humour the officious young men with a response.

Quarantine was simple enough. The ship had visited and been registered before. Within a few hours, they were flagged up and obelisk moored and ready to climb to ground.

"The good thing is, we aren't inside the plague zone yet." Rue leaned against the railing and watched their heavy rope ladder get lowered.

"Wasn't that the point of bringing your father here?"

"Yes indeed, and he spends much of his time just inside it, with my mother just outside of it. It's a compromise. She can't stand being inside for too long and he isn't sane outside. They keep moving house to stay exactly on the border, as the plague zone shrinks southwards. We'll need to find out where they are, at the moment."

"Awkward kind of marriage."

"Too true." Rue looked pensive. "But it's the best solution they could come up with. They were already an odd match, preternatural and werewolf. I shouldn't really exist, you realize? Not practically."

"You're a miracle of the modern age."

"She is *the* miracle of the modern age," said Rue's husband, coming up and kissing her cheek.

Rue grinned at Quesnel, but continued blathering with Arsenic. "Will it hurt the child, do you think, going inside the zone? I can try to avoid it if necessary."

"How does it make you feel?"

"Sort of buzzing and odd. It's not as unpleasant as my mother finds it, apparently. Or Rodrigo."

Rodrigo, hearing his name, swaggered over to them.

Rue turned to him. "Are you going to come meet Mother? You're related, after all."

Rodrigo raised one eyebrow at her. "And how would I do that?"

"Oh yes, of course." Rue shook her head at herself.

Arsenic had been doing her reading and understood the particulars now. "Two preternaturals canna share the same air."

"Although," said Rue, cheeky, "they might be able to share the same pond."

"What?" asked Arsenic and Rodrigo at the same time.

"Water mitigates preternatural abilities."

"Aye, so you said before." Arsenic considered. "*Share the same air.* I wonder if it means literally that there is something in the air that makes preternatural abilities work or na work, and also metanaturals. Captain, can you change shape inside the plague zone?"

"I don't know. I never tried. And how could I, if it makes immortals mortal? Now that I think on it, it does feel a little numbing, like preternatural touch."

Arsenic let her mind wander. "I wonder if one might apply something akin to germ theory to the supernatural state. Meaning that preternaturals act upon supernaturals na unlike a medicine. That the state of undead is essentially an illness of the very air around us."

Percy's voice drifted down towards them from the navigation pit. "Have you read Weismann's challenge to Lamarckism, Doctor? It's a bit old. But we know that preternaturals breed true and mostly men, so there might be something in the blood."

Arsenic had, of course, read the paper. She drifted away from the group at the rail and towards Percy's pit. "The germ plasm theory of inheritance? It *might* apply. You're suggesting preternatural abilities are some kind of inherited disorder, and that the capacity for excess soul is similarly transferred?"

Percy nodded. "It might not be germane, but a man named Mendel did some very interesting work with pea plants a few decades ago. Solid stuff." He shook his head. "Never got the recognition he deserved, poor sod, but he showed that it's possible to pass certain traits from one generation to the next, even to skip a generation in defiance of blending theory."

Arsenic agreed. "Makes sense. Na all children are exact mixes of their parents."

"Eye colour, for example." Percy was looking into hers earnestly. Arsenic settled at the edge of the pit, not wanting to intrude, but this was fascinating. "I've my mother's eyes. So, if we combined these concepts with a supposition that preternatural, and therefore metanatural and associated abilities, are inherited traits that dictate certain skin-to-air reactions? Much in the manner of those allergic to wool."

Percy's eyes lit up. "The God-Breaker Plague means that there's a prevalence of wool in the air and thus preternaturals react badly, because that prevalence is them, and they can't share air with other preternaturals. Thus supernaturals react to the plague zone much as they would to preternatural touch."

Arsenic was getting excited by this theory. So was Percy, if the light in his eyes was anything to go by. She couldn't pinpoint exactly when they'd become chummy, probably shortly after she realized his apparent disdain was only an awkward shyness. She had started regularly leaving him pocket scones. The man loved a pocket scone. Now they were cohorts, although nothing more intimate as Arsenic hadn't figured out how exactly to coax him past intellectual hypothesis into something less hypothetical and more, well, scientifically rigorous – so to speak. The scones didn't seem to be sufficient.

"We always think of preternatural touch as taking the soul away from the supernatural. What if 'tis more physical? What if they dampen a supernatural's defences, somehow?"

Percy followed her idea exactly. "Interfering with an existing skin-to-air bond?"

"Aye!"

"Is it odd how comfortable they are with each other?" Anitra wanted to know.

Arsenic looked up, only then noticing that Rue, Rodrigo,

Quesnel, and Anitra were all standing around the navigation pit looking down at them.

"It's almost like Percy has a *friend*," said Quesnel.

"Oh my heavens, are you two *friends?*" That was Rue.

"Do they speak in English?" Rodrigo wanted to know. "That is not real English."

At this juncture, Tasherit appeared abovedecks. It was now after sunset and evidently they were far enough away from the aetherosphere for her to be awake and moving about.

"Good evening, my lovelies," said the werecat. "What have I missed?"

Arsenic looked up at her. "Good evening, Tasherit. May I ask, what does the God-Breaker Plague feel like to you?"

"Like preternatural touch."

"Aye, but what does that *feel* like?"

"Like I'm human again."

Arsenic frowned.

Percy said, "That's not at all helpful, since we *only* know what being human feels like."

"Perhaps we are na asking the right question." Arsenic regarded the werecat. "What does being supernatural feel like? How is it different from before metamorphosis?"

"Doctor, that is a conversation that would take many nights."

"Could we have it sometime?"

"Of course, but now it seems you're leaving the ship?" She gestured to where the decklings were attempting to get Rue's attention and let her know that the rope ladder was down and ready for embarkation.

"You willna be coming with us?"

"That close to the plague zone? No. I've been around it enough to last all my lifetimes, thank you. I'll stay here on the ship like the sane supernatural creature I am."

"Never did I think I would agree with a monster. But she speaks truth," said Rodrigo.

"I'm coming." Percy climbed out of his pit.

"You are?" Rue was shocked. "I mean to say, I know I ordered you to, but I didn't think you'd listen."

Percy was a little red. "Well, yes. I feel like it."

Arsenic noticed he was looking at her from under his lashes.

"You *feel like* visiting my parents? You barely tolerate them. Percy, are you being noble?" Rue put a hand to her chest. "Protecting our new doctor from my mother?"

"Someone has to." Percy was truculent.

"She's that bad?" wondered Arsenic.

Rue glared at Percy. "She's a bit *much*. I don't see what Percy thinks he can possibly do to help. Most of the time, with most people, he makes everything worse."

"Your mother likes me," said Percy.

"My mother has horrible taste."

Percy only changed into a visiting jacket. Virgil had been lurking and proffering it up hopefully.

"I'm grateful, for my part," said Arsenic, because she was. She was flattered that the professor, who seemed to bestir himself for nothing and no one, was moved into some gallant action on her behalf when faced with the most noted harridan of the era. Of course, he hadn't met Arsenic's own mother, and he didn't know what kind of resources Arsenic had as a result. But it was terribly sweet of him.

Since she'd as lief have his company either way, Arsenic allowed Percy to be gallant and didn't tease him for it. She wished Rue wouldn't. Percy seemed interested in her as more than a friend, and Arsenic rather liked the idea. She found his awkward mannerisms endearing, his conversation stimulating, and his skeletal structure pleasing. She'd never thought to pair up with a man, but he was exactly what she'd pick, if she did think about it. Also, she liked his cat.

There came a funny squawk at that juncture. (Not from Percy, as it turned out.)

What appeared to be some form of mechanized parrot fluttered down to land on the railing nearby. Arsenic thought mechanicals were illegal, but perhaps not in Egypt.

"Stay back!" yelled Tasherit, dashing forward with supernatural speed.

She caught it up with alacrity, and unceremoniously ripped its head off. Well, it was a bird and she was a cat.

"Was that strictly necessary?" asked Rue.

Tasherit handed her the broken pieces.

Rue poked about for a moment, finally extracting a note. "It's from Mother. It's their current address."

Tasherit remained unrepentant.

"Give it here, chérie. I'll see if I can repair it." Quesnel held out his hand.

Rue passed the decapitated bird parts over. "No time, darling. They want us now, tonight. In fact, we're already late."

"How can we be late when we just got the message?" wondered Percy.

"You know Mother."

Percy sighed.

Primrose appeared abovedecks perfectly turned out in a visiting dress of soft pink muslin, a matched beaded reticule, and an ill-matched but serviceable-looking parasol. She made a grabbing gesture with her pink-gloved hand at Quesnel. "Give it here? I'll put the parts in my bag. You are a vicious thing, aren't you, Tash my darling?" There was approval in her tone.

Tasherit grinned at her.

"Poor petit oiseau. He was only doing his job." Quesnel passed the parts over.

"Well, Aunt Alexia should know not to send birds to this ship. It's lousy with cats." Primrose was staunch in her defence of her lover.

Arsenic tilted her head, hearing a funny ticking sound. "Um, does anyone . . . ?"

Tash apparently did, because she grabbed Prim's reticule and hurled it full force up into the air.

The reticule exploded, showering them with pink beads.

Arsenic was amused to see that no one had flinched.

"For goodness' sake," said Rue.

"Self-destruct mechanism," explained Quesnel.

"Yes," snapped Percy, "we did deduce such."

"Should have known, with my parents." Rue was philosophical.

Primrose sighed. "I'll never be able to find one better matched to this dress. Do I have time to change?"

"Don't know why you were bringing a bag, anyway, Prim. Your parasol has more than enough pockets." Rue didn't sympathize with her friend's accessory murder.

"There *was* an offering in my bag from my mother. I was to convey her warmest regards to Aunt Alexia... with fruitcake."

"Your mother, the vampire queen, made fruitcake?" Arsenic wondered.

While Rue said, "Aunt Ivy baked? Well then, that might have been what exploded."

Percy let out an exasperated breath. "Meanwhile, could we get on? Aren't we already late?"

Tasherit was looking guilty. "I didn't know it would explode."

"Of course you didn't, darling," replied Prim.

"I'll buy you another baggie thing, little one."

"Pray don't trouble yourself," consoled the captain. "I'm sure Prim will find another reticule even better than this one, next time we are in Paris."

"With tassels," added Percy, in a certain flat tone Arsenic was beginning to realize passed for his version of humour

"Baggies come with tassels? Why did no one say?" Tasherit brightened.

"All reticules possess the possibility of tassel-dom," added Percy, as if waxing thoughtful on some serious philosophical point.

Arsenic tilted her head at him. *What was he about?* "Are you claiming, Professor, that the tassel possesses, intrinsic to its nature, the ability to both exist and na exist, at the same time?"

"Where handbags are concerned, yes."

"The professor reads Plato, I see."

Percy's lips twitched. "So does the doctor."

Rue was glaring at them. "You two have to stop this kind of thing, at once. It's most unnerving."

Tasherit had big brown eyes fixed on her lover. "More tassels?"

"Percy! What have you done?" Primrose glared at her brother.

Arsenic tried unsuccessfully to hide a smile.

CHAPTER

SEVEN

Bobbing for Parents

It was an exercise in drama and balance and, in the case of Quesnel, tolerance, getting Rue down the rope ladder (as opposed to the more civilized gangplank). She categorically refused to be lowered as if she were chattel. She would not use something called *The Porcini*, either, because it would take too long to inflate.

Arsenic insisted on going first, so that if Rue did fall, a professional would be there to pick up the pieces. Not that she thought it likely. In her opinion, pregnant women were more capable than most believed. It was only that this was a first for everyone, so all of Rue's friends were overly concerned.

Nevertheless, the captain climbed down in one piece. Quesnel was next and the twins after, making that the sum total of their expedition party.

Arsenic wasn't entirely sure why she'd been pressed into accompanying them, but she did admit to a certain curiosity over Rue's parents. *How does someone like Rue happen?*

"How did your mother know we'd arrived?" it occurred to her to ask, as they walked through the city.

"I sent an aetherogram before we left London. She likely had the obelisks under observation too. But honestly, how does my mother know anything?"

Primrose nodded. "These days she's almost as bad as Lord Akeldama."

"What does she do, exactly, your mother?" Arsenic asked Rue.

"She and Paw run a tea business."

"Oh aye, I remember someone said something about that. 'Tis na, uh, odd for an aristocrat?"

"To be fair, Mother's only gentry, Paw holds the title. And in the end, tea gets shipped practically everywhere, and so goes Mother's network. It's called Tarabotti's Tea."

"Oh! I've heard of it. Excellent Assam."

"See? Everywhere. Even Scotland."

"And you want me along to meet her. Why exactly?"

"Arsenic, you're part of the family now. You should meet our impossible matriarch. Everyone must."

Percy looked like he was trying not to grin – an odd expression on his normally sombre face, as if he were attempting to swallow a live mouse. "Aunt Alexia is like an inoculation against smallpox, best to meet her at least once."

Arsenic nodded. "Very well then."

They hailed a steam-assisted camel cart of some mildly confusing arrangement, half modern technology, half old-fashioned pack animal. The camel and a steam engine existed in strange equilibrium. Arsenic was disposed to be pleased she wasn't spat at, and happy to see Rue comfortably ensconced and not slogging along in heat and defiance.

Eventually they arrived at their destination.

"Well, that's one solution, I suppose." Rue regarded her parents' new residence suspiciously.

It was not what Arsenic had expected. It was not what anyone ought to expect. She'd thought perhaps a palatial house, or a suite of rooms in a fancy hotel.

Lord and Lady Maccon appeared to have taken up residence in a house that was also a boat. Or a boat that was also a house. Like the narrow boats of the Thames dockworkers – only bigger.

It was, without a doubt, the oddest residence Arsenic had ever clapped eyes on. She supposed that if one *had* to move one's house regularly up the Nile, as the plague zone shrank, and if proximity to water would make it easier on a preternatural to tolerate proximity to said zone, a boat did rather make perfect sense.

Rue rolled her eyes. "Of course, a boat, what else would they live in?"

Primrose was shocked. "My word, Rue! Your parents are itinerant vagrant river rats!"

"Prim darling, we live in a dirigible, what does that make us?"

Prim looked struck. "Good gracious me. We're *vagabonds*! We're essentially vagabond pigeons."

Rue winced. "Can't we at least be robins or something cute like that?"

Percy said, with a grin, "Anitra would call us Drifters."

"It's a loveliness of ladybugs. So can we be ladybugs?" offered Arsenic.

Quesnel cocked his head to one side. "It looks like a well-designed kind of boat."

The Maccons' boat-house-floating-thingy was about a third the size of the gondola section of the *Custard*, which made it respectably big, since presumably it didn't have to house a massive engine room and boiler and storage and crew and so on.

There was no way to get onto it, however. The residence bobbed a ways away from the embankment.

"Tally-ho," yelled Rue.

"Tally-ho yourself, Infant!" came an autocratic female voice back. Her tones were melodious and her intonations similar to those of Rue. Arsenic assumed that must be Lady Maccon.

"Rue, that you?" This time a loud male voice reverberated across the water. It was brash, deep, and raspy – very much as one imagined a werewolf voice ought to sound. Except this one was also distinctly Scottish.

"Paw, Mother, could we maybe come, uh, aboard? It seems silly to carry on yelling at each other over the Nile."

"Oh yes, of course. Conall, would you be a love?"

There was a heaving sort of creaking noise, and a massive plank came whizzing down and hit the embankment with a crash, stretching over to the boat.

It didn't look entirely stable but Arsenic supposed the worst that could happen was that one of them might fall into the river. She wasn't the best swimmer herself, but she could mostly float. It was also hot enough that she wouldn't mind cooling off. Why was sportswear always tweedy? She should have some bicycling outfits made up in muslin – in defiance of fashion.

Quesnel went first, although he ought not to, as he kept twisting about and nearly falling in an effort to keep an eye on his wife.

Said wife got mildly exasperated. "I'm fine, dear. I'm going slowly and I'm accustomed to being a bit off-balance. The plank makes no difference."

Quesnel looked panicked by that.

"She's not helping at all, is she?" said Primrose to Arsenic.

Arsenic shook her head.

After Rue went Prim.

Arsenic exchanged glances with Percy.

"I wish I'd asked you what I was in for."

Percy grinned at her. "Lady Maccon? She's a lot like Rue, only bigger and bolder and more practical. She's all right so long as you don't take offence easily."

"Very astute summation of character, Professor."

The man shrugged. "I don't like people and I prefer not to interact with them if I can help it. Doesn't mean I don't understand the ones I grew up with."

"Why did you really come along, Percy?"

"Honestly, for moral support."

"Figuratively?"

"Literally. Lady Maccon has no soul, remember?"

"I wonder what you'd say about me, Percy, if someone asked."

"So do I." Percy's voice had a funny note to it.

"And Lord Maccon?"

"He's a big old softy, really. Adores his wife and daughter. Large. Scottish. Werewolf." This observation was decidedly less astute.

Arsenic nodded. "Verra good then."

"You go, I'll come last."

"Why?"

"Seems like the gentlemanly thing to do."

"Ladies get to walk the plank first?"

"Isn't it always ladies first?" Percy looked perplexed.

Arsenic decided they were running the risk of being rude, blathering on with hosts awaiting. She walked lightly across the plank to the house-meets-boat. Percy followed.

They were then treated to the sight of Lord Maccon, clearly in full possession of his werewolf abilities, simply lifting the massive plank, swinging it around, and sliding it along one side of the hull into a specially designed cradle. It was quite the display of supernatural strength.

His wife, one must presume, put her hand to his arm as soon as the wooden beam was settled. This must be for preternatural reasons, as they were not inside the plague zone, and her touch would keep him human and safe from Alpha's curse. Clearly, they were temporarily in this location in order to meet up with Rue.

Rue ran at her parents. Well, waddled at them enthusiastically. She was absorbed into a three-way hug, one arm from each as they bent over her, both being considerably taller.

It was an egregiously open display of affection for British aristocrats – how Continental of them.

After a long moment of softly murmured greeting, they broke apart. Arsenic admitted to wiping a mote of sentiment from one eye, since Lord Maccon reminded her a bit of her own da, who was large and Scottish and a big advocate of hugs.

Rue backed away and Quesnel made his greeting, for the first time, as her husband. Despite the fact that he was an intellectual, middle-class tradesman with no peerage and foreign heritage, Lord and Lady Maccon welcomed him with evident approval.

"They support the match?" Arsenic whispered to Prim, seeking confirmation.

"They do indeed. Lord Maccon would let Rue do most anything, so long as it made her happy. Lady Maccon is great friends with Quesnel's mother. I think, as well, they did not anticipate the possibility of grandchildren, so all around this is a welcome event."

After Quesnel, the twins issued pleasantries with all the forwardness of domestic intimates and the stiff awkwardness endemic to their personalities. Primrose was painfully polite and well-mannered. Percy was his usual half-shy, half-arrogant self, unable or unwilling to interact easily with others, even old family friends. Arsenic felt a bubble of pride that she'd managed to crack his shell, if only a little.

Lord Maccon treated the twins with open affection, as if he wanted to give them hugs too, but was tolerably certain one or both might swoon if he tried.

Lady Maccon gave each Tunstell an exhaustive once-over and a supportive smile, much in the manner of an affectionate teacher.

Then it was Arsenic's turn.

"Mother, Paw, may I present the latest addition to my crew, Dr Ruthven? She's a pip, even Percy likes her. Arsenic, this is my mother, Lady Maccon, and my father, Lord Maccon, formerly of the London Pack."

Lady Maccon offered up her free hand in the manner of Americans. Arsenic shook it, noting the firmness of the grip and the sureness of her stance. A vigorous woman, Lady Maccon. Her figure was well padded, her complexion robust if rather tan, and her black hair only just beginning to grey. Arsenic thought her likely in possession of a resilient constitution. She was the kind of female one could imagine taking up mountain climbing in her eighties, or retiring to a desert country and living in a boathouse, for that matter. In other words, a bold eccentric.

"It's a pleasure to meet you, young lady. And to see my daughter is being sensible with her safety at last."

"Mother! I did it for the crew. It was Quesnel who got shot recently, not me!"

"But you are the one unexpectedly inconvenienced. It's just as well to have a physician aboard."

Arsenic hastened to correct any misconceptions. "I'm a *surgeon* by training, Lady Maccon. I will do my best for your daughter and her crew, of course, but trauma is my specialty. I was with the military for years."

Lord Maccon looked pleased. As a werewolf, he would have served himself. There was an innate camaraderie among those who'd been to war, regardless of which war. Even those like Arsenic, who'd merely been adjunct, were acknowledged as having shared experiences with soldiers.

"Delighted to hear it!" he boomed out. "I think injury is likely more frequent than childbirth, given my daughter's proclivities."

Lady Maccon looked between her daughter and Quesnel, who had a hand to Rue's lower back in a manner that ought to look supportive but actually looked libidinous. "I don't know, Conall. This may not be our only grandchild. Our son-in-law is French."

Quesnel blushed quite red.

"Mother!" said Rue.

Arsenic could be diplomatic. "Let's see how this one goes, shall we, before we consider the next?"

"Wise words. I like you, girl," said Lord Maccon.

"Thank you, sir."

"Come inside, you lot, do." Lady Maccon had apparently decided they'd spent enough time dawdling on deck.

Indoors, the house-boat was designed not unlike a standard English country home. Lady Maccon led them to a parlour-meets-sitting-room-meets-conservatory, hand firmly holding her husband's. The room was decorated with light rattan furniture, sumptuously thick rugs, and hanging plants. There were large windows opened wide to harness the breeze off the river and displaying a spectacular view.

Rue and Quesnel sat together in one settee, with Arsenic and Primrose in another, while their hosts and Percy opted for chairs.

The chairs were a little spindly. Arsenic feared for their survival under the Maccons' bulk.

An Abyssinian cat wandered in at that juncture, big, orange, arrogant, and clearly master of the place.

"Mother, when did you get a cat?"

"Ossobuco found us. Years living with Lord Akeldama and I could only accept my fate."

"Paw?"

Lord Maccon shrugged. "I spend little time as an actual werewolf anymore, no cat could object. Besides, cats are adaptable, even to living with larger predators."

Percy said, "Footnote barely tolerates Tasherit. He will leave any room she walks into, whether she's lioness or human."

"Yes," said Primrose, "but that's two cats. Different thing entirely."

Ossobuco made the rounds about the visitors, sniffing feet and expressing a general opinion of disinterest. He rolled a bit on Quesnel's shoes, something appealed there, and then padded over to the window, where he jumped onto the sill, and sat in picturesque elegance licking a paw and keeping one eye to the river, and the other to the humans.

Lady Maccon turned her large nose upon Primrose. "That's right! Dearest girl, I hear congratulations are in order."

"What could you possibly mean, Aunt Alexia?" replied Prim, rather unguardedly, Arsenic suspected.

"I hear you have found yourself *a lover.*" Lady Maccon waggled her eyebrows.

"Mother! You can't simply *say* those things out loud!" Rue was aghast.

Prim looked like she was halfway between hilarity and hysteria.

"Obviously I can, because I just did, Infant. It's true, Prim dear, isn't it?"

Primrose extracted a fan from her many-pocketed parasol, and in the manner of all elegant females, hid behind it, crimson faced.

Percy was trying not to smile.

Quesnel said, staunchly, "We all like Tasherit very much. Rue has made her first mate and she's taken over ship's defences and militia training."

Lord Maccon's yellow eyes narrowed. "Militia?"

Rue jumped to the defence. "Everyone *will* keep shooting at us. It's not our fault. It's where we get sent. Blame Mother or Dama for that."

Lord Maccon glowered at his wife.

Lady Maccon looked complacent. "Prudence can take care of herself. Look how well she's done. So far, no one important has died. I call that a win. And she's managed to recruit a werelioness to defend them; a noted spy to interpret for them; a paranormal assassin to do whatever it is that he's doing on board; and now a doctor. Rue is fine, dear. Perfectly fine."

Lord Maccon looked like he would enjoy arguing any number of those statements but in the end chose Rodrigo as the scapegoat.

"Aye, daughter dear, what is Rodrigo Tarabotti doing, exactly, aboard your ship? Dinna he try to kill you?" Lord Maccon's Scottish accent, Arsenic noted, was stronger than her own. But she'd worked to shed hers, scared of losing the respect of the medical community. Lord Maccon need not fret about such things.

"Well, yes, Paw, but that's all in the past. Percy saved him with philosophy. He's on our side now. There was a book club involved. It's all perfectly in order."

"And he married Anitra," added Primrose, clearly thinking that should help.

"The assassin married the spy?"

"They're sweet together. And they like it aboard the *Custard*. We're family." Rue was adamant about this.

Her parents didn't seem wholly convinced. Arsenic understood their concern. However, after two weeks aboard Rue's dirigible, she could also see that there was little need for it. Whatever Anitra and Rodrigo had once been, they were now part of Rue's crew.

Anitra gave language lessons that anyone could attend. Half the decklings were learning Italian at the moment, with Rodrigo's help, of course. They wanted to know what he said when he swore. And Rodrigo seemed willing and able to put his hand to anything, from helping the sooties in the boiler room to describing foreign ports, to telling tall tales to decklings on slow evenings.

The whole time, both Anitra and Rodrigo tended towards that slightly shocked air of unexpectedly having found a place to belong. They lived with people who enjoyed their society and wished to keep them. It was a sensation Arsenic occasionally enjoyed herself these days. To be *wanted* was an extraordinary gift.

The thing about *The Spotted Custard* was its general aura of welcome. So long as one was willing to tolerate the foibles of the staff and crew, the ship forgave you yours. No one minded Arsenic's propensity for sportswear or the way she always looked to physical fitness and health, before seeing the personality of the actual human. No one cared that her mother killed people. *The Spotted Custard* was the kind of place where exceptions were made, because everyone was strange and exceptional.

Surely Lord and Lady Maccon could understand that? For lack of a better analogy, what their brash and rather impulsive daughter had done was build herself her own pack.

"Anitra used to work for Lord Akeldama, you know that?" Lord Maccon pressed his point. Divided loyalties bothered werewolves.

Rue shrugged. "Still does, I think, but we keep her busy. I don't mind. He was bound to have someone in his silken pocket aboard my ship, keeping an eye on me. Better to know who it is than not know."

Lord Maccon turned to his daughter's new husband. "Lord Akeldama hired you and your mother to make the preservation tank for Floote, and Floote adopted Anitra as his granddaughter before he died. You aren't perturbed by questionable allegiance?"

Quesnel shook his head.

Lord Maccon glared at his daughter.

Rue only shrugged. "I am less concerned by Formerly Floote and his machinations than you are. After all is said and done, he and his schemes were for the good of Grandfather Tarabotti, and now they are for the good of me and Rodrigo. We are the last of the Tarabotti line and we are together on my ship. I believe he always intended to see us united. He's vested in our safety. I'm Lord Akeldama's adopted daughter. I've been raised to question motive, including his and yours. But I've never doubted your love, none of you."

Lady Maccon looked pleased. "Yes, we made sure of that. Children should know they are loved. But that doesn't mean you should forget other lessons concerning caution."

Rue actually paused to consider this. "I believe that now we all share the same goals, such as they are. We enjoy one another's company, and we have, I hope, a purpose. So it will all work out in the end. Speaking of which, I hear you've a task for us?"

Lord Maccon waved a large hand dismissively. "We'll get on to that in a moment, and I want to hear all about the wedding. But I've one question for you to consider, daughter mine. Did Lord Akeldama send Anitra to Floote or did Floote hunt out Anitra?"

"What does it matter except that they found each other? And that she found Rodrigo?"

Lord Maccon was going to press the point, but Lady Maccon squeezed his hand. "Enough for now, husband. Let her make her own choices."

"Rodrigo sends his familial regards, incidentally, Mother," said Rue.

"And I return them, of course. It's difficult knowing that I'll never meet my only nephew. Rodrigo is, so far as I can tell, my last living relative on my father's side."

"Speaking of relatives, your mother turned up at my wedding." Lady Maccon made a face. Lord Maccon practically growled.

Arsenic tried to exchange a significant glance with Percy, but he was staring at the cat.

"What did she do?" Lady Maccon was prepared to get upset.

Rue grinned. "That's the fun bit. She fell into a fountain! Or more precisely, Aggie pushed her. Never been so happy to have that woman around. Did you know we were related on Grandmother's side to Aggie? I didn't."

Lady Maccon frowned. "Your head greaser is a relative? What's her surname?"

"Phinkerlington?"

"Ah, that's Mother's maiden name. She must be a second or third cousin."

"Were you bad to them?"

"Not so as I'm aware."

"Well, Aggie's never liked me. I think it has to do, in part, with relations. I can understand simply not liking me on principle, but her animosity always seemed to be rooted in something more."

Lady Maccon shrugged. "There was some scandal with Mother's side. Serious scandal. She never talked about it. Lost two brothers, I think. Although I'm unclear exactly how they were lost – dead or disowned. She got stranded and married Alessandro Tarabotti, as an odd kind of rescue. He died, and she never recovered from the embarrassment of it all. So far as I can tell from her treatment of me, she regretted it. I thought the Phinkerlingtons cast her out, but perhaps it was something else. Perhaps it was the other way around, and that's what has your greaser's bloomers in a twist."

"Families are awfully challenging," said Rue with feeling.

Arsenic considered her own, with her mother's covert activities and all her sisters and their agendas, and had to agree. Even her father had once worked for the War Office.

The tea tray was brought in by a bonnie-looking butler, who was immediately dismissed.

Arsenic wondered if Lady Maccon trusted her servants, or if it was simply her way.

"This is delicious!" Arsenic couldn't help but say, sipping the golden-tinged scarlet brew, which was light with almost sweet notes. "It looks like Darjeeling, but it dinna taste like it."

Lady Maccon smiled. "You have an interest in tea, Doctor?"

"Aye, a little."

"Infant, I approve your new crewmate. This, Doctor, is my current favourite, Jaekseol from Choson."

"Mother, never say you've thrown over Assam!"

"Infant, even I am allowed to broaden my tastes upon occasion."

Rue looked at her mother suspiciously. "Is that where we're going next then, Choson?"

"Ah, you see my scheming ways, Infant. Not Choson exactly, but close, Japan."

Arsenic was excited. She'd never been to Japan. The others looked interested, surprised, and resigned according to their natures. Except Percy, who looked like none of those things, but just like Percy.

"That is, if you accept the mission."

"You can always say no." That was Lord Maccon, glaring at his wife.

His daughter did no such thing. "Why are we headed to Japan?"

"There are rumours of a new kind of supernatural."

"Like last time in Peru?" said Rue.

"Or the time before in Sudan?" said Primrose.

"Or the time before that in India?" added Quesnel.

Arsenic looked at them all. How many different kinds of supernaturals had they uncovered?

She'd heard, of course, of all the new shifters and bloodsuckers and so forth coming to light in the second age of exploration. Monkey shifters and werecats, of course, and wasn't there some kind of fat-sucking vampire reported recently?

"Is it always you who find them?" she wondered.

Rue shrugged, no doubt a mannerism she'd picked up from her husband. "Seems to be our custom, these days, to unearth new types of supernatural creatures. Sometimes literally."

"The *Custard*'s Protocol, if you will," suggested Arsenic, with a grin.

"I like it!" said Rue.

"So what kind are we after this time? The immortal flesh-consuming kind or the changes-shape kind?"

"Is one worse than the other?" wondered Arsenic.

"You never know until you meet them," said Primrose, darkly.

Percy was holding his tongue and looking smug. Arsenic recognized that expression – he knew something.

"Form-shifter this time, dear, or at least we think it's a form-shifter. Lord Akeldama had a report but since then, silence. So we thought you'd like to go after it."

"And he couldn't tell me this himself? I *just* saw him!"

"You know I like to give the orders," said Lady Maccon. "Besides, I wanted to ensure you visited us."

"Oh, really." Rue looked a little choked up. Quesnel put an arm about her shoulders.

"You'll bring the grandchild to Egypt, after it arrives?"

"Of course I will, Mother."

"Of course you will, Infant."

The rest of the visit was mainly a retelling of the wedding, which was amusing in spirit if not content, as it exposed the opinions and biases of Arsenic's crewmates. Their descriptions of the event were materially different from her own, in style if not substance.

After several hours they rose to leave. Arsenic found herself held back with a firm brown hand, while the others took to the deck and watched Lord Maccon wrestle the plank into place.

"A word, please, Dr Ruthven." Lady Maccon was not asking, she was insisting.

"Aye?"

"Lord Akeldama wrote to me of your mother. He said that despite her profession, she has some admirable qualities."

"Some."

"He explained that he hired her once. Did you know?"

"I ken that he might have."

"Did she give you, erm, what do they call it, *training*?"

"She has four daughters, Lady Maccon. She gave all of us training. She dinna trust the world."

"Sad but wise. Have you ever had to use it?"

Arsenic looked at her, so much larger than life, so worried for her daughter yet so proud of her. "Every day, Lady Maccon. Every day."

Lady Maccon looked briefly old and lost, then said, "It is a gentleman's profession, medicine."

"Exactly."

"You'll look after them?"

Arsenic knew Lady Maccon was referring specifically to her daughter and her new husband.

"'Tis my duty now." Arsenic, however, was thinking about the entire crew. Bossy and efficient Primrose, precocious Spoo, dour Virgil, and grumpy Aggie – all of them. Even awkwardly sweet Percy. They were all hers to care for.

"See that you are very good at that duty, then, Doctor." There was no mercy in Lady Maccon's eyes. This woman would be ruthless in defence of her family.

Arsenic understood perfectly. "I willna fail them."

A slight clearing of the throat caused Lady Maccon's hard stare to swing to the door.

"Plank's down," said Percy, looking scared but defiant.

Lady Maccon squinted at him. "So go cross it, Percival."

"Can't without our doctor. Ladies first and all that rot."

"Percival Tunstell, are you being a *gentleman?*"

"Will that persuade you to release our doctor, Aunt Alexia?"

"Are you being pert with me, young man?"

Percy arched a brow.

"Oh go on, both of you. Keep my child out of danger, and prison, and death, and such, would you?"

Percy sniffed. "I make it a point never to make promises I can't keep, Aunt Alexia."

Percy hadn't particularly enjoyed the social call on Rue's parents. Not that there was anything wrong with Lord and Lady Maccon. They were certainly easier to take than most of their generation, and definitely better than his mother at more than double the effect. It was simply that Percy did not enjoy any kind of social call. He'd only gone along to keep an eye on Arsenic, good thing, too.

Lady Maccon had managed a private conclave. Not that Arsenic had been at physical risk, but Lady Maccon could eviscerate emotions with little effort and no compassion. Fortunately, Arsenic seemed perfectly capable of standing up for herself. Impressive. Percy was left wondering if she would do equally well against his own mother, and then got angry at himself for entertaining the very idea. Poor Arsenic.

The *Custard* was off refuelling, so they dawdled returning through Cairo. Quesnel found them a nice watering hole on a lamp-lit square where he puffed on something quite smelly while the ladies indulged in coffee so strong no one could possibly actually enjoy it. They nibbled on a lovely flakey pastry drenched in honey and nuts. Percy thought gloomy thoughts about his mother meeting Arsenic Ruthven. Then he considered them never having reason to meet, as he couldn't gather enough courage to actually court the chit.

Rue seemed happy to sit and more fatigued than she ought given her customary propensity for charging about. Percy gave her his piece of the honey pastry, she clearly needed sustenance. He also observed Arsenic whisking Rue's coffee away and replacing it with coconut water in a masterful sleight of hand.

"How do we feel about Japan?" Rue asked, grimacing at the water but drinking it obediently.

Primrose beamed. "I've always wanted to go. I hear the embroidered silks are unparalleled."

Quesnel nodded and blew a perfect dirigible-shaped smoke ring into the night air. "We studied the Paper City in engineering school. I look forward to seeing it first-hand."

"Will we get to see the countryside, do you think?" Primrose sounded oddly wistful, as if she missed some supine country lifestyle, even though it had never been their lot.

Everyone looked at Percy. He was expected to be up on all information about other cultures. Luckily, knowing they were headed to Japan weeks before the rest of his compatriots meant Percy now had the opportunity to appear the miracle worker. He did enjoy lording his knowledge over others – precognitive perspicaciousness.

"It's unlikely we'll be allowed out of Edo. The Japanese authority is quite xenophobic, even after the Americans insisted they open up to trade. They confine most interactions to the Paper City. But everyone writes that Edo is something to see, even if it's all we get. I've a number of guidebooks in my collection." Which he'd purchased, of course, shortly after his conversation with Aunt Softy.

"You'll be happy to know it is a culture that cherishes tea," he added.

Primrose nodded. "Good. A sensible people then."

Arsenic smiled, watching him from under long dark lashes.

Percy swallowed on a suddenly dry throat. It did glorious things to her eyes, that smile. And those lashes. *Like the legs of a cellar spider, long and elegant. Erm*, he considered, *that's probably not a compliment.*

Arsenic said, "They're reputed to be inclined to share medical knowledge. Is that true?"

Percy nodded. "Knowledge in general, actually. Where other countries trade for weapons or technology, Japan, as a rule, is more interested in intellectual tomes and intelligent conversation. A policy I greatly admire, *in libris libertas* and all that."

Arsenic raised her brows at him. *"Helluo librorum."*

Percy blushed. "A bookworm? I stand justly accused." He became conscious of paying her too much attention and turned to Rue. "I'll comb through my library to see if I've any double volumes or others that we might use for trade and goodwill."

"Percy, you're willing to sacrifice your library for the good of our mission?"

"Within reason."

Rue grinned at him. "And how are the Japanese concerning the supernatural set?"

"So far as we can tell, they're accepting bordering on reverent. Spiritualism has been integrated into Japanese culture as a matter of both worship and history. It's difficult, scholars say, to distinguish between what is real and what is fancy in many texts. Some of their mythologies are so outlandish it's assumed they couldn't possibly be based in supernatural truth. Their shifters, for example, are supposed to defy the laws of physics, gravity, and thermodynamics. It was thought they were mostly imaginary. But with these new rumours from your mother and Lord Akeldama, who can tell?"

"We are to tell, apparently," said Rue.

"It's going to be a long time getting there. It's the other side of the world." Quesnel glanced at his wife.

Primrose allayed all fears in that way she had of being profoundly stable. "Percy will chart us a nice safe route, won't you, brother dear?"

Percy glared at her. "Efficiency is my preference, sister, you know that. Besides, I've all the currents mapped and the charts prepared already. Why should I change them now? We can leave immediately."

Everyone stared at him like he'd put the milk in *after* the tea or something equally damning.

Rue's eyes were narrowed. "Prepared *already*, did you say, Percy? How's that?"

"How's what?" He did wish people would be more precise with their questions.

"How'd you know we were going to Japan?"

"You have precognitive abilities?" suggested Arsenic.

"Oh no, nothing so unscientific. Aunt Softy told me."

"Who on earth is Aunt Softy?" asked Quesnel.

Primrose explained. "Our great aunt on our mother's side. Grandmother Petunia's younger sister."

Percy nodded. "Lady Kingair and Madame Lefoux talked to me about Japan too. At the wedding."

"What?"

"Who?"

"Percy!"

Percy held up a hand. "They want us to rescue this friend of theirs. The same one who's gone missing in Japan hunting rumours of shifters."

"Percy, really."

"So, you see, I knew we were going to Japan next."

"You did?"

"I should have mentioned this sooner, shouldn't I?"

They all tutted at him, except Arsenic, who had her nose in Rue's coffee and seemed to be shaking slightly. Was that amusement?

"Percival Tunstell, you do take the absentminded professor thing a little too far sometimes. Honestly." That was, not unsurprisingly, his sister.

"Has he always been like this?" wondered Arsenic.

Percy was pleased she felt comfortable enough among them now to tease, but a little unhappy that she was teasing *him*.

Prim sighed. "Always. When we were little I think it was a defensive mechanism against Mother, but now it has become an indelible part of his personality. You're not as annoyed by it as the rest of us?"

Arsenic shook her head. *"Alis volat propriis."*

He flies by his own wings, translated Percy. He flushed with pleasure.

Then she added. "'Tis rather bonnie."

"I say!" Percy was offended. *Bonnie! I'm not bonnie! I'm wise and intelligent and insightful. Bonnie, my arse.* He paused his internal diatribe. *Although perhaps that's better than not bonnie?*

He looked at Rue. "Lady Kingair, *your* werewolf relative, said we should go to Japan next. So did *my* aunt. And so did *Quesnel's* mother." He gestured at the repugnant Frenchman, who was leaning back and dimpling at Percy's discomfort. "So I deduced that was where we would be going. Pardon me for forgetting to mention it, but you know now, don't you? Isn't that enough?"

Quesnel's dimples deepened. "Of course my mother is involved."

"'Tis na odd?" wondered Arsenic.

"Not if you know them," said Percy vaguely.

Arsenic nodded. "I sat with them a bit, at the wedding. Peculiar group. Powerful. They went to school with my mother. Did you ken?"

"Did they indeed?" Rue blinked at her.

"The assassin?" Primrose pressed.

"Aye."

"Coils within coils," said Prim, ominously.

Percy couldn't see that it made any odds. Arsenic's mother, Madame Lefoux, Aunt Softy, Sidheag Maccon – they'd all been trained as spies, hadn't they? What else could one expect from spies? Or was that one of those things he'd deduced and no one else had? He opened his mouth to explain, but Rue cut him off.

"To get back to the point, what did they tell *you*, Percival Tunstell, about going to Japan?"

"They've lost one of their number. A lady who goes by the

moniker *the Wallflower*. They want us to find her and bring her back." Percy produced the photo of the matron from his waistcoat pocket, where he'd stashed it originally. Although, of course, that was a different waistcoat, which meant Virgil had been faithfully transferring the photo from one waistcoat to the next for weeks. *Good lad, that Virgil.*

He handed it over. "There, see? She went missing in Japan. Probably the spy Lord Akeldama sent."

"A rescue mission as well as one of discovery? Only we're after a woman who trained all her life to stay hidden. They don't ask much of us, do they, the previous generation?" Rue looked resigned.

Primrose took the image and studied it. "Percy, occasionally you're a complete ninny-hammer."

Percy bristled. "I don't see how. You said we were going to Japan, didn't you, Rue? I just got us prepared."

"You're utterly impossible," said Rue.

He had no idea why everyone was so vexed with him. Certainly he'd forgotten to mention it, but they knew *now*, didn't they? It wasn't as if the knowledge would have materially changed any actions prior to this moment.

Percy turned desperately to Arsenic. "You talked with them too, at the wedding?"

"Aye I did, but they said nothing of Japan. One of them was your aunt?"

"Great Aunt Softy, well, Sophronia really."

"Sophronia? I believe my mother hated her. Or, more precisely, she hated my mother. Which is a perfectly respectable reaction to my mother. She's quite prickly, and all the pricks are poisonous."

Percy nodded, as if he could even hope to understand what it was like to be the daughter of a killer. Although his mother was a vampire who did, occasionally and with great delicacy, kill people, so perhaps he could comprehend it.

Arsenic gave one of her throat-drying smiles. "Mother used

to call it *annexing. Don't mind me, darling,* she'd say, *nipping down to London. I've a foreign dignitary to annex."*

"And how did she feel when she found out you wished to be a doctor?"

"Delicious irony. She's an odd sense of humour. I told her that someone had to balance all the death she dealt. She laughed and reminded me that she only killed bad men. Was I going to find out the moral character of my patients before I cured them? I told her that wasna how the Hippocratic oath worked. She called me a *strange little mineral* and accepted my decision. After all, arsenic is also medicinal."

Percy nodded. "Logical."

"Homo sum humani a me nihil alienum puto?" suggested Arsenic.

"Exactly!" beamed Percy. He did so admire a sagacious woman. Admittedly, Arsenic was the first to match him Latin-to-Latin, but he'd always suspected such females must exist. He was seized by the horrifying suspicion that she may be the only one. *She must be protected,* he decided. *A unique specimen among humans. Should I write a paper?*

Rue looked at Quesnel and then Primrose. "Are they *flirting?"*

"It's like watching dirigibles crash midair, filled with hot air, slow and horrible yet inevitable," said Quesnel.

"I don't think it can be flirting when it's done so badly, can it?" Primrose finished her coffee, eyes wide with wonder.

Percy glared at them all. It was all very well for them to pick on him, but they shouldn't pick on Arsenic. She hadn't the appropriate defences in place. "We are having a perfectly respectable intellectual conversation. Just because you lot are too dim to follow the nuances."

"Definitely flirting." Rue grinned at them.

Fortunately, at that juncture *The Spotted Custard* depuffed to its mooring obelisk, presumably stuffed to the gills with coal and water and suchlike necessities.

Percy was grateful it wasn't part of his job to oversee the logistics of supplies. He was more of a theorist than a list maker.

He stood. "Shall we head back to the ship?"

Primrose stood as well and poked him with her elbow, hissing into his ear rather too loudly, "Offer her your arm, you goose."

Percy, blushing hotly, offered the doctor his arm.

Arsenic took it with a shy smile and a lowering of her spidery eyelashes.

They led the way back to the ship.

"Complete ninny-hammer," asserted his sister, behind them.

"Flirting," confirmed Rue to her husband, who no doubt nodded wisely.

Percy stuck his nose in the air and ignored them, face hot. But not feeling overly distressed, for there was a small capable hand on his arm. And, after all, Arsenic thought he was *bonnie*.

CHAPTER

EIGHT

On Handmaidens, Hats, and Hasty Marriages

Travel to Japan took the better part of a month, and Percy wasn't thrilled about it. Really, at that rate, they might have gone by sea! But bits of the aetherosphere weren't charted as well as they ought, and (in deference to Quesnel's spousal concern) Percy altered some current choices and refuel stations to ensure the safest route.

Percy didn't tell Quesnel he'd made adjustments, of course. Let the Frenchman stew.

With so much time idle in the grey, Percy organized an intensive study of the Japanese language with Anitra. She already had a bit, and he'd been at it since the wedding, but now they focused. Others joined them, when their duties permitted, including Arsenic. She also continued to disturb the peace of his library, in the best of all possible ways, in honeysuckle-soaked silence and the occasional scone.

To Percy's delight, Arsenic staunchly resisted developing any possible chatterbox tendencies. Their long silences might have become uncomfortable, except for their mutual joy in quiet and the ameliorating presence of Footnote. The cat divided his time between them. He showed a marked preference for Arsenic's lap and Percy's feet, and happily basked in the attention of whichever human was most easily distracted at any given moment.

Percy came in for additional teasing anytime Rue, Prim, Quesnel, or Virgil caught him with Arsenic. Philosophical to the last, Percy figured this was making him less likely to blush about it. Although no less fascinated by those spider lashes, and no less likely to swallow dryness when she smiled.

Rodrigo and Anitra, who were sensible sorts, made no comment. They occasionally joined them in the library, although it really wasn't big enough for four (five, counting Footnote). If any discussion resulted and got too lively, they adjourned to the stateroom for tea (including Footnote). Rodrigo brought a much more mercenary perspective to any intellectual debate, being invested in seeing things dead. Also, he came from a background of religious belief in the supernatural, so he understood some of the Japanese mindset with regards to spirituality. After all, one had to *believe* in something in order to kill it, so Rodrigo's perspective on the probable existence of various Japanese spirits and monsters was eye-opening.

Percy did find himself struggling to reconcile the written record with reality, but he'd met enough unexpected supernaturals by now to be sympathetic to the possibility of their actuality, in a way he certainly wouldn't a mere three years ago. Still, physics demanded that fox shifters be scientifically impossible. The biggest fox recorded in his natural history volumes weighed in at forty-two pounds. A human toddler might weigh that much but not an adult. Should they exist at all, fox shifters couldn't have hidden themselves among humans.

Unless they did so by pretending to be children, of course.

Which was an interesting possibility.

He made a note.

Arsenic added her own frisson of biological practicality to any debate. She was delighted to learn that the shape of a pishtaco's fangs differed from that of a British vampire's. She immediately theorized that it had to do with the difference in the chemical structure of fat versus blood.

Percy liked it when she went into gruesome physiological

detail, Rodrigo tolerated it, and Anitra would duck her head and hide behind her veil. Percy was charmed by most anything Arsenic said or did, which was irksome but inevitable. Because she was smart in ways he was loath to admit he wasn't. There was little Percy found more admirable in another person than that.

"What happens," Arsenic wanted to know, "if Rue touches both a vampire and a werewolf at exactly the same time? What happens when she touches one and then another, or if they touch each other and then she touches them? Has anyone studied the preternatural effect on two supernatural creatures at once? Have the Templars?"

Rue was on restricted touch until after the baby, but Rodrigo said he was willing to experiment if they could get Tasherit and some other supernatural to play with him. He said this with an unpleasant gleam in his eye. But they hadn't another supernatural aboard (Floote didn't count, because his body had to stay en-tanked). So Arsenic's questions remained unanswered. Percy admired her for thinking them in the first place and hoped they might get to try her experiments, and write papers on the results. They might even, he blushed to say it, co-author something?

She said, without any concern whatsoever, that he was welcome to write anything he liked, and take credit, she only wanted to know *how things worked*. Percy decided he would share the byline with her, whether she liked it or not.

A thought that was startling in and of itself.

He was a little sad, though, that despite a distinct sympathy of intellect, and a profoundly high quality of debate (and the fact that she had called him *bonnie*), Arsenic did not seem inclined to further their association beyond convivial friendship and scones. He supposed it was for him to pursue further intimacy, being the gentleman in this equation. But Percy was entirely unsure how to go about that. He might need to actually talk to his sister on the subject. Primrose had, after all, successfully courted a woman herself.

He couldn't bear that idea, so decided to ask Rodrigo's opinion instead. After all, he was an Italian, weren't Italian men supposed to be the best lovers in all the world?

"You must woo her with the tongue," was Rodrigo's disgustingly crude advice.

"I *beg* your pardon!"

"Bah! You English. So stiff."

That gave Percy even more graphic ideas. "I say, that's going too far."

Rodrigo snorted. "Seduce her. Love her. Kisses! You talk and talk and talk and talk. Too much talk. More kisses."

So much for Rodrigo's advice.

Unfortunately, Primrose, while delighted to be asked, was equally unhelpful.

"Oh, Percy, simply see if she'd like to be wooed and then woo her. Must you make everything so complicated?"

"I hardly think wandering up and saying, *Pardon me, Dr Ruthven, but would you like to be courted by, well, me?* is particularly romantic. Or is it? I really don't know."

Prim rolled her eyes. "Say it in Latin."

Percy actually considered that. But it seemed just as daunting. If not more so. Latin made it *real*.

The thing was, his entire life Percy had been good at anything he put his mind to. But *only* those things. He was perfectly well aware that in matters convivial he was an abysmal failure. Arsenic was important, so he didn't want to fail her. It was a bitter pill to swallow, doctor pun intended, but he figured he ought to read up on such things as love poetry and romance before he attempted anything like a direct approach.

His much-vaunted library was sublimely lacking in these arenas. He'd have to expand his collection as soon as may be. The question was: Byron or something Greek? The French were supposed to be good at love, surely one of them had written a guidebook? He could, of course, ask Quesnel but the very idea of approaching the man, hat in hand, on such a matter was profoundly horrific. So it was that Percy decided to pine quietly,

and think a little too much about the shape of Arsenic's mouth
and the trimness of her figure and the sharpness of her mind, and
hope against hope that she would make the first gesture.

Arsenic was not ignorant of Percy's interest. And since she found
him attractive, even in his acerbic awkwardness, possibly because
of it, she was also not averse to his overtures.

Except, of course, that he didn't make any. Despite many a
pocket scone.

He seemed to genuinely enjoy her company, which was rare
for him, according to Spoo. He snapped at her a great deal less
than he snapped at everyone else, but it stopped there. They
spent the month in and out of the grey floating around the world
by stages, progressing towards their destination, but not really
progressing towards anything else.

She had visions of convincing him out from behind his desk
and into the wingback chair. Of dumping Footnote out of his
lap and sitting there herself. Or pressing her cold nose into the
warmth of his neck. Of something less bold, simply smoothing
the wrinkle in his forehead when he was reading so hard.

She considered asking his sister about it all, but that felt a
little too wicked and underhanded, rather too much like something her mother would do. Arsenic tried hard not to be that
kind of woman. Although occasionally she would lick her lips,
as Mother had taught her, and watch his eyes dilate and his
breath shorten.

So she bided her time and wondered about simply creeping
into his bed one evening and seeing how he might react. But he
was so proper, he might experience a fit of the vapours.

So they circled each other in mental harmony and physical
frustration, a kind of dance Arsenic was unsure of finishing, only
knowing it was a waltz to which she had never learned the steps.

Percy wasn't given to flights of fancy. He would never call himself a student of aestheticism and he was perennially more intrigued by the function of the world than by its appearance.

However, even he could appreciate the utter glory and breathtaking beauty of the Paper City. When seen from above, Edo the floating metropolis, the cloud of lanterns, was like a constellation of flying flower-buds. It was brilliant and colourful and impossible.

The whole ship's complement, even the most pragmatic and business-minded of the decklings, stopped in awe and stared down at Edo the moment they depuffed into the atmosphere above Japan.

Percy was so stunned he didn't even think to close down the Mandenall Probe, or keep a hand to the helm, or really, do anything at all but stare across the deck and out over the railing at the bit of Edo that he could see from the navigation pit.

Then, as if compelled by some mystical force, he found himself climbing out of the pit. Leaving *The Spotted Custard* entirely without guidance, he joined Rue and his sister at the railing of the poop deck.

"I've never seen anything like it." That was Arsenic, coming to stand with them. The doctor's mellow voice was deepened by awe.

Rue nodded. "One of the Seven Wonders of the Age of Steam. And I thought the Maltese Tower was something special. This... This is..." She was at a loss for words.

Miracles do happen.

Edo was a city above a city. The memory of an ancient time made light and rising towards the heavens, it floated by means of brightly coloured paper lanterns. The technological mystery of their phosphorescent lift-lights was jealously guarded, and Percy was greatly looking forward to sunset when they would flicker into self-illumination. But even in daylight they were miraculous, celebratory and cheerful, and impossibly vast under the bright sun.

The lanterns supported, swaying below each, the fine light-coloured and lacquered houses of Japan's elite, like so many gilded birdcages.

Far below Edo, nestled in the curving island that was mainland Japan, sat Tokyo, the new city built on the ruins of Old Edo, after the salvaged pieces had taken flight. Tokyo was a shining example of modern technology, smoky at the edges but bright and spired at its heart, even under the rainbow light filtering through the Paper City above. Tokyo's busy seaport was a forbidden fantasy of prismatic light, while Edo's float-port above was a thing of welcoming ethereal wonder.

Thus far no Westerner had ever visited Tokyo. But of all the thousand travellers who had visited and described Edo, not a one had done it justice.

The lanterns were fixed by multiple ribbons to one another, paper flags fluttered from the lines connecting them. Tassels, kites, and hanging plants decorated the bottoms of Edo's residences, draping and waving in a slight breeze.

Percy noticed instantly the thing that always caused comment among the scientific community. Edo had no anchor to the ground. Nothing, apparently, connected the Paper City to its Tokyo counterpart. Yet it stayed in place. In Japan this was called magic.

Percy did not believe in magic. He wanted badly to know how it was actually done.

But the people of Japan were notoriously closed-lipped, remaining autonomous and disconnected from global society. The Paper City was their compromise and the only place where Japan mingled with the outside world, tightly controlled and extremely polite.

Percy became nervous simply looking at the precise fragile beauty of Edo. He was phenomenally bad with restrictive manners, having assiduously avoided those places where etiquette was most required. He'd never even been presented at court. He'd better try to keep his mouth shut in Japan. He was self-aware enough to know that talking inappropriately was a Percival Tunstell character flaw. When he saw something worthy of comment, he usually, unfortunately, commented.

"Do the colours have meanings?" Arsenic wondered.

It was Rodrigo who answered her. He was the only one among them who'd visited Edo before. "In Japan, everything has meaning."

"It looks so fragile and unstable. I feel as if tossing aside a peach pit might tear through everything and cause a grand collapse." Primrose fiddled with her hat.

"I'm certain it's more sturdy than that. Edo has, after all, existed for a while." Rue was frowning.

Percy explained, because he'd read about it. "It's coated with a kind of glue made from seaweed and then also wax. The lanterns are actually quite strong, and many of the largest and most important ones, like that one there that looks like a huge red sphere? Those aren't paper at all, but silk, which makes a stronger balloon than the canvas we use for the *Custard*."

"Percy, why do you always have to spoil beauty with explanation?" Primrose didn't look away from Edo.

"One would think it might enhance your appreciation."

"No, one wouldn't, you puffed-up chump. The mystery is all gone now!"

"I appreciate knowing," said Arsenic, giving Prim a side-eye.

"Well, you would, you're an intellectual too." Percy said it without realizing he'd extended praise, and blushed to hear the admiration in his own voice.

"Of a type, you two. It's exhausting. Go talk about technicalities on the other deck, would you? Let us bask in wonder." Prim, apparently, had reached a state of such comfort with their new doctor that she felt fine snapping at her.

Rue looked up. "Wait a second. Percy, what are you doing here? Who's flying the ship?"

"Ah, yes right, we're drifting." Percy made a face.

"Are we indeed? Do you think you might want to go stop that?" Rue made a face back at him.

Percy glared at her and then gestured around where the entire crew stood pressed along the ship's railing, including most of engineering, who'd come up to see why they weren't being shouted at down the speaking tube on a depuff.

"You expect me to run the old girl all on my lonesome, do you, Captain?" Not that Percy didn't feel a little pang at deserting his post. Usually, he was above fascination with the extraordinary, except where it afforded him a scholastic paper and academic advancement. But Edo really was remarkable.

Spoo put it best. "Golly, that's a piece of *something like*, isn't it?"

"Yes, Spoo, it is, but in order to prevent us crashing into one of the most famous cities in the world, we should probably resume our positions and pilot an approach, yes?" Rue was being sensible.

Since it wasn't that common for Rue to be sensible, everyone took heed, and jumped to work. Only those who had no depuff duties were left staring.

Stratocumulus lux, thought Percy, trying to remember his cloud terms. *Only made of paper and colour.*

He resumed his place at the helm and guided them down slowly, keeping a watchful eye for the Imperial vanguard. This would be a thousand times worse than the customs check in Egypt. Japan held its secrets close and guarded, but that didn't mean it respected the secrets of others. Nothing was allowed to put the Paper City at risk and odd things were considered dangerous.

Sure enough, well before they were in Gatling-gun range, let alone hailing distance, they were approached by a sleek black dirigible, lacquered shiny and svelte. It looked not unlike a gleaming crow with a bird figurehead at its prow, feathers painted orange on the black balloon, and trailing wings of fabric on each side that presumably helped with guidance, and made it look like it was wearing an opera cloak.

The officials who hailed them from its deck were also dressed in black. The military uniform was inspired by the Americans, with flat cap and orange sash across the front, and plenty of gold epaulettes at the shoulders, and a bit of a cape at the back.

There was a great deal of bowing and exchange of civilities, with Percy himself leading while Anitra assisted, as it became abundantly clear that despite her superior mastery of the language, the officials preferred to communicate with a man.

This made Rue sneer and Prim smile. His sister liked to be underestimated, Rue did not.

It took several hours for the officers to search the ship. After a great deal of discussion, they confiscated all the bullets for the Gatling guns, although it was clear they would have preferred to seize the guns themselves. They also tried to find and remove every other gun aboard the ship, including Tasherit's rifle from the corner of her room while she still slept, curled in a ball in the middle of the bed.

Weapons seemed to be their main focus. They refused to allow *The Spotted Custard* any closer to the Paper City with even one projectile aboard.

Quesnel managed to keep his dart emitter, which looked enough like an elaborate bracelet to escape suspicion. Spoo reported that Aggie made a great show of annoyance when the guards searched engineering, abusing the small kettle boiler in the guise of repairs. Aggie being female, the authorities tried to ignore her, but Aggie persisted in a great deal of banging. The end result was the boiler room was less well searched than other parts of the ship.

Rodrigo sneered while the officials removed a small mountain of weaponry from his and Anitra's quarters. But Percy had no doubt there were more still available to him elsewhere. He was also the kind of man who could turn a diminutive potato into a means of mass decapitation. Primrose also maintained possession of her battle parasol. No doubt that was a result of its innocuous appearance as a mere feminine frippery. So, all was not lost. Also, when Tash woke up they had a lioness. Which wasn't quite a projectile but almost as good.

There was a great deal of fuss over Percy's library, where the guards clearly wished to confiscate a number of his precious books. Percy glared at them and spoke eloquently of fair trade, *The Spotted Custard*'s significant political connections back home, and his own academic prowess. Upon learning that they might be permitted access to information in a more legitimate (and polite) fashion, the officials relented. Then they proceeded to undertake the same rigmarole with Arsenic and her medicines. She responded with the same defence, stressing that she was eager to share her knowledge with her physician colleagues among the Japanese. She managed to be both demure and charming while she spoke, a tactic the officials responded to positively.

As the vampires were wont to say, sweet blood beats rotten flesh every time.

Her feminine wiles and genteel appearance did something to excite official interest. Percy was frightened at first that they might perceive her negatively as an uppity scientific female who should not even think of communicating with Japanese male doctors. Then he deduced that their excitement revolved around the fact that she *was* female. Apparently, they wished to retain her in a medical consult as soon as may be.

Arsenic stiffened. "Is Edo suffering from a disease or illness? Because, if so, I willna allow my ship to dock."

The officials hastened to reassure her that no, there was nothing plaguing the Paper City. One of their great noblewomen was afflicted with a mysterious lethargy, and they hoped Arsenic might see to the lady's comfort, given that their own doctors had proved ineffectual.

"We believe," the officer whispered, as if greatly embarrassed, bowing so low Percy had a challenging time interpreting his speech without visible mouth movement, "that it is a *female* complaint."

Percy himself blushed as he said this to Arsenic.

The doctor nodded and agreed to visit the afflicted lady as soon as they were safely docked, before Percy could stop her from being rash.

Rue took her to task, later, of course, after the officials departed with a float-trunk full of the *Custard's* best deadly weaponry. "We could have traded your services!"

Arsenic drew herself upright. "I will help any in need, Captain! I am na a diplomatic trinket to be exchanged, and you shouldna barter with the health of others. Besides, my skills have eased our way."

As indeed it did appear to be the case. After discovering Arsenic, *The Spotted Custard* was rushed through the rest of customs with unseemly haste. Everything that he'd read about the process assured Percy that customs in Edo were the worst in the world, sometimes taking the better part of a week, and yet they found themselves safely moored to a friendly little plant-strewn dock by the time the sun set.

The lanterns around them glimmered into life. The one directly above casting the *Custard* in a red glow.

Everyone let out an *ooo* of appreciation.

Tasherit came abovedecks, blinking at the colourful lights, to find herself in a world unlike any even she had seen in all her long years on earth.

Primrose went to her. "Isn't it lovely?"

The werelioness looked pale. "It is, little one, but, oh—" She stumbled to the side. Prim caught her up.

His sister's face wrinkled in concern, or stomachache, Percy wasn't great on expressions.

Arsenic ran to the cat shifter. "What's wrong?"

Tash shook her head. "I'm feeling a little groggy."

"The long sleep in the grey?" wondered Prim, while Arsenic touched Tash's forehead and checked the pulse at her neck.

Tasherit batted the doctor away. "Don't fuss. It's not serious."

"Can you shift?" Rue asked, no doubt thinking of ship's defences.

The cat shook her head. "Unlikely."

"Does it feel like him?" Arsenic pointed at Rodrigo, standing innocently some distance away.

"No. It's not preternatural or metanatural."

Arsenic summoned Rodrigo over. "Are you experiencing any strange sensations as a result of your unnatural state?"

Rodrigo made a funny face. "What?"

"Is your preternatural side feeling weird?" Percy translated Arsenic's frantic words into Italian.

"No."

"Stop, Captain!" Arsenic turned back in time to interpose herself between Rue and the werecat. "You might still be shifted by touching her. You must stay away."

Rue frowned, then nodded and backed off.

"You're feeling normal yourself?"

Rue nodded again.

Arsenic turned back to the werecat. "You canna shift. 'Tis connected to the woozy feeling?"

"No. I think we're simply too high. The aetherosphere may dip low here and be close to us, affecting my abilities. I'm not sure. I don't think the two sensations are connected." Her shoulders slumped. She looked almost human frail. "I feel quite tired for having recently slept nearly a month."

Percy noticed that his sister's knees buckled slightly as Tasherit gave her even more of her weight.

Arsenic moved to slide under the werecat's other arm, supporting her as well. "Let's get you back to bed."

A polite cough interrupted them.

A small group of beautifully dressed Japanese women stood before them on the dock. The *Custard*'s gangplank was down, but thus far not a single person had approached out of Edo.

Apart from the military confiscation, they'd not seen anyone since the depuff.

Percy thought the ladies looked about Aunt Alexia's age, but delicate with it. They moved with small steps on high sandals. Their faces were painted white with red lips. Their hair was dressed high and overly elaborate. They looked like dolls.

Rue regarded them for a moment and then gestured Anitra forward as speaker.

Anitra bowed deeply and made her opening remarks.

There was an elaborate exchange of formal greetings, but unlike the guards earlier, these ladies seemed eager to speak to Anitra rather than Percy. If anything, they gave him, Rodrigo, Quesnel, and the deckhands wary regard.

Rue noticed. "Percy, you and Quesnel help Tasherit belowdecks. Rodrigo, Bork, Willard, move to the other side. Prim, you're now first line of defence. Parasol at the ready, please. Although I don't believe these ladies are a threat."

"Oh, but..." Primrose clearly wished to go with her lover.

"Wait, Captain, I need to..." Arsenic as well.

Anitra turned from talking with the newcomers. "They are here for you, Doctor."

Arsenic was clearly torn.

Tasherit settled it. "I'm fine. You think that after hundreds of years on this earth I don't know a real risk to my survival? This feels tether related. I likely need earth under my feet and a good hunt by moonlight. This is no concern of yours, Doctor. See to your duties, ladies. Gentlemen, shall we?"

Prim nodded and ceded her place to Quesnel. Arsenic did the same to Percy.

She gave him an unfathomable look as they brushed arms. Percy tried to reassure her with a tip of his head. She chewed on her bottom lip, smiled at him softly, then turned to their visitors.

Together, Percy and Quesnel helped the werecat across the deck and down the ladder to her quarters.

Arsenic regarded the three women before her. Their manners were diffident. Their eyes were eager on her face and very focused. Despite a certain doll-like impassivity, these ladies could not disguise their delight in seeing her.

Arsenic had experienced various reactions to her chosen profession over the years but never before joy. Relief, on occasion, especially with female patients whose complaints related to procreation, childbirth, or sexual encounters. To these ladies, she represented something more like hope.

"Sisters of the afflicted?" she asked Anitra.

Anitra translated for the women. "Handmaidens."

Arsenic took a second look at the ladies. Their hair was exquisitely arranged and decorated with silk flowers and sticks from which ribbons dangled. Each wore two or three layers of embroidered silk. Robes that looked not unlike dressing gowns, but of such stunning quality they were obviously designed for public show. They wore wide belts as well, coordinated but not exactly matching the robes. These were tied at the back around a large cushion, creating a massive puff with trailing ends. This resembled something like the bustle of England's previous decade, only higher up at the small of the back. The sash wound up and over the shoulders. Arsenic wondered if that was to assist in support of the bustle.

It was a great deal of fabric and fuss and expensive cloth for three servants.

"Are you sure? They look like royalty."

Anitra crooked an eyebrow. "You wish me to press the question?"

Arsenic thought better of it. "Nay. May I ask a little on the nature of their mistress's affliction? It'd help me know what to bring for treatment."

The handmaidens were amenable.

Arsenic dug a bit into the manifestations of the lady's illness.

Determining quickly that it was unlikely to be respiratory, skeletal, or skin related.

"Is she eating? Does her stomach ache?"

Their answers steered her in no better direction, until finally Rue put a stop to it.

"This is getting you nowhere, Doctor. Please go collect your basic supplies."

Arsenic did so, collecting only her telescoping travel kit. Chronic lethargy could be anything from emotional withdrawal to a tumour of the lungs. It was likely that she'd need to convince the patient to return with them to visit her swoon room for a proper examination.

Arsenic checked on Tasherit while she was belowdecks. The werecat was asleep, once more curled in a ball in the centre of her bed. Arsenic worried but didn't know how to help a supernatural creature. *Here's hoping I can prove my worth with a human patient.*

Abovedecks, Rue and Prim were engaged in a hissed argument, apparently about something one of the handmaidens had said.

Arsenic trundled up, carrying her kit.

Rue looked at her. "You don't have to go, Doctor. They are insisting that you go alone."

Arsenic shook her head. "I canna. I need at least Anitra. I studied the language but I'm by no means fluent enough to ask useful questions."

"The handmaidens claim that the patient herself speaks perfect English."

"Aye? Verra interesting. Weel then, I should get on."

Rue put her foot down. "No, Doctor. You aren't going alone into Edo with three strange women in embroidered night attire. I'm sorry. I know they look harmless, but . . ."

Arsenic quirked a brow. "Captain, I'm entirely aware of the fact that the most beautiful and delicate looking among us are often the most deadly. What do you suggest? Otherwise, we are at an impasse."

Rue considered the gentlemen standing off to one side. Quesnel and Percy had returned up top and joined Rodrigo near navigation, where they were trying to look unthreatening. Only Percy succeeded.

"I shall send one of the men with you. You might require the perceived authority of the male animal."

Arsenic gave their three gentleman officers a sceptical look. "From them? Authority?"

She turned and considered the handmaidens, all standing patiently with mouths hidden behind open fans. "I doubt they will allow him into the patient's presence."

"They must have allowed male doctors in at one point. Otherwise they would not now be resorting to you."

Arsenic wrinkled her nose. "The question becomes, then, which one do I take, and what subterfuge do we use to persuade these ladies that 'tis vital I have an escort?"

Rue considered. "Rodrigo is the most physically powerful but also the least predictable. Quesnel would be good as a general rule."

Arsenic disagreed. "I'm afraid it must be Percy. He speaks the language near as well as Anitra, and he can tell me if they say anything important between themselves."

"I suppose you're right. Pity we can't send him armed."

Arsenic blinked at this. "Aye?"

"Oh yes, he's a crack shot."

Rue gave a nod to their visitors and then dashed across the deck, leaving Arsenic, Anitra, and Primrose staring awkwardly at the three Japanese ladies.

"I like your bustles," said Primrose via Anitra, pointing to the puffs of fabric at their backs.

"Obi," corrected one of them. Then gestured to the robe part of her outfit. "Kimono."

"Very pretty," asserted Prim.

The handmaidens exchanged glances with each other from

behind fans, and then bowed at Prim in what was probably their version of graciously accepting a compliment.

One of them responded with marked interest in Prim's hat, which was a wide straw affair decorated with multiple ostrich feathers and having more fluff than application. It was night so Prim hardly required the shade, yet the handmaidens looked upon it with frank approval.

Rue returned, pulling Percy alongside. She said, much to everyone's surprise, except Percy, who looked resigned, "This here is Percival Tunstell. He is our doctor's husband. Lord and master and so forth. He must, perforce, accompany her. In our culture, husbands go everywhere with wives."

Anitra translated the blatant falsehoods with consummate smoothness.

Percy jerked to a stop next to Arsenic.

Arsenic couldn't help it, she grinned at him and batted her lashes. "Dinna look so miserable."

"Rue's making me."

"I know she is, husband darling. Light of my life."

Percy groaned softly but offered her his arm, as if dredging up some forgotten memory of what a man was supposed to do with his wife.

The handmaidens spoke briefly among themselves and then said that this was acceptable. Of course a husband would not permit his wife into an unknown city without him. They were impressed that he'd married the doctor and yet allowed her to continue practicing.

"Are women not permitted professions in your culture?" Primrose asked.

The ladies did not respond, exchanging glances.

Finally one said, "We are not to be doctors, which is why you are so welcome as a visitor." She bowed at Arsenic.

Arsenic bowed back. "Speaking of which, you are no doubt eager for me to see your mistress. As she is in great need of relief, should we perhaps get on?" The rules of polite behaviour seemed even more strict in Japan than in the finest dining rooms of London's high society. If she did not press them to leave, the handmaidens might stand making niceties with the crew all night.

The handmaidens' faces remained impassive but Arsenic sensed that they were relieved. They bowed low to Rue and Primrose and then turned to bow to the men left standing on the poop deck. The decklings received shallower bows.

Spoo bowed back. Following her lead, the rest of the deck crew did the same.

Rue and Prim curtsied, Anitra bowed, and after a few rounds of this silent farewell abasement, the handmaidens turned and began moving away, their tiny steps making them appear to glide down the *Custard*'s gangplank.

Arm in arm, Arsenic and Percy followed them.

NINE

Arsenic Has a Patient

Percy found the Paper City as stunning inside as it was from without. The lanterns cast colourful light on the streets, while the night sky beyond twinkled with stars.

They followed the handmaidens over roads that were made of stiff slatted reeds and arched, one after another, like a chain of perfect bridges. The storefronts and houses alongside were colour balanced and complementary to the balloons above, so that everything was aesthetically cohesive. They moved from the red zone to the gold, to the green, to the blue in seamless beauty. Each different neighbourhood was decorated, beribboned, and stylish like the best Worth gown. There were only a few people here and there, all of whom bowed low as they passed.

"'Tis like a set dressing for a stage play," Arsenic said to Percy.

He looked closer at the gilded elegance. He hadn't noticed the stilted nature of its appearance, but she was right. Edo was very stage-like – self-consciously cultivated and uncomfortably false.

Arsenic snorted softly. "You were wondering how it stays up and together, aye?"

"And what keeps it from drifting."

"Whereas I was wondering – where are all the people?"

It made an odd kind of sense to Percy. "It's a port city, for show, for foreigners to use. Sanitized. Everyone here is likely to be carefully vetted diplomatic representatives."

"'Tis *actually* a stage, in its way?" Arsenic nodded. "You're suggesting that the Americans whisked in twenty years ago and by dint of foisting trade upon the Japanese, encouraged a performance city?"

Percy nodded. "Show only the best to outsiders. The whole place is the Japanese version of a London receiving room."

They spoke frankly to each other, but in hushed tones. The ladies were in front of them, and they didn't want to appear rude. But Percy was also careful not to say anything that might be misconstrued. They were speaking English, but this was a port city.

"'Tis verra beautiful." Arsenic seemed to understand his careful phrasing.

"And here, I think, beauty has a way of meaning moral superiority," replied Percy.

"As though London high society dinna believe the same. Vampires have much to answer for."

Percy frowned. "You think they are at work here in Edo?"

"I hadna considered that. Look at you, Professor, coming over with a bout of cultural perception."

"I can analyse culture when it's required."

"When 'tis scientific and logical."

"Same difference."

Arsenic paused in their banter and her steps. This allowed their guides to get a little ahead. Her attention was arrested by the open storefront of a nearby shop.

Percy followed her gaze. Bundles of dry herbs hung from a framed doorway, with beautifully arranged wicker baskets of more stretching back into the shop. Paper bags filled with mysterious items were stacked in rows on shelves. There was something about it that screamed medicinal, rather than culinary. One might expect glass bottles of tinctures, but Percy supposed they would want to keep everything as light as possible in Edo.

"'Tis remarkable," said Arsenic, big eyes even bigger in awe. "I wonder what they..."

A wizened gentleman came to the fore. He wore a kind of robe, only shorter and with wide-legged trousers beneath, like a lady's split skirt for riding, with a sash for a belt.

Percy greeted him with a bow and the formal words of strangers opening a dialogue of mutual interest.

The man bowed low in response. "Welcome. You wish to trade?"

Percy screwed his courage to the sticking point and decided that since he was speaking Japanese (and could be overheard *and* understood) he should adhere to the fabricated relationship. "Your wares interest my wife." To claim her so made him flush furiously.

"She has knowledge of medicine?" The apothecary looked with shock at Arsenic.

"She does."

"Not you?"

"Not me."

Arsenic began sniffing herbs and muttered to herself. "Is this cardamom? What could it be used for?"

"You are permissive with your womenfolk. You foreigners."

Percy bowed again, trying to think of a good answer. "I think you will find it is the other way around."

The man started. "We rarely meet the women of the West, except for those who travel for pleasure."

"Tourists," agreed Percy. "Are all your women such? Surely some must work." He was trying to make a point.

The apothecary spread his hand. "Only those of the highest rank float among the lanterns without labour."

"So" – Percy smiled – "we are not so very different."

Arsenic came over to them, proffered up a seedpod. "Ask him what they use it for, please, Percy."

Percy asked.

"Your wife is not a good doctor if she does not know jehotang, for cooling of the mind."

The handmaidens, having noticed they'd lost their foreigners, backtracked and now stood watching with interest.

Arsenic noticed them and the apothecary's sneer at the same time. "I must prove my mettle."

She whirled about and perused the assembled plants, seeds, herbs, and powders. Finally she settled on a gnarled yellowish-brown root. It looked like a deformed carrot with pigmentation issues. She picked it up and sniffed it.

"Angelica root," said Arsenic. "Different from the Nordic kind but still smelling like celery. Perhaps this is a local variant?" She seemed to be asking herself, so Percy did not translate.

She made a gesture at the apothecary, directing the root to her mouth. He nodded. She smiled. "Tell him it is used to stimulate appetite and improve digestion, for stomach complaints and colic in babies."

Percy was finding his mastery of Japanese insufficient to meet this conversation, but he did his best, and the wizened shopkeep inclined his head in approval.

Arsenic picked up a seedpod, and made a gesture with it towards her ear.

The shopkeep tilted his head again.

Arsenic dipped her chin and smiled at him.

He said to Percy, "Your wife, she is not so ill trained, only a stranger to some of our plants."

Percy could not help but admire both Arsenic's knowledge and her charm.

"I have medicine she does not recognize," the man continued.

"No doubt she has the same," said Percy with confidence, pointing to Arsenic's kit.

The man's eyes became calculating.

Percy looked around nervously. They were under close observation from the handmaidens and anyone else walking by. Three Edo natives had stopped to watch the English doctor and the Japanese apothecary. There were likely other eyeballs on them as well. There were buildings all around them with vellum windows, slid aside to peek through.

Percy felt exposed. "Arsenic, I believe it would be best...That is to say, wife, we should perhaps move on to your patient?"

"Dear me, of course! I was distracted. Perhaps we could stop by again on our return?" Her eyes were intrigued and hopeful. Percy wanted to buy her every herb in the shop.

Instead he made such intentions known to the proprietor and bowed.

The apothecary bowed back and murmured an eagerness to renew the acquaintance.

Percy led Arsenic away and gestured for the handmaidens to proceed. "Please excuse our distraction."

One of them gave him a grave look. "Your wife has a passion for healing, such should never be stifled."

Percy murmured politely, "But your lady awaits."

"Our lady does nothing but wait."

They continued down the slatted street.

As they got deeper into the city, the walkway became less firm and supportive, and more like a suspension bridge. The handmaidens appeared to not notice the difference, their steps small and light. But the street swayed as Arsenic and Percy walked on it. Percy caught his breath. He did not mind heights. He was, after all, the navigator of a dirigible, but there was something about *swaying* and heights that did him in.

Arsenic firmed up her arm in support and smiled shyly up at him.

He was grateful when they diverted onto one of the solid arched bridge-ways again. This one was so steep that it formed the top half of a circle and required tiny steps for them to climb up. A big golden lantern was above them now, the house hanging from it, directly in front of them. It was impressive in an airy way. Its walls were made of paper or fabric, opaque and colourful, but flimsy.

He wondered about crime in the Paper City.

The handmaidens approached the door and at some unseen signal it slid smoothly to one side. A servant knelt near the opening. The handmaidens moved swiftly in and past her. Percy and Arsenic followed.

They all paused while the servant slid the door closed behind them and the handmaidens removed their sandals. They waited expectantly.

Arsenic and Percy exchanged looks. With a shrug, Percy toed off his shoes. Virgil would have his ear for the smudges this left on the heels but there didn't seem to be a shoehorn about.

Arsenic looked desperate. "I'm wearing bicycle boots. They lace all the way up. I need to sit to take them off and there's no chairs. What do I do?"

Percy figured he'd better do valet duties and dropped to one knee before her. He looked up at her expectantly.

Of all things, the doctor blushed. "What are you doing?"

He patted his knee. "Give it here."

"Oh dear." She raised one dainty foot to his thigh. A slim hand pressed on his shoulder for balance.

Percy unlaced her boots carefully. They were the tall kind, going most of the way up her calf, and he, who had never cared for gentlemen's shoes, let alone ladies', found them quite fascinating in their meticulous construction. Or perhaps it was simply that the leg beneath was shapely and silken. His stomach went slightly queasy.

He pulled one boot off and set it aside.

"This is so embarrassing, as if I were a child." Arsenic gave him her other foot.

"I know you're not a child," he replied, gravel in his voice.

He made quick work of the other boot, knowing he was red about the ears.

The three handmaidens watched this exchange with interest, but no censure.

"You are a good husband," observed one.

Percy stood and bowed in reply and tried hard not to think about the delicacy of the ankle so recently in his hands.

At first, Arsenic was tempted to believe this was a household of women, but there were two large men stationed at the entrance to her patient's room. Guards. Whoever she was, the ill woman was important.

The door slid aside to reveal a room of consummate style and essential barrenness. There was no furniture beyond a low bed in one corner, sumptuous and beautiful, and walls made up of the most stunning tapestries Arsenic had ever seen. The landscapes they depicted were flowing and entirely alien. There were sharp red mountains, high white clouds, and trees made of flowers weeping into the wind and becoming butterflies. The Paper City was depicted too, seen from below and far away, a cluster of colourful bubbles. Arsenic moved to look closer and realized that they were not tapestry at all, but shimmery painted and embroidered silk. Silver was threaded throughout, wefted into the fabric, and embroidered around the images as if forming a window frame. She wondered if it were a special kind of thread, or actually metal. From the way they hung, heavy and still, she suspected true silver. She wanted to linger, they were so stunning, but her patient waited.

The lady was almost as beautiful as the walls surrounding her. She was tiny as a child, frail under a mound of blankets. Her face was not a painted white like her handmaidens', but her black hair was equally elaborate, woven through with coloured ribbons. Her eyes were wide and black, sparkling with humour.

She was awake and alert, her gaze focused and interested, clearly neither her mind nor her vision were afflicted. Arsenic approached, turning at the last to ask a question of her escort, only to find that the door had been slid shut behind her. The handmaidens hadn't followed. They stayed with Percy and the guards.

Arsenic thought she was alone with her patient and was startled by such trust. But then from behind her, in the corner, a man stepped forward. He was fierce looking, tall as Percy but a great deal bulkier, and wore a long vest made of blue and purple lacquered scales, as if he were a fish. His expression was stern, but if Arsenic had to guess from the shifting of his eyes, she would say that he was more frightened. He carried in his hand a long curved metal sword, naked and gleaming. Its hilt was elaborately bound in gold and ended in a gold tassel.

"I do apologize," said Arsenic, "but I dinna speak your language. If you're na fluent in English, French, or Latin, then we'll need someone to interpret."

"I speak your mother tongue," said her tiny patient from the low bed. "I make it a practice to study the newer languages."

Arsenic nodded and stepped towards her.

The man moved quickly to intercept. The room shook about him as he walked, for he had a heavy tread.

The lady spoke to him in lyrical flowing sentences that did not sound at all familiar.

"'Tis na Japanese?"

"No." The patient offered no further explanation.

"Does he speak English?" Arsenic was concerned as to the privacy of her examination.

The woman didn't answer and Arsenic interpreted that as an urge for caution.

Lacking any tables or chairs, Arsenic set her kit down on the corner of the bed. There was more than enough room, the tiny woman took up so little. Arsenic clicked it to telescope open. Both the lady in the bed and the man in the scales gasped, impressed by the fluid beauty of the technology.

"I'll need to ask a number of questions," said Arsenic.

"Ask away, young one. I am at your disposal. I am going nowhere."

Arsenic took hold of one thin wrist to check for a pulse – it was slow, thready, and weak. The man shifted uncomfortably as if he did not like them touching. Arsenic gave him a side-eyed look.

"Do not mind my Lord Ryuunosuke. He worries, always, for my safety. I am important to him. You might say . . . necessary."

There was something in her tone that made Arsenic look around, and wonder if the sumptuousness of the room did not belie its purpose.

"You're his wife?"

The woman's lips twitched infinitesimally, which Arsenic suspected was her version of a wide grin. "No. I am geisha. I do not marry."

"Geisha?"

"An entertainer of wealthy men."

"Oh, I see," Arsenic said, although she wasn't entirely sure she did. The woman acted like royalty, not like an actress or a courtesan. Although some opera singers Arsenic had met could out-snob the queen. "You sing?"

"Among other things. I have never met a woman doctor before. Are you unable to bear children?"

"That is an interesting assumption. Why would one presuppose the other?"

While they spoke, Arsenic checked the clarity of her patient's eyes, the pinkness of her tongue, the cleanliness of her ear canals. Nothing was amiss. If anything, the woman was too healthy. Almost ageless. Except for the state of her pulse. Also her breath was slow and shallow, her skin nearly transparent.

"What's your name, madam?"

"You may call me Lady Sakura."

"Fair enough. You may call me Dr Ruthven." If they were going to be formal about it.

The graceful head inclined towards her.

Arsenic began asking questions, delving into the nature of any discomfort. Any tenderness, difficulty with food or waste? Any digestive or respiratory complaints? Any mysterious bumps or rashes?

All such enquiries received negative answers.

"I feel as if I am fading. Stretched. We all do."

Arsenic started. "All? Who all?"

"Well, there is me up here, and then all the rest of us down below."

"'Tis spreading, this lethargy? 'Tis catching?"

"Only to my cousins. Not to you."

"To me?" Suddenly, and for some reason, Arsenic thought of Tasherit, crumbling under the unseen weight of the Paper City. Then she thought of the tapestry walls around them, threaded with silver.

"Your cousins? This is a familial complaint?"

"We are not related by blood but by state of being." The geisha looked from under her lashes at the man nearby.

"Are they being helped?"

"No, hindered. I am hoping, if you save me, that I may convey to them the cure."

More than one life, apparently, hung on Arsenic's ability to treat this lady's ailment.

Arsenic was getting frustrated. How could she cure anything without *all* the necessary information? Was this woman even human?

"Say *ahhh*." Arsenic checked Lady Sakura's soft palate, her gag reflex, and her teeth. Those teeth were small and sharp, but not fanged. So if she was anything inhuman, it was meat eating, not bloodsucking.

The beautiful room began to feel sinister. *Silver in the walls.* Arsenic was grateful to know Percy stood just the other side of the tapestry and that the silver could not harm either of *them*.

"I need to take you back to my ship, for a proper examination."

"They will not let me go."

"They may surround you with guards, if they wish. How could you possibly escape, anyway? Quite apart from your weakened state, you are leagues up in the air. Where would you go? Can you fly?"

"Perhaps I am tired enough of this condition to walk to the edge and jump?"

At that statement Arsenic wondered if this were a mental complaint, like hysteria. "Are you so inclined?"

"I am not suicidal, if that is what you are asking."

"What do *you* think is wrong with you?" It was a question so few doctors remembered to ask their patients. To give them agency in their own illness.

"If I knew, I would not be so upset. If there were not others of us afflicted, I would not be so eager to see a strange Western doctor who smells of foreign flowers."

"I smell, do I?" Surrounded by silver, obsessed with scent. Before meeting the werecat and reading about her kind, Arsenic would not have thought it possible. But if there was one that could travel by dirigible, might not others float in a Paper City? If there was one shifter species where bite survivors were mostly female, then there might be others. Simply because one grew up surrounded by werewolves, and knowing that they were predominantly large men, did not mean it translated to a place like Japan. Perhaps here shifters came pint-sized and female.

"Are your cousins all women?"

"Mostly."

"Are your handmaidens also your cousins?"

"I am the only one of my blood kept in the City of Paper."

Arsenic bent, in the guise of pressing her ear to the woman's silk-covered chest. "Are you a hostage?"

The lovely head inclined a fraction.

Arsenic stood and turned to face the man in the scales. "I must get her to my ship."

Not a flicker from the man. He did not even acknowledge that she'd spoken.

"You brought your husband with you?" Lady Sakura asked.
Arsenic nodded.

"Use him to convince my lord. Do this outside my room, please, and send in my handmaidens. If I am to go out, I must be properly dressed."

Arsenic resealed her kit and marched to the door, gesturing for the lord to follow. He gave Lady Sakura a look of mixed gentleness and exasperation. It was all in his eyes, his face remained unmoving.

Arsenic flapped at him with her hands, shooing him out.

He side-eyed her in surprise. Or annoyance. Or approval.

In the vestibule, Percy was sitting cross-legged on the floor. The three handmaidens were kneeling to face him. The guards stood to either side of the door, unmoving and unmoved.

"Percy, would you persuade this gentleman, Lord Ryuunosuke, that I must take his Lady Sakura back to *The Spotted Custard*? I require my swoon room to make a proper diagnosis."

Lord Ryuunosuke barked an order at the three handmaidens. They all stood and glided into the sickroom, bowing before closing the door behind them.

Percy stood to face the lord and began garbling at him in Japanese.

The lord crossed his arms and glared at Arsenic's ginger boffin. The two guards stepped forward and began to argue with Percy. It made her feel protective.

This went on for a while.

Eventually the sickroom door slid open and one of the handmaidens re-emerged and approached. She said something too quickly for Arsenic to follow.

Percy interrupted his rapidly escalating one-sided argument with the lord, to tell Arsenic that she, and she alone, without her kit, was required back in the chamber.

Lord Ryuunosuke whirled and made a gesture with his hand to the guards, indicating that the door be left open. Then he returned to listening to Percy, glowering and granite, unmoved.

Lady Sakura was sitting on the edge of the bed when Arsenic re-entered. She was wearing two elaborate embroidered kimonos. Her face was now painted – skin white, lips red. Her hair had added decoration, trailing gold leaves and pink silk flowers.

One of those massive bow belts was around her waist and the puff was a thing of beauty at the small of her back.

"Should you be walking?" worried Arsenic.

"I will be carried, if they permit me to leave at all." She gestured with one tiny frail hand. "Come. You, too, must wear an obi."

The handmaidens approached Arsenic. One of them held a large pillow-like thing. Another held a length of that wide stiff highly decorated belt-cloth. The last held some kind of tool presumably designed to fasten everything in place.

Arsenic looked down at her sensible bicycling uniform of brown tweed – it had nice green buttons down the front, and green braid coiled at the hem, but it was nothing compared to even the simplest outfit she'd seen in Edo.

"It willna match."

The geisha laughed. "It will be fine, child. Put it on."

Arsenic assumed this was an important local custom, or great honour, and so stood obediently while they pressed the pillow to her lower back, binding it there with straps over her shoulders. It was a little like the hiking packs army foot soldiers used, not uncomfortable, but heavier than expected.

"What's it stuffed with?"

"Safety," replied Lady Sakura. "Be still, child."

The three handmaidens wrapped Arsenic with the belt and arranged it artfully over the pillow in what was likely a big bow. It was behind her back, so she couldn't see, and there were no mirrors to be had.

Arsenic was amused to think it rather like a version of the cravat. "Must I wear the high sandals, too? I have no practice walking in such things."

"The obi is enough. See here?" Lady Sakura pointed to her own belt. It was embroidered with trees in full bloom.

"A fruit tree of some kind?"

"Cherry blossoms. Look closer, Doctor."

Arsenic squinted. The blossoms were all falling as if scattered on the wind, but as they fell they turned into white birds and flew away.

"I dinna understand."

One of the handmaidens took Arsenic's hand and guided it behind her back, to a small corded ribbon dangling from beneath the pillow, stiffer, more sturdy.

"You pull it," said Lady Sakura.

"And what happens?"

"You float."

Arsenic suddenly understood – the elaborate weight of it, the straps over her shoulders. "'Tis a parachute."

"I do not know that word."

"A huge parasol of fabric to catch the air and carry you to the ground."

"Yes."

Arsenic looked at the three handmaidens.

"Are all the ladies of Edo so equipped?"

"Yes."

"You dinna trust the Paper City?"

"Would you?"

By the time they were finished, the handmaidens easily taking Lady Sakura's weight to help her from the room, Percy had convinced the austere lord (or perhaps more importantly, the guards) that visiting an airship was not only a good idea but vital to his lady's survival.

"How did you do it?" Arsenic asked Percy in French, hoping it was the least spoken language here.

"Not entirely sure. I praised the advancement of our technology. We may have to show them the boiler room or something."

"That's all?"

"Well, I wouldn't want to tell Quesnel, but our boiler room is impressive."

"But not medical."

Percy winced. "Make certain you use every ridiculous gadget you have, even if it's not necessary. Make it *look* good. Their only concern is her health, so their belief in our technological advancements is paramount. I preyed upon both."

"Will do."

"She does look ill. And she's very small."

"She's also a hostage."

Percy hardly changed expression. "Ours or theirs?"

"Theirs."

"For what purpose?"

"I dinna know, but she isna the only one ill. There's more of her family, on the ground. Also sick."

"Why can it never be simple?"

"I've been given the impression that *The Spotted Custard* takes extraordinary measures to avoid *simple*."

"You'd think we'd have grown out of it by now."

Arsenic shrugged. "Think they'll have found the missing spy by the time we get back?"

"Doubtful. I forgot to remind them that was part of our mission."

"Good point."

Percy would rather not remember putting the bicycle boots back onto the doctor. It was almost as erotic as it had been taking them off.

On the walk back, the Paper City continued to impress them by being slightly too empty and slightly too perfect, and thus eerie.

The wind had kicked up and was brushing by them, an odd sensation, as most of the time a dirigible was not windy because it nested *inside* a breeze, like a boat upon a current. But in Edo air rustled the dangling jewellery in Lady Sakura's hair, making it tinkle merrily, even inside her litter.

The handmaidens did not make the return journey with them. The lord, whose name was impossible for Percy to pronounce, marched in front, the street quaking beneath him. The two guards carried the lady in her elaborate litter behind him. They did so with remarkable ease, as if it weighed nothing.

Percy offered Arsenic his arm and together they brought up the rear. Nervous and silent. They did not stop at the apothecary shop.

They found the *Custard* unchanged. The crew was mostly standing around abovedecks. There was none of the customary activity of being in a port – no refuelling or restocking. Everyone was sipping tea and making an appearance of relaxation. Percy automatically looked to Rue for reassurance, but for once her round face was set and serious, no smile to be seen.

An array of what could only be military men stood in formation dockside facing *The Spotted Custard*. These soldiers made no pretence at appearing relaxed. They stood to attention, facing the dirigible and its tea party, hands to the guns at their hips. As if the act of drinking black tea in the European style were a punishable offence.

For all Percy knew, it might well be.

The Japanese did not put milk in their tea.

Lord Ryuunosuke had an extensive ritualized conversation with the military fellow in charge, eventually convincing him that he and his party should be allowed to board. Apparently, this would only be permitted with a full complement of soldiers accompanying him.

Thus, *The Spotted Custard* was invaded.

Everyone was made tense by this, although Percy was pleased to see the crew made no outward show of it. The tea continued apace. Primrose attempted to foist beverages upon the new arrivals, as if the soldiers were merely guests paying a call.

In the companion hubbub activity, Rue managed to pounce on Percy.

"What on earth, Percy?"

"Arsenic wants her patient in the swoon room for a proper examination."

"And they're allowing it?"

"As you see."

"With restrictions."

"As you see."

"And?"

"The patient is a little thing, one of those geisha I told you I read about. But that seems to mean more than my research initially suggested. I had thought geisha were entertainers of the elite and—"

"Percy, do *not* get distracted right now."

"I beg your pardon, Rue. Where was I? Oh yes, the scaly lord chappie that's with her, he owns her, or has her trapped, or something. Anyhoo she's a hostage, says Arsenic. Should I make introductions?"

Rue looked over at Lord Ryuunosuke, who was squaring off with his two guards (the litter having been set down) and his newly acquired military enforcements, against Rodrigo and Quesnel, the decklings, deckhands, and a few stalwarts from the boiler room. Aggie was there too, spoiling for a fight.

Primrose offered more tea.

Percy frowned. This was not going well. "We don't look very threatening."

Rue looked over her stalwart crew, plucky, but honestly not all that vicious without weaponry or werecat.

"I see your point, Percy."

"I had a point?"

"Different tactics are required."

"Oh yes?"

"Like delicacy."

"Don't strain anything, Rue."

"Your faith is heartening, Percy old sod."

"Did you find any word of the Wallflower?"

"We haven't been able to leave the ship, get word off it, or meet with anyone. How would we do that?"

"You have your wily ways."

"I do?"

"They seem wily to me."

"That's because you have no guile at all, Percy."

"Are you calling me honest?"

"No, dear, simply obtuse."

"That's fair."

"So, the doctor wants us to rescue this patient?"

"I believe so. There's definitely something wrong with her."

"Percy, there's always something wrong. Now introduce me to His Lordship so I can beat him over the head with diplomacy and delicacy."

"I don't think it works that way."

"How would you know?"

"Fair point, come on." He started and then stopped, remembering one last thing. "And I think that the ill lady is one of those fox shifters we were meant to find."

"What? What!"

"You know, the—"

"Yes, Percy, I *know*. I meant you couldn't have started with that little fact?"

"I only just deduced it."

"What, just now?"

"Well, yes. You see, I've been neglecting something quite simple all along. To do with physics, I mean. I forgot that preservation of mass can be nothing more than a matter of density."

"What?"

"When they lifted her litter, it was very very light."

"Light?"

"She weighs less than forty pounds, easily."

"Light enough to shift into a largish fox?"

"Exactly."

"Density? Of course. Oh, Percy, I hate it when you're right."

He patted her shoulder. "I know, Rue, apologies."

Percy led his captain over to the visiting Japanese lord, bowed deeply, and made what he thought was a reasonably good introduction.

Lord Ryuunosuke, however, did not seem at all impressed with Rue. Which was not unusual. To be honest, as captains went, Rue was one of the least impressive he'd ever encountered. It took knowing about her metanatural abilities, or her parents, or her connections, or her attitude, or her unexpected success rates, to really be impressed by her.

Nevertheless, Rue must have access to some kind of diplomacy because she managed to get Lady Sakura, Lord Ryuunosuke, the two guards, and three of the military men belowdecks to Arsenic's swoon room.

Percy didn't follow, choosing to stay abovedecks and relay as much as he could (mostly in French and a little Italian) to his friends and crewmates about what had happened.

Primrose attempted to distract the remaining officials with ever more tea and even some biscuits.

The Japanese soldiers were bewildered by the biscuits, and then scandalized when Spoo demonstrated the dunking procedure favoured by decklings. Primrose ordered her to stop. Percy thought the decklings were perspicacious about biscuits, as ship's biscuits were horrible hard old things after a month of travel. Cook made them that way on purpose, so they'd keep.

Although Percy would never have dared dip a biscuit himself, he did grab a few extras and pass them along to Spoo, who he knew had a love of the ghastly things.

CHAPTER

TEN

How Not to Arrive Gracefully

Having access to her swoon room didn't increase Arsenic's ability to determine the nature of Lady Sakura's illness.

She used every analytical device that she had, especially the most technologically impressive ones with long names and complicated patents. But they only told her what she already knew, that Lady Sakura was exhausted, driven to a weakened state by some draw on her system. There was no definable disease, it was a state of being or mind. And she was probably a supernatural creature.

The lady herself was of no help. She was even more peely-wally and fragile after the journey through the city, looking almost paper herself.

Frustrated, Arsenic turned to the lady's keeper, using Anitra as interpreter. Lord Ryuunosuke looked as if he would prefer to ignore them both, but he was smart enough not to discount women entirely – anyone could be a threat.

"Have you tried taking her ground-side, consulting a doctor in Tokyo?"

"What good is that? All the best doctors are up here."

"Perhaps she needs soil under her feet. Perhaps this is homesickness."

"You speak as a scientist? Homesickness, pah."

Anitra was funny, trying to express the Japanese lord's disgust.

Arsenic did not take offence. "She is weakened by some pining that even my science cannot understand. She is fading. Why do you keep her up here anyway?"

"I? It is not I . . . Pah. She must stay in Edo and you must cure her, here."

"Saying something *must be* dinna make it so. Her own body contradicts her condition. Is she eating enough protein?"

"She eats everything. Her kind always does."

"Her *kind*? Geisha?"

His face went stony and withdrawn.

Arsenic considered her options. She wished Tasherit were awake. She'd like the werecat's opinion on the matter. Supernatural creatures had extraordinary olfactory abilities, perhaps Tasherit could smell something.

I'm grasping at straws. And I'm running out of delaying tactics. She could no more determine a way to rescue Lady Sakura than she could cure her.

Lord Ryuunosuke seemed to sense her frustration.

"You've no idea what's wrong, do you? So much for all your vaunted Western science."

The only thing Arsenic could think to say to that, was something along the lines of, *Well, if you gave me any information to work with, I could have success.* This was entirely too rude, so she held her tongue.

"I must get her home."

Lady Sakura opened her eyes. She was lying on the cot, so still only her eyelashes fluttered. "Thank you for trying, Doctor."

"You're sure there is nothing more you can tell me?"

The lady shook her head. "Perhaps it is my time."

Arsenic winced. "I dinna accept that!"

"Very few can thwart death, child."

With much pomp but admirable care, Lord Ryuunosuke carried the lady back up on deck.

The contingent of Japanese had begun bowing their way to

departure when a shimmering in the deck, and a certain spiralling of cohesive aether, indicated Formerly Floote was about to make an appearance.

Arsenic tensed. If Tasherit was having a hard time being awake, no doubt ghostly manifestation would be even more challenging.

So it appeared to be the case. Or *not* appeared. Formerly Floote struggled valiantly to coalesce but in the end, he was nothing more than a loose amalgam of non-corporeal mist. He'd lost track of both eyebrows, they formed expressive articulations of emotion over his left shoulder. His arms and legs were much longer than they ought to be. Overall, he appeared stretched.

"He is either closer to poltergeist stage than we thought or whatever put Tasherit to sleep is pulling on him, too," Arsenic said to no one in particular.

"I thought such things wouldn't be possible with your tank," said Percy to Quesnel.

The chief engineer got defensive. "The tank does its best, but even Lefoux technology cannot keep back the natural state of decomposition forever. It was bound to happen. Also, there is something wrong with the aether here."

Lady Sakura held up a hand to stop Lord Ryuunosuke from closing the curtains of her litter.

"What did you say, young man? About the aether? That is the European word for spirit realm, is it not?"

But Quesnel never got a chance to answer, because Lord Ryuunosuke looked up from settling Lady Sakura and noticed Formerly Floote's ghostly form.

At which juncture, he proverbially lost the plucked chicken.

He'd been, until that moment, such a solid stoic presence, Arsenic would have thought nothing likely to ruffle his feathers.

Ghosts, apparently, ruffled them. Or should one say shivered his scales?

He roared, gave a hissing shout, and flinched back, looking as if he might run to the railing and cast himself over the side of the *Custard* in horror.

The Japanese soldiers and guards also saw and reacted badly to the ghost. Some drew their weapons, others cowered back, but Lord Ryuunosuke's reaction was the most extreme.

He began yelling in Japanese, as did many of the others, with Percy and Anitra trying to translate the diatribes. But they were speaking too fast for the two interpreters.

"Soooo," said Arsenic, "they're scared of ghosts."

Only Percy paid attention to her. "Or *our* ghost. The lord keeps saying something about the masculine nature of the manifestation."

Arsenic shrugged. "Male ghosts are less common than female."

Rue was barking orders at their visitors, in English, so she was being ignored (even presuming that they would ever listen to a woman). Anitra was attempting to explain that Formerly Floote was a member of their crew, which only seemed to cause more horror. Primrose was waving biscuits around.

Lady Sakura fell back into her litter, hand to her heart.

Only Arsenic thought to go up to the ghost himself and ask why he was trying to manifest when conditions were obviously not conducive? Wouldn't it be best, safest, and most comfortable for him to stay dead awhile longer?

Formerly Floote looked at her, wild and confused. He kept opening and closing his mouth.

"What is it, Formerly Floote?" Arsenic used his full title so that he might remember himself. Remember his cohesion.

"Little doctor?"

"Aye."

"I have to. I must say . . . What did I need to say?" His voice was an echo of itself, the memory of words rather than the real thing. "Oh yes. There are threads here."

"Threads?"

The ghost bobbed and stretched, becoming translucent in patches. His voice was almost inaudible with all the yelling around him. "*Threads* between paper and spirit."

"Paper and spirit, sir?"

"Yes, little doctor. Remember."

"Aye, I shall. Now would you mind returning to your tank, please? It seems you're upsetting the locals."

"Am I? Oh dear. How embarrassing." He twirled around in the air, noticing the chaos, which flustered him further.

Arsenic had little contact with Formerly Floote but she got the impression that he had excelled, in life and in death, at being *capable*. To cause a fuss was an embarrassment.

Formerly Floote murmured, "Oh, I beg your pardon!" Then he wafted down through the deck, and was gone, presumably to the relative safety of his tank.

Silence fell.

Percy said, in that way he had of being inconveniently late with an explanation, "Ghosts are greatly feared in Japan. One of the reasons to have a floating city at all is that there are no spirits possible in the skies."

"Oops," said Rue, "guess we just proved that wrong."

"The military representative is accusing *The Spotted Custard* of being cursed and demanding that we leave Edo as soon as Lord Ryuunosuke and his lady disembark. They are revoking our permission to dock. Anitra, would you take over, please? I wish to talk to the doctor."

Anitra did in fact take over, interpreting as the military captain and Lord Ryuunosuke continued ranting.

Percy touched Arsenic's arm. "What did he say?"

"Formerly Floote?"

"Yes."

"He thinks it verra important that we ken there are threads in Edo between *paper and spirit*. Whatever that means."

Percy frowned. "Threads?"

"Aye."

"For a ghost. Could he mean tethers?"

Arsenic considered. "Or perhaps there are strands of aether coming down here into the city, and that's what's giving Tasherit issues."

Percy pursed his lips. "We met pockets of aether in Peru. So it's not unlikely. Aether doesn't stay confined to the aetherosphere as completely as we once thought."

"Wouldna Rodrigo or Rue sense something, if this were true?"

"Maybe, difficult to know. We don't have enough case studies. We need another supernatural creature aboard. One who doesn't sleep as much as a cat."

Arsenic nodded towards Lady Sakura. "Weel, she's a supernatural. Aye?"

Percy wrinkled his nose. "Obviously. She's one of the fox shifters we were meant to find."

Arsenic was pleased to have confirmation. It made her feel a lot better about her inability to diagnose the patient. She didn't ask how Percy figured it out, she trusted him.

Arsenic fell back on their customary exchange of ideas. Bouncing her thoughts off him as soon as they appeared. "And she's ill because of aether exposure. The same that's impacting Tasherit. But she's been here longer so it's got her worse."

"Or it, whatever *it* is, affects different types of supernatural creatures differently." Percy's red eyebrows were drawn down in thought. The light of the red lantern above made his face devilish. As if he were the malignant spirit, and not poor old Formerly Floote.

Percy continued speculating. "*What if* Edo is tethered the same way a vampire queen is tethered to her hive or an Alpha werewolf to his pack? What if there is no visible connection keeping the Paper City from drifting away, because it's aetherically based and therefore invisible to the naked eye."

Arsenic liked that idea. "As if this whole city were charged with aether?"

Rue interrupted them. "Are you two theorizing? Now is not the time for rampant hypothesis! We are in a precarious position. Next thing you'll both descend into Latin while the rest of us are assassinated around you."

Arsenic looked up.

There appeared to be some sort of stalemate.

Rue explained. "We're refusing to leave without return of our weapons. They don't get to keep everything they confiscated!"

"Canna they boot us regardless?"

Rue grinned evilly. "Nope. Turns out we have a few more bullets than they thought stashed aboard. One Gatling gun is loaded and pointed at their biggest lantern. I don't know for certain, but Lord Ryuunosuke's attitude would seem to indicate that whatever keeps the lanterns alight and afloat is also explosive." Her tawny eyes were filled with glee.

"You saying that we are currently threatening their entire city?"

"Might be." Rue looked sublimely casual about it.

Arsenic turned to see who manned the guns – Spoo and Virgil. "With children?"

"They're excellent shots," said Rue.

Arsenic tilted her head and took a deep breath. "We are at an impasse?"

"Indeed we are." Rue was a little too cheerful.

Primrose was attempting to pass around fresh tea.

Arsenic glanced back at Percy. "Does your sister never stop?"

"Tea is her answer to everything. I once broke my arm and she tried to give me Lapsang souchong."

Arsenic gave his arms an appraising look. "Healed straight?"

"Pray don't concern yourself, Doctor, I had an excellent surgeon. Amazing how efficient people get when one's mother is a vampire queen."

The main deck was a tableau.

A massive glittering gun was aimed at the red balloon above them. The Japanese soldiers, for their part, were pointing wicked-looking handguns at the *Custard*'s officers. Arsenic was shocked to find one pointed at her.

Lord Ryuunosuke still looked shaken after his ghostly encounter.

Lady Sakura had reappeared in the door of her litter, reasonably calm.

Arsenic walked over to her, ignoring Lord Ryuunosuke's warning hiss and the gun pointed at her.

"She is still my patient," she said to him, via Percy, who walked with her.

She bent down to look inside, shielding the tiny woman from outside view with her body.

"What are you, Lady Sakura? What species?"

"Kitsune," said the lady, no shame or dissimulation. "The best species, of course."

"And you're the leader of the kitsune in this area?" There was no other explanation for keeping one such as her hostage than that they wished to guarantee the obedience of others with her presence.

The tiny woman inclined her head.

Arsenic could not see how this dignified yet meek immortal could be so much a threat. But then again, vampires could often appear unthreatening, yet they were the most dangerous of the supernatural set. Countess Nadasdy was reputed to look like a dairymaid, yet she'd killed thousands without mercy over the decades.

"Help them, Doctor. If you cannot help me, help them."

Arsenic was shoved aside by Lord Ryuunosuke.

Percy, silly man, yelled and tried to step between them.

Lord Ryuunosuke was not quite so tall as Percy but he was more substantial. He brushed the ginger academic aside with a flick of his wrist, at the same time pulling Arsenic up and holding her with one hand to the front of her bicycle suit.

"What are you doing, little doctor?" He spoke English after all.

"One might ask the same of you, my lord. What do you need her for, so badly?"

His face remained impassive.

"Edo is killing her. Whatever it is that separates her from her people is making her weak."

"That's your professional opinion?"

"How fare the rest of her kind below? I hear they are ill too? She is their queen, is she not? Their Alpha?" Arsenic wondered what it would be like for a werewolf pack to be separated from their Alpha for years or decades, knowing she was right there, far above them. Or vampires separated from their queen, the tether still present between them but stretched, constantly stretched.

Percy raised himself on both elbows. "Goodness, that's not it, is it?" He looked at Arsenic. "It is possible to do that?"

Percy's mind buzzed with the possibilities. Could a single tether hold an entire city in place? Was it strong enough? Was a tether so solid a thing as to profoundly affect the tangible world? He supposed it must be aether that facilitated form-shifting. Aether must be both particulate and wave, both reality and probability. So it had some substantial physical manifestation.

"Arsenic!"

"Aye, Percy?"

They were crouched together, having been thrust aside by Lord Ryuunosuke.

"You think it's possible that Lady Sakura herself is being used to keep Edo from drifting? That it's her tether to her pack that is keeping the Paper City in place?"

"Aye, Percy."

"That's brilliant!"

"It would account for her illness. It would account for the effect on Tasherit and Formerly Floote."

"But can one tether interfere with another in such a way?"

"I think if it is fraying. It is like aether, leaking. Aether that is meant to hold a kitsune to her people. Who knows what kind of effect such a thing might have on those around. Perhaps there is something more tangible than simply culture that keeps packs and hives apart."

Percy nodded. It was well known in England that vampires and werewolves took many lovers, but never each other. His mother described the very idea as *revolting.*

"They are using a supernatural like an anchor." Percy's mind boggled.

But then again, it was not so improbable as pockets of aether. As fat-sucking vampires. As anything else they'd encountered in their various adventures. Ugh, he hated the word *adventure.* So threatening. Although this would make an excellent paper.

Except, of course, there was a niggling concern. Poor Lady Sakura. Percy could not help but imagine someone doing such a thing to his own mother, trapping her and using her as a lynchpin. It was outright abuse.

Percy was sickened and offended. It was out of character for him to be so overwrought. Yet he was. To understand the supernatural from a dispassionate outsider perspective was one thing, but to manipulate it for one's own ends? Well, that was downright *ungentlemanly.*

Percy stood, drew himself up to his full height, and ignoring the tension about him, and the guns pointed at him, and everything else, he thrust an accusing finger at Lord Ryuunosuke.

"How could you, sir! You torturer! You malignant, nasty, despotic..." He was running out of terms and searched for the right phrase in Latin. But even Latin deserted him.

Lord Ryuunosuke crowded him back, using his bulk and proximity to force him and Arsenic away from Lady Sakura, until they were pressed against the railing on the side of the deck.

"Uh, Percy..." said Arsenic, clutching his arm.

But even Arsenic's touch did not distract him.

Percy was angry. Percy rarely got angry. But such a thing! To trap an innocent supernatural creature and keep her prisoner, use her in such a brutal way. Even Percy had a moral compass. And this flipped the pikelet!

He switched to Japanese and tried to remember every mean word he'd learned. Which hadn't been a lot, but he could get creative. He called Lord Ryuunosuke a rotten fruit, and a limp cherry blossom, and a dead dog, and a flat dumpling, and then...

All breath left him at the force of the shove. He was airborne and he was falling.

Arsenic was a decent student of human nature but even she had no idea why it was the dumpling insult that did it.

Nevertheless, apparently it was *flat dumpling* that drove Lord Ryuunosuke to physically shove Percy overboard. He may, or may not, have intended to kill him. She'd like to give him the benefit of the doubt. He did not know his own strength, or he did not realize Percy's fight was all mouth and he had no physical defences.

But he shoved hard enough to tip the professor. And Percy was tall enough for the railing to be hip height. He stumbled over his own feet. Arsenic knew it was going to happen a split second before it did. Since she was there, close to him, touching, she did the only thing she could think of.

She dove after.

Of course, this was a daft thing to do. She was a doctor and her instinct was to try to save people. But honestly, she couldn't fly.

Above them everyone screamed.

Or Arsenic assumed they screamed. She was too busy listening to the sound of air rushing past her ears.

She folded herself tight so as to gain a tiny bit of momentum, because Percy was right there, falling too. He wasn't screaming, but she suspected that was because Lord Ryuunosuke had knocked the wind from his lungs when he shoved.

She hit Percy, thank heavens, and wrapped herself about him tight, one arm and both legs. They were lined up so she was plastered against his front, like lovers.

Instinctively, if convulsively, Percy wrapped himself around her. Long gangly arms about her neck, legs twined with hers.

"Dinna strangle me, Percy," she yelled, "but hold on!"

She reached behind, above her bottom, where a thick corded ribbon flapped. She tugged at it, pulling hard.

The obi about her waist unfolded and the pillow beneath unfurled. A huge silken parachute deployed above them, sky blue and beautifully wide. It flapped a moment and then caught.

They jerked. Percy coiled himself even tighter around her. His eyes were screwed shut. He seemed to have recovered his breath because he was muttering over and over again, "Oh no oh no oh no oh no."

"I got you, m'eudail," said Arsenic, feeling proud of herself. Her mother's training had come in useful, remembering all those times she'd been made to climb up walls and swing from ropes, and jump from one roof to another.

"Mother, must I?" she'd always said. "I hardly see how this sort of thing will help a doctor."

"You'll learn what I have to teach you, Nic." Preshea had insisted, eyes hard.

Her mother wasn't loving but she was often right. Not that Preshea had shoved her daughters over the sides of airships on the regular. But she had taught them how to stay calm in a crisis, and how to weigh and balance options, and how to make use of the tools provided.

The silk held them steady, slowing their descent. Percy stayed wrapped firmly about her. The dark of Japan below stopped rushing towards them and instead began to sway gently as they got closer.

Arsenic calmed enough to enjoy the sensation.

Flying, she thought. *I'm basically fall-flying.*

She threw her head back and yelled into the night, "Wheeee-eeeeee!"

Percy had never been so scared in all his life.

It wasn't that he had a particular fear of falling, until he was, in fact, plummeting to his death from a dirigible.

This is it, he thought. *Lose my temper and here I am.* He hadn't even managed to dredge up any famous Latin insults.

Then thin strong arms were twined around him. And legs, too. And in midair he was in an intimate embrace with a doctor. He was even more horrified by the idea that he'd somehow pulled Arsenic overboard with him. Worse than his own death, he'd caused hers, too! He moaned in misery and opened his eyes.

I should apologize before we both become eternally procumbent.

Except she was giving him instructions to hold on. Like he would ever let her go. And calling him *m'eudail*, which was wonderful, whatever it meant, but she couldn't have called him that while they were actually still alive?

He closed his eyes.

He heard something louder than the rush of the wind. He heard a hollow flapping cracking sound, like the biggest kite in the world.

Then Arsenic gave a tremendous jerk, and his arms tightened about his lady reflexively.

The air about his ears quieted.

They were no longer falling. They were no longer rushing full tilt through the air. He was drifting, cradled in Arsenic's arms.

He cracked one eye and then the other. Above him the stars were gone. He expected to see the rapidly disappearing Paper City but he saw nothing, emptiness.

Not emptiness, fabric. Like a tent. He twisted his head. There was the moon, not quite full, near the horizon, glittering over the ocean. There was Japan, a dark blob against the shimmering sea, moving closer to them. But slowly, illuminated by the prismatic colours of Edo. Colours that they interrupted in part, a smudge in the filtered light, because above them, supporting them, slowing their descent, was a massive . . . pillowcase?

Parachute? supplied his addled brain.

"Wheeeeeeeeeee!" said Arsenic.

He gripped her tighter. His muscles convulsed, semi-frozen in fear. Also, it was cold.

Percy shifted his gaze to look at the woman in his arms.

Her eyes were bright over his shoulder, watching the land they were floating down towards.

"It looks like we'll land just outside of Tokyo, in the country-side," she reported, happily.

"Where? What? How?" he babbled at her.

"Lady Sakura gave me a parachute."

"Oh." For once in his life Percy really couldn't think of anything to say. "Sorry about the, erm, intimacy of our current predicament."

"Dinna let go!"

"Never!" Percy hooked one hand into the belt at her waist, which seemed to be holding them both up.

"I dinna mind," she added. "If you dinna."

Percy snorted. "I'd respond in Latin, but my Latin has entirely deserted me. Suffice to say I should like to have embraced you under less dangerous circumstances."

"Would you?"

"Absolutely."

"Bonnie. Now, hold on, we're down in a few moments, could get bumpy."

"Delighted to be alive, frankly, Doctor. Bring on the bumps."

"Good, because you're on the bottom."

"A model for our future life."

"Is it?"

"Anything you wish."

"Right now, ground would be good."

Thump.

CHAPTER

ELEVEN

Temples in Motion

The thing is, one never expects to see someone *actually* fall out of an airship.

Spoo racked her brain. She'd been a long time aboard dirigibles, ever since she was old enough to know a puffer from a probe, but in all that time she'd never seen someone tumble overboard. Certainly not someone she liked.

To see the doctor follow immediately after old Percy, apparently of her own will, was even more startling.

Spoo might have screamed.

Fortunately, everyone was screaming so no one noted her moment of weakness. Spoo was well aware of the ragging that she'd endure from fellow decklings, if they ever found out. She had a reputation to maintain.

Everyone rushed to the edge to watch them plummet to their deaths, because who wouldn't? It wasn't as if humans could look away from horror.

Plummet they certainly did, for seemingly long moments, and then a poof of fabric bloomed above them like a massive bathing cap and caught in the wind.

"By Jove," said Spoo, to no one in particular, "that's a parachute, that is! Did you know they had themselves a parachute?"

No one answered her but there were a great many sighs of relief.

The railing was crammed with Spoo's crewmates but also the enemy. Spoo defined *the enemy*, for the time being, as the Japanese soldiers, one tarted-up lordling in a suit made of fish scales, and his ladybird. Spoo knew she was supposed to be impressed by all the fancy fabrics and gussied-up noggins, which was why she wasn't.

After all, she'd once seen Lord Akeldama up close and all sparkles, so it'd take a deal more than robes to impress *her*. Something *like*. These Japanese folks were *like* something, but Spoo wasn't sure what just yet.

Spoo's immediate thought was of Virgil (since she couldn't do anything for the poor sods gone parachuting). She glanced about to see her friend with a shaky hand pressed to his chest, beads of sweat on his brow, and as near to an actual fainting fit as Spoo had ever seen in a non-aristocrat.

She marched over to him, shoving Nips out of her way.

"All right there, ol' Verge?"

"He's alive?"

"Here's hoping."

"You're not very reassuring, Spoo."

She tried an awkward pat to his shoulder.

The fussy coot only glared at her. "Don't mess up the line of my jacket."

"I'm trying to be nice."

"Nice would be if we had handguns aboard, and that puss-nodule in our sights." Virgil pointed at the fishy lordling who'd shoved his master overboard.

That was what Spoo liked about Virgil, he only *pretended* to be proper. Underneath it he was delightfully ruthless. The best sorts were, in Spoo's experience, ruthless. One had to be, if one wanted to accomplish things in this world.

The general sense of relief was short-lived, of course, because everyone started looking about and realizing that they were still at odds.

Spoo gave Virgil a nudge. The enemy was regrouping. "Best get ourselves armed."

Virgil nodded and made for the Gatling gun. They only had a few bullets, and those could only be fired away from the ship, but he'd make them count.

Spoo let out the low long whistle that informed her decklings to make themselves scarce. They obeyed instantly, disappearing up into the rigging. The soldiers ignored them. Spoo was used to that. She liked it, usually worked out in her favour.

Meanwhile, the nobs were focused on silly things like verbal blistering. Lady Captain was red faced and high volume while their enemy seemed to take stony silence as a heavenly mandate.

Aggie's red head popped up out the hatch.

Spoo sprang at her.

"Got your shinks on you?"

Aggie glared.

Spoo glared back. "No time to be a tosser. You can yell later, things 'ave gone wonky. We lost the professor and the doctor. Captain won't play nice for much longer."

"Dead?"

"Overboard."

Aggie didn't stay to talk. She was a right namby pill, but terribly good with a crossbow, and at least she knew when the bow was more necessary than her winching.

"Be soft about it, ginger," Spoo hissed after.

Aggie made a rude gesture above her head, but didn't stop climbing back down the ladder. Presumably in pursuit of her crossbow, wherever she'd managed to hide it.

Spoo's eyes sought the captain. Captain was this small round hot cross bun of a toff, wearing a military-style head consequence, with the three big white floofy feathers. Made her a top target, it did, but also made her easy to spot in a crowd. Spoo supposed that was important in a leader.

Lady Captain was yelling at the fishy lordling so hard her feathers quivered. She was using language Spoo was tolerably certain no quality ought, which was mighty impressive. Fortunately, the man in question didn't speak English. 'Specially fortunate since he was armed and Lady Captain was not. If he knew what she was barking at him, he'd have shot her on the spot. Spoo could sympathize with her captain. She, too, would be driven to berate a man who pushed her professor overboard. Assuming she had a professor of her own. Added to which, losing the new doctor like that. Rummy thing.

Miss Prim was indulging in a bout of hysterics over losing her brother. All over tears and shrieks, and waving about her battle parasol in a manner that seemed entirely unthreatening, unless you knew what that parasol was capable of.

Spoo wondered how much of the performance was genuine.

Their Frenchie still had his darts, but he was doing that oily charming thing instead. He could be deadly with his charm. While the ladies blistered, he applied the balm of persuasion.

Spoo assessed the situation. The *Custard* held the inferior position and the enemy had only one apparent weakness. Everyone was overly concerned for the wellbeing of the tiny lady. And she was, currently, simply sitting in her carrier thing, unguarded.

Aggie's head reappeared.

Spoo gave what she hoped was a meaningful glare and small head tilt.

Together, they ran to the tiny lady.

At that juncture, they were noticed. Guns were pointed at them, but too late. Spoo had out her fish-gutting knife; it was long and thin and wicked sharp. She was pretty good in a knife fight, had to be, growing up dockside.

Spoo scooped up the tiny lady and held her upright and in front, like a shield, one arm about her middle for support. The lady was sick, that much Spoo had gathered, but the lady must stand so Spoo could make her a proper prisoner. Spoo was strong, but it was still remarkably easy to support the lady with one hand, and press a knife to her throat with the other.

Aggie, making things clear, stood next to her, crossbow pointed at the fishy lordling.

"He's in charge?" Aggie hissed at Spoo.

"He's important, I know that much."

"Good enough."

The soldiers and guards responded by aiming even more guns at them, but Spoo's knife was awful close to that white neck.

And so, impasse.

Spoo stayed focused on the tiny lady, who seemed pretty relaxed for a toff with a gutting blade at her throat. Mayhap in Japan these things happened to toffs? She was also the lightest thing Spoo ever held, like one of them white feathers in Captain's hat.

Mayhap she was sicker than she looked?

To be on the safe side, even though it was a fib of the first water, Spoo said, real loud into the now silent deck, "Anitra? You tell 'em my knife's silver. You say that sure and clear. And you tell 'em Aggie's got rowan and silver bolts too, ya hear?" As if either of them could afford silver, let alone get the permits out of BUR.

Anitra looked at the captain.

Lady Captain nodded. Her face was all stiff and serious, but she'd left off her yelling. Spoo hoped that was approval in her eyes.

Even Miss Prim had given up on caterwauling.

Anitra was spouting forth in that singsong language they insisted on speaking round these parts. Whatever she said, it didn't stop things from being tense. But it did cause a shift in attention, negotiations began in earnest. Good, they should want that. Spoo and Aggie were providing incentive.

The fishy lordling, wary eye to Aggie's crossbow, was busy

talking with Anitra. He sure was happy to talk now that the professor was gone and his life was in danger.

Spoo shifted her grip on the tiny lady.

"All right there, little flower?" she asked, knowing the lady couldn't understand her, but feeling she ought to say something under the circumstances.

"Yes, dear, thank you," replied the tiny lady in clear, if accented, English.

Spoo started but kept her grip. "You speak Queen's."

"Some."

"You human?" She reminded Spoo of Tasherit, or Lord Akeldama. So still and calm and superior.

"Not exactly."

"You shift or suck?" No response at that so Spoo pressed on. "You could get away from me then, no? Being all strong and such."

"If I wanted, but I really am ill. And I like where this is going."

"Do you now?"

"I do not want to die. Not yet. Not for this."

"I can't make promises."

"No, dear, not your knife. I mean the city."

Spoo didn't understand, so she tried to soothe. "You just lean up against me then. I'll make certain sure you don't get actual hurt. Sound tops?"

"Tops?"

Spoo took that as agreement.

Anitra, the captain, the fishy lord, and now the head guard were in deep discussion.

Aggie gave Spoo a baleful glance. "This is fun."

"You love it," snapped back Spoo. "Never so happy as when you might get to shoot things."

"Says the girl with the knife."

"Think I can't recognize my kind?"

Aggie sniffed. "We're nothing alike, scrapper."

"Oh, shut your maw and prepare to kill someone."

"Don't tell me like it's your idea."

Spoo considered turning her knife on Aggie. She certainly deserved it more than the tiny lady, who seemed like a good egg. Spoo wondered what kind of supernatural she was. Mayhap a fairy of some kind? Were fairies even real? She'd seen some belter undead floating with the *Custard* but nothing with wings, not yet anyways.

"Sure wish we had our werecat right about now." Of all the toffs, Spoo liked Tasherit best. She was easiest to rub along with. Frenchie was fine, but he was a tradesman so not really a toff-lofty, and the new doc seemed solid, but she was basically in service. Of the aristocrats, the lioness was Spoo's favourite. Frankly, things were never good on deck when she was asleep.

Aggie ignored Spoo's statement.

The tiny lady didn't. "What is a *werecat?*"

Spoo saw nothing wrong in issuing another threat. "Lioness, lion, you have them?"

Shake of the head.

"You got cats?"

Nod.

"Well, then imagine one ten times larger. Big teeth. Human during daylight. As you do."

The little lady looked startled. "They are still alive?"

"In some parts of the world."

"But that is wonderful."

"Like cats, do you?"

"Of course."

"What kind are you, then? I mean to say, you a vampire? You're awful pale."

"Jikininki?" The tiny lady shuddered against Spoo. "No. Kitsune."

"Oh? Whatsat?"

"Fox."

"Belter," said Spoo because that explained why the lady was so light. "Foxes are awful pretty."

The tiny lady preened. "Why, thank you."

The kitsune was starting to shake a bit and lean more heavily against Spoo – out of need or greater trust or both. Spoo was uneasy. She should let her sit but that wouldn't be threatening enough. So she took on as much of the fox's weight as possible.

Spoo turned her attention back to her surroundings.

The fishy lord made a sudden move towards Lady Captain and the lead Japanese soldier, as if he were going to draw his sword and lop off both their heads.

Aggie shot a bolt at him, missing his head by an inch. She loaded in another and took aim without even checking where the first had gone.

"You tell them," said Aggie to Anitra, "that I only miss once."

The lordling looked at Aggie. His expression was pretty impassive but Spoo suspected he was impressed. He stopped reaching for his weapon.

Spoo rolled her eyes. "I thought you hated the captain."

"It's the principle of the thing. I have a prior claim to decapitation."

"That's fair," said Spoo. "You were here first."

"Exactly."

Suddenly all the Japanese soldiers relaxed. At a gesture from their captain, two of them turned and ran down the gangplank, apparently in pursuit of something important.

Miss Prim rang the bell for *more* tea.

Before the two guards returned the tea materialized, Spoo took this as a point of pride. Honestly, it mattered not what occurred abovedecks, Cook was ready to serve at all times.

Tea was poured and passed to all the toffs, including the fishy lordling and the head soldier cove. A footman even came over with a cup for Spoo's charge. They were using the best china.

"You can lower your knife now, Spoo." Miss Prim followed the footman.

Lady Captain yelled at Spoo and Aggie, "We're keeping both of them."

"Who?" yelled Spoo back. "Who are we keeping?"

"Lady Sakura and Lord Ryuunununununu, oh dear, that is a worrisome name. The lord chappie." Captain gestured to the fishy lordling.

Miss Prim explained further. "But keep your blade ready. They've gone for a contract and a clamp."

"A what and a what?"

Miss Prim gave a small sigh. "Big on honour around these parts. Apparently, since we lost two of ours with one push, we're allowed to keep two of theirs of equal value. Anitra negotiated for the lord there and his lady here. So long as we stay docked in Edo, we can keep them aboard. In exchange, the government is going to track our people down below and get them back to us. We're to wait here until they do. Rue's signing a contract about it all. To ensure we don't float away with our hostages the *Custard* gets bolted down to the dock. Hence the clamp."

Spoo was not best pleased. "*Clamp* sounds hard to break free of."

"Yes, Spoo, I believe that's the general idea."

"I don't much like it."

Miss Prim's expression indicated that she felt similarly but was too ladylike to agree. "Until the clamp arrives, we're still in a standoff. So if Miss Aggie will keep with the crossbow and you with the knife, though not quite so threatening, that would be good."

Aggie relaxed her stance but stayed focused on the lord.

Spoo let her hand fall to her side but stayed supporting the lady and didn't sheath her knife.

"You two did good," said Miss Prim, who never stinted on praise when it was due.

"Belter," said Spoo, happy her instincts had been correct.

Aggie didn't say anything, but Spoo suspected a little flush of pleasure. Hard to tell in lantern light.

Miss Prim trundled off to do whatever it was she was always

bustling about doing that revolved around manners and etiquette and silly suchlike.

The lordling looked torn, like he wanted to come over and take the tiny lady away from Spoo, but also like he wanted to fight the captain. Or the Japanese soldiers. Or both.

The tiny lady said something sharp in her native tongue at the man. The fishy lordling subsided.

"That man," the fox-lady said to Spoo.

"Difficult?" suggested Spoo.

"The best ones always are. But he might let me sort it out sometimes, after hundreds of years."

"Hundreds? He undead too? Also a fox? He's too big, right?" She ignored Spoo. "After all, he got us into this mess."

"But that means he wants to be the one to get you out of it. Otherwise he'd be asking for help. He don't like that part, I wager. Pride, I'm thinking. Pride's a rummy old thing with gents."

The little lady grinned. "Yes."

"How long you been stuck?" Spoo wasn't sure if the fox-lady was stuck with the lord, or stuck in the city, or some other kind of stuck. But stuck she certainly seemed to be.

"Too long."

"We'll help," said Spoo, with confidence. Because whatever it was that had the fox-lady trapped, Spoo was convinced her captain would want to break her free. Lady Captain loved to meddle in the affairs of foreign countries and supernatural creatures.

"You will? Why?"

"It's Lady Captain's favourite thing." Spoo gestured at the captain with her knife. "Well, after puff pastry and shoes."

"Helping?"

"More meddling *and* helping."

"She could be kitsune," said the lady, as if this were a compliment.

Given the captain's particular set of abilities, that was an entirely true statement. So Spoo agreed, "She could."

After what amounted to a not very bad fall out of the sky (parachutes certainly helped in that arena), Percy became rapidly and personally acquainted with the fact that actually landing a parachute was perhaps not so easy as the deployment part of the equation.

It transpired that (as Arsenic informed him kindly later while she splinted his ankle) the problem with parachutes was one needed to be trained in the final descent. Since neither of them were, they mostly ended up crashing. Percy landed quite hard, one leg twisted under him. It hurt enough for him to be in no fit state to appreciate Arsenic's weight atop him. Not that this lasted overlong, because she recovered from their fall, and rolled off him to commence doctoral fussing.

"'Tis na broken." Small firm hands efficiently checked over his trousers. Her touch was nice, even if it was impersonal, perhaps slightly too nice. Percy was happy for the pain as this kept said trousers under control. He distracted himself by noticing that the trousers themselves were a great deal worse for wear – torn and soiled. Whatever they'd landed in was damp. Silty moisture squished through his fingers as he levered himself upright.

"Dinna sit. I've na checked the rest of you."

"It's only my leg. And my attire." Percy wrinkled his nose. Not that he was a fancy lad, but he couldn't abide being mucky.

"The mud cushioned our fall, otherwise your leg would be broken."

"I'm to be grateful for the squelch?"

"Aye, m'eud—" She stopped herself.

"You can call me *m'eudail*," said Percy, feeling quite bold. Perhaps the result of a near-death encounter.

Arsenic wrapped his lower leg with the belt part of her obi. If she blushed to touch him so intimately, he couldn't tell in the dark.

"I mean to say, if you wish to call me *m'eudail*. I like it, you calling me that. I don't know what it means, I don't speak Gaelic." He stumbled on the dismount.

Percy wished he could be charming. But of the many insults and superlatives that had been used to describe Percival Tunstell over his lifetime, *charming* had never been among them.

"*M'eudail* is like *dear*. I'm glad you like it. And what should you call me?"

Darling? That seemed somewhat formal. Percy wondered what it was in Latin, but he'd never had cause to study endearments. He supposed *dulcis* was sweet, but *dulcissima* seemed a bit of a mouthful.

Unfortunately, he'd now been thinking too long on the subject and things were awkward. She was looking disappointed in his lack of response.

He might have apologized but he wasn't sure for what, so he gave credit where it was due instead. "I do believe you just saved my life."

She flashed him a smile while she tied off the improvised bandage. "No need to fawn upon me as a result."

Percy grinned back. His whole leg throbbed, migrating up from his twisted ankle.

"Look here, I liked you before you saved me. This simply makes it better."

"Because you owe me a favour?"

"That would be silly, you're a doctor. I'd always end up owing you. How'd you know how to do that?"

"Tumble out of a dirigible?" She sat back on her heels, giving his leg a critical once-over. "A girl learns odd things when her mother is an assassin. Surely you've some strange skill or another connected to your mother being a vampire?"

"A healthy disregard for hats."

"Percy, you're quite diverting when you wish to be."

Regrettably, they were back to *Percy*. *M'eudail* had been abandoned.

Percy was sad. "It's the pain, throws me off. Are you injured at all? The parasol jerked you about when it deployed."

"A little bruised at the shoulders and I dinna think I'll be hungry anytime soon, since the belt bit into my waist, but no serious damage. Thank you for asking."

Percy nodded, taking her at her word. "What do we do now?" He was no man of action to seize the moment as an excuse to make ill-informed decisions.

Arsenic pursed her lips. "I dinna think we'll get verra far. There's na to make a crutch of."

Percy looked around. It was dark, the rainbow lights of the Paper City far above were faint. They hadn't landed in the middle of Tokyo but well outside of it. They were sitting in a field of grain – a damp tallish grasslike crop. *Rice paddy*, Percy supposed.

"We should stay here?"

Arsenic's eyes were bright on him, reflecting what little light there was in an eerie manner. "We both read the warnings in the travel guides. The people may na be xenophobic but the government certainly is. Outside contact is restricted to the Paper City, and foreigners found on Japanese soil without permission are imprisoned or killed."

"But we fell by accident."

"I hardly see how that will matter to the local militia. And if we're found by anyone else we canna predict the reaction. Hopefully, Rue will come up with a means to extract us, but until then I suggest we make for the city." She pointed towards the soft yellow light some distance away. Percy was terribly disorientated and never very good with directions at the best of times, odd in a navigator (although he was excellent at reading charts). However, given his general sense of the water, he thought that they were northeast of Tokyo.

Percy was, by upbringing and inclination, inclined to let ladies lead where matters of adventure were concerned (and this was definitely one of those unfortunate *adventure* situations). If Arsenic wanted to relocate, he would relocate.

He hoisted himself to his feet. His trousers gave an ominous ripping sound. A light breeze in places where breezes ought not to go indicated that his posterior was now on display to the Japanese countryside. *I shall make a most excellent impression.*

"Oh dear," said Arsenic.

Percy sighed, took his jacket off (it was ruined anyway), and tied it about his waist by the sleeves.

"I wouldna have minded," said Arsenic, under her breath. *"Felix culpa."*

Percy, pleased, gave her an arch look. "That is not a part of my anatomy I generally feel needs an airing."

"How about a private viewing?" Arsenic shot back and then covered her mouth with her free hand as though it had spoken without her consent.

Percy sputtered. That was bold to say the least – serious flirting. He supposed they were on more intimate terms than they had been a mere fifteen minutes prior. They'd only recently been wrapped in an embrace, admittedly a hazardous one, but still . . . One might say that Arsenic knew the exact cut of his trousers. He supposed it was only one step removed from wishing to peruse the territory beneath. If he were lucky.

She lowered her lashes. "Too much?"

Percy shook his head, grateful for the night as he was certain his cheeks were crimson. "Perhaps when we aren't in a dangerous and unknown country having fallen out of a dirigible?"

"You can think of a better time?"

"Well, yes, at any point in the last month."

"You would have dropped your trousers for me shortly after my interview, then?"

She'd clearly discovered boldness. She also got more Scottish when she flirted.

He adored it.

She helped him to stand and slid herself under his arm. They began a shuffling hobble towards the far-off city. Well, he hobbled, she walked like a normal human.

"Absolutely," he said. "I might have been surprised, but I assure you I'm well educated."

"What does that have to do with it?"

"I'm no idiot, not to recognize a good thing when she shows interest in bits of my anatomy." He paused. "In a non-medicinal way, of course."

She laughed. A small hand reached down and patted him. Over the jacket, more was the pity.

Percy decided that was more than enough of something that couldn't be pursued just yet. Given the ephemeral state of his trousers, one didn't wish to encourage undue movement in that area, sadly.

Besides, he had questions. "How did you end up wearing a parachute?"

"Lady Sakura insisted. I wonder if she knew this would happen."

"So far as I'm aware, supernatural abilities do not include precognition."

"I dinna mean that. I mean, I wonder if she thought it likely someone would push me off an airship."

"It was me who got pushed."

"True, but to be frank, Percy, I'm surprised it hasna happened afore."

"Me too. I don't mean to be so obnoxious."

"'Tis one of your more endearing qualities."

"You're the first to think so."

She hummed. "Materially mitigated by the fine cut of your jib and a bonnie pair of eyes, and the fact that you mostly talk sense, even if you explain overmuch afore you get there."

Percy suspected that was a compliment. "Uh, thank you?"

She continued. "Also, I ken you have a good heart. 'Tis thoroughly hidden, but 'tis good."

"For pity's sake, don't *tell* anyone. My reputation will be in ruins."

Without turning to look at him, she smiled. "You should court me, Professor."

"From the look of things, you're hell-bent on courting *me*. Quite well, I must add. The direct approach is best for someone with my condition."

"Your condition?"

"Uh, socially rummy and easily bewildered by females."

"On the contrary, I ken you understand women verra well. You've simply never bothered to apply your understanding."

Percy narrowed his eyes. She was awfully perceptive. "So you, erm, want courting? What kind? I hardly know how."

"A little effort, please."

He stumbled and then coughed out a laugh. She was playing with him. "You think I'm lazy?"

"I think you've had it quite easy, m'eudail. Aye."

That particular application of *m'eudail* was condescending, but he still preferred it to anything else, coming from her. He noticed a bit of plant matter caught in her braid and removed it gently. Her hair was knotted from their fall but silky soft.

Percy considered as they trekked along in silence. How to court a doctor and an intellectual? Arsenic was a practical female who probably saw him as quite frivolous. She clearly liked the way he looked, but Percy didn't know how to flirt using that, so perhaps conversation was best? They had a firm grounding in that after all their afternoons spent in his library. How to start without a book?

He coughed, not sure if they were trying for stealth in the quiet night. It seemed they had not only the rice paddy but the whole world to themselves. It was difficult not to squelch as they walked. Perhaps idle conversation was permitted?

"Tell me about your family. Are you close to your father?" He asked, of course, because Arsenic's feelings towards her father, and her parents' relationship, might give him insight into her expectations on such matters.

Arsenic knew exactly what he was getting at. She laughed. "A good first effort, shall I tell you how they met?"

Percy, pleased with himself, nodded and said, "Please?"

"It was on a train platform..."

Spoo watched from the main deck as the two missing Japanese soldiers returned, floating between them a massive clamp supported by a balloon. It looked like the kind of clamp used to lock together two pieces of wood – a big C-shape of metal with a screw part to tighten. Only this one was made to winch shut with a windlass. It was massive and lodged over the rail of the *Custard* and onto the deck flange, next to the starboard Gatling. The other part fit around the dock, bolting the airship to the city.

Once the clamp was secured and locked, the soldiers retied the weight-relief balloon to the dock, not the clamp.

Spoo was impressed despite herself. The lock looked near impossible to cut though, melt, or pick. Sure *The Spotted Custard* might rip free, but if it did the clamp would come along without its balloon, and it no doubt weighed enough to tilt an airship and render it unsafe for floating.

The Japanese soldiers bowed in a modest way to Lady Captain and Miss Prim and then left down the gangplank.

Miss Prim came bustling over with Anitra and the fishy lordling in her wake. "I'll take our guests to quarters. The sun will be up soon."

Aggie hoisted her crossbow, giving the fishy lordling one last glare, before swaggering off to Frenchie to see if he had any instructions for the boilers.

Miss Prim said to Spoo, "You're to pull in the gangplank and post guards at the clamp. It connects us to the city and presumably someone dexterous could climb aboard using it, if they really wanted, to try to free our hostages."

"Rather spiffy, to have hostages." Spoo frowned. "This our first time?"

Miss Prim said, "It worries me that you had to ask that."

"Where you stashing them?"

"Supposedly they are staying by choice, so guest quarters."

"You might wanna see if old Tash will wake up, sniff at 'em some. This one speaks the Queen's." Spoo let the tiny lady go. The fox-lady stumbled slightly, and the fishy lordling scooped her up in his arms, like a child. His face softened when he looked down at her.

Footnote appeared abovedecks. Tensions had relaxed enough for the cat to be interested. (Cats were sensitive to such things, they didn't always care, but they did know.) Yet there were still enough people to give him due attention.

Footnote swaggered around, tail crooked, sniffing feet. He didn't notice, or mind, that his master had fallen overboard. Spoo had made swift friends with the cat from the start, through judicious application of dried salt cod and the occasional kipper. She'd done this as a means to needle Virgil, to ensure that Percy's cat liked her best.

So when he spotted Spoo, Footnote trotted over, whiskers twitching.

Then he caught a whiff of something, probably the fox-lady. Spoo didn't know how cats felt about foxes. She assumed that any affection professed by the lady was entirely one-sided. As was often the case with cats.

Footnote went bottlebrush, hissed in a mighty way, and made for the mast and up it to the crow's nest, where he no doubt cowered. Nips would have to pacify him with nibbles. Nips also kept dried fish about to bribe cats. He was all right in the noggin, was Nips.

Spoo supposed Footnote might have reacted to the fishy lord. If Footnote hated him, *fishy* was a bad moniker. Spoo supposed she should call him the *scaly lord* instead.

Miss Prim took Footnote's disgust in stride. "Percy would say

that's a bad sign. He trusts Footnote's character assessment." She
turned baleful eyes on their guests. "Then again, I suppose you
pushed Percy overboard, Lord Ryuunosuke, so perhaps Footnote
is spot on?"

"She's a fox-lady, you know, a kissy-something," Spoo explained,
in case they didn't know.

Miss Prim nodded in that superior way of hers. "Yes, we learned
this. And important to Edo, for some reason. And this man is her
husband, or guardian, or something like that."

"Not husband," said the fox-lady. "And it is *kitsune*, if you please.
I do not go around calling your werewolves *wolf-lords*, do I?"

"They'd probably enjoy it if you did," grumped Spoo.

"*Kitsune* is the proper name. And names have power. So use
them with care, child of the skies."

Spoo waggled her eyebrows. "Do they really?" She wasn't sure
about being called *child*, but she thought *of the skies* was rather
grand. "What kind of power does *Spoo* have?"

"The ability to annoy everyone," replied Miss Prim. "Now go
pull in the plank, do. I'm taking our guests belowdecks."

"Hostages, not guests," crowed Spoo as she scampered off. *I
have taken my first hostage.* She was pleased with herself.

Miss Prim's sigh followed her.

Percy thought Arsenic had a nice childhood. Her parents' initial
courtship notwithstanding and her mother's profession to one
side, she'd grown up in the Scottish countryside under idyllic
circumstances. It seemed, from her descriptions, that her father
was warm and doting, and her mother a little cold, but practical
and helpful. He almost envied her.

He contributed some bits and bobs concerning his own
childhood, but he was ill equipped to convey what it was like
to grow up inside a hive, surrounded by adults all overly vested
in his safety and education at the expense of his autonomy and

wishes. The fact that he'd become withdrawn and insular was no surprise to Percy. He'd few examples of affection to call upon. Aunt Alexia and Lord Maccon being the singular exception. Their marriage, to his outside eye, had always been combative but never lacking warmth. Percy could admit to himself, if not to Arsenic, that he was attracted by their model of a profound and loving relationship, if perhaps hoping for a little less rushing about and banging of heads together.

To be honest, he liked what he and Arsenic had begun aboard ship. Quiet evenings reading. Perhaps his imagination could stretch to more than one cat? Perhaps to not going to sleep alone. Perhaps those evenings might include a bit more touching and kisses and such. He wasn't a complicated man. He didn't think this desire far-fetched. But it might seem tame to a lady of Arsenic's upbringing.

So he didn't mention it, merely prodded her for insight into her family, her sisters, her life. Hoping he might better understand her wishes and compare them to his own. He was not above modifying his hopes in order to accommodate hers. After all, he'd once imagined himself a solitary Oxford don, lording his intellect over rooms of terrified students, and retiring alone to his dusty quarters. That future had moved location to *The Spotted Custard*, where he still lorded his intellect and retired alone, but perhaps the alone part might be reformed?

They were many hours plodding (in Percy's case limping) in the direction of the city, mostly through fields until they came upon train tracks. These were a promising indicator of civilization, so they followed them as best they could.

They made a positive wreck of the paddies, clearly indicating their path, not to mention the huge sprawling flop of the parachute. Percy could understand the urgency to keep moving, to get to a place where they might hide, but they were terribly exposed in the interim.

As the horizon began to pinken, Percy found himself exhausted. They'd fallen quiet. Arsenic's posture was more bent than when they started. He tried not to lean upon her too much but his ankle seemed to have become one massive throb of agony.

They began to see small signs of human life.

Steam puffed into the sky ahead of them, marking the outskirts of Tokyo. A train station and possibly a village of some kind were just ahead of them. Structures at least.

"What do we do? Do we approach?"

Arsenic bit her lip. "Your guess is as good as mine. We need food. You need clothing. And if we could find a safe place to sleep for a bit, that'd be beneficial."

A huff-puffing noise rent the early morning air.

They froze.

Percy glanced behind them to see an engine chugging towards them.

They shifted off the track and kept walking. It wasn't like a train would stop for them. It was unlikely to be military, going so slowly and at such a time of day. Freight, probably. Surely the engines of industry were the same in any country?

If the train paused at the station ahead of them, they might be able to catch it there. If they wanted to stow away.

"Should we hop it?" He was nervous, that seemed a very athletic endeavour.

"If it is low enough to hoist on to? Then aye, we should. You canna keep walking on that ankle. If we lie flat to the top, we might na be noticed before we get to the city. 'Tis a risk, but the best option we have."

Percy pushed himself to move faster, queasy from the pain.

The engine chugged by him. It was a brightly painted particularly attractive version of most steam engines of Percy's acquaintance (Quesnel no doubt would've had more to say on the subject). Percy could see instantly why it wasn't in a hurry. It wasn't a passenger train. It also wasn't freight or cargo or anything one might expect. It was something else entirely.

Something he'd never seen before.

And he'd seen a train in the sky shaped like an elephant.

"Is that a *temple?*" Arsenic's big pansy eyes were even bigger in awe.

Percy nodded. "It certainly looks like. Do you remember the sketches in those travel journals?"

Arsenic nodded. "A temple on tracks. I suppose that's a little like those roving tent revivals in America. It makes odd sense."

Percy thought it quite practical, actually. Why not take the gods out and about, as it were? That way everyone got a chance to visit them. The reverse of a pilgrimage.

"I wonder whose temple it is?"

Arsenic was more focused. "If worshipers are expected, it means the train might pause awhile at that platform. Perhaps we can climb on." She was looking at the temple roof. It was that curly pagoda style, quite steep and slippery and difficult to stay on top of when in motion.

Percy got distracted by the architecture. It really looked like someone had uprooted a temple and put it onto tracks, with little concession made to the fact that it was a train car and not an actual building. Although the structure was longer and narrower than he supposed one might expect of a stationary temple.

It pulled into the station in front of them in a measured way.

The platform was raised above the surrounding fields, and designed like a village green. It had the air of a formal garden about it, with beautifully tended trees, topiary, carefully smoothed gravel, and artfully arranged boulders. When the train stopped, the temple was sitting within quite pretty grounds.

"Pretty." Arsenic's voice was low. "No one is there to meet it."

"That's interesting, isn't it?"

"Aye, but it means it might na stay long."

"Excellent point." Percy hobbled faster.

Then they heard a loud whining horn – akin to the mating cry of a constipated bagpipe. It struck something deep in Percy, a reminder of unbearable country house parties when the local gentry insisted on riding the hunt. A horrible custom that Percy objected to on principle because it occurred at inappropriately early times of day, and required both an entirely new wardrobe (including a crimson jacket, indeed!) and an excellent seat. Percy was, much to his embarrassment, a *very* good shot, but he couldn't ride a horse any more than he could ride a limp baguette.

All to say that although it was not the *same* sound, it was certainly a noise that reminded Percy of the hunt, and he knew without any question that he and Arsenic were the ones being hunted.

TWELVE

Kitsune Are My Weakness

It was not a pleasant noise. It was the sort of sound that shivered the hairs down the back of Arsenic's neck in a way that heralded *threat*. Militia or constabulary or the equivalent.

Arsenic straightened under Percy's weight and tried to chivvy him along. Poor sod, his ankle had to be killing him. It hadn't been in great condition to start with and they'd just walked miles and were now running.

Over her shoulder she could see kicked-up dust and bouts of steam, chasing them. Not on the track, but next to it.

Arsenic kept glancing back and eventually the figures became more distinct. It was definitely militia, possibly military. They moved as a cohesive group and sported some kind of uniform. Could be both, of course, in some countries there was little distinction between local constabulary and standing army. The men moved together in such a way as to suggest that either they were highly trained, or their transportation devices were attached to one another. Since their attire was mostly black and yellow, they unpleasantly resembled swarming wasps.

They rode what seemed to be bicycles but with the assist of a steam engine, or multiple small engines, because of the smoke and general speed of their approach.

Arsenic and Percy attained the hopeful safety of the train platform-garden before the wasps. They had to hoist themselves up. Both of them struggled, Arsenic because she was short, Percy because he was injured. Also, neither of them was as fit as they ought to be. Too much sitting around in libraries, Arsenic remonstrated with herself. They were both in for a world of aches and pains tomorrow, as their bodies reminded them that they'd recently trekked a vast distance after months of walking no further than the poop deck.

That was assuming they got a tomorrow.

A loud *whizz* and *bang* rent the early morning air, and a garble of Japanese meant that the wasps were within shooting range.

Arsenic and Percy were horribly exposed, running across on top of the platform to the temple. Percy clearly ignoring his ankle in favour of his life.

More gunshots.

Fortunately, none of them hit anything living.

The temple doors were those big double kind, much less flimsy than in the Paper City. She and Percy tried to slide them to the side, but nothing happened. They tried pushing and pulling, still nothing.

Arsenic banged on them while Percy looked around and began poking and prodding at anything that stuck out or looked movable. He was trying for a release valve, or a door pull or a butler bell. Finally he latched on to a long luxurious thick gold embroidered ribbon, not dissimilar to the obi currently wrapped around his leg. He pulled it down so hard he almost swung from it.

Inside the temple train a tremendous gong reverberated.

The doors to the temple slid aside.

Two ladies stood before them, or Arsenic thought they were ladies. They were dressed not unlike Lord Ryuunosuke in scaled shiny armour, only they were about Arsenic's height. Everything they wore was white or cream, and it occurred to Arsenic that this was the first time she'd seen a lack of colour in Japan. Everything so far had been bright and cheerful, from the lush

green of the fields to the red of the temple roof. Each guard
held a long staff in one hand with a wickedly curved blade at
the top.

Arsenic bowed low and poked Percy in the hip so that he did
the same.

Fortunately, the guards made concessions to their foreign
appearance and spoke Japanese slowly.

"Strangers?" said one.

"Westerners," said the other.

"Do you seek mercy?"

Arsenic thought quickly. "This is a temple to the goddess of
mercy?" she asked or hoped she asked.

"It is."

Behind them, the wasps had attained the platform and were
rushing towards them.

"Please, help us. Mercy." Arsenic waited for the next gunshot.

"We aren't criminals," added Percy. "We have done nothing
wrong except fall from the sky."

"You come from the Paper City?"

"Sort of, yes. Before that England."

The guards exchanged looks.

"The girl is welcome. The boy . . ." The guard looked at Percy
with great suspicion.

Arsenic pressed. "Is my husband and he is injured. He needs
mercy more than I." She pointed to Percy's ankle with the obi
wrapped about it.

One of the guards bent and examined it. "Lady Sakura
sent you?"

Arsenic decided lying was the better part of valour. "She did."

The guard straightened.

Simultaneously, both guards banged their staffs to the floor
and spoke in unison. It was a single long word that Arsenic
hadn't heard before.

Percy shook his head before she could ask. He didn't recognize
it either.

The guards stood aside. Arsenic pushed Percy to enter, just as the wasps came up behind them. She felt the rush of air as she evaded grasping hands.

There was a *shink* noise. They whirled to find the staffs lowered across the entrance, protecting their backs with sharp blades. The wasps were stopped dead at the door.

"I believe we've been given sanctuary," said Percy.

"Lucky break."

"I assure you, not customary in my experience. You must lead a charmed life."

She snorted. "Not so far as you'd know it. There's something more going on here. They werena surprised to find us."

Percy nodded. "Agreed. I wonder if they saw us fall and came to collect us."

All the while they murmured back and forth in English the guards and the wasps argued in Japanese.

It was a sublimely polite argument, but an argument all the same. Arsenic was nowhere near fluent enough to follow. But she stopped talking, in case Percy could garner anything.

There was no doubt that the wasps wanted to take them into custody, but the guards were against this. Or perhaps it was simply that the guards had taken them into custody in the guise of sanctuary, and they were now merely bones to argue over.

Several more temple guards appeared, also women in the white scaled armour, who looked them over with interest, and then took up position to support the first two.

Arsenic liked the idea of a female warrior force. They moved well, battle-hardy and fit, with muscles under those scales. They were not very big but they were sturdy. One had a scar on her cheek.

Arsenic had known a few female soldiers in her day. Hidden, of course, but they found their way to her when they could.

She tried a small smile and another deep bow to the new guards. It was silly of men to think women couldn't fight or wouldn't want to. She wished to show support and gratitude.

Percy noticed they had more company, and also more protection, and bowed himself.

Arsenic was relieved, at least he could be trained.

The argument continued.

Arsenic looked to one of the newcomers and tried hesitant Japanese. "Perhaps if we were removed from view, we would be less tempting?"

The woman's eyes narrowed.

"This is a good idea," said a new voice.

Arsenic turned slightly, still vested in keeping an eye on the wasps, to find they'd been joined by a lady. Or she assumed this was a lady, for she was dressed much like Lady Sakura in layers of robes and a wide obi with that big poof out the back.

Unlike Lady Sakura she looked healthy, tired but not ill, and her eyes were bright in a way that suggested something otherworldly. Either human power or supernatural ability.

The sun was up, not something most supernatural creatures could tolerate. So Arsenic went with assuming this was a very important human person. Perhaps head priestess of the temple?

The lady was also quite androgynous, and after weeks spent socializing with Anitra, Arsenic's doctor's eye took in a certain arrangement of bones and throat and hands that might indicate biology and dress were more complicated than at first glance. Still, if Anitra had taught Arsenic anything, it was to respect presentation, so she bowed. "Lady."

Percy followed her lead.

The lady's responding bow was almost curt, foreshortened, which Arsenic knew had something to do with social rank.

"Lady Manami," she introduced herself.

"Arsenic Ruthven, Percival Tunstell," replied Arsenic.

"You're not Japanese," sputtered Percy. Thank heavens he hadn't said anything more dire.

"Neither, fire-hair, are you." The lady did not seem to take insult at Percy's blunt statement. She turned to the guards. She spoke Japanese more slowly and carefully than the locals, and Arsenic was grateful for it. "Shall I remove temptation?"

One of the guards answered, "This could become complicated."

"Did they cry mercy?"

"They asked, but the formal words were never spoken."

Lady Manami turned back to them. "Do you seek refuge, strangers?"

Arsenic flinched. "Does it come with obligations?"

"Of course. But we could hand you over to them, if you prefer." She gestured to the wasps. "And we will have wasted our journey."

"So you did see us fall. Why na stop on the track and pick us up there?"

"This temple must be at rest in what you would call consecrated ground. Otherwise authority overrides mercy."

Percy said, "And what will they do to us?"

"Prison, death, difficult to tell. There are factions with conflicting perspectives on foreigners. It's untidy."

"Politics," said Percy in an exhausted tone of voice.

Lady Manami inclined her head, elegant and sure. "As you say. So, us or them?"

Percy looked to Arsenic, eyes desperate.

She wondered if this was a sign of their future life. She did not deny that she wanted the prickly ginger boffin for herself. She'd accepted her fate the moment she called him *m'eudail*. Percy would have his opinions, of course, and much to say on all subjects, but in the matter of safety he would yield to her expertise. He'd decided to trust her, and for Percy that meant trusting his whole heart and body.

He let Rue boss him around as navigator, and Primrose boss him around about his personal affairs, and Virgil boss him around about his wardrobe. Percy was the kind of man who identified an expert and then ceded control, complaining all the while. He'd apparently decided that she was the expert on his safety. That, she'd been trained for, his heart was another matter.

The safeguarding of another's emotions was a serious undertaking. Arsenic could only hope she was up to the task. Although she realized she wanted to try.

His eyes were big on her face and she wanted to smooth over his red eyebrow, or stroke down his neck, like comforting a bird. "Arsenic?"

In this decision she had some measure of confidence. She couldn't explain why, but she liked Lady Manami. And she definitely approved of the guards.

"You," she said, without hesitation. "We pick you."

Lady Manami spoke the same long Japanese word that the guards had before they crossed staffs to defend against intruders.

The new guards instantly stepped forward to back up their colleagues.

Lady Manami turned and, using small tight gliding steps, led them to the side and into the temple.

The sun rose over a *Custard* clamped tight to the most beautiful city in the known world and an excess of birdsong.

Spoo slept. It was the deep sleep of one who knew that decklings and deckhands were keeping an eye on her airship. Even a few greasers, firemen, and sooties were up top through the morning, to watch over the clamp and the safety of *The Spotted Custard*. Some out of duty, most out of curiosity.

They shared out Quesnel's dart emitter and Aggie's crossbow, much to Aggie's horror. Frenchie had to issue an *order* at her. Because if Lady Captain had ordered Aggie to give over her crossbow, the head greaser would have gnawed the captain's face off. Aggie slept nearby, because she didn't trust anyone shooting it except her. Interesting to note that she slept at all. Spoo had thought Aggie spun herself a chrysalis and hibernated inside like a grub once a year.

Lady Captain muttered something about buying Aggie two

more crossbows simply to stop her fussing, which was just *like* Lady Captain. Reward grumpy behaviour. Honestly, Spoo sometimes wondered if Lady Captain actually liked Aggie, or if she was nice in order to annoy the redhead.

Before she dozed off, she heard someone report that the hostages were asleep. Which made sense, seeing as they were both supernatural creatures and the sun was up.

Spoo thought she'd only rest her eyelids for a bit, swinging in her favourite hammock. But she slept like the undead. She woke only once, when the lantern lights blinked out, because the birds started chirruping as if it were their duty to the Great Almighty. Then she remembered that they were docked in an air city and of course birds would be all in with that concept, and promptly went back to sleep.

By luncheon everyone began to stir, and by afternoon tea, the crew was back in form. They'd also managed to draw a bit of a city crowd. The dock filled with fancy local mucky-mucks and tradesfolk and such, all wearing brocade robes and stony expressions. They came, stood in silent interest, and then drifted away again, only to be replaced by others. Never too many at once, and never rowdy like dockside most cities. Still, it was clear that word had spread of an English ship clamped down to Edo – foreigners of interest.

A crowd, even a small polite one, put Spoo's people on high alert. She sent Nips, who'd once *mayhap* been a bit of a pickpocket (though they never mentioned that to the toffs), to walk among them. He caused a bit too much of a stir for stealth. He didn't pinch anything, not even information, since he didn't speak Japanese. He climbed back aboard via the clamp (proving how easy it would be) looking shamefaced.

Spoo slapped him on the back. "Can't win every port."

"Never happened to me afore, Spoo. They all up and *saw* me!"

"Taste of adulthood, I suspect."

"Horrible."

"Too true. Could even get too big to float."

"Not me," said Nips proudly. "Me da never went much over ha'penny size."

Spoo nodded, pleased for him. He'd stay slight and nimble. And he knew his dad. Spoo had no idea what she was in for when she turned all over woman. No idea at all.

It was a horrible slow day because they hadn't *anything* to do. Lollygagging about was only good for short spurts. Normally when they were in dock, Spoo and her fellows ran the restock, explored the city, or otherwise adventured. This was as bad as being in the grey. Only in the grey at least she knew they were heading *somewhere*. Right now they weren't moving.

Spoo hated being still.

So she did what any deckling of sense would do, she set to figuring out how to break the clamp. The thing was designed well, and so far they'd hadn't found any weak spots. Eventually she decided that they'd best involve their Frenchie in the matter.

Quesnel got all twinkle-eyed over the idea. "Could you make me some sketches, Spoo? Without anyone noticing."

Spoo wasn't an artist but she said she'd do her best.

And she did. Trying to get as much of the workings as she could with a bit of paper and stylus, then she brought her drawing down to engineering.

Quesnel was as flummoxed as the rest of them. "We know what the material is?"

"Steel most like."

"Hard to even melt that. Any weakness in the welds? The design itself is spot on." His tone was all genuine admiration.

Spoo shook her head. That had been her first thought too. "Brute force ain't the answer. We need us something *refined*."

"Ask Rodrigo, sabotage is more his kind of thing."

So Spoo went to the Italian next.

Rodrigo was weird. He was extra grumpy about the fox-lady being aboard, since he objected on principle to Tash. Another shifter was adding insult to injury. When Spoo woke him up to ask about clamps, he threw a shoe at her.

Spoo supposed that was fair. She'd busted into his private quarters, with his lady right there and without her veil and all. Aristocracy got odd about privacy.

Spoo wondered if there was a way to cut out a big circle where the clamp fastened to the *Custard*'s deck. It would weaken the ship's structure and it was right next to Spoo's beloved Gatling gun. But it was only clamped to the deck and flange of the railing, and honestly they didn't exactly need all their deck to float. Did they?

She went off to ask Lady Captain if she might start sawing around the clamp. Did they have a wood saw to do this with? And would the captain mind if Spoo basically made a ruddy big hole in her airship?

Of course Spoo would have to do it in such a way that it wasn't obvious to the crowd below, which now included more military men and other official-looking types.

Her afternoon was looking up.

Percy paid attention to interior decoration insomuch as to investigate other people's libraries but nothing else. He was well aware of social status conferred through opulence. He had, after all, been raised by vampires. But he could never bring himself to care.

However, if he were to enjoy any interior it would be the one afforded by the Japanese temple train. It was sumptuous without being garish or cluttered. The temple managed to convey a restful beauty and a sense of welcome. He couldn't pinpoint the details, and it wasn't in his nature to do so, but he *liked* it. Since he rarely liked *anything* (apart from his cat, his books, and Arsenic) this surprised him.

Lady Manami led them around a corner out of sight into what

amounted to a receiving hall. She then stopped and instructed them to remove their shoes.

Percy wasn't sure how to proceed. Exercise and now the sudden sense of safety had rendered any weight on his ankle unbearable. He was wearing a jacket tied about his waist to avoid exposure. Any action he took to remove shoes would be ungentlemanly. He decided to throw all sense of decorum to the winds and simply sat on the floor to pull them off.

Arsenic, with a shrug, did the same. She sat next to him, bent double to unlace her bicycle boots.

No corset then.

Percy approved, *practical.* He'd never understood stays.

Lady Manami managed to loom over them and smile down in a slightly aggressive way. Percy concluded that the smile was a surer indication than anything else that she wasn't native to Japan.

"Where are you from, originally?" He'd never learned to button up his curiosity.

"Oh, all over." She was as evasive as Aunt Softy. "Come along, child. Let's get you cleaned up and that leg tended."

"I'll do it," insisted Arsenic, helping Percy to rise. He supposed a thousand Englishmen around the world cried out that he took aid from a woman, but he was never one to accept lightly the illogicality of custom. Tradition seemed to him a poor excuse for inconvenience. Also he rather enjoyed her fussing over him.

"Wifely duty?" wondered Lady Manami, eyes sparkling with some hidden amusement.

"Professional courtesy," replied Arsenic.

Lady Manami was surprised, in the manner that indicated this was an unusual sensation. "You are a doctor?"

Arsenic nodded.

"Fascinating. I did not think Westerners allowed such." She led them further down the hall and into a small side room.

Arsenic tilted her head. "Says the roving temple with the female guards."

Percy looked around. The decoration was not dissimilar to the entrance of Lord Ryuunosuke's residence in Edo. There were stiff cushions on the floor and low tray-like tables set around. Lady Manami gestured with one graceful arm to two cushions. Percy sat. He was grateful for the low seating, as it allowed his injured leg to stay relatively level.

"There is a great deal you do not know about Japan. The English are not so secretive. So I have the advantage. You *are* English, yes? All Europeans look alike."

"English," said Percy.

"Technically Scottish," replied Arsenic.

Lady Manami tilted her head. "It is not the same?"

"Na if you ask a Scot." Arsenic was intractable on this subject.

"Ah yes. We have that here, too." Lady Manami pulled out a tiny gold bell which had been hanging in a cluster from a stick in her elaborate hair arrangement. She rang it.

Immediately a young lady in simple robes came in. Lady Manami issued a set of instructions in rapid Japanese that Percy followed only loosely. She was asking for hot water, and probably bandages, and he suspected if they were lucky, comestibles.

"If I may?" Arsenic asked, gesturing to Percy's leg.

The lady inclined her head.

Arsenic bent to unwrap him.

The release of pressure made his ankle hurt worse. Percy only just managed to hold back a yelp. A few tears leaked down his cheeks.

"I'm a terrible baby," he admitted to the two women in profound embarrassment.

Arsenic glared at him. "Dinna be a ninny-hammer. You're in pain. 'Tis perfectly natural." She turned to their hostess. "She's bringing hot water for cleaning? Can I also have cold for soaking?"

Percy looked down and was impressed despite himself. His ankle was three times its normal size and a spectacular purple colour. *At least it looks as bad as it hurts*, he thought, smug.

"When she returns. Meanwhile, perhaps you might tell me how two Westerners fell out of the sky. And why one of them is wearing Lady Sakura's gift as a bandage."

"You know the lady?" Arsenic prodded.

"We are friends of a kind."

"Of a kind. Are you supernatural?" Percy was being too blunt, but he wanted answers.

"Are you?" Lady Manami responded. A fan of the Socratic method, apparently.

"Perfectly human, but my mother is a vampire." He used the word *jikininki* for vampire, because so far as he could tell it was the closest they had in Japan. Although his reading suggested they were more like the flesh-eating breeds found in India, and regarded with similar abhorrence. He wasn't sure if a familial association would stand him in good stead or not.

Lady Manami started. "That is not possible."

Percy grinned at her discomfort. "My sister and I were born before her metamorphosis." He used the English word, because he had no idea what it was in Japanese. "She was bitten shortly after, so we've only really known her as a vampire."

"A queen, she would be."

Percy nodded. "Like your Lady Sakura."

"She told you that?"

Arsenic interjected, "We guessed."

Lady Manami nodded. "So, children, if you will tell me all you know from the beginning I will try to honour you with the same. Is that a fair exchange?"

The servant girl came back into the room followed by several others. They carried two bowls of hot water, several rags, and some long clean strips of silk to act as bandages. Another had food and the last a tray with what looked, to Percy's delighted eye, like tea things. He suddenly realized how hungry he was.

Lady Manami sent the servant girl back out for cold water and a bowl large enough to fit his whole foot.

"And a splint," added Arsenic, using the English word.

Lady Manami was perturbed. "I do not speak your language, girl. I only know your important words. Like *tea* and *jewellery*."

Arsenic looked to Percy for aid. Percy consulted his brain. "A stick of wood about this long." He made a shape with his hands, looking to Arsenic for agreement.

"A little longer," she amended. "To wrap with cloth to keep the leg from moving."

It was the best they could do, but Lady Manami seemed to understand. She said something more to the girl, who Percy supposed was the butler for the temple. All the young ladies trooped out, leaving the three of them alone.

Arsenic began cleaning his ankle and feet.

Lady Manami left her to it and began to pour tea.

The pot was strange, spouted like an English teapot but with a top handle made of rope and an egg-like shape. The cups were small, almost demitasse, and with no handles or saucers. The tea appeared to be green and served without milk or lemon, but Percy was disposed to be pleased with whatever was put before him.

"We do not have time for a proper ceremony," lamented Lady Manami, "not that foreigners would know to expect such."

Percy said, hoping it wasn't rude, "Much more interested in simply getting tea into me. Thank you."

Lady Manami regarded him with amusement. "Sensible boy." She passed him the tiny cup.

Percy sipped, eyes closed, happy.

It was perfumed and quite grassy in flavour but warm and necessary and comforting. Percy drank gratefully.

Arsenic took her cup with a polite thanks, but put it aside to continue her ministrations.

The possibly-a-butler returned with a large bowl of water.

Arsenic arranged Percy so he might bend his leg and plunge his foot into the bowl. It was shockingly cold but the horrible throbbing in his ankle faded to aching numbness.

"Have you willow bark for pain?" Arsenic asked.

"Vi-yow?" replied the lady, thrown over by the word.

Arsenic sighed. "Of all the things we might have right now, I find myself wishing for a Japanese language book the most."

Percy nodded. "It's always a book one misses." He tried to help. "A tree, lots of leaves, each one long and thin and light green. Grows near water, sometimes it weeps." He made a gesture with his hands to show the curve of a weeping willow.

Arsenic added, "The skin is boiled and used for pain or fever."

Lady Manami shook her head. Either they hadn't communicated properly, or she didn't know medicine, or there were no willows in Japan.

Percy resigned himself to pain and enjoyed the cold water while he could.

"Just a splint, please, and I'll stop making demands," said Arsenic.

"I highly doubt that from a doctor," replied Lady Manami, dismissing her servant. "Now, explain your presence here."

So Percy and Arsenic attempted to do so. Starting with Edo, and the general excitement in the Paper City when they found out *The Spotted Custard* had a woman doctor, and moving to meeting Lady Sakura and Lord Ryuunosuke.

The head servant interrupted them only once, carrying a flat wooden cooking utensil that looked to be a good length and stiffness to become a splint, and another pot of tea, smaller and with only one cup, which she placed near Percy, eyes lowered, as though she were scared of him.

Percy thanked her gravely.

She hurried out, sliding the doors closed.

"Lady Sakura is worse?" Lady Manami resumed their conversation.

Arsenic sipped her tea. "She's fading. Silly of them to keep trying human doctors. Her illness is clearly supernatural."

Percy added, "They are using her to tether an entire city. What do they expect?"

Lady Manami's eyes were sharp. "Your mother is a vampire queen, of course you would understand and sympathize."

Percy resented being accused of either.

"That's how we ended up here," said Arsenic. "Percy got angry about it. Percy never gets angry."

Percy hung his head. "I overreacted." He said it in English, for Arsenic's benefit. This was all his fault. The one time he let his emotions get ahead of him.

"What happened?" pressed Lady Manami.

So they explained about returning to the *Custard* with Lady Sakura, and the soldiers, and everyone getting angry. And them figuring out that Lady Sakura's link to her people was being used to keep Edo in place.

"Kitsune," explained Lady Manami, "are bonded strong. From what I have read it is not unlike your werewolves."

"Are you one of them?" Percy asked. "You are not as small, but I wager you're very light."

Lady Manami laughed. "Smart boy. What gave me away?"

"*Súilean geala*," suggested Arsenic.

"Gaelic again?" Percy put down his empty cup.

"*Bright eyes*, but the implication would be *otherworldly*."

"Do you *read* Gaelic, perchance? I've this manuscript I'd love your help with. Well, if we ever get back to the *Custard* I'd like your help with it. It's this fascinating little thing that—"

"Percy, focus." Arsenic was grinning at him.

"Oh right, sorry, Arsenic." Percy jumped back to explaining matters. "With Lady Sakura I didn't know to look, now I'm on watch. You're of a type." He didn't want to outright say she was arrogant and autocratic and capricious, like a tiny goddess.

"Am I? I should like to talk more on that subject but not now."

"No," agreed Percy gratefully because he didn't want to insult her, "not now. But are you kitsune? You must be very old to function so well in daylight, unless that rule does not apply to your species."

She gave him a thoughtful look. "I am *huli jing*. It is similar.

You might say fox spirit so *kitsune* is good enough. Some have called me *jiuweihu*, but you would have to test me to find the truth. I am not part of Lady Sakura's obi."

"Her pack?"

"Good enough. My kind of fox, we travel, do well alone. Hers no. She has been separated from them, and stretched because she misses them. Without them, she is too much trapped. And without her, they are too much free."

Percy considered. "Do they go mad?" *Like packs without Alpha or an Alpha gone too old.*

"Kitsune are tricksters by nature, without their lady it is more that they go evil. The lady is the moral heart. She is the honour of the kitsune. With her gone, there is no good left in them."

This was fascinating, and Percy wondered if he might get a paper out of it. Really the different types of supernatural creatures were intriguing. Perhaps adventuring wasn't so bad. His ankle throbbed at him.

"Yet somehow a tether based in goodness is concrete enough to hold a city in place?" He had to use the English word *tether*. He could not keep the suspicion from his voice.

"You speak of *chi*."

Arsenic started to giggle. "Percy, 'tis a *moral foundation*! The church was right. Soul and all."

"Stop it, woman." Percy rolled his eyes. "I'm trying to understand the science in play!"

Lady Manami looked almost pitying. "Poor boy, to try to make logic out of magic. We will talk philosophy later."

Arsenic tapped Percy's foot to lift it out of the bowl. She dried it with a rag.

Lady Manami passed her a pot of salve. Arsenic sniffed it and then with a shrug applied some to his ankle. She then used the wooden cooking tool to splint up his leg, wrapping it tight.

"So, you, Lady Manami, are neither weak nor evil because you aren't part of her pack, her obi?" Percy pressed for comprehension.

"Exactly."

"Yet you're *involved*."

"Foxes like to meddle. Now is a time of change in Japan. Much meddling is needed. But with Lady Sakura otherwise occupied, her kitsune are meddling in bad ways."

"And this temple?"

"It is one of mercy and sanctuary, especially for women."

"Is the rest of her pack here?"

"They are all wild now. It is not good."

"Why not jump out of Edo, like we did?" asked Arsenic. "She has her special obi."

"Worse things would happen if she left. Lord Ryuunosuke, he would..." Lady Manami was darkly mysterious.

Percy wondered how wrong he'd been to hate Lord Ryuunosuke. Perhaps he too was acting against his will.

"Politics." Percy was unable to keep the disgust from his tone. He was eternally grateful that his mother's title was one of conference and not inheritance. He need never take a seat in the House of Lords.

"Politics," agreed the lady. "You should be warned, child, that you were permitted into the temple only because you were injured and claimed marriage. Yet I see no ring."

"You know our customs?" Percy felt a twinge of guilt at the deception. Or perhaps it was simply that he liked the idea of strangers thinking him good enough to marry Arsenic.

"I pay attention to those who conquer."

"Will you expose us?" Arsenic moved closer to Percy, put her hand over his. Percy welcomed the contact, accepting that he liked it when she touched him.

"Not yet, but I like knowing."

"You too are a trickster?"

"Did I not say I liked to meddle? And I have no obi to keep my moral code, perhaps I am evil." Lady Manami stood with infinite grace. "I think we must find you clothes, young man. I should check with the guards as well."

It occurred to Percy that she'd never answered his question about her being awake during daylight. She reminded him more and more of Lord Akeldama. Yes, a small cheeky version, full of mischief, but manipulative and measured and deft. Players of power did love delicate manoeuvring.

Percy wished fervently for his sister. He was horrible at delicate manoeuvring.

THIRTEEN

Breeches and Rutabaga

Percy quite dreaded what he might be given to wear. Not that he was averse to those relaxed-looking robes. Simply imagining his sister's reaction (if she caught him in one of them) was a joy. But he thought they might insist he wear scaled armour and what was an ordinary Englishman to do with *scales*? It seemed overly flashy.

Instead of scales, one of the servants proudly offered up a stack of carefully tended and well-preserved gentleman's attire. *British* gentleman's attire. And by *preserved* Percy meant for decades. The clothing, and he was hesitant to use such a moniker, was perhaps a hundred years old. He thanked her as earnestly as possible under the circumstances.

Perhaps he exaggerated a touch, but the jacket was of the kind one's grandfather wore in the 1820s. It was blue with puffy shoulders and large collar, and cropped in such a manner as to exaggerate certain frontal sectors of a chap's anatomy, sectors Percy was tolerably certain a respectable gentleman ought not to be exaggerating. Which was to say, he had received compliments in the past, but only from ladies who were monetarily encouraged to be positive on the subject. The jacket had tails like a wedding suit that flapped over his posterior, which was a little disappointing as Arsenic had indicated her interest in that portion of his anatomy and he now appeared to be offering up the reverse. Perhaps she was egalitarian in her taste with regards to the male form?

The vest was brocade and similarly tight. There was a stock involved, and a fluffy cravat. The fawn-coloured buckskin breeches were exactly that, and the Honourable Percival Tunstell had *never* worn anything like leather trousers in his life. He supposed they'd be less likely to rip open when tumbling out of dirigibles, but *honestly*!

Arsenic turned her back on him and bustled about with the food, while he squeezed himself into the attire and felt quite as if this were an opera costume and he ought to start grandstanding about with delusions of tenor.

"I seem to be decent again," he said. "Although only nominally."

Arsenic turned, regarded him. Her eyes went big. She unsuccessfully smothered a giggle.

"I know," he said, with as much dignity as he could muster under circumstances of *fawn-coloured* buckskin breeches.

"Percy, m'eudail, those are . . ."

"I know, *breeches*."

"Very tight."

"I know!" He was grateful the ruddy things stopped at the knee. They'd been challenging enough to get on with his splinted ankle. Whoever had owned them originally must have been about his size, with perhaps a little less meat in a few key areas.

"And *fawn-coloured*," Arsenic persisted.

Percy wondered if it was a doctor thing to be driven to blurt out the blindingly obvious, or perhaps it was a method of coping with shock. The breeches were shocking.

He made his opinion clear. "I *know*."

She pursed her lips together. "They're verra fetching."

"I know . . . wait, they *are*?" He couldn't tell if she was being serious or not.

"Mmm-humm."

"I'm ridiculous." He languished. Percy wished to impress

Arsenic. That seemed unlikely to occur, ever in his whole life, at this juncture. Fawn-coloured breeches were the definition of unimpressive.

She laughed. "Aye. But on the bright side, you're also fully dressed."

He perked up. "True. Very well then, but you'll explain to my sister? I mean if we are ever fortunate enough to reunite with them, she'll mock, and I'll come off as defensive."

"Aye, I'll explain."

He tore his eyes away from her delight in his misfortune, which made her eyes bright and her smile easy. The outfit could not possibly be that bad if it pleased her so much.

He realized that there was something quite exciting set out on one side of the room.

"Food!"

Not that he hadn't seen it earlier, it was only that he finally noticed it. There were little dumpling-like things in wooden bowl-baskets, some slightly mysterious-looking fruit, and vegetative matter. Some of the produce he supposed was for display purposes, as it was offered up whole and in naked glory.

Rather like his posterior only moments before.

Percy scooted on his cushion across the floor, so as not to bother with his leg.

Arsenic walked back to her cushion and sat with a lacquered tray-plate in her lap from which she began daintily sampling foodstuff. Her peaked eyebrows occasionally wiggled in interest. "This bright yellow thing is pickled, I think. Sour and a little salty. Are you a fan of pickling?"

Percy could murder a gherkin given the slightest opportunity. "Absolutely."

He grabbed up a bowl, because it felt safer than the tray-plate and more familiar, and dumped some of the yellow pickled vegetable into it. He added a few other things, pleased to find recognizable white rice, dismayed to find only squat ceramic spoons for utensils.

He admitted to sampling a few things right there at the spread, which was bad form, but he was hungry and bewildered, and he didn't want to have to scoot back to get more of something he unexpectedly enjoyed.

His eye was caught for a long moment on a spectacular mound of root vegetables. They were arranged as if for the paintbrush of an Italian master. They looked faintly familiar and yet not, thus holding his attention rather long.

Percy had gone through an admittedly somewhat depressing agricultural phase, with a particular focus on researching root vegetables. He couldn't remember why. It had lasted only a few months, but one of the offerings on the table reminded him vividly of a vegetable that he'd studied in depth. He simply couldn't remember *which* vegetable. Perhaps a radish of some kind? He tried to recall the name.

"M'eudail, you're meant to *eat*, na stare."

Percy plucked up the confusing root and scooted himself back using his good leg, carrying his bowl in one hand and the root in the other. "Darling, what about—"

"Not *darling*. Darling is what my mother calls my father when she's cross with him."

He stared at the root. *A turnip of some kind?* "I did ask what form of endearment you'd prefer."

"Dinna think endearments ought to come along naturally?"

"Arsenic, I hate to say it, but endearments, as a general rule, may come naturally to some stout gentlemen of fine moral fibre, but certainly not to me." He set the root on his thigh, which was not at all slippery because *buckskin*, and grabbing up the stubby spoon, tucked in.

"Give it time. Now, how long will we be safe in this temple? Will an ordinance be required to extract us? A higher power? Or could it be stormed by the army or an angry mob?"

Percy blinked at her. "Do you think that likely?"

"Weel, clearly some authority knows that we're here and wants us. We're na supposed to be in Japan at all. The temple canna simply dash around, scooping up any peely-wally foreigner it wishes. That grossly undermines government authority."

"Unless there are politics to that effect in play?" Percy liked the rice, it was a little sour and sticky. The root continued to confuse him. It had what looked like more roots at one end. Was it a tuber or a large legume?

"Weel, I suppose we're safe for now, but we should probably suss out passage back to Edo, or better yet the *Custard.*"

"Rue will come for us." Percy was convinced on this matter.

Arsenic put down her spoon and stared at him intently. "The captain will *try* to come for us, no doubt, but if the entire Japanese government is set against her? What can one ship do? An unarmed ship, no less. In fact, the *Custard* might have already been hounded into the aether."

Percy was incensed. "She would never abandon us and I resent the implication!"

"You are delightfully loyal, m'eudail. I only meant to imply that they could be lurking in the grey, scheming on how to extract us. We must determine how to get back to them. And I ken we must save Lady Sakura as well."

"Absolutely," Percy agreed. *What was that one root called? Rotunda? Roberta?*

"Percy, are you following?"

"Rutabaga!"

"Absolutely not," said Arsenic instantly.

"It *isn't* a rutabaga?"

"You canna use *rutabaga* as a pet name. Na even for a façade marriage."

"No, no. This root thing." He waved it at her. "It's a rutabaga, isn't it? Or perhaps mangelwurzel?"

"'Tis lotus root. Water lily, aye?"

"One can *eat* water lily? Remarkable."

"If you cut it open 'tis full of holes, like a loofah."

"So not rutabaga?"

"Nay."

Percy sighed at the root. "Would you include Lord Ryuuno-suke in your scheme to save us all?"

"I thought you hated him."

"He did push me overboard. But I'm beginning to think I was mistaken in his character." With the root quandary solved, Percy let his mind finally latch on to the thing that was bothering him the most. "Married werewolves, you know, they're always *better*. They work more for the common good, they fit easier into mortal life. It's like pack, only civilized. We talk about it as being *tamed*. But it's not that simple. It's being *loved*. It makes werewolves fit."

Arsenic's eyes were sharp. "It makes them good. Like a moral compass for a diminished soul."

"Lady Sakura is staying in Edo for *him*. Lady Manami said *goodness*, remember? Lady Sakura is her pack's tether, but something else is holding her there, in the Paper City. Her own tether. Her own *reason*. She stays because she needs to and that can only mean one thing."

Arsenic blinked spider lashes. "Love."

Percy nodded. "And they may act like vampires but *kitsune* means *fox*. She's a shifter. And shifter means that any hold over Lady Sakura has got to include Lord Ryuunosuke because he's her, you know . . ." He let himself trail off, hoping Arsenic might follow his reasoning.

"Mate," she said. "Oh dear."

Shortly after they finished eating, whatever was going on with the soldiers in the courtyard got sorted, because the temple closed its doors and departed the station. Arsenic and Percy stayed aboard.

Arsenic suspected that the authorities would follow them, but for now the temple won the day. She and Percy were safe.

Percy, silly man, returned the lotus root to the table as if it had disappointed him. He then rearranged the cushions a bit to lean back and, without any apparent effort at all, fell asleep.

Arsenic was also exhausted. The terror of having run across rice paddies, not to mention the fall that preceded it, rather rocked her mind and body in such a way as to weigh her eyelids down.

Percy had co-opted most of the available cushions to make himself an improvised bed. For lack of any other option, and because he looked ridiculously inviting, Arsenic curled up next to him. His normally frowning, mobile face was at rest. Up close she noticed that his eyelashes were red as his hair and his cheeks faintly freckled.

There was something about the man, secretly sympathetic, or emotionally harmonious. Others seemed to find him frustrating, but Arsenic found him restful. Touching him was comforting, and from the little smile and the way he curled an arm about her, she thought he might feel the same. She used his chest as a pillow and enjoyed his warmth. He was not entirely asleep, as it turned out. For as she nuzzled tentatively, Percy wound one long arm about her and tugged her close until she pressed against his whole side.

And it wasn't, it fairly wasn't that Percy made her feel safe, it was more that she made him feel that way. He valued her, for all he nearly called her *rutabaga*.

She had a sudden thought of curling up against him just so, in the library while they both read and petted the cat. Perhaps she might persuade him to get a bigger chair. If they ever made it back.

Arsenic dozed off, the motion of the train lulling her to sleep.

Arsenic woke to find her body had become one massive ache. Under her ear Percy groaned.

"I feel like a potato."

"Why the sudden affection for root vegetables?" Arsenic levered herself to one elbow and looked down on him.

It was still light in the room. The place was illuminated by high windows. She supposed it must be afternoon but it was disorientating, not to know how long she'd slept.

"A potato." Percy did not open his eyes, but tugged her back against him in a proprietary way that Arsenic found she didn't mind. She leaned on his chest with her forearms and looked down at him.

"Why a potato?"

"I feel as if I'd been boiled to within an inch of my life, then mashed, then whipped with butter."

"Sounds tasty."

"Painful was what I was alluding to."

Arsenic tensed suddenly. There was someone else in the room, someone watching them.

She forced herself to sit up. "Who's there?"

Percy remained lying down. "Are we under threat again? I'm too tired, let them have us."

Arsenic assessed the room. It wasn't big. It was well lit. There weren't exactly places to hide. Yet, when a strange woman appeared, it was as if she'd materialized out of the tapestry on the wall. Or as if she'd been there all along, yet so calm and quiet that the eye simply skipped over her.

Arsenic forced herself to look at the stranger. Her gown was simple and made of Japanese embroidered cloth, but cut in the manner of an Englishwoman's day dress. It was entirely devoid of fancy-work, almost painfully plain. The stranger was Arsenic's mother's age, but whereas Preshea kept herself trim and spent hours with cold cream of an evening, this lady did neither. She was matronly, well padded but over muscles, in the manner of a farmer's wife. She seemed the type of redoubtable woman who might whip up a custard with one hand and plough a field with the other. Her face was forgettable. Her hair had started life blond or red or somewhere in between but was now predominantly grey.

Her eyes were on Arsenic. They were not friendly. "Of all the ones they might send after me, they send Preshea's get?" She moved a little closer.

Arsenic stood defensively in front of the still reclining Percy. Her thigh muscles screamed at her, but she relaxed back to the balls of her feet and prepared to kick.

Her mother was a noted proponent of kicking, should physical combat become necessary.

"Dinna get ornery. He's the one they sent." Arsenic pointed down at Percy. "I'm an unplanned addition."

"A coincidence of such magnitude cannot possibly be unplanned," replied the Wallflower, husky-voiced and narrow-eyed.

Percy explained, from the floor, "It's complicated. But basically Aunt Softy sent me. Aunt Alexia sent Rue. And Arsenic is here because of a letter from my mother, which is probably also Aunt Softy's fault. But it seems the Kingair Alpha might be involved because she lives close to where Arsenic grew up and they all went to school with her mother. And there's also Madame Lefoux to take into account."

"Honestly," added Arsenic, "I'm beginning to question whether any of us actually have free will at all."

The Wallflower sighed and the strain in her voice faded. "They like to organize the world, my friends."

"Don't they just," grumbled Percy.

The Wallflower continued as though he hadn't grumped at her. "A long way of saying that the people who love me sent me a rescue. But you're veritable children and I'm doubting their methods. Neither of you seems particularly capable of a sophisticated extraction."

Percy said, "Fair point, since I'm currently doubting my ability to sit upright."

It was Arsenic's turn to bristle. "You're the expert who got stuck."

The Wallflower winced. "Terribly careless of me. My transport, erm, exploded."

Arsenic pressed her advantage. "Weel, we brought along the finest in modern dirigibles to fetch you back. We simply canna determine how to get us all up to it. And we're still trying to untangle the Lord Ryuunosuke situation."

"You're wondering what hold the government has over him that keeps him in Edo?"

"And by default Lady Sakura."

The Wallflower moved closer and it was almost as if the room brightened with her trust.

Arsenic pulled a cushion out from Percy's hoard and tossed it to her.

The Wallflower sat, oddly graceful for a matron taking up position on the floor.

"Will you tell us what you know, please?" Arsenic asked.

"It's not in my nature."

Arsenic sighed. "I'm Arsenic Ruthven."

"Yes, clearly. Preshea's girl."

"One of them."

"You look like her."

"I ken that makes things challenging."

"She was horrible."

"I'm na my mother."

"Understood. And you, boy? You're connected how exactly?"

"I'm Percy Tunstell."

"One of the twins. Thissleweight or Wisstlestop or ..."

"Hisselpenny. Mother was a Hisselpenny."

The Wallflower looked at them silently for a long time. "I find your generation exhausting. Was I ever so young?"

It was a rhetorical question but Percy took it literally. "Must have been. Still are, if that wedding is anything to go by."

"Wedding? Never mind."

The Wallflower was not the type of woman Arsenic would suspect of being an intelligencer. She was the type of woman who ought to be home in Cornwall with too many cats and a lapful of something chartreuse and badly knit. Which was, no doubt, exactly what made the Wallflower an effective spy. If Arsenic Ruthven knew anything, it was how to manage a spy.

So Arsenic was generous with information. She explained exactly what she and Percy had determined about the Edo situation. She articulated probable risks and likely prospects of rescue, and what they did not know and what they'd only guessed.

The Wallflower listened, face impassive but focus infinite. "You've done better than I thought."

"So tell us what we dinna know?"

"That is mathematically impossible." The Wallflower tried to be funny.

"You ken what I mean – about this situation."

"Lady Manami is strong. Alpha if you like. She might take over the kitsune pack, if Lady Sakura dies. Or has to die, to solve the tether problem. But that is only half Sakura's function in Edo."

Percy opened his mouth but the spy held up her hand. "Death is not my recommended solution. Just a conditional outcome. The kitsune *are* causing strife. Japan's government is fracturing. Those who want to open up entirely to foreigners, versus those who wish only the Paper City open for trade, versus those who want Edo destroyed. And that's the progressives. There are also those who argue for more secure borders and increased isolation. The kitsune go out among them all, needling and prodding, whispering in ears, seducing and manipulating with no other goal than chaos. Imagine, if you will, a pack without their Alpha but all of them disinclined to outright battle, and more inclined to social mischief."

"So what else holds Lady Sakura in Edo?"

The Wallflower stared at her own hands. Finally she said, "We British learned the wrong things from our supernaturals. We went out into the world with no idea but them. We built our armies around werewolf packs. We built our government around vampire hives. We failed to realize that it could be different. We failed even to understand there might be others. Supernaturals are not the same the world over. Any more than countries, governments, or people are the same. Our failure as a nation is in thinking not only that our method is best, but that it is the *only* option."

Arsenic tilted her head. "That's na verra patriotic."

"I'm not a patriot."

Arsenic tried to understand what the Wallflower was implying. *What's the weirdest pairing I can imagine?* What would be strange about Lady Sakura and Lord Ryuunosuke? A vampire and a shifter pairing, that would be madness. Or perhaps two shifters of different species? She knew that werewolves took wives, and even vampires married on occasion. But that was humans, they married *humans*.

"Is Lord Ryuunosuke a vampire of some kind?"

Percy said, "That seems unlikely, I'm thinking shifter. Snake or something, with that scaled armour."

The Wallflower nodded. "Yes, close enough. My research suggests, uh, dragon." She sounded unhappy to admit it. Probably because the very idea was something the English would find absurd. Because it *was* absurd – fantastical and mythological.

Which meant it was probably true.

"Oh dear," said Arsenic, "that's going to upset people." Poor Percy would have a devil of a time writing an acceptable paper on this revelation.

Percy grinned. "And I thought fox shifters were an outlandish concept. But dragons?"

Arsenic tried to keep them focused. "So what traps a dragon in a Paper City? Do they have his hoard or his egg or something to blackmail him with?"

The Wallflower shook her head. "Dragons are aquatic creatures. Forget everything you think you know from Western mythology."

"It does open up the possibility that we had them too. In the past. At least at some point." Arsenic's mind boggled thinking about Arthurian legends and winged iconography. "How could something that massive even fly?"

Percy, being Percy, explained, "It would be similar in principle to the kitsune. Control over density in order to shrink and expand apparent mass. I wonder what it is that allows shifters control over such in this part of the world, whereas in England there is a clear preservation of relative size. If Rue touched a kitsune would she change into a human-sized fox or would density control somehow transfer to her along with shape? Arsenic, what do you think?"

"You have the metanatural with you?" For the first time, the Wallflower's tone showed surprise.

"Aye. But we canna run that experiment. She's pregnant and any shifting could risk the bairn." Arsenic was firm on the matter.

Percy's sigh was sad. "Could we stay in Japan until after the baby comes? It would be awfully fun to experiment. The scientific community would find the information invaluable."

Honestly, Arsenic adored the blighter, but sometimes Percy could be exasperating. "Could we please concentrate on the matter at hand?"

"Oh yes, dragons. Lord Ryuunosuke has a dragon form, and when he shifts it's basically a big sea serpent that probably doesn't weigh much. Either that or one of the reasons there aren't any people in Edo is because he weighs about as much as a whole crowd of normal humans. Which would explain why the city was prone to shaking when he walked. In which case, if he's married to Lady Sakura, how would they even copulate? The weight difference alone. He would crush her and..." Percy seemed to realize he had gone rather too far in a conjugal direction, with two ladies in attendance. He flushed and lowered his voice to mumble to himself, "There must be an equation." And then, "I require a notebook."

"She could be on top," said Arsenic, because, well, she could.

Percy blinked at her. "She could? Oh yes, she could! Would

you, is that" – he cleared his throat – "Would you maybe like to try that sometime?" He went even redder.

"I would," said Arsenic, because she liked the idea.

"Oh," said Percy. Then softly, "Good."

The Wallflower said, "So you two are genuinely married? I thought that was a front. Lady Manami said that you wore no rings."

"We're na married," Arsenic assured her.

The Wallflower was appropriately shocked.

Arsenic pulled them all back to the point. "What is the hold on Lord Ryuunosuke? Because clearly that's our priority. Because of him, Lady Sakura is trapped as the Paper City's tether. Because of him, the kitsune are mucking about with politics."

The Wallflower looked ever-so-faintly smug. "That's the question, isn't it?"

"Is it also the objective?" wondered Percy. "I mean are we getting involved? Are we going to free the dragon and cause a revolution or what have you?"

"Generally speaking that's too bold an action for me," said the Wallflower.

Percy looked up at the ceiling as if he might see all the way through it to *The Spotted Custard* above. Presuming it was still there. "Well, it's not too bold for us."

"Your generation is very dramatic."

"I dinna ken what you're grumbling about," replied Arsenic. "From what I've garnered, all our drama might be construed as your generation's fault."

Things got progressively more peculiar from there on out.

The oddest thing, so far as Percy was concerned, was that he had evidently accepted the idea that dragons existed. He found himself seriously pondering how dragon metamorphosis might work. Were they bitten? Were they born? Was egg gestation involved? Perhaps the hold over Lord Ryuunosuke was, in fact, egg based?

It was *bizarre*.

Percy was finding, much to his distress, that the more he thought he knew about the world, the less he actually did.

The temple train chugged along, destination unknown.

The Spotted Custard floated far above them, location unknown.

Dragons and foxes were trapped in Paper Cities, reason unknown.

Percy was positively overwhelmed by things *unknown*.

It was not a comfortable position for an academic. So he focused on what he did know. The fact that apparently, Arsenic wanted to ride him in a decidedly explicit way. That he now knew what a lotus root looked like. He wondered if the two were connected. Then he had a sudden sense of inferiority, since a lotus root was quite large, by comparison.

In other words, Percy was undergoing a profound crisis of confidence while wearing buckskin breeches in a foreign land. He supposed he'd been in worse situations, but he couldn't remember them at the moment. And he missed his library.

What he got instead was a very large bathtub.

Occasionally in one's life, it turns out, one ends up in a large round wooden cistern of hot water, with a fox spirit and the woman one hopes to marry.

Or one does if one is Percy.

The temple train ended its lugubrious chugging run at sunset, at a station that was, if possible, even more unusual than the first. Instead of a courtyard arrangement, this one was landscaped with the express purpose of illuminating and celebrating, so far as Percy could tell, *water features*. Not waterfalls or birdbaths or fountains, but sinks and bathtubs. Things that ought to be hidden safely away behind firmly closed doors.

True, there were well-tended trees, clusters of exotic plants, mossy pathways, and beautifully arranged piles of stones, but then... there were large wine barrel contrivances which proved to be enormous bathtubs.

Communal bathtubs.

Percy found himself directed to strip and immerse himself in hot water – with other people. With women! The hot water was, quite frankly, not unwelcome, but to do such a thing in public when he was the *only* gentleman present?

Now, Percy knew perfectly well that there were such things as communal bathhouses during Roman times. He also knew that such structures still operated in certain countries formerly part of the Persian Empire. But these establishments were always described in Percy's books as being divided by sex.

Fortunately for his strained sensibilities, those wandering around outside of said tubs donned short robes. Unfortunately, those present were the ladies of the temple – priestesses, staff, and so forth.

Never in his life had Percival Tunstell voluntarily showed ladies his *bare* arms and legs by traipsing around an open-air garden in a smock. He was horribly conscious of the fact that his limbs gangled and his skin popped against the darkness, for he was unconscionably pale.

He blocked out any memory of the act of walking through the trees, removing his robe behind a bush, and scuttling into a wooden tub in which Lady Manami and Arsenic already reclined. He did not look at them. He could only hope they tendered him the same courtesy.

He would hold on to that hope for all his remaining years.

What he did remember later, was being in the hot water and trying desperately not to *notice* anything. When he looked around, as common courtesy required for conversation (because the ladies insisted on *talking* while they bathed), he made a point of meeting their eyes but *nothing* else.

Desperate for a distraction, Percy focused on trying to understand the plumbing of his current predicament.

The big wooden cistern was round and deep with a faucet part that was more an open-topped spigot that never stopped supplying fresh hot water. This suggested to Percy that there was a natural hot spring nearby to be tapped so indiscriminately. The general boiled-egg smell permeating the air supported this hypothesis.

As a result of the constant inflow, there was also a constant outflow via a spout-shaped drain to one side.

Percy had to admit that the hot water felt wonderful on his sore muscles (if horrible on his throbbing ankle), and he was delighted by the idea of becoming clean even if he must to do so in the company of two females.

Lady Manami appeared to find his discomfort diverting.

Arsenic seemed more comfortable than he, but Percy supposed that as a doctor she was accustomed to the naked body in its many forms.

To top it all off, the Wallflower joined them. Not in the hot water, but simply sitting off to one side, fully clothed, like a nanny keeping them company during bathtime – to prevent them from drowning.

Percy wanted to drown himself in embarrassment. "I mean to say, I'm open to new experiences but this is really beyond."

"Beyond what?" asked Lady Manami.

They were speaking in Japanese in deference to her presence, but Percy's mastery of the language was insufficient to cope with this crisis.

"The limits of my tether," said Percy at last. Tilting his head back and looking up through the leaves into the starry sky, hoping against hope there was a fat ladybug dirigible coming to rescue him.

Honestly, he'd sooner be hobbling across a rice paddy.

"Chi," the kitsune corrected him.

Percy latched on to the word. "I wonder if you might explain your understanding of this *chi?*"

The amusement in her tone suggested she was onto his diversionary tactics. "This is a good place for philosophy."

Percy supposed he often had epistemological revelations in the bath so he could see her point.

"Think of chi as the water around us. The tub is the kitsune, or one of your werewolves. The stronger the spirit, the bigger the tub. What you might call Alpha. Or queen. Lady Sakura's tub is big."

"So is yours," suggested Arsenic.

"Just so." Lady Manami nodded. "The chi comes from all around us – the world, living things. Spirits collect it, where humans cannot. This collection gives us immortality, certain abilities, like changing shape. But we cannot keep chi. It is always there, filling us up, but we must also let it out, overflow. That is what you call tether, the draining of the tub. For some the water is moved from one tub to another, or to many others, like a pack."

"Or hive." Percy frowned in thought. "And when there is an imbalance between too much flowing in and too little going out, that causes problems."

"Or vice versa." Arsenic was excited too. They both liked the scientific implications of the metaphor. Her eyes were bright and pleased on his face. Sometimes not just his face. Percy squirmed a bit but he liked it.

Percy switched to English to better articulate his thoughts. "So what would Rodrigo be? If the working hypothesis is that preternatural touch interrupts the flow of aether, then do preternaturals turn off the chi spigot?"

Arsenic grinned. "And metanaturals take over the whole tub?"

Percy wrinkled his nose. "I'm not sure if the metaphor can stretch that far."

The Wallflower spoke from the shadows. "I don't think Lady Manami knows what preternaturals and metanaturals are."

They switched back to Japanese.

Percy tried to explain. "We know others. Not *spirits* as you say. Human, but who take away the ability to change."

Lady Manami nodded. "We have legends for that. Japan has no word that I know for them. I might say *fangxiangshi*."

Percy pressed her. "And do you have legends of those who can become spirits for the space of a night? Humans who could be fox?"

Lady Manami looked surprised. "You know a flesh thief? I thought they were myth."

Percy was hesitant. "So we thought dragons. Would either a fangxiangshi or a flesh thief be useful in dealing with Lord Ryuunosuke's problem?"

"Fangxiangshi disrupt the chi. They do not break that which holds form."

Arsenic nodded. "A preternatural dinna break a pack tether merely by touching a werewolf. Rue dinna destroy the fabric of what it means to be a werecat when she borrows Tasherit's shape. Metanaturals and preternaturals interrupt the supernatural state but they dinna change the fact that their victims *are* supernatural."

Percy was uncomfortable with the word *victim*, but he let it rest.

Lady Manami smiled. "But a shakubuku might still help Edo's prisoners."

"What's a shakubuku?"

"A breaking of chi, an awaking."

"Tether snap, or something less severe?" Percy looked to Arsenic.

She wrinkled her nose. "Not sure, let her continue."

The kitsune did. "The dragon and his mate are stuck in the Paper City in all ways – spiritual, emotional, physical. A fangxiangshi might slice them free."

"So we should set Rodrigo at them?" Percy shuddered to think what their Italian might do if let loose in Edo.

Arsenic ruminated. "I've always wondered if supernatural abilities are basically an allergic reaction to aether. Instead of breaking out in a rash, they turn hairy on full moon. Too much aether, like the grey, and they go into shock, or fall asleep, or go mad. Preternatural is a momentary inoculation to aetheric allergies."

Percy was intrigued. "So how does tether to pack or hive fit into that?"

"It dinna, especially when it has physical components that react to the natural world, like holding a city in place." She sighed and swished about in the hot water. "I need to work on my theory."

The Wallflower said, "The longer I live and the more I travel the more I find that practicality is the enemy of wonder."

"But we *need* to understand," insisted Percy. "It's the only way to fix anything." He switched to Japanese. "The question is, Lady Manami, what exactly is the problem with Lord Ryuunosuke's chi?"

"Yes, fire-hair, that is the question."

"Is someone fiddling with his spigot?" Percy wondered, in English, causing both Arsenic and the Wallflower to chuckle.

Lady Manami said only, "Lady Sakura is sharing chi with her dragon."

"They are tethered to *each other*?" Arsenic's tone was all surprise.

Percy swiped a wet hand through his hair. "I've never heard of interspecies tethering before."

"Just because you've not heard a thing, doesn't mean it can't be true." The Wallflower waxed philosophical.

Percy pressed on. "She stays with him to keep him connected to chi, at the same time stretching her own? No wonder she is unwell."

"With only the little he's getting from her, Lord Ryuunosuke probably dinna have enough to shift forms or help," added Arsenic.

Lady Manami nodded.

"The solution," said Arsenic, "is to give Lord Ryuunosuke back his chi?"

Percy agreed. "Which is where, exactly? Is there a dragon pack? Or a dragon hive house?"

"Well," said Lady Manami, sounding cheeky, "you're sitting in it."

The Wallflower explained. "Dragons are water spirits. I believe she's implying that Lord Ryuunosuke's tether is to a hot spring. It's no more odd than a vampire queen being tethered to a London town house, is it?"

"The hot spring is not in good working order?" Percy didn't get the problem.

"What happens to a vampire queen taken from her house?"

"Oh! He's *swarming*? But slowly, because what? The locals have been piping away all his water?" Percy's brain hurt a little. "Are you saying this is a *plumbing* issue?"

Arsenic said, "The government imprisoned a water dragon in an air city because bathing is important. And his mate went with him to keep him safe and accidentally tethered Edo in place. The whole infrastructure grew around their tethers. So what do we do?"

"Destroy all the plumbing?" suggested Percy.

"And end civilization as we know it," added the Wallflower, in a tone that suggested she was being facetious.

Percy was tolerably certain spies shouldn't be facetious.

FOURTEEN

Dunking Is an Act of War

Arsenic supposed she'd had more peculiar conversations in her lifetime but not under more surreal circumstances.

The shared bathtub experience was odd and, to be honest, somewhat enjoyable. She thought a tub of such a size had some interesting medicinal applications. She wondered if she might build one for an infirmary someday.

Poor Percy remained deeply uncomfortable throughout. His muscles probably needed the soak – hers fairly did. With his hair wet, she noticed he had a nicely symmetrical skull. She did eventually use his ankle as an excuse to get them out.

The lad gave her a look of mixed horror and gratitude. Horror, presumably, at now having to determine how to extract himself *and* dress without complete exposure, and gratitude to have the trial by bath concluded.

Arsenic found Percy's awkward attempts at modesty endearing, if mainly useless. She was doctor enough to evaluate his frame medically, and woman enough to appreciate it. He had nothing to be embarrassed of, so far as she could tell both professionally and aesthetically.

She kept Lady Manami and the Wallflower talking as a distraction while Percy limped behind a bush after his robe. It transpired that Lord Ryuunosuke's tether source was a volcano of some ilk, west of Tokyo near a place called Hakone. Arsenic supposed if a dragon were to be tethered to a hot spring, volcanoes made perfect sense.

They now had to get to the other side of Tokyo. And convince *The Spotted Custard* to meet them there, with both dragon and fox. Her life seemed to be turning into an Aesop's Fable.

Lady Manami said she thought that Lady Sakura's pack should be summoned as well. She dressed and disappeared, presumably to send out invitations.

The Wallflower followed them back to the temple and asked, before they parted ways in pursuit of sleep, for the name of their preternatural.

"I'm aware of the metanatural, of course."

"Who isn't?" muttered Percy.

"She's not supposed to be kept secret?" The Wallflower seemed sublimely uninterested in their captain. Arsenic suspected this meant she knew everything there was to know about Rue.

Percy shrugged. "Imagine Rue keeping anything secret, least of all her own nature?"

Arsenic smiled. "Fair point."

"She keeps getting in trouble with the queen. Her marriage was pronounced *a good thing* because it might *settle her.*" Percy unsuccessfully tried to hide a snort. "Preposterous sentiment."

Arsenic agreed. Ten minutes in Rue's company was sufficient to divine that nothing would ever *settle* Lady Prudence Akeldama.

"Oh?" She pressed to see what Percy would say.

"A heap of flimflam and nitty-water, if you ask me." He did not disappoint.

They turned back to the Wallflower, remembering she was there.

She's verra good at being forgotten. Must get annoying, that.

Percy finally answered her question. "Our preternatural is

Rodrigo, Rue's cousin. Rodrigo Tarabotti, decent chap, once you get over him having dispatched so many people in his youth."

Lady Manami returned in time to catch the tag end of this explanation. "What did you say?"

Percy turned to her. "Rodrigo Tarabotti. That's our, how you say, *fangxiangshi*."

Lady Manami shook her head. "Tarabotti? Of course it is Tarabotti." She gestured for them to follow into the temple.

Percy stopped Arsenic with a touch and a question in his eyes.

"Aye, m'eudail?"

Percy dipped his head and hid a smile. It was rather adorable how much he liked the pet name, and how much he struggled to find one for her. Arsenic supposed she must have a tiny bit of her mother in her, that she enjoyed engendering discomfort in the man she adored.

Percy pontificated. "We must orchestrate a gathering. How do we convince the *Custard* to meet us at a volcano west of Tokyo?"

The Wallflower cleared her throat. "I might be able to get word to them."

"How? And why didn't you say so sooner?" Percy was understandably annoyed.

The Wallflower only became more bland in tone. "It's an illegal technique fraught with difficulty, only good for relatively short distances, and it presupposes that you have a certain individual aboard. I've been in the field awhile and I don't keep a close eye on logistics. That's what Goldenrod is for."

Arsenic didn't know that name. She looked at Percy.

Percy shrugged at her. "It's probably a secret, but honestly I can't remember what I'm supposed to hide and what I'm allowed to talk about. Goldenrod is Lord Akeldama, which means she's likely referring to Anitra. Anitra is his spy. Or we believe she is. She's never outright admitted it."

Arsenic nodded. "Better the spy you know than the one you dinna notice."

"Besides, one assumes Lord Akeldama knows everything or will soon enough. It's his only hobby. Well, that and absurd clothing." Percy shook his head. "I don't understand the man at all. He has all the time in the world. He could be doing *science*."

The Wallflower looked like she was hiding a smile. "Not all of us are cut out for academia."

"No? Pity."

"What should I put in the message?" she asked.

Percy looked at Arsenic for help. Arsenic was getting used to that. Poor m'eudail, he needed a keeper. Fortunately, he seemed to realize that, most of the time.

She helped. "We have the location. We need a time to meet up. Then we hope Rue's adept enough to get there, and to bring the kitsune and the dragon. When's full moon?"

"Tonight," said the Wallflower. "It should be up soon."

"Can you get them a message and can we get to the dragon's source before moonrise?"

"Maybe," the Wallflower replied, cautious.

"How many hours should we give?"

"Four should do it."

"Four it is. You'll need to tell them to bring Rodrigo, Lady Sakura, and Lord Ryuunosuke to Hakone at full moon." She turned to Percy and tucked a lock of wet red hair behind his ear. "They can figure out where that is?"

Percy accepted her touch without question. "It's on the map I left out in the library. Before Japan closed its ports, there were enough visitors to write something down, and hot springs were of interest. Now I understand why." He gave a disgusted gesture towards the bath.

"Trust the English to be fascinated by communal bathing," replied the Wallflower.

"I notice you didn't partake," snapped Percy.

She ignored him. "Shall we tell Lady Manami of our plan?"

"Do you trust her?" Arsenic asked, pulling her hand away from Percy. Really he did have a very nicely shaped skull. She wanted to keep touching, but they were in public and she liked it too much.

"I'm an intelligencer, girl, I don't trust anyone. I don't trust you. That's how I stay alive."

"Sounds lonely." Arsenic was glad her mother, for all her failings, had allowed herself to trust one man long enough to marry and be happy. Didn't the Wallflower even have that? "Have you no one at all?"

The Wallflower rolled her eyes.

"Are you ever going to tell us your actual name?"

"Since I have seen you both starkers, I suppose we can dispense with the formalities. You may call me Agatha."

Arsenic thought it exactly the right name, which made her wonder if it was the real one. Since Percy was looking grumpy, she answered. "Thank you. And you may call us Arsenic and Percy."

"Whoa!" said Percy.

"Oh, dinna fret. We're clearly on terms of some intimacy."

Percy wrinkled his nose.

The Wallflower drifted off, presumably to wherever she spent her time when she wasn't skulking near them in the shadows being cryptic. And to send a message to *The Spotted Custard*.

They made their way to the receiving room in the temple, which for lack of any other options, they'd adopted as their own. It was still full of root vegetables and cushions.

Percy wondered out loud, "So how do *we* get to Hakone? Is the temple taking us? Do train tracks go to dragon volcanoes?"

"I guess we'll find out."

"I like it when you touch me."

"I like it too. Your skeleton must be very symmetrical."

Percy grinned. "That's a nice thing to say, dearest."

"No, not *dearest* either, keep trying."

"Of course, my little mangelwurzel."

Arsenic was ridiculously pleased with him.

Sunset brought the lanterns back on and the Japanese captain and his soldiers back aboard the *Custard*. The two hostages remained below.

Spoo overheard Lady Captain instruct Miss Prim to wake up Tasherit and introduce her to the fox-lady. Even if the werecat fell immediately back to sleep, the captain wanted Tasherit's perspective on their guests. Spoo wondered if Tash would puff up like Footnote, metaphorically, of course.

Something happened, because the scaly lord came up on deck, looking shaken, or what Spoo assumed was the Japanese equivalent of shaken. Otherwise known as his helmet thingy being slightly askew.

He seemed not best pleased to see the soldiers. Lady Captain wasn't best pleased either, as Spoo gathered through the judicious application of eavesdropping on Anitra's interpretation efforts. Apparently, the Japanese had deployed troops to hunt Percy and the doc ground-side. But the two had managed to escape and hide in a roving church or something odd like that. It was all rather confusing.

Lady Captain expressed her opinion that if an army was after *her*, she, too, would run and hide, so really what *did* they expect? Especially when one of them had been pushed out of an airship. *Yes*, she now knew the scaly lord wasn't part of the army, but Percy didn't know that.

Spoo wondered why the scaly lord had pushed Percy. The lord couldn't have gotten emotional, that didn't seem like something he got. She wondered if he knew there was a parachute in play. She wondered if this was all contrived. Had he planned to be taken hostage? Whose side he was on, apart from his own?

The scaly lord revealed nothing. It was maddening. But he had brought his sword with him. That was telling.

It appeared that negotiations were not going well. Lady Captain expected to have her professor and doctor back by now. The guards expected to have their hostages back. But Lady Captain was refusing to give over the hostages.

Miss Prim returned abovedecks and relayed Tasherit's opinion on their guests. It was a cryptic, "Foxes and reptiles are annoying but not amoral." Miss Prim was now carrying her battle parasol.

Spoo crossed her fingers that they'd be able to negotiate one more night of grace. It being full moon and all. Except that the captain was a lady of action. *Leap first, everything else later* was her motto. If the army below had failed to retrieve her friends, then she would bally well do it herself!

Spoo began to inch away, towards where the clamp was fixed. Aggie and her crossbow were there, as well as a few other decklings, and a defensible position.

Everything quieted with the toffs.

With exaggerated care, Lady Captain picked up a large hard biscuit. She weaved this back and forth in the air in front of the Japanese captain's face. Ostentatiously, she dipped it into her cup of tea. She then withdrew it with a flourish and raised it high into the air. It sagged, dropped, and then disintegrated and fell to the deck with a *splat*.

All hell broke loose.

Apparently, in Edo, dunking one's biscuit was tantamount to a declaration of war.

Every soldier drew his gun. The deckhands stood ready to fight. Rue and Anitra looked fierce. The tea things scattered. Biscuits shattered. The carnage was unnecessarily tragic.

Spoo whistled three sharp short blasts. Tasherit Sekhmet might be incapacitated in their hold, but she'd trained them hard over many months. The decklings hadn't any guns, but they had mops, and knives, and all sorts of useful tools stashed about the deck. The *Custard* might have been stripped of obvious weapons, but no ship could be stripped of *all* weaponry. Decklings were nothing if not resourceful. *Make do* was essentially their battle cry.

They all knew what Spoo's whistles meant, even if the officers didn't.

The decklings quietly and efficiently armed themselves and shifted position. Spoo knew where every single one of her friends would go. Whether in the rigging (the better to swing around for dropdown access) or near the gangplank (the better to trip anyone trying to board or escape). One was behind a large barrel – bucket of slop in hand, prepared to render slippery disservice. There were many ways to fight, and when one was young and undersized, sabotage was the best option.

Lady Captain didn't know what her decklings were capable of. She didn't need to know. Spoo had made it her business to ensure that decklings were, above all things, *capable*. Their captain trusted them because of this, and that was good enough for Spoo.

With Percy gone, Lady Captain gestured Virgil into the nav pit. He was their next best navigator, assuming Quesnel stayed with the boilers. Their Frenchie had come over all odd since the captain got corked up, so he might defy orders and come above-decks if he thought she was in danger. But Spoo hoped he'd stay below. He was a better engineer than he was a scrapper.

Virgil would stay out of the brawling. He'd sprouted in the countryside, like a turnip, and couldn't fight any better than one. Spoo would never have thought she'd be friends with a valet from West Wittering.

Bork and Willard were good in a brawl, but they'd a dozen trained and well-armed soldiers occupying their deck. Not to mention the lord in scales with a ruddy big sword and no sense of his allegiance. They were outmatched, out-bladed, and out-gunned.

Anitra, the captain, and the head soldier were in fierce argument. Spoo realized she couldn't see Rodrigo. She suspected that with Anitra in the thick of things he was around, only hidden. This was good. Tasherit had taught them a lot, but she'd trained as a knight, or whatever her people called knights hundreds of years ago, old-fashioned military. Rod wasn't so fussy. He was all dirty fighting, designed to go up against monsters. He and Tash had done some display fisticuffs for them once. They were well matched, which was saying something because Tash was supernatural fast and strong, and Rod was only human. Spoo was beyond glad he was on their side. If he was off being stealthy, well, *good*.

"Ho there, Spoo," Nips hissed at her from behind the railing near the clamp. Unobserved, he'd snuck around from the other side of the deck. The boy was part spider.

Spoo didn't show in any way that he was there. Aggie didn't change her stance either. Finger to the trigger, bolt trained on the lordling.

Spoo whistled a long low note of understanding.

Nips said, "Herself wants us prepped to break free of the clamp."

"She does?"

"And a rescue option in place."

Spoo said without hesitating, "Get the mushroom filled."

"*Custard*'ll droop." The helium would be taken from the main balloon, which meant their airship would sink.

"Not with this clamp still holding."

"Then it'll tilt all over wonky."

"That's the idea, put some strain to it. So, go fill the dropsy. Stop flapping at me. She wants her prof back, she does."

"And we might be needing a doctor soonish."

"Go, Nips."

"But what if there's fighting?"

"Rod is nearby."

"He is?"

"Must be."

"Then I suppose a few of us can drop position."

"I'll explain to Tash why we did, if she ever wakes up and demands explanations."

Nips climbed away.

Spoo bent to check the state of the clamp. They'd sawed most of the way around it. The only bit left was where it held to the flange of the deck, the point where the railing attached. She thought it was pretty much ready to rip free. She hoped.

The crow's nest gave a warning holler.

Spoo braced for a cannonball impact. Instead a great flapping raptor bird of some ilk appeared off the port side, hurtling towards them. It was an eagle or falcon, only very large and definitely focused on *The Spotted Custard*. It whooshed close, under the balloon and right over the main deck where they all stood. A couple of the soldiers shifted to aim at it, although it was only a bird.

"Is that a pigeon?" screeched the captain. She had a horror of pigeons.

It was clasping something in its talons. Mayhap a big dead critter? Then the critter gleamed metallic in the light of the lanterns. Spoo wondered if it was an explosive.

Who sends a falcon to explode an airship shaped like a ladybug? It was all very animalistic.

The bird was near enough over the toffs that they ducked. Most of them. Lady Captain didn't bother, she was too short to mind, even with her big hat.

The bird dropped its prey, which landed with a clatter and rolled across the deck, coming to rest against Miss Prim's shoe. She shrieked and swung at it with her parasol as if it were a golf ball.

It skidded across the deck towards Spoo, stopping near Aggie, who, keeping her crossbow pointed at the lord, strode forward and glanced at it quick. Since it was made of metal, a gadget of some kind, and that was basically her whole world, no doubt she was mighty interested.

The object unfurled, revealing itself to be a toy. A clockwork dog. One of those sausage-shaped ones. It had four short legs and a small, spiky tail. Spoo thought it was kinda charming.

Steam emanated from its underbelly. Smoke came out from under its leather earflaps. It started tottering about, all on its lonesome.

Aggie reared back in horror and pointed her crossbow at it. She was terrified. Spoo didn't think Aggie could *get* that scared.

"Mechanimal!"

Everyone looked startled, but no one was as upset as Aggie.

Lady Captain yelled across the deck, "I thought those were illegal."

Spoo said, "Guess they aren't in Japan."

Aggie backed away as far as she could. "That's not Japanese. That's old Euro-tech *and* it's pre-compliance. In fact, it's English made, unless I really don't know my cog-and-bolt styles. Rhetorical statement, Spoo, because I *do* know them."

Spoo didn't want to set her off. "It's cute."

"It's a menace to society and a danger to all civilization, is what it is."

"Still cute."

The sausage dog swayed about a bit and then trotted hopefully away from them and towards the larger crowd, mechanical tail wagging in a reassuring ticktock manner.

The Japanese soldiers parted for the mechanimal warily, some guns pointed at it.

The only person who didn't move out of its way was Anitra.

Upon reaching the Drifter's feet the mechanimal stopped. Anitra wasn't in the least upset. Her eyes above her veil were crinkled in pleasure. He (Spoo decided the dog was a *he*) squatted down and emitted a tube of glass out his backside. The offering was shaped like a valve in one of those aetheric communicators.

Spoo found this act slightly disgusting and rude, and thus, of course, liked the little dog even more.

"Can I keep him if no one else wants to?" she asked Aggie.

Aggie snorted at her.

Anitra bent gracefully and retrieved the tube, not at all concerned by its source.

One of the soldiers made as if he would interfere, trying to grab the tube from Anitra.

Miss Prim bolstered up her parasol, flipped it spray-side and pointed it at him and his cohorts. They likely didn't know that there was acid inside. But the action was threatening. Well, it was threatening if you were the type to be scared by an inside-out parasol pointed at you. The parasol spray mechanism was pretty indiscriminate, and the acid was strong enough to hurt humans, even if it was intended for vamps. Miss Prim may look like a silly fluff muffin, but secretly Spoo thought she was a bit of a bruiser.

Something in Miss Prim's expression conveyed this to the soldier and he backed away from Anitra.

Anitra pulled a cork stopper out of the tube and fished about inside, retrieving a tiny roll of paper with a printed message. She read this quickly, and from the sharp liquid look she gave Lady Captain, she understood it, too.

Before anyone could take it from her or do anything, she ate it.

"Interesting choice," said Spoo.

"You think it's from Percy?" asked Aggie.

"You actually want my opinion?"

"Everyone else is occupied."

"How'd old Percy get himself a sausage-dog mechanimal?"

"Good point."

"Someone is helping us. Or them."

Aggie looked glum. "It's probably Lord Akeldama related."

"Isn't it always?"

Aggie nodded.

The guards were not pleased about the sudden interference of a flying dog, nor were they best pleased with Anitra eating his message. Not that they would have understood it. No doubt it was intended for Anitra or Lady Captain, and therefore in code.

Toffs were like that, not enough to write plain English, had to learn to write a secret version of English, too.

A few soldiers lurched at Anitra, annoyed.

Then things began to happen fast.

One of the guards shot at Anitra. She dropped to the deck. Not because she was hit, but because she knew how to behave in a gunfight.

Aggie didn't approve. Aggie didn't like many people, but she was nicer to Anitra than most anyone else. So Spoo wasn't surprised when Aggie shot the soldier who'd shot at Anitra.

She didn't miss. The man collapsed, bolt lodged in his shoulder. His gun clattered to the deck. One of Spoo's decklings dove for it, tumbled, scooped it up, and leapt back up into the rigging. Another guard fired at him, but too late.

"One down," said Aggie with great satisfaction. She angled and fired at another guard. Dead on and deadly. Aggie had no mercy.

"That's two."

Several guards fired in their direction.

Spoo and Aggie took refuge behind the clamp, which provided excellent cover as it was made of solid steel.

Spoo peeked over the top while Aggie took the port side and fired from around it with her bolts. She didn't have that many, so she took her time and aimed with care.

"That's three."

Miss Prim swept around, laying down a spray with her parasol, covering the three soldiers nearest the gangplank. The horrid smell of acid and burning rent the air. The soldiers screamed and those that had sense ran off the ship.

"That's six down total. Only six left."

"This is fun," said Spoo.

Aggie glared at her, no doubt offended that Spoo had the temerity to say anything positive.

Willard grappled with one of the other guards, trying to muscle away his gun. Bork took one of the others straight on, clipped him hard under the chin. He used to box in the ring.

The man had a set of fists on him, he did. Spoo thought he was just about the cream on the top of the milk.

"Look at that hit!" she crowed.

Aggie was glaring at her.

"Righto." Spoo whistled out a series of piercing instructions. Her decklings swung into action.

Some of them actually swinging.

Whoever had the filched gun was firing it, although not well, and clearly, he wasn't confident about firing down into the now boiling crowd on the deck.

The soldiers' bullets kept flying. It looked like a few *Custard* crew were in danger. Spoo, however, had little doubt in her airship's ability to win the day. She let her decklings cause havoc for a few minutes, to even the odds. Then she whistled them back out of harm's way and into the rigging.

The whole ship lurched suddenly.

Virgil yelled a question from the pit.

A deckling yelled back from the squeak deck.

Spoo and Aggie held on to the clamp while *The Spotted Custard* listed hard, losing height on the port side.

The deck around the clamp began to creak loudly as it buckled and splintered along all the weak points Spoo had cut.

Nips appeared. "Dropsy is ready."

"You don't say? Pull in the gangplank then, quickly now."

Nips glanced around and then scuttled down the clamp to the dock, ran through the city, around to the gangplank, and then back up to the crank. He was called Nips for a reason.

Lady Captain's strident cry rose above the fray. "Pull the plank!"

The captain, Miss Prim, Anitra, the scaly lord, the Japanese head soldier and his six remaining compatriots, *and* the deckhands were all mashed together, skidding towards the port railing while still grappling with one another. Luckily, most of the guns had stopped firing as the soldiers scrabbled for purchase and defence. Those guns had all run out of bullets or been dropped when the ship tilted.

The Spotted Custard listed further. Spoo noted the dropsy bobbing off the forward bow.

Lady Captain yelled, "Spoo, cut the clamp! Virgil, get us out of here. Depuff like you mean it!"

Spoo whipped out a crowbar and started wrestling it into the torn deck. The tilt had done its worst, but the *Custard* was mainly made of bamboo and that was darn flexible stuff. Holding on to the clamp, to keep herself from sliding, Spoo used her free hand and her weight to try to encourage the deck to split further.

"Give it here." Aggie latched her crossbow to her belt.

Spoo frowned but handed the crowbar over. Aggie's arms were twice as big as Spoo's, if not more so.

Aggie started in on the deck.

Spoo crawl-climbed up to the railing.

She braced herself on the clamp, knowing it was a risk because if they managed to get free, she might go with it. Using her legs, her strongest assets, she began to beat the *Custard*'s flange and railing, hoping to break the last solid hold the clamp had on her ship.

She felt the rumble of the main boiler kicking in and hoped they weren't too off-kilter. There came a point, if the kettles tilted too far, that the safeties would shut the boilers down.

The airship lurched violently.

A loud *clunk* indicated that the gangplank was up.

A great gout of steam wafted around them, which meant the boilers were fully operational.

Aggie let out a whoop of delight. "That's my boffin!" She resumed crowbarring with a fierce expression.

The *whump whump* of the propeller shivered across the tilted deck. Spoo prayed they were in a position that kept the blades from hitting Edo.

The *Custard* lurched and began to right herself.

"Come on, old girl," shouted Spoo, kicking at the railing with everything she had.

The deck underneath her rippled, and then came the horrible wrenching sound of fracturing wood.

"Roll, Spoo!" cried Aggie, letting go of the crowbar and allowing herself to slide across the deck towards the opposite railing.

Spoo gave one last mighty kick, then bounced herself up to a crouch.

"Oui up!" came a cry. A rigging rope hurtled towards her. Spoo caught it, looped it into a hold, and kicked herself to swing free. Behind her the deck broke apart. The railing splintered off and peeled away from the ship with a screech.

There was now a massive gaping hole where the clamp had been. Spoo could see right through to the stateroom.

The Spotted Custard lurched to right herself.

Immediately Virgil depuffed, the propeller ramped up, and the ship let out her customary farting noise. Never before had Spoo been so pleased to hear that sound.

They floated away from the Paper City, sinking fast. Virgil, smart lad, steered them quickly in and directly under Edo, where it would be hardest for city defences to shoot them.

The fight, which had descended into a port-side crush, resumed as the deck levelled out. It was mostly fists and blades now, which Spoo preferred, it meant the odds were better.

Primrose was laying about with her parasol. She'd presumably used up her spray and darts, but she had other defences. Lady Captain was grappling unsuccessfully with the head soldier. Captain wasn't a fighter, not in her human form, and she was pregnant, too. But she was doing her best. Anitra was right there, trying to help.

Bork, Willard, and the decklings swarmed the remaining soldiers.

The scaly lord righted himself with dignity and stood a little apart from the scrapping, apparently *still* undecided as to which side he was on.

Spoo had a feeling he could sway the tide. Especially if he was

a form-shifter of some kind. It was a full-moon night, after all.
The moon wasn't up yet and she hoped he wasn't one of those
who went mad.

Then there came this funny sort of yodel, and Rodrigo
Tarabotti leapt into the fray.

Finally!

The man moved through the crowd as if the people he hit
were helping him shift position, like an acrobat at the circus.
He had two double-sided knife things. Silver blades – real *actual*
silver – on one side and hard wooden spikes the other. Sundowner
weapons.

Rodrigo Tarabotti had trained his whole life to kill only two
things, vampires and werewolves. And mayhap his grandfather
had known there were others, and mayhap his father had known
and not said anything. But the Catholic Church saw only vampires and werewolves. So that was what he'd killed.

But those skills turned out to be pretty darn effective on other
kinds of shifters and flesh eaters, and he was bloody brilliant
against humans.

Spoo never understood the term *cut a swath*, something to do
with fields and harvest, Virgil likely knew what it meant. But
Rod sure *cut a swath* through the crowd.

Anitra said something to her husband, something in Italian,
and Rod turned in the direction of the scaly lord.

This seemed to make up the man's mind. He unsheathed his
long sword and swung it out in a wide arc, taking a defensive
stance behind the naked blade. Then he waded in, clearly intent
on the Lady Captain or the Japanese head soldier. Unfortunately
for him, that meant he was also threatening Anitra.

Rodrigo was there.

Spoo dangled from her rigging and watched in awe.

Rodrigo leapt in front of the lord, catching and deflecting his
sword. He made this twisting movement with his double-edged
blades that slid the sword harmlessly away and would have shattered a lesser blade.

The scaly lord twirled, supernatural fast, and came at him again.

But just as fast, Rodrigo's blades were there to intercept. He ducked out and away, assessed the lordling out of dark eyes, then flipped one blade so it was wooden end forward. He drove the stake in and down hard as he could, hitting the man heart-side, in the chest.

Spoo winced. But the sharp stake was deflected by the lord's armour. It cut in and down along his left shoulder, tearing his robe sleeve and opening a long gash along his upper arm.

The blood that beaded forth was dark and slow. The cut instantly started to heal.

Definitely a supernatural.

The lord gave a roaring hiss noise.

Rodrigo reassessed his approach. He dropped one of his knives to the deck and reached out fast, touching the man's bare cheek with his fingers. Then he raised up the wooden stake again.

Then Anitra was there, a hand to her husband's arm, calming and sure. Voice low, she spoke intently in Italian.

Spoo leapt to the deck and ran over to them. She slid in and retrieved Rodrigo's dropped blade. The balance was topping. Following his example, she held it pointed forward, but with the silver end to the back of the scaly lord's neck. He might not notice her but Rodrigo and the captain did.

"He's not on their side," explained Lady Captain. "Apparently, he's as much a prisoner as Lady Sakura. Has been all along. In fact, she is held trapped by her connection to him and is being used to keep the city in place. He is held trapped by his connection to the city, which has something to do with plumbing. Apparently, when Edo was on the ground, before it split and floated up into the air, he provided the water. It's confusing. He's not on our side either. But there's no need to kill him."

Rodrigo looked at his cousin. "You're sure?"

"Yes."

"Pity."

Spoo saw him realize then that the lord's blade was up against his own back. It would have taken little effort to split him open. Rod wrinkled his nose at his predicament.

"I call it a draw," said Lady Captain, ruefully. "But we've subdued the others, so the whole fight is ours."

Spoo maintained her position and looked around.

Bork and Willard were sitting on top of the head soldier. Of his six remaining compatriots, one was curled over an Aggie-administered crossbow bolt, one was collapsed insensate (possibly from one of Miss Prim's darts), two were trussed up by deckling artifice, and the other two had their hands loose and open while Nips stood before them, shaky hand holding the retrieved gun. Aggie went to join him, crossbow at the ready.

Nips was a terrible shot.

Anitra said to the captain, "The message inside the metal dog was from a contact ground-side, using Goldenrod's code. Intended for me."

"You trust this contact?"

"The Wallflower? Yes."

Miss Prim started at that. "Didn't Percy say . . . ?"

"Yes, Prim. Anitra, go on, please." Lady Captain was in full command snobbery.

Anitra continued, "She has Percy and Arsenic safe. They want us to meet them in two hours, at Hakone hot springs. We should be able to find it on a map. She specifies they need Lady Sakura, and Rodrigo must go along to balance the lady with preternatural touch."

Lady Captain nodded and looked hard at Rod. "What took you so long?"

Rodrigo glared at his captain and spoke in his strongly accented English. "Full moon, little cousin. If we drop low, we got the werecat going mad. And that new lady beast. I locking down monsters."

Anitra pointed at the lord. "He, too, becomes beast."

Rodrigo swore in Italian.

Spoo thanked heaven that the moon wasn't up.

Lady Captain made a tutting noise. "I thought he was a vampire type."

"No," said Anitra.

"What beast, exactly?" asked Miss Prim.

"The Wallflower did not say." Anitra looked at the scaly lord, then asked him something in Japanese.

He cracked a smile, an actual smile.

Spoo was amazed.

He didn't answer, but he did bow at Rodrigo.

Rodrigo gave him a narrow-eyed glare.

"Play nice," ordered Lady Captain.

He bowed back.

The lord rumbled out something.

Anitra interpreted, "He said there is nothing on this ship that could hold his beast."

"Well, that's awfully arrogant. We do have the Lefoux tank."

"Stick him in with Formerly Floote's decomposing body? Isn't that rude?" asked Miss Prim.

"To whom, him or Formerly Floote?"

"Would he fit?" asked Spoo, making her presence known at last.

The lord turned, then started to find a silver blade at his back.

Spoo gave him an apologetic grin and handed the fantastic weapon back to Rodrigo. "Nice poker," she said, reverently.

Rodrigo gave her an oddly impressed look, and then holstered the blades. They seemed to vanish somewhere about his person in a seamless manner. Spoo was suitably awed.

The scaly lord gave a slow blink at Spoo, then turned to Anitra and spoke again.

The Japanese soldiers within hearing distance cried out in fear or horror or anger.

Anitra interpreted. "He says that it matters not. He cannot shift this high up. If we get him home before moonrise, all will be well. He is free now. His contract is broken. Edo will run dry."

"What contract?" said Miss Prim, who worried about such things.

"It seems that the moment they let the Lady Sakura leave the city, his indenture was broken. Or whatever they call indentures in these parts. Us breaking free of the clamp counts as them letting her leave the city."

"He's on our side now?" Spoo pressed.

Anitra squinted. "I wouldn't go that far."

Spoo said, "Dropsy is ready when you are."

"No need. We'll depuff the whole ship and—"

A tremendous staccato cracking rent the air at the same time as the crow's nest let out a holler of warning.

A military dirigible had dropped down and under Edo, found them hiding, and opened fire.

Bork and Willard leapt to their one gun and fired, but that was all they had. They'd no more bullets and no way to further defend themselves.

"Orders, Captain!" came Virgil's frantic voice.

Rue winced. "Guess hiding isn't working. We can't outrun them, not crippled as we are with extra bodies aboard. Virgil, make for the grey. Spoo, ready the dropsy!"

CHAPTER

FIFTEEN

It's in the Plumbing

It became abundantly clear that with both fox-lady and scaly lord susceptible to full moon they needed Lady Captain and Rodrigo with them for *balance*. Assuming the Wallflower's message about *balance* meant neutralizing any tethers with preternatural touch. Considering the fact that no one had any idea of how long it would take them to get where they were going, better to be safe than sorry when trapped with supernaturals.

Spoo had overheard the doctor's warning to the captain on the risks of form-shifting. But if the captain was disposed to ignore it, who was Spoo to gainsay? Lady Captain rarely listened to anyone. Quesnel was the only one who might stop her, and he was dealing with advanced boiler tilt. Also the *Custard* was struggling to stay the course, wobbling rather badly (possibly due to a ruddy big hole in her main deck). Their chief engineer must remain belowdecks.

So the captain, Rod, the fox-lady, the scaly lord, and all seven of their Japanese prisoners (for ballast) were loaded into *The Porcini*. The lord insisted on climbing in last, and with good reason as it turned out. He must've weighed a great deal, because the dropsy immediately began to sink, no venting needed.

"It's going to be hard to steer, Lady Captain," warned Spoo. "*Porcini* isn't designed to be nimble."

"We'll be all right, Spoo. You'll look after things up here?"

"Can't do much worse than I already did, creating that huge hole and all."

"You got us free, Spoo. That's what matters."

"Take care down there, Captain."

Miss Prim appeared. She thrust a rolled map at her friend. "Here, Rue, I circled Hakone but you can see it there." She pointed southwest of the big city, along the coastline.

"Once you get closer, you should be able to make out that it's a mountain. That's near where his hot springs are. Lord Ryuunosuke can guide you."

Miss Prim looked at the scaly lord.

Rod had his hand firmly around the man's exposed upper arm, inside the cut in the sleeve that Rod himself had made. But all the lord's attention was on his lady, the expression in his hard eyes almost tender. Spoo wrinkled her nose. Adults were odd. Immortals were even odder.

The fox-lady said, "We both know where it is. And I can speak your language well enough to get us there."

"Can you indeed?" Lady Captain gave her a quizzical look.

Well, Spoo could have told her *that*.

"I hope this works." Miss Prim stood back.

Spoo unhitched the dropsy from the *Custard*.

Lady Captain looked hard at Miss Prim. "Come back for us?"

"Never doubt it. I've been following in your wake my whole life, Rue dear. I'm not stopping now. Get the dropsy back up and we'll nip down and scoop you in quick as may be. That's assuming Quesnel doesn't kill me when he finds out I let you go."

"Blame me."

"I will."

"He'll fight you to come after me right away."

"I'm well aware."

Lady Captain looked at Spoo. "You tell Virgil that navigation is to obey Primrose, not Quesnel, got it?"

"Aye, aye, Lady Captain."

Another barrage of artillery fire came at them, the black sleek dirigible was back in range and taking potshots.

Spoo let loose the dropsy.

Rodrigo pulled on the release line with his free hand. *The Porcini* sucked in the cold night air, weighing down against the helium reserves, and began to drop.

"Not so much at once!" yelled Spoo.

Too late, the dropsy plummeted, not quite falling, but faster than would feel comfortable.

Miss Prim shared a look of exasperation with Spoo before leaving *The Porcini* to its own devices, and turning her attention to the *Custard*'s predicament.

She began gesturing with her parasol and issuing orders. Perhaps not so autocratic as Lady Captain, but forceful and direct.

"Spoo, get four decklings positioned for balloon repairs. We can't afford to lose even the tiniest bit of helium to bullet fire. We've given everything we can spare to the dropsy. Have the rest of your people prepare to assist with speed and puffing. You know where best to place them."

Spoo did and went to do just that.

Prim yelled at Virgil to take evasive action and puff them away from Edo and into the grey as quickly as possible. They would hide there, dropping out occasionally to check for *The Porcini*'s return. It would be work for Virgil, not to get caught in any currents and dragged away. They'd use a lot of fuel but having to run the boilers at capacity would keep Quesnel busy. Something to be grateful for.

They needed to draw enemy fire away from *The Porcini* as much as possible in the interim.

Which seemed to be working. There was only one enemy airship after them, and it didn't divert to chase the dropsy. It couldn't have missed seeing *The Porcini* descend, but it was sinking too fast for a large dirigible to easily follow. Also, there was a good chance the enemy ship thought it was a distraction and intentionally stayed focused on *The Spotted Custard*.

The *Custard*, drawing fire all the while, made its way up towards the grey in jerky stages.

The military dirigible followed them as close as may be.

Never before had Spoo wanted to man a Gatling so badly. Looking down over the railing, she noted the dropsy was no more than a small speck, and yelled to Prim that they were clear.

Virgil puffed them up and they hit the grey.

The enemy ship didn't follow.

Numbing nothingness surrounded them and everything went quiet and still, except Virgil, still muscling the helm and muttering to himself.

Everyone held their breath and waited for Quesnel to come up and yell at them.

Spoo went hunting for the cute little dog mechanimal, hoping he was still somewhere on deck.

Despite Arsenic's fears, it was relatively easy to get to Hakone. Lady Manami informed them brusquely that *yes, of course* the temple train went there. Her tone of voice suggested she found it insulting to have it implied otherwise.

Apparently, the Temple of Mercy train went to most of the major hot springs in Japan. Maybe it was part of the condition of being a temple train. Or perhaps hot springs were considered particularly merciful? Or it had something to do with dragons.

Dragons, mind you. Arsenic shook her head in awe. *The idea!*

Sometimes she found it terrifying to live in an age where science must grapple with mythology. Other times she found it glorious. Dragons fell into both. Perhaps it would've been better for them all if the monsters had stayed in the shadows. But such secrets would always out themselves, eventually.

Nevertheless, dragons!

Arsenic and Percy were still cooling their heels in the receiving room. Literally, since they'd not been given socks or slippers after tubbing. Guards occasionally walked by the open door, exchanging nods with Arsenic.

Nice work if you can get it, she thought, watching them with interest. Not a bad job, she supposed, had she some other life to live. Presuming they allowed non-Japanese women to take the position. She liked the spear as a weapon. Not that she'd learned to use one, her mother was more about small sharp knives. Oddly tangential to life as a doctor, as it turned out. Arsenic's scalpel technique had excelled from the start.

She'd grown rather fond of the stoic temple guards. They were so fierce and sure of themselves.

Percy napped while they wended their way around Tokyo, along the coast, and finally up the mountain. He possessed the magical ability to sleep anywhere, as needed. Arsenic envied him. She also suspected he'd enjoy a long and healthy life as a result.

They made Hakone in good time and Percy awoke looking refreshed just as the train wheezed to a stop. They went to find a window and see what Hakone looked like.

Hakone's hot springs were entirely different from the ones they'd recently visited. Instead of tubs and sculpted grottos, the station was built outwards like a dock, over a beautiful lake with a truly stunning snow-topped mountain in the distance. "Mount Fuji," explained Percy with a note of awe in his voice. Between them and the water were lovely arches and large pots filled with tiny trees forming pleasing vistas.

The lake beyond steamed.

"Shall we brave the entrance?" Percy offered her his arm.

Arsenic took his hand instead, which was soft and strong in hers. His fingers were long and capable and surprisingly firm. Hand holding seemed to both startle and please the ridiculous man. She merely led him to the temple entrance facing away from the lake.

This view was no less beautiful. Before them was a steep

sulphurous mountain peak that had been sculpted by both man and nature into ledges. Each ledge was decorated differently with a tree or moss, a fern or small shrub, and a stunning bronze sculpture. But the bulk of each ledge was a rock-carved pool, presumably filled with hot water. Stone stairs cut into the mountainside connected them. It seemed idyllic.

Arcing over them all, both part of the mountain and wrapped around it, was a vast hydraulic plumbing system. It coiled down along each side of the peak, flowing over the train tracks in elegant arches. It delved deep down into the lake, presumably drawing water away into aqueducts. It was clearly powered by advanced steam technology that took advantage of the volcanic heat of the location. They needed no actual boilers here, only the pumps and engines that could run off perennially boiling water – for the water was naturally boiled. It was ingenious. Arsenic wished, for one of the only times in her life, that she had a better understanding of engineering.

Percy, who was apparently only shaken by things like hand holding, looked mildly interested.

"Amazing, aye?" She nudged him.

"It's certainly very large." He squeezed her hand.

"I wonder how it works?"

And Percy was off on some elaborate explanation as to probabilities, hydraulics, and temperature controls. As he talked, he got more excited. For Percy, appreciation would always involve comprehension. He would never be the type to immerse himself in wonder without understanding. She was lucky she found this appealing, and had already learned how to guide him towards joy.

Arsenic smiled and half listened to him natter, while she absorbed the beauty of the technological marvel. No attempt was made to hide the pipes, instead they were glorified. The tubes were made of iridescent glass, so one could see the water moving inside. They shimmered. The metal supporting them was all curved and swirling, filled with swoops and organic shapes. Shining under the light of floating paper lanterns, filled with the same lighting technology that kept the Paper City aloft.

Arsenic realized, without much surprise, that everything was formulated into artistic interpretations of serpents. She had seen much plumbing in her day and many a steam engine and boiler arrangement, but never had she seen them turned into art.

She tilted her head and leaned back, trying to take in all of the peak with its ledges of hot springs as well as the massive tubes draped around it. She realized that, when seen from far enough away, it would look like two dragons wrapped about the mountain.

Percy shifted so he could support her as she leaned. He did it naturally, as if he didn't even realize he was inclined to be supportive. She nestled against him happily. He was still prattling on about the complex functionality of large-scale hydraulics.

"I think the whole thing is designed to look like dragons," she interrupted.

He didn't mind, of course. That was the thing about Percy, he merely wanted to convey as much information as possible because that was what he needed from the world, so he assumed everyone else needed it too. But he was never offended when she stopped him. He also knew he had a propensity to waffle and that sometimes convention dictated he stop. He might not understand why, but he had learned to accept it.

"It must be beautiful from the air," Arsenic mused.

"It is indeed." Lady Manami appeared like magic near her elbow.

"My crewmates are in for a treat." Arsenic gave her a friendly nod.

"You do not doubt they will come for you?"

"Nay." Arsenic was confident.

Lady Manami lowered her lashes. "One hour until moonrise, I can feel it in my bones."

"Are kitsune subject to moon sickness, like werewolves? Must we see you locked away?"

"Not just yet, but soon. Even should I change accidentally, it matters not. I am fox, my instinct will be to run and to hide, not to fight or hunt humans. I can be vicious, but it is not my instinctive state, even under the influence of the moon."

"Interesting," said Percy. "What other differences are there between kitsune and werewolves? Are you omnivorous?"

"Indeed."

"And the conservation of mass? I've been formulating a theory on shifting density, is that what you do?"

She looked at him out of bright eyes.

Percy took that as agreement. "How much do you weigh, then?"

"Percy!" said Arsenic.

"What? Oh! My apologies. One doesn't ask a lady her weight, does one? Silly that. Why not apply basic understanding to both the sexes equally? Especially in these days of dirigibles, when weight is of general concern. Where was I? Oh yes, Lady Manami, if you don't object, I simply want to know if you weigh the same as a normal fox when you are a human, or the same as a normal human when you are a fox? Or do you split the difference, so to speak?"

The lady in question seemed more amused by Percy than offended, thank heavens. She came all over furtive, in that way that supernatural creatures got when asked directly about their abilities. "I weigh more than a normal fox and less than a mortal woman."

"Remarkable," said Percy and then, because he really never did learn, "Can I lift you up?"

Arsenic poked him in the arm. "Percy! One dinna simply ask to lift up random females."

"One doesn't? Oh, pardon me! But if she faints I can catch her, no? Isn't that basically the same thing? Lady Manami, would you please faint for me?"

Fortunately, Percy was saved from further blundering by the appearance of a small airship, *falling* more than floating, in their direction.

"That is *not The Spotted Custard*. Is it for or against? And why that shape?" Arsenic gawked at the peculiar mushroom-shaped contraption with no propeller headed at them. It was more like an old-fashioned hot-air balloon.

"That's *The Porcini*, our dropsy. For escaping and whatnot. We stole it from a wheystation in Singapore. Or my sister did, after she made Tash dress like a fish."

"Please stop explaining, Percy. You're only confusing matters."

"So I've been told. I do beg your pardon."

"All is well, m'eudail. I ken you mean a kindness. 'Tis only that we dinna always have time to learn everything all at once, sometimes you have to relay only the important bits."

Percy frowned, concentrating, and then said, clearly and distinctly, "That's the airship that we use in emergencies or when we need to retrieve something but can't risk the whole *Custard*. It's called a dropsy. It's always looked like a mushroom, which is why we named ours *The Porcini*. That's an Italian mushroom. It's probably carrying Rodrigo, the two shifters, and anyone else the Wallflower asked for."

"I didn't ask for anyone else," said the Wallflower, who had, of course, somehow appeared out of the shadows to one side of the temple door. Because where else would she be?

The dropsy was moving a bit too fast and possibly out of control. But it managed to crash not into the lake, but down in front of them, narrowly missing one of the swirls of serpentine plumbing.

Two of the temple guards pushed Percy and Arsenic aside and ran towards it, spears drawn.

Lady Manami said, "We cannot step out of the temple. Look there?" She pointed to one side, just off the platform's sacred ground. There waited a large group of wasp-dressed men.

These soldiers were also focused on the dropsy.

The temple guards got there first but the soldiers were mobilizing.

Until something stopped all of them in their tracks.

As expected, the dropsy contained Lady Sakura and Lord Ryuunosuke. Both of them were in human form, despite the proximity of moonrise and freedom from imprisonment.

Because they had help.

In Lord Ryuunosuke's case, he was being gripped by Rodrigo Tarabotti. The preternatural had skin-to-skin contact with the man's upper arm. Even had he wanted to, Lord Ryuunosuke could not shift.

Arsenic found this display of power impressive. To have biological control over another being, how remarkable from a medical perspective.

But next to Lady Sakura? With its paws up on the edge of the dropsy basket was a fluffy red fox. A *human-sized* fluffy red fox.

It was, frankly, startlingly huge.

It took Arsenic only a moment to understand. Then she became both angry and distressed. That was Rue. That was a *pregnant* metanatural Rue, shifted into an enormous Japanese fox. Because, why not?

There were a thousand reasons why not!

Arsenic resisted the urge to run to her. It wouldn't do any good. Honestly, being a medical practitioner would be a whole lot simpler without ruddy patients!

Fortunately, the presence of an enormous fox in the basket of a mushroom-shaped airship seemed to arrest everyone.

The temple guards, sufficiently awed to be in the company of what could only be an engorged fox-spirit god, had each taken a knee, spears planted and heads bowed. The wasp military men fell back. They didn't bow, but they also didn't attack.

It was all too much.

Lady Manami gave a tinkling laugh. "Oh dear, your flesh thief has miscalculated."

"'Tis worse than that, she could miscarry."

"She is with child?" Lady Manami's lovely face registered fleeting surprise. "Human father?"

Arsenic nodded.

"Interesting."

"Aye."

"You have concerns?"

"I do."

"You're worried about the impact of form-shifting on a baby inside?"

"Aye."

"You should be. I know of only one incident of a shifter female carrying a human child and she stayed human the entire time."

"How?"

"What do you think started the God-Breaker Plague?"

Percy said, without inflection, "Alessandro Tarabotti. At least, that's the rumour."

"Ah, no. He resurrected lost knowledge, and figured out how to extend it. But before him, there was *them*. Three of them – the lioness, the vampire, and the fangxiangshi."

"How do you know . . . ?" Percy glanced at her.

"Child, immortals like to know everything, particularly about one another. It's how we stay immortal. Speaking of, tell Alessandro's grandson there to let go of the dragon, before the moon strikes."

Percy yelled to the dropsy. "Rodrigo, old chap! Welcome to Japan."

Rodrigo looked over to the temple, squinting. "Buonasera, Percy!"

Percy cleared his throat. "Would you be so kind as to let the dragon chappie go?"

"Sì?"

"Yes please."

"Sì."

Rodrigo withdrew his hand.

So that's a dragon.

As weird as Percy found a human-sized fox, he found a massive serpent even weirder. Of course, control over density went both ways, but Percy didn't realize how far that control might stretch.

The dragon was huge, easily the size of the temple train itself.

Obviously, a serpent of such proportions didn't fit inside a dropsy basket. Instead he rather draped over it, so whoever was inside with him was now crouched under his belly.

Percy turned to Lady Manami. "Would you please ask the temple guards to lash down our dropsy? See the dangling ropes?"

Lady Manami did as asked, issuing a set of requests in Japanese to the guards. The guards, despite the dragon oozing out of the basket and the fox now hidden beneath him, did as requested, each one tying *The Porcini* down – one to a tree, the other to a large boulder. The military gentlemen sort of stood around, stunned.

Percy sympathized.

The dragon coiled and slithered himself to flop to the garden below. His movements were not exactly graceful, like an eel on land. A really, really big, scaled eel. His body was all iridescent blues and whites and purples, gleaming in the lantern light. He had feathery fins all along, like a lionfish.

He certainly was beautiful. If one was inclined to find serpents beautiful, which Percy was. He'd wager the dragon was a marvellous swimmer.

The dragon paused outside the basket and looked back at it. Lady Sakura's face popped up over the edge. The dragon's massive head tilted back to her, and they touched noses, a sweetly affectionate gesture.

Then the dragon slithered around the temple and across the tracks, disappearing into the steaming lake beyond with the softest of splashes.

He was gone.

"*Omnia iam fient quae posse negabam*," said Percy. Only Latin could possibly apply at a time like this.

Lady Manami glanced up at him. "A language I have not heard in hundreds of years, and I never learned to speak it. The Romans, after all, were a vampire concern. They did not like shape changers."

Arsenic translated for Percy. "Everything I used to say could na happen, will happen now. An old proverb."

Lady Manami laughed. She was much more animated than her Japanese compatriots. "Saying something cannot happen practically guarantees that it will. Terribly short-sighted of mortals to believe that the shifters they know are the only shifters there *are*."

Percy nodded. "So we learned when we began our travels. But a dragon seems that much more improbable. What's next? Griffons? Unicorns?"

"Do not be silly. Mermaids, however." Lady Manami slid sly eyes over to Percy.

Percy suspected he was being teased.

"Look!" Arsenic pointed.

The serpent figure of Lord Ryuunosuke was visible slithering through the pipes draped over the mountain peak.

"What's he doing?" Percy had assumed the lake itself was the dragon's home. Like a vampire queen safely back in her hive house, why leave again so quickly?

"He has things to fix before moonrise. He will not go far. Lady Sakura is here. He will not leave his mate."

Percy frowned. "It seems an odd pairing."

Lady Manami shook her head at him. "The heart is an unfettered thing when spirits are involved. Had you not noticed, we love where we will? We have learned that love happens so rarely, we should value it beyond all things when it lands upon us. It is the only thing that keeps us young and sane."

Percy thought about Lord Akeldama and his drones, not to mention his adoration for Rue as his adopted daughter and his loyalty to Lady Maccon. He thought of Tasherit and her delight in his sister and her ready affection for the *Spotted Custard* crew. How strange that the knowledge of immortality was bundled up not in intellectual pursuits but in emotional acumen.

"Is that wisdom?" he asked, because Lady Manami was old and must perforce have something to teach him.

"It is the only wisdom worth knowing."

"Oh." Percy looked down at Arsenic, who was still leaning against him, her eyes wide and full of wonder.

He followed her gaze and watched a dragon negotiate plumbing.

The world was indeed a wondrous place.

The dropsy strained against its cords.

Percy's friend, his actual long-time true friend, Rue, was in there, shaped like a massive fox. She'd put herself and her child at risk, to see a kitsune safely home. To see a dragon reunited with his hot spring. Because they loved each other. Because Rue was like that. Because Rue, for all her enthusiasm and all her silly antics, had learned such wisdom as to trust in love.

Lady Manami patted his arm. "I know, it's confusing. You'll figure it out eventually. You're young."

The dragon vanished behind the peak, following the piping.

Percy squeezed Arsenic slightly to get her attention, and because she felt good resting against him. "What should we do for Rue? Safer to let her stay a big fox, now that she's already done it, or better to get her back to human form?"

Arsenic frowned. "Human. I'm concerned about her internal anatomy as a fox and how it will affect the baby, better to limit exposure."

Percy nodded and yelled over to Rodrigo. "Rodrigo, would you mind touching Rue for us?"

Rodrigo did as requested.

Rue returned to human form.

Lady Sakura popped back up next to them, she seemed pleased with the outcome, although it was difficult to tell for certain on her perfect impassive face.

Percy could only see the three of their heads inside *The Porcini* but he suspected there were others, otherwise the weight would be off.

From the shadows next to the temple, the Wallflower spoke in that pointed way of hers. "About twenty minutes until moonrise. In case that was something to think about, Lady Manami."

SIXTEEN

Reunions, Crisis, and Crumpet Requirements

Released from metanatural tether, Lady Sakura transformed into a red fox. Normal-sized, mind you. With the moon still not quite up, Percy assumed this was a voluntary choice. It certainly made her nimble, or perhaps that was simply freedom from all those robes and elaborate baubles.

She leapt easily over the edge of the dropsy and landed to stand directly in front of it. Her big ears were perked and she had one paw up, poised, her bright dark eyes intent on the incoming military.

She looked to be slightly bigger than any other red fox of Percy's acquaintance. Certainly nowhere near as big as Rue had been in fox form. Although her tail was impressively puffy. Percy always admired foxes' tails.

"Isna she cute?" said Arsenic.

Percy was pretty certain that wasn't a very respectful description of an immortal trickster spirit creature.

Lady Manami seemed to agree. "Kitsune are not *cute!*"

"Bonnie," Arsenic offered, making things worse.

Percy was amused to note that for once he wasn't the one making the social gaffe by voicing indiscriminate thoughts.

There were now only two, apparently, normal humans left

inside the dropsy. Foreign humans at that. The military seemed to think it was now safe to attack and made for *The Porcini*.

The temple guards weren't foolish. They were dedicated to the goddess of mercy and had no reason to protect random foreigners in baskets who had not officially been granted sanctuary. They left the wasps to it, returning to take up a defensive position at the temple doors. Percy gave them a polite nod of thanks anyway.

Rodrigo was not shy in a fight, even under overwhelming odds. He jumped to the ground brandishing two long double-sided knives as if he'd been born holding them. (Which he might well have been, knowing Templar training.)

Rue stayed behind him in the basket, looking pale and forlorn and most unlike herself.

Rodrigo took up a defensive stance, as if he might fight off the whole military troop himself. But even Rodrigo wasn't that good a fighter.

Percy sighed and looked around for a weapon. He loathed fisticuffs, but those were his friends and if fighting was the only option . . . A gun would be best. Guns, of course, were a coward's choice but he *was* a remarkably good shot. And a bit of a coward.

But someone else came to Rodrigo's aid before he could.

A red fox.

Percy wasn't certain why, or even how much human capacity Sakura kept in her fox form. Werewolves ranged quite a bit, depending on rank, mental stability, and age. But despite what Lady Manami had said about fox instincts, Sakura seemed to have decided it was her duty to defend Rue, Rodrigo, and the dropsy from wasp attackers.

Except that she was only one small fox.

Until she wasn't.

It was impossible to know where they came from, or if they'd been there all along, because foxes were nothing if not stealthy, but suddenly red foxes were materializing all around them. They ran out from behind bushes and boulders and trees.

They came in a small river, over a dozen of them.

Lady Manami said, by way of explanation, "Lady Sakura's obi. They have been waiting a long time for their vixen to return to them."

Percy remembered that Lady Manami had said she would send word calling for the rest of the kitsune. Apparently, it worked.

He wondered how much they functioned like a werewolf pack. "Will they lend her strength?"

"Lady Sakura has *six* tails. How else could she have held an entire city in place for so long? They *are* her strength. Watch."

So they stood in the temple doorway and watched as the foxes (small though they may be) moved like a weapon of umber fire through the soldiers. They darted in and about, tripping the men up, nipping at their ankles. The kitsune drove the men back, as if they were sheep being herded by very small collies.

It was nothing like a werewolf battle. There was little bloodshed. No one was torn asunder, no throats were ripped out, no limbs were lost. Yet, somehow, the foxes prevailed. They drove the soldiers back through sheer aggravation, teasing as they fought, dividing them apart from one another, nudging and tripping. Three of the kitsune forced the military leader to stumble into the lake. The rest applied such persistent needling pressure, most of the soldiers ended up fleeing in sheer surprise.

Eventually, the few soldiers left were panting, bruised, and confounded, weaving about in circles.

Lost to all sense, these men simply turned away from the dropsy towards the temple and stopped fighting, as if whatever was happening was beyond their ken.

Dreamlike, they bowed deeply to the temple, and as if wanderers in a fairy tale, they set out away from the lake, abandoning all duty there.

Lady Manami said, "Each will walk home, however far away that home may be, and tell a story to his family of this night, when the kitsune defended a floating mushroom. The legends will live large. Each man will be thought spirit-touched, or crazy,

or prophetic – and the kitsune reputation will continue eternal."
She looked smug.

Percy decided he liked her.

Percy wasn't surprised to learn that kitsune strength was in
their ability to befuddle. He was never one to believe power
resided in brute strength, physical prowess, or technological
superiority. Often it was more effective to mystify people. He
should know, he did it all the time. All he need do was open
his mouth.

Feeling lucky to have witnessed such a thing, Percy wondered
if he might publish a paper on the subject of kitsune magic, or
if that would come off as too outlandish for academia. Best to
call it something other than *magic*.

Left safe and alone with their dropsy, Rue and Rodrigo
exchanged glances.

Arsenic said, "Rue looks unwell. I should go to her."

Lady Manami agreed. "Go."

Arsenic sprinted across the platform.

Rodrigo leapt back inside *The Porcini* in time to catch Rue as
she folded backwards and out of sight. He then reappeared to
offer Arsenic a hand up. She grabbed it and he hoisted. Arsenic
almost walked up the side and over.

Percy trundled after. He wasn't sure he'd be much help, except
he did speak Japanese and he could request medication of the
temple, since Arsenic didn't have her kit.

Percy was tall enough, and *The Porcini* strapped down to the
ground tight enough, for him to peek over the side and see
inside.

There lay what he assumed were prisoners, trussed up and
strewn about.

Something rather drastic must have happened aboard the
Custard, for they'd dropped off a half dozen or so Japanese guards
along with the fox and the dragon.

"That's a lot of prisoners," he said to Rodrigo, while Arsenic
checked over Rue.

Rue was whiter than normal, and sweating a bit, but awake and grumpy and batting Arsenic off. Arsenic, of course, was having none of it.

The Italian answered him in Italian. "It was good fun. The battle up there." A pause and then he added, "We won."

"So I deduced." Percy supposed that was sufficient information to be going on with.

Rodrigo ambled over to lean against the side of the dropsy near Percy's chin. Together they watched the ladies and felt ineffectual.

Percy said, "Can I do anything to help? Should I fetch something useful? Root vegetables? Hot water? We seem to have a great deal of both."

Arsenic looked over. "I'm thinking she merely pushed herself a bit much." She turned back to Rue. "No contractions? Ache in the lower back? Nausea? Dizziness?"

"No. I told you, my knees gave out. Sudden upset after returning to human form. Not to mention being nearly smothered by a bloody dragon! It's not like that happens every day."

Percy sniffed. "Certainly seems like."

A small throat was cleared near the vicinity of Percy's chest. He looked down to find Lady Manami had left the shelter of the temple and joined them.

She'd paused to put on yet another colourful robe and some of those high sandals and was looking up at him expectantly. Or perhaps not at him but at Rodrigo, who turned to stare down at her with equal interest.

Lady Manami blinked slowly, bright eyes curious on the preternatural's face. Finally she said, "You look like your grandfather."

"You knew him?"

"Percy here is wearing his clothes."

"Of course he is," said Rodrigo.

Rue said, attempting to sit up while Arsenic clucked in disproval, "That sounds like Grandfather. From what I can gather, he travelled around shedding his clothing all too often. I'm surprised there aren't more by-blow cousins turning up. Or maybe not. It's supposed to be difficult for preternaturals to breed."

Percy looked between Rodrigo and Rue. "There are more of you?"

"No," said Rodrigo.

"Not that we know of," added Rue, with a cheeky grin.

Percy shrugged. "You could ask Formerly Floote."

They both looked at him.

"Don't stare at me like I'm cracked. It's obvious he keeps track of stray Tarabottis. Isn't that why he's done everything? Honestly, you two. Isn't that why *everyone* has done *everything* all along? You name it, from God-Breaker Plague to my outfit, from sea to desert to island nation."

"Percy, stop waffling." Rue was out of patience with him, as usual.

Percy shrugged. No skin off his teeth. Not like he could get a valid paper out of *that* theory even if it was evident to him that there were connections (all kinds of connections, all over the planet), and most of them could be laid squarely on two sets of shoulders, Alessandro Tarabotti and Lord Akeldama. But if no one else wanted to play the game, he'd write notes and ask Aunt Softy about it later. Or maybe the Wallflower.

Speaking of, where'd she gone?

Rodrigo glared at Percy. "Why *are* you wearing Grandfather's clothes?"

Arsenic stood up. "Honestly, you lot. 'Tis a wonder you've survived so long. Shouldna we be getting back to the ship? Rather than havering on about fashion?"

"My father would say there can never be anything more important than that." Rue was obviously referring to her vampire father, not her werewolf one.

Percy levered himself into the dropsy. It took a bit of doing, he wasn't graceful about it like Arsenic or Rodrigo. He got a little caught up on the side, with his still bare feet and his injured ankle. His breeches didn't rip or even threaten to. Clearly buckskin was more practical than he gave credit. *Maybe I ought to don leather trousers more often.*

He squinted his eyes into the shadows around them, finally spotting a subtle blob. "You coming, Agatha?"

The blob materialized into the dumpy form of an elderly aunt-type female who one expected to find leading the trifle committee at the local ladies' aid society, not tromping the wilds of Japanese lakes.

Rodrigo issued a surprised snort.

"Rue, stay sitting, for pity's sake. 'Tis only the Wallflower we were meant to find." Arsenic kept her charge in check through dint of explanation.

Rue relaxed back. "Oh yes, I forgot."

Percy said, "That would seem to be the point, with Agatha."

He and Rodrigo bent to offer the Wallflower assistance climbing into the dropsy.

Agatha rolled her eyes at them and through some improbable feat of athleticism, jumped and twisted herself over the edge of the basket, skirts and all, to land perfectly inside.

Percy was very impressed.

She and Rodrigo, quickly in non-verbal accordance, began hoisting the prisoners overboard.

The Porcini began to bob and strain against its anchors as its load lightened.

Percy looked over the edge at Lady Manami. She was the only one left standing outside now. Except for the temple guards, of course.

He surprised himself by saying politely, "It has been an honour to meet you, Lady Manami."

"Actually . . ." The kitsune was looking speculative. "Might I come along? I should prefer not to overstay my welcome here, and I have been in Japan for several decades. It might be time for a new adventure."

Percy wrinkled his nose. "Really? I rather loathe adventure, but if you're sure."

He turned to look down at Rue. "Erm, Captain? Can we adopt a fox shifter for a bit?"

Rue was looking a bit more perky, although since Arsenic kept glaring at her, she wisely stayed seated.

"She'll be well in the grey?" Rue asked.

Lady Manami shrugged. "I've never tried, but you do have the fangxiangshi aboard, in case things go wrong."

Percy explained. "She means Rodrigo."

Rue nodded. "Fair point. Climb on in then, happy to have you."

Percy reached a hand over to help the kitsune aboard. This only required one hand as Lady Manami weighed so little.

Percy was delighted to continue the acquaintance. He would get to ask her questions about manipulation of density and study her. He might get a decent paper after all.

The last of the prisoners tipped overboard, they were ready to float.

Rodrigo lifted Lady Manami up, so she could see over the edge of the basket to yell back to the temple guards. Apparently, it was acceptable to lift a lady under certain circumstances.

"Are they na sorry to let you go?" asked Arsenic.

"Why should they be?"

Percy was confused too. "Aren't you head priestess or mother superior or something?"

Lady Manami laughed, a bright tinkling sound. "Of course not. I was only a visitor, like you, taking sanctuary, like you. I am not a pet to be kept by mortals. Kitsune cannot be tamed."

Rue said, "Well, you'll behave yourself aboard my airship, please. No fur in the bathtub."

"Certainly not." Lady Manami's face was serious but her eyes sparkled.

The temple guards came over to cut them loose with their sharp spears. They gave a kind of salute as *The Porcini* started to float away.

Rue said, "Percy, you know how to work this thing? Take the lines, would you?"

Percy did know so he took the lines accordingly.

"We've minimal helium. We can't afford to lose any."

Percy let out a bit of air ballast and *The Porcini* rose slightly faster.

"Rue, you only had a few more people coming down, why'd you have such a fast descent?"

Rue was happy to explain. "That Lord Ryuunosuke weighed a ton."

Percy nodded. "Of course. I wonder what the conservation-of-density ratio is? Is it similar across all density-sensitive shifter species? I mean to say, one assumes there must be a minimum and a maximum allowable size versus density at each end of the supernatural spectrum. One must still yield a viable human form during daylight that satisfies the parameters of basic bipedal appearance. Unless there are some shifter species that make for giant humans or others that look like children."

He turned slightly towards Lady Manami. "Are there?"

"Not that I know of." She seemed a little awed by Percy's overabundance of speculation.

He was doing his academic rambling thing again. "You'll let me run some calculations on you, Lady Manami, won't you?"

"Will they hurt?"

"Well, there are some who find the mere presence of advanced mathematical equations painful, but I don't think that you'll be materially damaged in any physical manner. Oh! Can I ask how the relative densities affect buoyancy? I mean to say, do kitsune bob something fierce?"

Arsenic cleared her throat.

Percy, attuned to her as he was to no other person, instantly paused to look at her expectantly.

"Perhaps this could wait until you get near notepaper and a scale, m'eudail?"

His stomach contracted into a tight pleased knot at the pet name in so public a forum, but his attention was still on floating foxes. "And maybe a bathtub?"

"No fur in the bathtub, Percy!"

"Yes, Rue, but, I mean, we were in a tub of hot water together and she didn't seem to me to be excessively buoyant in human form." He turned back to Lady Manami. "Are you excessively buoyant in fox form?"

"M'eudail?"

Oh, I'm asking rude questions again, am I? "Yes, Arsenic. Sorry, Rue. Sorry, Lady Manami. I'll navigate the dropsy and think about it quietly for a while, shall I?" Percy hoped that was the right choice, and when Arsenic beamed at him, he knew it was.

He rather enjoyed the sense of pride this gave him, and the realization that Arsenic had guided him away from one of his gaffes. He might trust her to do so in the future.

"Did Percy just apologize?" Rue asked the world at large. "Hang that, did he just stop talking without being yelled at? Doctor, what have you done to him?"

"Nothing, yet."

"You're amazing. Please don't fall overboard again."

"I shall endeavour na to, Captain. Although to be fair, I jumped, Percy fell. Ah look, there's the *Custard.*"

Far above them, *The Spotted Custard* popped into existence. It had dropped down out of the grey.

Unfortunately, there was a mean-looking, angular, black, military dirigible that took offence and floated straight at the *Custard.* Even a ways below, *The Porcini* could hear the *rat-tat-tat* of gunfire.

The Spotted Custard disappeared. Percy could only hope someone had seen the dropsy.

It seemed they had, because the *Custard* reappeared about five minutes later, in much the same spot, clearly checking on their progress, drawing attention and fire, before vanishing once more.

It was a funny game of cat and mouse.

Honestly, Percy was impressed. He owed Virgil a raise. The boy was doing a bang-up job of navigating some tricky currents.

The ones closest to the atmosphere were always a challenge, and to keep the *Custard* steady enough to pop in and out like that took profound skill with the puffer *and* the helm.

Still Percy worried. Virgil must be running the propeller at full spin, which meant the *Custard* was using up a lot of coal and water. Not to mention that kind of pacing put stress on the hull. It wasn't what the dirigible was designed for.

Percy started running calculations in his head. Wondering how far the airship would be able to float without a refuel. He envisioned his charts, determining the closest friendly whey-station. *Hong Kong, perhaps?*

They were close enough now for the military ship to spot *The Porcini*. It swung in their direction as if trying to decide whether to depuff towards them or stay high stalking the grey.

The Spotted Custard depuffed out of the aetherosphere, directly above *The Porcini*.

The enemy ship was on the *Custard*, guns blazing. Percy couldn't determine a way for them to rope in and board safely, not under heavy fire.

They were close enough now to see the frenzied activity on *The Spotted Custard*'s decks. Decklings crawled the rigging, making frantic repairs. As soon as a bullet hit, one of them was on it. Primrose was striding around the main deck, waving her battle parasol and issuing orders. Even Virgil's intent and terrified face could be seen, the rest of him safely inside the navigation pit, as he desperately muscled the helm. Occasionally, his head disappeared as he reached down to the puffer.

Then, suddenly, all the shooting stopped.

The black airship turned away from them and back towards Edo, kicking up its own propeller. Smoke flowered from its stacks as it sped away. Or to be more precise, floated away as quickly as a dirigible could, which wasn't exactly *fast*.

Lady Manami said, "Look. She's begun to drift."

They turned to stare at the Paper City, which did indeed appear to have moved from its old position above Tokyo. All of Edo was floating slowly away from them, northwest towards Choson. The city was untethered.

Percy wasn't certain what the military airship thought it could do to help. But clearly losing an entire city was a darn sight more important than terrorizing one chubby foreign dirigible.

"And there they go," said Lady Manami, smugly.

Figures began to jump over the sides of the Paper City.

The ladies of Edo with their beautiful fluttering robes, and their wide, stunning, and oh-so-useful obi.

Like cherry blossoms they fell, and then one after another the bloom of a parachute deployed above them. They weaved back and forth, decorating the evening air, heading towards Japan far below.

"They stayed for her, you know? Lady Sakura. And now they are free."

Percy was confused. "Why would they do that?"

Lady Manami looked over with a smile at Rue and Arsenic and the silent forgotten lump that was the Wallflower. Percy suspected that Lady Manami always knew where Agatha was standing.

"Because we women must help each other. And because it never hurts to be owed a favour by the kitsune."

The Porcini gave a sudden lurch.

Percy's attention was drawn outside the basket. They'd been grapple-hooked by a couple of decklings on the squeak deck and were being winched in under charge of a determined-looking Spoo.

Rodrigo vaulted out of the basket as soon as they were close enough and grabbed Anitra up into his arms. She bracketed his face with her hands and stared into his eyes a long moment. They engaged in that silent communication some couples have where words were unnecessary. Percy didn't get it, he always needed words. Even with Arsenic. Especially with Arsenic.

Arsenic was helping Rue out of *The Porcini* and into Spoo's tense arms.

"Lady Captain, good to have you back. Old Q gave us a right haranguing, he did."

"He's in engineering?"

"'Course he is. He might be all over grumpy, but he knows his duty. We're under attack. He wants to yell at you something fierce but he'll do it later, when we're safe. Though I suppose we aren't under attack anymore. I'd take cover if I were you. Oh! Did you see the ladies jumping? Prettiest thing."

Percy climbed out.

Already, above them, two other decklings were pulling the sipper tube over. Collapsing the dropsy's balloon and porting the helium back into *The Spotted Custard.*

Agatha vaulted to the deck, before turning to lift out Lady Manami. She set the kitsune down quickly and then backed away.

Lady Manami didn't look well. Her face was warping and white-furred. She had great big semi-present ears on her head and not one, but several puffy fox tails spouting from her posterior.

"Moon's up." Agatha exchanged a nod with Anitra. "You might wanna let your man do his business."

"Oh, yes!" Anitra pushed out of Rodrigo's embrace and turned her husband bodily to point him at the suffering supernatural creature.

"Is that a kitsune's Anubis Form?" wondered Percy. Yes, he knew it wasn't the right time to ask about such things, but, well, *was it?*

The *Custard* lurched slightly and Lady Manami stumbled. Unfortunately, Rue was nearest and she automatically reached out to steady the kitsune.

And turned into a massive white fox.

Rodrigo leapt and clapped his own hand to the kitsune.

Rue turned back to a human and Lady Manami returned to normal. Looking shaken and frightened.

Arsenic yelled, "Spoo, get my kit!"

Spoo ran for the swoon room.

Rue collapsed to the deck with a surprised expression. She looked, if possible, worse than she had before.

Arsenic bent over her, calling her something in Gaelic.

Rue coughed and waved a limp hand. "Percy, take over the helm. Get us into the grey as fast as may be. Hopefully it'll put her to sleep like it does Tash." Her voice was weak.

"Yes, Captain." Percy was worried but he knew how to obey orders so he made for the navigation pit, where his valet was looking tired but determined.

"Virgil, fantastic floating that was."

"Thank you, sir."

"My turn now."

"Thank goodness, sir. She's all yours."

Virgil handed over the helm with relief in every line of his small frame. Considering how long he'd likely been at it, his arms were probably sore. Steering a dirigible took more strength than most gave it credit.

Percy was embarrassed to admit he even had a few muscles from his time as ship's navigator. He hoped Arsenic wouldn't find this off-putting. A gentleman ought not to mess up the lines of his jackets with muscles.

Not that she hadn't already seen him naked. He shuddered to recall.

Percy took over and began puffing quick as he could, back into the aetherosphere. Should they hop a full current or risk something small, local, and uncharted, and then depuff quickly for a refuel?

Virgil sat on the edge of the pit, looking exhausted.

"You all right there, Virgil?"

"Been a long few days without you, sir."

"Sorry about the whole falling overboard thing, old chum."

"Don't do it again, sir."

"I certainly didn't intend to the first time."

"Very good, sir."

A pause.

"Virgil, why is there a whopping big hole in my ship?"

"Spoo, sir. Couldn't be helped."

Another pause.

"Sir, what are you wearing? Where are your shoes? What happened to your foot?"

"Long story. But now, I think, tea?"

"Tea? Tea started it all, sir. Don't talk to me about *tea*." Virgil sounded particularly gloomy.

"Well, perhaps fetch us both some to be going on with anyway? There's a dear chap."

"We're in the middle of an escape, sir."

"You're absolutely correct. Crumpets are also required under such trying times. Tea and buttered crumpets, please, Virgil. And for Arsenic as well. We all need restoration."

"Yes, sir. Right away, sir." Virgil tottered off, muttering something dark about Percy wanting dipped biscuits. As if Percy would ever do anything that shocking with biscuit integrity. He wasn't a monster.

Arsenic was rather concerned about Rue.

The captain was in a cold sweat and emitting funny tiny moans. She was also attempting to give orders.

Fortunately, they made it into the aetherosphere. Percy dexterously puffing them up and hitting some useful current or another. At least she hoped it was useful, she couldn't pay attention to that right now.

Unfortunately, the grey didn't sooth Lady Manami. Even though Rodrigo was touching her, once they hit the aetherosphere she started keening in pain.

The Italian glanced desperately around for some kind of guidance. He was a preternatural. He didn't know how to *help* people. Rue was breathing in little pants, her eyes tightly closed, and Anitra didn't know what to do.

So Arsenic made the decision.

"Let her go, see what happens." She was hoping the kitsune would simply drop into a deep slumber, like the werecat. Unfortunately, different shifters had differing physiology.

When Rodrigo let go, Lady Manami got worse. She clutched at her head, messing up the stunning and elaborate hair arrangement, and started screaming.

Rodrigo grabbed her again, looking wide-eyed and perturbed by the whole situation. Arsenic felt sorry for him. He was rather like her mother in that he felt most comfortable when he was killing something. He was completely out of his depth when someone was upset and he needed to assist.

"So you canna simply fall asleep?" Arsenic divided her attention between the collapsed metanatural and the suffering kitsune.

Spoo appeared with Arsenic's medical kit.

Arsenic spiralled it open, looking for anything that might ease either patient.

Spoo gave an impressed whistle.

"'Tis a bonnie design," Arsenic agreed.

She hadn't any painkillers for supernatural creatures. She didn't want to give Rue anything that might further traumatize the bairn. Poor unborn mite had been through enough what with the mother becoming a gigantic fox...twice.

Lady Manami managed, through the pain, to say sharply, "Is that what your werecat does? Sleep? Lucky her."

Primrose appeared next to them. "Cats do well in high places."

"Foxes like to den underground." Lady Manami's voice was sharpened by agony.

Prim crouched down on Rue's other side, wisely staying out of Arsenic's way. "What can I do?"

"What does it feel like, Lady Manami?" asked Arsenic, dealing with what seemed to be the most urgent situation first.

"Like thousands of hairpins pressing into my mind. It's also buzzing, and whining, like it's perforating my ears."

Arsenic nodded. "And when he lets go?"

"Many times worse, unbearable pain and pressure."

Rue still seemed to need to always be involved. "Even if he wanted to, Rodrigo can't stay touching you for the duration of the grey. It's far too long a journey."

Arsenic agreed. "And Lady Manami, you canna take the pain even with his touch, na for verra long. No one wants that. To stay aboard and fly the aetherosphere, you'll need to share Floote's tank. You're small enough. 'Tis odd to think on, but you did share a bath with Percy."

"Did you? Peculiar choice." Primrose was arrested.

Arsenic inclined her head. "I was in it too. 'Tis a cultural phenomenon."

"If you say so. Rue, stay awake now, darling, please."

Arsenic glanced back down. "We should get you to the swoon room, Captain."

Rue shook her head weakly. "Take me to engineering. The entrance platform, that's how we get to Floote's tank. And Quesnel is there. You'll need his help to get Lady Manami safely into the tank. He designed it. I want to be there." She winced noticeably and a tear leaked out her eye. "And I want to see him."

Arsenic nodded, of course she'd want her husband.

Rue was clearly scared. *Finally.* Arsenic wished the captain had gotten scared a bit sooner, before she shifted shape.

"I'm coming too," insisted Primrose.

"You're leaving Percy in charge?" Arsenic wasn't really interested but she wanted to keep Primrose distracted.

Prim nodded. "It's only the grey, he can handle it. Spoo, you coming?"

"I'd as soon not be involved." Spoo had a mildly disgusted expression on her face.

Arsenic glanced at the deckling. She had a funny-looking metal dachshund strapped to her belt, as if it were a pouch. Odd choice of apparel. Where'd that come from?

Anitra was off to one side in deep discussion with the Wallflower, Spoo went to join them. Since they were already a crowd, Arsenic left them to it.

Accordingly, they made their way over to the ladder and down two decks to engineering. Rue managed to climb, slowly, with Arsenic's help. Rodrigo carried Lady Manami. Primrose carried Arsenic's kit, which probably weighed more.

They made it to the upper part of the engineering platform, which also acted as a lookout over the boiler room. Quesnel noticed them arrive and headed up with a concerned expression.

As Arsenic had anticipated, Rue's water broke right about then.

SEVENTEEN

On Birth, Death, and Decomposition

Things came over rather chaotic and messy after that, as births tend to do. Arsenic consoled herself that it wasn't any worse than some of her battlefield surgeries. Although the smoky, steamy, hot confines of the boiler room, even the upper level, were not ideal for bringing new life into the world.

"It's too soon," Rue kept saying. And, "What have I done?" in between contractions and screaming.

Quesnel was, as husbands often were under such trying circumstances, entirely useless. Arsenic set him to helping Lady Manami and Rodrigo prep the tank, and insisted that she and Rue would do fine without him cursing in French every time Rue winced.

At some point, the chaos calmed slightly because, frankly, these things always took longer than anyone expected.

Arsenic consoled Rue that the baby was a touch early but would likely be fine, and that things were proceeding as per normal. Rue admitted that the pain was bad, worse than shifting shape, but not unbearable. She was rather a tough little thing, was the captain. Arsenic tried to persuade Rue to relocate but the captain was adamant they stay until Lady Manami was sorted. She refused to cede her captain's duty to the minor inconvenience of an onset child.

Prim stuck close, a comforting support for her friend.

The rest of engineering stayed below, going about their jobs, ignoring the dramatics on the platform. Occasionally one of the sooties appeared with a bucket of hot water, which they had in endless supply. Said sootie would give the party a terrified look and then hurry back to more quotidian duties.

Lady Manami was still not in the tank, there seemed to be some difficulty about sharing with a corpse. Which was understandable, but if there was a better solution beyond dumping the kitsune overboard, Arsenic would like to hear it. Arsenic paused in her birth ministrations to look over.

Rue had calmed enough to occasionally emit an articulate sentence and her current obsession resolved itself into one continued question, "What is Formerly Floote doing here?"

"'Tis his tank, dear." Arsenic worried that Rue might be running a fever or becoming demented.

"No, he's manifested. Why?" Rue pressed.

"Well, he's a ghost and 'tis nighttime. They do that."

"No! We are *inside* the grey. He *can't* manifest! Ooooch. Bollix that hurts."

Arsenic finally understood Rue's concern. They were no longer inside the aetherosphere, because there was a ghost present. She caught a bit of non-corporeal white above them out of the corner of her eye.

"She's right, you know." Virgil appeared with a tea tray and a lachrymose expression. "Good evening, Formerly Floote. Tea, Doctor? Percy sent me. Thought you needed it. And crumpets. He was most insistent."

Arsenic did, but wondered if it might be considered rude to pause a birthing to consume tea and buttered crumpets.

Also she must keep her hands clean.

Virgil, carefully not looking at the captain's supine form, poured Arsenic a cup and then held it for her to sip, as if Arsenic were the invalid. She drank the whole cup down in one dredge. It was delicious.

Virgil was scandalized by her gluttony, but they were both glad to have it over with.

He then fed her the crumpet as though this were the most embarrassing thing he'd ever had to do in his life.

Arsenic ate it as quickly as she could, and felt substantially better for the sustenance. She'd been languishing.

"Ho there!" said Rue. "Do I get tea? I'm doing all the work."

Arsenic glared at her. "You can have water."

It was then that Arsenic noticed that not only had Floote materialized but Lady Manami was calm under Rodrigo's touch. She was no longer in pain.

"We must be quite low down," Rue concluded. "I hope Percy hasn't put us in danger. Quesnel, darling, would you call up to navigation and find out where we are and what he's about?"

Quesnel probably wanted to glare at his wife, but under the current circumstances, he reached for the speaking tube with alacrity.

After some tense back-and-forth over the tube, Quesnel reported that Percy had decided to get them out of trouble by taking them away from Japan, south over Formosa and the open ocean. They were quite low, just dodging the waves. Percy was committed to keeping them there until everything got sorted.

"He insists on holding position, but we need to hurry up and make choices, because we're running low on fuel."

Rue took her husband's hand when he came back to her. "Coal or water? Oh ouch, darling, don't take this wrong but I think I rather dislike you right now."

"It's not my fault we're running out of fuel, chérie. And both, I'm afraid."

"That's not why I dislike you. Tell Percy to make for the nearest friendly wheystation. Hong Kong, I suspect. Barring that, we'll take a nice lake and a forest in welcoming territory."

Quesnel was scandalized. "Can't put trees in coal burners! It'll bung up the works. Really, mon petit chou!"

"Needs must, my love. Just tell Percy, please."

Primrose gasped. She'd been silently helping with hot water and swabbing Rue's brow and other capable nurse-like duties. "Oh no! Tash'll be awake and it's full moon! She's not in her cell. She'll destroy all my hats! You'll be all right while I just run and secure them?"

Rue waved a hand.

Arsenic agreed. "Things will likely take a while."

Prim bustled off, climbing up off the platform with remarkable dexterity for one in full skirts and puffy sleeves.

Rue clicked her tongue. "I don't know what she thinks she can do about it. Tash makes for a big mean lioness."

Virgil brought them back around to the important things in life. "Anyone else for tea?"

Rue made a beseeching face at Arsenic.

Arsenic said, firmly, "Some fresh drinking water, please, Virgil."

No one else seemed inclined for tea, although Rodrigo snagged a crumpet as Virgil made his way out.

Rodrigo and Lady Manami were standing to one side now, out of the way, and in awkward conversation with Formerly Floote, who was near poltergeist stage and therefore only loosely cohesive and not at all communicative.

Quesnel picked the tube back up and began arguing with Percy about flight patterns and propeller usage.

Primrose returned carrying all manner of items – blankets, pillows, soap, cognac, vinegar, bicarbonate of soda, a flowery sun hat, and a bottle of rose water. Arsenic wasn't certain about any of it, but if it made Prim feel good.

Quesnel started yelling at Percy about the fact that Rue was busy giving birth and did he have to be so difficult? That appeared to perturb Percy no end, because he hung up on Quesnel. Then the engineer was suddenly looming over them.

Arsenic put him and Primrose to work creating a bed out of blankets for Rue. It made them feel better and it would make the captain slightly more comfortable.

In the manner of many first babies, not to mention those early and traumatized, this one seemed likely to be difficult. Rue's contractions were getting closer.

Percy tubed back down. Quesnel picked back up. In a matter of moments they were yelling at each other again.

Arsenic consoled herself that at least they were out of her way. Eventually Quesnel's end of the conversation got loud enough for Arsenic to summon the tube to be stretched to her ear.

She was going to settle this matter.

"M'eudail?"

"Oh, Arsenic, how is Rue?"

"As well as can be expected, Percy. Do please stop yelling at poor Quesnel."

"But he got her into this mess."

"In a manner of speaking. But 'tis rather her own fault, too."

"I suppose so. But I enjoy yelling at Quesnel."

"Weel, stop it. Now is na the time."

"He won't tell me what's happening down there."

"Because *nothing* is happening. These things take time. Now, be nice to the man." She looked at Quesnel while she said this, meeting his eyes firmly. "You both love her. Stop fussing."

"If you insist. I'm taking us to Hong Kong."

"That sounds lovely. You do that."

"Did you get tea?"

"I did, thank you."

"I thought it might be necessary. And crumpets."

"Verra buttery, but now I must be off. Birth and such."

"Oh! Yes, of course."

Sometime later, difficult to tell exactly how long, Arsenic held a wriggling baby girl in her arms. The child had some lungs on her, rather like her mother.

The bairn passed a quick inspection, after which Arsenic cleaned her best she could, swaddled her in a pillowcase, and passed her off to smudged and exhausted parents.

Quesnel's eyes were incandescent with love. He also seemed pleased his child had been born in engineering.

"Look at that grip on her. We shall have you holding a wrench in no time, petite fleur."

Primrose had remained the entire time, holding Rue's hand when needed, encouraging her to drink water and soothing her with a damp cloth. Now she helped Rue to sit up, propped against Quesnel, and placed the baby in her friend's arms.

Arsenic, having dealt with the afterbirth and ensuing mess, was busy cleaning herself up in one of the sooties' buckets using Prim's soap. Sadly, her bicycle suit had been through more than enough for one lifetime. She'd have to get a new one.

Primrose asked the inevitable question. "What will you name her, darlings?"

Rue and Quesnel exchanged a look.

"Alexandra Constance," said Rue after a moment.

Which seemed a mouthful to Arsenic, but who was she to criticize names? After all, hers was *Arsenic*.

Rue explained. "After various sets of grandparents. Close enough to Alexia to make Mother happy, but also it's basically the translation of *Alessandro*." She nodded over to Rodrigo, who was grinning in pleasure. "And, of course, it's really for my Dama. He'll be chuffed."

Primrose was nodding, face pressed next to her friend's, looking down at the newborn with worshipful eyes. "And *Constance*?"

"Well, I had to suffer *Prudence* my whole life. Can't let her escape codswallop free. Also, I was thinking of Paw, since he's a Conall."

"Nothing for Quesnel's side?"

Rue smiled. "She's a Lefoux, isn't she?"

Rodrigo and Lady Manami came over and stood looking down at the new family.

Rodrigo greeted his baby cousin with a string of lyrical Italian and those funny faces adults will make at babies before finally he said, "I think Formerly Floote has a request."

It was then that they all remembered the ghost.

He'd been there for a while, of course, witnessing everything. Arsenic thought he might even be aware of it, or *mostly* aware of it.

Formerly Floote's limbs were stretched and his eyebrows drifted, but he was managing to keep his non-corporeal form cohesive. His ghostly apparition wore old-fashioned dress, something on the order of what Percy currently wore. Only of a style meant for valets.

He wafted above them, his shape misty and easy to see through, his tether frayed beyond repair. Truly, the Lefoux tank was a thing of great technological achievement to have kept him this long.

Rodrigo said, carefully, "Rather than share the tank, I believe he wants to give it up."

Rue's eyes went wide as she looked up from her beloved new baby, to her beloved old ghost. "No!"

Quesnel had one arm about his wife's waist. His other hand rested on his child. "You need to let him go, chérie."

Tears streamed down Rue's face.

Arsenic was sympathetic. The captain clearly collected people and made them family. It was entirely against her nature to let anyone go. Especially not forever.

Rue took a shuddering breath. "It can't be my choice. It should be Anitra's. She's his granddaughter, after all."

Quesnel nodded and reached to unhook the speaking tube.

Percy answered, although Arsenic only heard Quesnel's side.

"Send down Anitra, please? Yes, everything is fine! Oh! Yes, the baby, she's a girl. No, I don't know *what* she is. What on steaming earth do you mean by asking a question like that? Why do we need Anitra? No, nothing to do with translating for the baby. Anitra doesn't speak baby, besides the baby hasn't said much, only drooled a bit. She's adorable. What do you mean, that doesn't matter? Of course it matters! Will you stop asking that? Send down Anitra! Merde!" Quesnel hung up the tube. "That man!"

Arsenic perfectly understood what had happened. Percy wanted to know if metanatural Rue and human Quesnel had produced a human baby, a metanatural baby, or a preternatural one. Arsenic was equally curious about this, but didn't want to press the matter.

Anitra climbed down to the platform a few minutes later. She looked with charmed eyes at the new baby and then with sad eyes at her grandfather's ghost.

"He's ready to go?"

Rodrigo nodded and held out his free hand, the one not keeping Lady Manami sane.

Anitra took it and pressed against him, cuddling her husband close.

She took a shuddering breath, then turned to face the others, looking down at Rue.

"He told me, before he started to slip into poltergeist, that he was ready. He's accomplished it all. He didn't think he'd see the next generation, and now he has. It's more than time."

Above them the ghost shivered, head nodding. He was lucid enough to follow Anitra.

Then Formerly Floote said, slowly and distinctly, "My duties are done." He sounded, if not happy, at least satisfied.

Anitra gave a little half sob. "He told me—" She stopped to collect herself. "He told me to tell you that he had a long life and a longer-than-expected afterlife and he's finished."

It was her soulless husband who broke the sombre mood. "Unfortunately, I am otherwise occupied and cannot free him."

Rue kissed the top of her baby's head. "It'll be me then. It should be me, anyway. Quesnel, help me over to the tank."

"Rue, chérie, is that wise? Doctor?"

Arsenic sighed. "Probably not, but I'm beginning to understand how she is. Here, give Alexandra to me, you help your wife."

Primrose and Quesnel helped Rue over to the tank suspended from the ceiling at the far side of the platform.

Fortunately, during the chaos of the grey, Quesnel had already lowered it down and cracked the lid's seal. The bubbles were still passing throughout the orange liquid, partly hiding the body within.

The hiss and screech of metal against metal with a hydraulic assist indicated the tank was now fully open.

Arsenic made herself look. She was a doctor, she'd seen many a dead body before.

The corpse was completely wrapped like a mummy, no parts visible. Presumably this helped to prevent decomposition.

Primrose made a tiny retching noise. She angled her body so as not to see into the tank. Although she stayed standing behind and supporting Rue.

Quesnel was the one who reached in, lifting the body up to the surface and into the air.

Arsenic smelled formaldehyde and other preservatives, but no stench of death.

Rue reached in and under the bandage-like wrappings so she might touch flesh. Arsenic had never witnessed an exorcism before but she understood the basic premise.

Above them Floote's long stretched misty body drifted apart, coiling and separating further. Until his essence joined the ever-present steam of the boiler room, and he was no more.

Arsenic, who was modern in her opinions on the matter of hygiene, insisted that neither Rue nor Quesnel touch the baby after performing an exorcism until they had washed, preferably with something stronger than soap.

Fortunately, there were buckets of hot water all about, with the sooties desperate to help. So the new parents scrubbed down and then doused themselves in Primrose's vinegar, which Arsenic doubted would do much good but couldn't hurt, and then again with the brandy. Which Arsenic thought should do the trick.

Meanwhile, Arsenic sidled over to Rodrigo and asked him to let go of Lady Manami for a quick moment. Lady Manami looked panicked and braced herself.

"'Tis only a test." Arsenic tried to sound confident.

Rodrigo let go.

Lady Manami instantly began doing that flickering thing, where she was both a small white fox, in between with the head of a fox and multiple fox tails, and fully human.

Arsenic touched the baby's tiny fist to Lady Manami's cheek. Nothing happened.

Arsenic nodded, pleased. Her theory confirmed.

Rodrigo grabbed the kitsune by the hand once more.

Lady Manami returned to fully human and let out a sigh of relief.

"Was that necessary, Doctor?" she asked.

Arsenic nodded. "We must know *what*."

Quesnel growled. "You sound like Percy."

"Sometimes he's correct, he's just na verra graceful about it. More often than *sometimes*, actually."

Quesnel sighed, drying himself on one of the clean blankets. "I know, I simply hate telling *him* that."

The baby hadn't cancelled out Lady Manami's transformation. She hadn't stolen her shape, either.

Arsenic handed the newborn to her now clean father. "She's human. *Only* human. Nothing special."

Quesnel cooed down at his daughter. She had a tiny tuft of blonde hair, his colour, but her eyes were almost yellow, like her mother's.

"Oh, she's special, ma petite fleur."

"She's perfect," avowed Primrose, who was helping Rue to clean herself and then settling her back into the funny bed-nest.

Quesnel sat down next to his wife and offered to return the baby.

Rue nudged up against him, clearly too exhausted. So Quesnel kept hold of Alexandra. Rue rested her head on his shoulder. She put out an arm and pulled Primrose down to join them.

"All right, Prim?" she asked.

"Perfect," repeated Primrose. She was only crying a little.

Rue looked up plaintively at Arsenic. "May I please have tea now?"

They gave Floote, what was left of him, a sailor's farewell. They wrapped his body in a nice quilt and set him out to sea.

Anitra said he would have liked it. He'd travelled the world with Alessandro Tarabotti, she explained, but he always loved the ocean best. It was a good resting place.

They put Lady Manami into the preservation tank in Floote's stead. Fortunately, Quesnel had reserves of the special orange liquid, so she didn't have to get into the same water. This seemed to please her more than the idea of sharing with a corpse.

After some consideration, Lady Manami elected to strip and pull on one of Prim's bathing costumes, a navy-and-white-striped affair which was rather large on a kitsune, but had enough stretch to fit well enough. She put one of her own robes over it, a pale blue one with lots of embroidered cherry blossoms, which she explained was her least favourite.

She floated in the orange liquid, the robe wafting about her as if she were some species of large preserved moth. When fully immersed the kitsune breathed evenly, asleep or insensate, the gas bubbles all around her glinting in the light from the boilers below. A truly remarkable invention. Technology that preserved the corpse of a ghost one moment and a supernatural creature the next.

Arsenic was impressed and told Quesnel so. "Ingenious device, something that maintains tethers."

Quesnel was pleased by the compliment. "Mother came up with the idea after Rue here had issues with bathtubs."

"I loathe bathing," confirmed Rue.

Arsenic blinked at her.

Rue blushed. "Oh, I use a sponge and such to stay clean. It's full immersion that gets me."

"I suppose that makes sense. It cuts off, or at least numbs, aetheric contact. Good thing it was Percy and I stuck wandering around Japan and bathing in groups."

"Yes, apparently they steal shoes, too. I love my shoes."

Arsenic only then realized she was still barefoot. She'd left her favourite bicycle boots in the temple. "Oh, bother."

Sometime later Arsenic finally chivvied everyone along to the swoon room, where she could weigh the baby and perform the appropriate tests on eyes, ears, nose, and throat. Despite being at least a month early, the infant seemed perfectly topping, as Percy might say. Arsenic wondered if perhaps Rue's inception calculations were off.

Primrose gave up her worship of Alexandra and went above-decks to sort out their travel situation. At which juncture Percy came limping down to meet the new addition. At some point Virgil had persuaded him into one boot, his bad ankle still splinted up, but otherwise he was still wearing antiquated dress, including tight buckskin breeches.

He looked down with an expression of mild censure at Rue, Quesnel, and baby. Only Quesnel bothered to glare back at him.

"'Pon my soul, it has fingernails and all such nonsense."

Arsenic nodded.

"Will it grow eyebrows or is it permanently surprised?"

"*It* is a *she*. And *she* will grow both eyebrows and eyelashes."

"Remarkable."

"Pretty standard, actually, m'eudail."

"Human, you say?"

"Aye," said Arsenic.

"Metanatural and preternatural must be deeply recessive characteristics, you suspect? In terms of that bally gene theory, the one the Mendel chap was bandying about a while back?"

"Aye."

"I agree. Good showing, her being human."

"I thought so too."

Rue said to her husband, "There they go again. Do you think they'll ever stop?"

"No, not now. You've gone and done it, chérie. Given them something to mutually hypothesize about until the end of time." He nuzzled Alexandra's tiny head adoringly.

"Do you think they'll pause long enough to kiss?"

"Stop matchmaking, they'll come around to it on their own time. Or not."

Percy was looking back and forth between Arsenic and the baby, a curious expression on his face.

He plucked at Arsenic's sleeve so she looked up at him. "Arsenic, petal, would you like one?"

Petal, hum? Arsenic considered the endearment and the question, decided she didn't object to either.

"We both keep rather busy but I'm willing to debate the idea."

"But you'd be, perhaps, interested in the activities that revolve around trying?"

"With you? Certainly." Arsenic could feel herself blushing. Trust Percy to ask her such a question while they had an audience.

"And perhaps, the occasional quiet evening spent reading with Footnote." Percy seemed to think this request even more daring.

Arsenic considered. "Who gets your lap, me or the cat?"

Percy gave a delighted smile and parroted her words back at her. "I'm willing to debate the idea."

Quesnel snorted loudly. "I may be in a constant state of

intellectual battle with that man, chérie, but I am unquestion-
ably superior at flirtation."

"Of course you are, darling."

Primrose reappeared. "What happened while I was away?"

Rue said, "Your brother seems to be attempting to seduce our
doctor. It's rather a catastrophe."

"Well, it would be."

Arsenic felt a slight tug on one hand. Percy had sidled close
and twined his soft capable fingers with hers. She cocked her
head and saw yearning in the way he didn't quite look at her.
She slid against him, trying to be reassuring. They were close
enough for her to see the three freckles on his ear that she liked
so much. Feeling brave, she stood on tiptoes and kissed his neck,
just there, below them.

Percy trembled slightly and wrapped his arms about her. It
was lovely, gentle, less stiff than she might have expected.

"We should, erm, marry, do you think?" He was endearingly
hesitant and he only winced a little.

"I look forward to you attempting to persuade me." Then
because she knew Percy would be in fits of nervousness about
the whole endeavour, she added, "How about I ask you, when I
feel persuaded? That way you dinna have to fret about it."

"I wouldn't."

She arched a brow.

"Well, yes I would, but you'll give me time to research?"

"Which part?"

"All of it, of course."

"I'll give you time, Percy. I know very little on the subject
myself. We should discuss."

"Library then?" Percy blushed quite red.

Arsenic pressed her advantage to see how much redder he
might get. "I ken the mechanics, na the practicalities." Quite a
bit redder, as it turned out.

"I have a book for you," offered Primrose.

"To be fair," said Rue, passing Alexandra over into Prim's eager embrace, "it's actually Quesnel's book."

"Can't blame a book for its source," replied Percy, philosophically.

"Why don't you two go off and talk about it *in private?*" suggested Quesnel. "We'll be good here for a bit."

Arsenic tore her gaze away from Percy to peruse her charges.

Rue and Quesnel were curled on the cot together, heavy-lidded and exhausted. Primrose was cradling the baby, rocking and humming softly.

Out the porthole behind them, the wide dark ocean was beginning to look actually blue. The sun was rising at last.

It had been a long night.

The library sounded like heaven.

Tasherit appeared, bleary and moon-worn, but pleased to meet the new addition to their crew. Primrose snuggled against her, showing off the baby, and refrained from asking about the survival of her hats.

Percy smiled to himself. His sister was growing up.

He led Arsenic out into the hallway and across to her quarters. She looked knackered and he thought it best that everything else wait until she got some rest.

Still he found himself sort of bending towards her hopefully, and when her eyes crinkled up at him, he decided this was a good sign and tried for a kiss. It came out more of an anticlimactic peck, but he felt like that was the challenging bit over with. He pulled back quickly, checking her eyes again.

Still crinkled in pleasure. *Oh good.*

"Bit more?" she suggested.

Percy took a breath, then applied what he had once learned, long ago, from a capable older female. He started soft, just a light pressure, then a tiny nip, so her lips parted in surprise. Then deeper.

This time, when he drew back, her eyes were wide but delighted. "You dinna need to read anything on the subject. Do you?"

Percy rewarded her for that by kissing her again. "It's always worth researching and discussing."

His ran his thumb down her lovely face, feeling the smoothness of her skin – pleased when her eyelids lowered under the caress.

"*Petal.* You wish ta call me *petal?*" she wondered.

He smiled and kissed her again, petting along her chin to her throat. "Your eyes are like a pansy and your skin is like a rose petal. It suits you." He carefully didn't mention the spider lashes. Maybe later.

Arsenic nodded, nudging into his hand, tilting her head back in request. So, he kissed her again, before sucking in a shaky breath and pulling slightly away.

"And," he added with what he hoped was a charming grin, "*rutabaga* for special occasions."

Arsenic snorted out a surprised giggle.

"May I try?" She reached up and drew him close and kissed him, harder than he expected. He gave himself up to her curious questing mouth, letting her have her way. Until it tested him rather much and he backed up, surprised and flattered by her intensity, but knowing they needed to take this slow. It was their way.

"What's this then?" He touched his tingling lips with curious fingertips.

Arsenic smiled, eyes full of joy. "Affection, possibly even love."

"How ghastly. Me too. Do it again?" Arsenic wrapped herself around him one more time. Her fingers threaded into his hair, and her lips went from his mouth to his neck. Percy was surprised by the heat in her. The heat in both of them.

Until behind them the baby started to cry.

And below them the boilers shook the ship as they began to run dry.

And a small black-and-white tomcat wound his way about their ankles and meowed imperiously.

Percy realized that perhaps he hadn't estimated properly and that they might not *quite* make it to Hong Kong, but he had no doubt at all, that they would make it *somewhere*.

They would make it happen.

They would make all of it happen, together.

And it would be glorious.

EPILOGUE

With a Neat Little Bow

January 1901
    A notebook, slim and leather-bound with a gilt flower pattern on the cover, was found alongside a velvet box.
An inscription at the beginning of the notebook read:

> *From the personal memoirs of Lord Akeldama, who was once Great and always fabulous.*

The box contained within it a small charm made of two interlocking parts. One slightly oval in shape, the other like a sword or a lowercase *t*. Locked together, the shape resembles the ankh seen carved into Ancient Egyptian tombs, only solid at the top rather than looped. It is not surprising for a vampire to possess such a symbol – eternity, immortality, and the supernatural. The charm is old.

Very old.

Ancient.

The meaning of the filled loop is undoubtedly significant but remains a mystery to scholars. Others have noted that the artefact also breaks into three parts, two crooks and a flail, for those familiar with Ancient Egyptian rulership symbols. Why three? Professor Percival Tunstell claims to have a solid working theory of a metanatural correlation, but for once he refuses to publish on the subject.

A selection from the notebook is presented here, for the good of posterity and the possible enlightenment of a few. Should any feel themselves able to understand the meat of the implications set forth, BUR is very interested in conducting interviews. Please find their offices in Fleet Street, London.

Excerpt...

> *Rodrigo Tarabotti will be the Mujah to the new king of England. I will see that bit finished. Anitra did well with him and they are happy together. I didn't anticipate that, not real love, but I know as well as others the lure of the Tarabotti line. Nevertheless, it's a neat bow there, if I do say so myself. Even if I can't take credit for all of it.*
>
> *I was always very fond of bows. They tell me the cravat is out of fashion these days and the tie is all the rage, but I cannot countenance a noose about the neck. Give me a silken fall in a perfect bow to end every outfit – wrapped about a throat like a gift just for me.*
>
> *I can change a whole look with a neat little bow.*
>
> *I can change the world with it.*
>
> *Aggie Phinkerlington has finally left* The Spotted Custard. *We are all grateful, although I did admire her skill with a crossbow. The crossbow is sadly undervalued in these days of flashy pistols and even flashier rifles. Being a vampire, however, I cannot but admire a weapon that delivers a stake to the heart across long distances.*
>
> *But, I digress.*
>
> *The last reported rumour of Miss Phinkerlington has her recruited by certain unsavoury northern elements, of which we are all very well aware. She went and found herself the only woman in existence as grumpy as she. A good match, I suspect. No one is too surprised, least of all me.*

Those ladies and I have been in such a dance these many years. A contest of wits the likes of which I've not enjoyed since Roman times. Life was so boring here in London before they started meddling. So few have challenged me of late. I am eternally grateful. Literally.

We have all, I think, been enjoying this game of ours. Us with our living players and tentacles that stretch ever outwards touching more and future lives.

To what end?

One might well ask, gentle reader.

Who can say? It's a matter of fate, I suspect. Who doesn't want to dabble in the outcome of other people's stories?

Who has won?

I always ask this of myself, because I once marched an army across the known world and winning remains embarrassingly important to me. A character flaw, I suspect.

Yet I find that in this matter, I do not know.

I have kept my boys safe, and my girls now too, as much as I am able. Safe by human standards, at the very least. And happy. And I have seen another soul-stealer into adulthood and this one will survive. My little puggle will live on to a ripe old age by mortal standards, surrounded by chosen family. I will make it so. Not for her lack of trying to undo my good work. Are they all born strong and fierce and reckless, these so-called metanaturals?

Two in my lifetime and both my daughters. I got it right the second time around. I'd say thank heavens, but heaven had nothing to do with it. It was all me. With perhaps an assist or two from the wicker chicken and one overly capable butler.

It was a good notion to add the Tunstell twins to the mix. I had no idea we needed them. Never discount humans, they try so very hard. Sometimes, they become something wonderful.

And what of the perfect spy in the shadows, the wolf queen in the north, and the inventor in the caravan? Why did they move their pawns about the board? I suspect it was for love. Or maybe that is simply what I hope it was for.

I am a foolish old vampire. But I am not yet lost.

And me? Why did I do it?

I played my game for love too. A love long lost, a man who made miracles with his touch, and a shifter who adored us both beyond reason. I did it for that first Tarabotti, who had me and a werecat in his bed. And we made a miracle child who became a Queen and a legend. Zenobia, our daughter. The first metanatural. We thought the world was collapsing and there was no reason left to exist at all, yet despair became passion, and the result altered reality.

Perhaps we will all change the world out of love.

Can you think of a better reason?

And there I go, being serious. I'm not at my best when I'm serious. I'll stop now.

Yours etc . . .
Goldenrod

Author's Note on Names

As with previous books in the Custard Protocol series, when not fictitious, I've used place names as if I were a Victorian (according to maps of the mid-1890s). Governments were changing a great deal during this time period and I'm well aware that what the British called places was, generally speaking, not what the residents of said places called the places themselves.

It is for this reason that Korea is referred to and spelled Choson, as Victorian travellers would still have relied on Percival Lowell's *Choson, the Land of the Morning Calm*, published in 1885. At least, that's what Percy had in his library.

Acknowledgements

This one is for you, eyeballs in the sky. Thank you for joining me on this amazing ten-year journey. I honestly wouldn't have kept writing it if you didn't keep reading. So this is all your fault. May your tea always be the right temperature, your book never boring, and your world changed for the better by love. Props to my amazing team of beta readers, after twenty-odd books, it's a lot for them to keep track of! And thanks to my darling Piper J Drake, her friend Miyuki, and the charming Mr Kato, who together found me Mr Fujishima, who kindly lent his expertise as a delicacy reader to the Paper City, the Meiji Restoration, and beyond. (I now know the difference between geta and zori sandals and am a better fashionista because of it.)

And for Davin.

May we all live life as he did, with more vigour.